FATHER TIME
LANCE PARKIN

Published by BBC Worldwide Ltd,
Woodlands, 80 Wood Lane
London W12 0TT

First published 2000
Copyright © Lance Parkin 2000
The moral right of the author has been asserted

Original series broadcast on the BBC

Doctor Who and TARDIS are trademarks of the BBC

ISBN 978-1-84-990178-9

Imaging by Black Sheep, copyright © BBC 2000

Dedicated to child of the eighties, Cassandra May.

Thanks to the usual suspects: Cassandra May, Mark Jones, Mark Clapham, Mike Evans, Kate Orman and Jon Blum.

And also to Lisa Brattan, Henry Potts, Allan and Charis Bednar, Lorraine Mann, Jonny Morris, Rebecca Levene, Graham Evans, Amanda Dingle, Lawrence Miles and Paul Griggs.

The cover is based on an original concept by Allan Bednar.

Chapter Zero
Planet of Death

It was a planet shrouded in fog.

Thick grey mists clung to the broken, rocky ground. Nothing but the simplest vegetation lived on the surface, although there were ruined walls and cracked roadways, evidence that a civilisation had once prospered on this world. At higher altitudes the fog grew thinner, but also more sulphurous. The sky was yellow, sickly. Even at noon, the sunlight was weak, filtered through layers of haze. Everywhere, the air was stagnant. There were no winds, not even the hint of a breeze.

But life still clung to this planet, dotted around in sealed cities, tunnels and bunkers.

A flying disc broke through the gloom and soundlessly approached the largest of these strongholds.

The palace was a collection of twisted silver spires, like fingers reaching up to grasp the stars. It was vast, the size of a city, with the tips of the tallest spires poking out of the poisonous atmosphere. There were signs of damage, and the metal surface had become tarnished over time, but it was an impressive spectacle, and the lights and air traffic were clear signs that this place was occupied, even vibrant.

The flying disc began slowing, altering its course ever so slightly. It drifted through a gap in the palace walls. As it passed, a transparent dome slid smoothly across, enclosing it.

The room smelled of cinnamon and sandalwood. He could feel the firm stone floor beneath his knee and his feet, and hear the hum of the ventilation ducts. Not even heavy robes could keep out the cold. None of this mattered.

His shoulder was aching again. He had a sharp pain in his stomach. The headache that had prevented him from sleeping hadn't subsided, despite the pills. None of this mattered.

He heard the footsteps, identified their owner while he was still fifty paces away. He didn't rise, but kept his gaze fixed firmly on the knife that sat on the family shrine. He resumed his prayers of dedication,

staring into the pitted blade, remembering.

Five paces away, and the footsteps stopped, as he knew they would.

'There is news, Eminence,' the Deputy announced.

He closed his eyes, prayed that after a lifetime this was the end.

'Tell me,' he commanded quietly.

'The Hunters are here. They say they have located the Last One.'

He nodded, gave silent thanks to the gods, and turned to face the Deputy. The old man was in his fatigues, ready for combat, even here. After all this time, the Deputy still relished the fight. This old man had been his rock all these years. There had been times – forgive him – when he had thought of abandoning his mission, renouncing his sacred duty, times when he thought there had already been too much killing, too much blood.

But you cannot escape the past: the great weight of decades of history and memory that shape you, make you what you are. Fate was the inevitable result of genetics and politics. The Deputy shared none of this heritage, at least not by birth, but knew what was important. What sort of man would the Deputy have been without the war? The Deputy wouldn't have the scar, but what about his permanently narrowed eyes or his hunched physique?

Only one more killing, and it would be over. He would have played his role to its conclusion.

'Where?'

'The planet Earth, in the twentieth century of the Humanian Era.'

'A precise fix?'

'To within ten square kilometres.' The Deputy sounded impressed, despite himself.

'They have done well. Authorise the second payment.'

'Sir...'

He laughed. 'I know: you are worried that they'll take the money without finishing the job. Authorise the second payment, but don't let them leave the palace.'

'I am uncertain of their loyalties.'

'You are right to be, they are not part of this. They require someone to keep them in check. We both know who would be best for that role. Commission him.'

'Yes, Eminence.'

He turned to the shrine, took the knife from its reliquary and slotted it into the sheath on his belt.

He took a deep breath. 'It's nearly over, old friend. Soon the last of our enemies will be dead.'

'It will be a new beginning,' the Deputy told him. 'The poison will have been drawn, the empire will flourish, we will prevent anarchy. We will be great again.'

He could barely remember what it had been like before the civil war. He looked around, saw the great cracks in the floor, the patches where the roof and walls had been crudely repaired. At least inside here the air was breathable. It was difficult to believe that they had been on the winning side.

The anger surged within him. He remembered what his enemies had done; he remembered his vow to end their rule, to hunt them down, to exterminate them.

'We will at least have that chance,' he agreed. 'Prepare for departure, prepare the timegate.'

Part One

'Battle of the Planets'

The Early 1980s

Chapter One
Knights and Castles

It was a planet of darkness, snow and hills.

Or so anyone arriving in Derbyshire that night would have thought.

There comes a time when the fall of snow is no longer the start of a marvellous adventure. There comes a time when it means scraping your windscreen and hoping your car starts. It means aching joints and throbbing sinuses and cold hands and feet. It means taking longer to get to work and spending all day sitting in an office where the heating isn't on. Grey slush and cracked pipes, cancelled trains and influenza, that's what snow means. You'll wake up feeling like that, one day, and it will mean you are grown up. I hope that day doesn't come soon.

This story is set in the last century. In those days, the Prime Minister was a woman, and there were no euros or pound coins, only pound notes. The Lords sat in the House of Lords, coal miners worked in coal mines, and ships were built on the Tyne. There were vinyl long-playing records, not compact discs, the space shuttle was shiny and new, there were only three television stations, and computers – hard to believe, I know – were black-and-white back then.

It begins with a teacher, a primary-school teacher, driving a tan Ford Cortina through a blizzard in the dark.

The teacher's name is Mrs Deborah Castle, and she hated to see the snow falling.

She remembered a story as she drove, and it made her cry…

Once upon a time there was a girl called Debbie Gordon who used to love to see snow fall. Debbie Gordon had long, long hair, which was as black as coal. Every winter, as soon as she saw it was snowing, she would press herself against the cold pane of the dining-room window, watching the flakes drifting down into the back garden, making her eyes go funny. The first snow didn't settle, although she never remembered that. The air was so cold she could see it in front of her when she breathed out, but the ground was still too warm for snow

to stick. However much snow fell, it vanished as soon as it hit the grass and paving stones. But despite that the first snow was never a disappointment.

Snow comes early in Greyfrith, high in the Pennines in the Northwest of England. The first snow can be at the end of September, while the rest of England has its first frosts. The children of Greyfrith don't understand the fuss everyone else makes about a white Christmas – every Christmas Day, without fail, there's snow on the ground. Not only does the snow come early, but you can never be sure it's gone. At the train station there's an old black-and-white photograph of a cricket pitch, covered in white. The scoreboard reads SNOW STOPPED PLAY – the only time that's happened to a county cricket match, anywhere in the world. June it was, the woman who runs the café at the railway station will tell you, if you ask – and often even if you don't. She's in that old photograph, but you wouldn't recognise her now, not unless you knew her granddaughter. It's not snowed in June since, but there'll be snow until April, most years.

Mrs Castle lived in Greyfrith, so it was a shame she hated it to snow.

Debbie Gordon and Deborah Castle sound like completely different people, and in some ways they are. Debbie Gordon had a big doll's house in her bedroom, a little cat, and a love of falling snow. Mrs Castle had none of the things that Debbie Gordon had, not any more, except the puppy fat. Once upon a time, not even twenty years ago, she did because – as you've already guessed – Debbie Gordon is what Mrs Castle was called before she became a grown-up. She got a new name on her wedding day. Gordon was a funny name, because 'Gordon' is usually a man's first name, but Castle was an even stranger name to have, and it made her think of medieval fortresses. For months afterwards she kept signing her old name by mistake – annoying her husband every time she did so.

Five years after her wedding day, when our story starts, she was used to being Mrs Castle, it didn't seem odd at all. Her pupils stood up and chanted the name every morning when she came into the classroom, it appeared on her pay-slips and phone bills. She'd forgotten what it was like to be Debbie Gordon; she'd all but forgotten that she once loved the snow.

Mrs Castle ignored the tears in her eyes, and tried to concentrate on the road in front of her instead of listening to her own silly stories.

Past the windscreen wipers and their battle with the snow, a mushy orange glow peeking over the hilltops marked her way. Those were the Greyfrith street lights. The road ahead was empty and unlit, all the way home. Mrs Castle's car radio was tuned to long wave and pop music was playing. Mrs Castle knew the people singing were a group called Adam and the Ants, because it was a new song all her pupils were talking about.

A red light appeared on the dashboard.

Mrs Castle tried to ignore it, tried to press on – even in this weather it would take less than ten minutes to drive the three miles to her house. She knew that her husband could sort out whatever was wrong with the car in the morning; it would be his problem, not hers. There was no other choice – she couldn't see any phone boxes, and this was many years before anyone but a millionaire had a telephone in their car. Mrs Castle didn't know if Adam Ant could drive, but if he could, and he had a car, she knew it would have a telephone in it. But no one in Greyfrith did, except perhaps the manager of the factory that made spark plugs, or Lord Wallis, who owned Wallis House.

Mrs Castle could hear every rattle her husband's car made now. She was acutely aware of every change in engine note.

Nine minutes. Nine minutes away from home.

Not far away, a man called Arnold Knight lowered his binoculars, disappointed. Arnold Knight was a UFO spotter – or would have been, if he had ever seen one.

Snow falling from a thick grey sky. This was not at all what he wanted. On the hillside, as Arnold was, the clouds weren't quite close enough to touch, but they looked it. For the last few days, with almost total cloud coverage, Arnold had convinced himself that the night's sky might be full of strange lights, there could be fleets of saucers flying in formation, all tantalisingly just a couple of hundred feet above his head, all swerving to avoid the occasional break in the cloud.

Arnold wasn't as fanatical as some of his fellow UFO spotters. Some of the men and women who'd congregated in Greyfrith after the initial reports of a flap thought they'd got it all worked out. They told stories about RAF planes chasing flying saucers, official cover-ups, a whole menagerie of plant men, robot men and spaghetti men from outer space, not forgetting the turtle men who lived under the sea. Arnold didn't believe any of that. As the famous scientist Carl Sagan

said, extraordinary claims required extraordinary proof. Arnold hoped he could provide some extraordinary proof. There were some interesting things happening in the sky. That seemed beyond dispute – lights, glowing balls, crosses... They'd all been seen over the years, by all sorts of reliable people. He was a good photographer – he made some money from it, doing portraits and work for the local paper. So, get a few decent photos of UFOs, done by a professional, and people might start to investigate the phenomenon seriously. That was why he'd travelled halfway across the country; that was what he was here for.

But that wasn't going to happen tonight, not with this weather.

It was dark, very cold, and it was still snowing, even though the weather forecast had said the cold spell was over. He knew how to stay warm, but the best way of all was not to go out on a winter's night in the first place. He found a fallen tree, checkèd it wasn't too wet and sat down.

It was very quiet tonight, and the low clouds were like a roof. It made everything seem unreal, somehow. It was calm. Civilisation wasn't far away – the outskirts of Greyfrith were only over the next hill, but it felt wild out here, as though there were things that *people* didn't know about. The hills themselves were dark. There were local legends that the hills and mountains were giants, curled up where they fell under some enchantment. Arnold could see where that had come from – the curves and undulations did make them look like fat people, fast asleep.

Arnold glanced over his shoulder and saw there was a giant standing behind him. Ten feet tall at least, and wearing angular armour. Two lights shone down, like the headlamps of a car, but they were the giant's eyes.

It was a machine, or a very tall man in a suit of armour – there was no way of telling which. Sensible thoughts crossed Arnold's mind: that this was a prank, a puppet or special effect of some kind. He'd spent enough time in the pubs of Greyfrith in the last week to know that the local lads regarded the UFO spotters with suspicion and derision.

But Arnold could tell that this wasn't some lashed-together farm machinery. It was dark, but he could see that it was elegantly designed, that its movements were fluid.

It was coming towards him.

Arnold screamed, and started to run.

* * *

Mrs Castle wasn't far away, and she heard the scream over the sound of the car radio.

It startled her for a moment, but only for a moment. She quickly told herself that it was nothing to worry about, just a noise like you often hear in the middle of the night. A sound like the cry of a fierce animal, or a strange aircraft. Perhaps just a bang or a thud.

Maybe you've heard a scream. When children play, it often sounds as if they are screaming. From a little way off, a playground can sound like a battleground. If children playing sounds like screaming, then, Mrs Castle thought, perhaps a field full of screaming children will sound as if they are playing.

It was a fox, she told herself. Or some sort of bird – a hawk or an owl. Or perhaps just something on the Kate Bush record that was playing now on the radio. Mrs Castle turned the radio up and tried to think of other things.

She concentrated on what was waiting for her at home. At first she thought of the nasty things. The washing-up, the hoovering, the mouldy grouting in the bathroom. Barry, Mr Castle, would be there, sitting in front of the television, telling her the commentators on *Rugby Special* were useless, and that he also had a low opinion of Paul Daniels, and that the licence fee was a waste of good money. But there would be nice things at home, too: a bath, a hot, soapy bath. A book – *Sense and Sensibility*, about a young woman who was out in the rain and was rescued by a handsome man on horseback. A fairy story. There was a Paul Newman film on later, and Mrs Castle knew not even Barry could spoil that for her.

There were now three red lights on the dashboard. Mrs Castle knew she wouldn't get home. Now she was looking for a phone box. She'd driven down this road hundreds of times, but because she'd never needed a phone box, she didn't know if there was one or not. And if there wasn't, then she'd have to hope that another car came by.

She could hear hissing. The engine was making a noise like a kettle. She pictured it, bubbling and churning. She imagined her husband shouting at her, telling her she only needed to stop to put some oil and water in it, but instead she left it running, she'd damaged the engine, it was going to take him all weekend to fix and it would cost them hundreds of pounds. She knew she had to stop the car as soon as she could.

And because she was looking at the dashboard, she didn't see the

man run out in front of her: she saw only his terrified expression, bleached by the headlights, as he turned to face her.

She slammed down hard on the brakes, without needing to think that she had to, but already knowing it would do no good. The road had been gritted, but it was still very wet, and the tyres barely gripped it.

The car hardly slowed before it hit him, sending him tumbling over the bonnet, rolling up the windscreen and over the roof. As the car stopped, he fell back on to the road.

For a moment, Mrs Castle just sat, clutching the steering wheel. Everything outside the car seemed so much slower – the snow, her windscreen wipers.

After a moment, her mind and the world outside it caught up with each other. Mrs Castle turned the ignition key, which shut off the engine and silenced the radio. The warm air from the heater died away, the boiling from the engine settled down. She took a deep breath and got out of the car.

She locked the car door without thinking what she was doing.

It was so quiet. It wasn't as cold as she thought it would be, despite the snow. There was nothing else moving here, of course, and it was too cold for animals and their predators to be out. The streams and brooks were frozen silent, the earth was solid as metal underfoot. The cold, snow-filled air seemed to dampen out any other sounds there may have been. There were gaps in the thick grey clouds, and through those gaps the night sky was the colour of Quink. The stars were sharp pinpricks. It was beautiful. It was just like being in outer space.

A broken body lay on the road.

Mrs Castle went over to it, knelt down. But before she had even touched the man's face, she realised he was still alive. Unconscious, but it was cold enough to see the man's breath coming from his mouth. Shallow breath.

He didn't seem to be bleeding, although he was wearing a thick parka and waterproof trousers, so it was difficult to tell. Mrs Castle had been given some first-aid training, so knew that he could be bleeding internally, and that plenty of serious injuries didn't lead to bleeding.

The man groaned, and tried to move.

Normally, she knew you weren't meant to move someone if they'd been knocked down by a car – they may have broken their spine, and moving them could permanently damage it. Here she didn't have a

choice: the pedestrian was in the middle of the road, and if another car came past it would hit him. So, as gently as she could, Mrs Castle helped to move him to the verge at the side of the road. He couldn't put any weight on his right leg – it looked like he may have broken it.

She asked him his name, he mumbled a reply, but she couldn't hear.

'Arnold Knight,' he repeated, straining to get up.

'Don't move,' she told him.

'We're in terrible danger!' he cried suddenly. 'It's after me. If it sees you…'

A part of Mrs Castle's brain, a small, primitive part at the back, right at the top of her spine, told her to get away from here.

She looked up into the darkness, up the hill in the direction this man had come from.

There was nothing there. Nothing she could see.

But whatever Arnold had seen, he'd preferred to run into the path of a moving car than to face it.

'What is after you?'

'A –'

'Animal? A person?'

'A monster,' Arnold told her. 'A giant metal monster.'

Mrs Castle smiled. 'You had a bump on the head,' she reassured him. Either that or he was drunk, or had been sniffing glue. He didn't look dangerous, she decided.

'I –' Arnold winced, unable to speak.

'Does it hurt?' Mrs Castle asked, knowing it was a stupid question.

'Can you get me away from here? If you can't, then at least you can get away. Tell people.'

'You shouldn't try to move unless you have to.'

He clutched her sleeve. 'We have to. It's after me.'

A car was coming. She could see the headlights and hear the faint sound of the engine.

'I'll get them to phone for an ambulance,' she suggested.

'Wait!' Arnold warned. 'You're in terrible danger!' His voice was almost comical – he was terrified, but nothing could be as bad as *that*, could it?

'It's *them*,' Arnold insisted.

The car was getting nearer, and so she began waving her arms. The circular headlights were getting bigger and brighter. At first she thought the driver hadn't seen her, or that he wasn't going to stop, or

even that it was the monster that Arnold thought had been chasing him, but the car came to a halt alongside her.

Mrs Castle found herself sighing with relief. It was a perfectly ordinary Volkswagen Beetle. It was matt black, almost invisible on such a dark night.

The window whirred down, smoothly – it must have been electric. Mr Castle was always talking about getting electric windows, but they were too expensive.

There were two people in the car. A man in the driving seat, a woman passenger nearer to the open window. They were in their early twenties, and they looked more like a twin brother and sister than husband and wife. They were both pale, with piercing blue eyes, and they wore identical plastic mackintoshes. They looked at her in a way that made Mrs Castle feel small.

'Good evening,' she said.

The two looked at each other.

'Good evening to you,' the woman said, her voice deeper than Mrs Castle had expected.

'Good evening,' the man echoed, with a voice that sounded almost like a woman's.

'There's been an accident,' she said. 'Could you telephone for help? This man will die if you don't.'

'Die?' the man said, peering over to take a look.

'Yes. He's already delirious. Talking about monsters chasing him.'

'And you don't believe that?' the woman asked hurriedly.

'Well… no.'

'Good,' the man concluded.

'You have to get help,' Mrs Castle insisted.

The two looked at each other again, and it was clear they found something about her amusing.

'We *could*…' the woman said.

'…could, but shan't,' the man finished quickly.

The car sped off, the electric window sliding smoothly up, and Mrs Castle could hear the man and woman laughing together as it went, the man's laugh sounding like a woman giggling and the woman's laugh like the deep guffaw of an old man.

She slumped her shoulders. There was a little nugget of cold in her stomach. She didn't understand why those two people would want to be so cruel. She knew there wasn't a reason, not really, they were just

'having a laff', as her pupils would have called it. That was what the children who pushed other children over in the playground said; that was what Greg had said when she'd caught him writing his name on his desk with a marker pen. That was what Barry said when he'd told everyone at her birthday party that her Purdey cut made her look like Velma from *Scooby-Doo*. 'Just having a laff.'

Mrs Castle felt like crying, but knew she had to be brave for Arnold Knight.

She went back to the injured man. He was cowering behind her car.

'You mustn't move,' she told him sternly.

'They didn't see me,' he said.

'I don't think so.'

'Were they the ones who were chasing you?'

'No… no, it was a –' He clamped his mouth shut.

'A what?' Mrs Castle scowled.

Arnold tried to sit up. 'It doesn't matter. It's gone.'

'Stay still.'

'It can't be doing me any good sitting down here,' he replied. 'I'll get frostbite.'

'You said someone was after you,' Mrs Castle said sternly. 'Who?'

Arnold looked down at his legs. 'They'd have caught up with me by now. I must have got away from them. You saved me. Thanks.'

Mrs Castle was grateful that he didn't blame her for running him over, but she found it hard to believe that she'd done him any favours. 'What were you doing out here?' she said.

Arnold chuckled. 'Looking for UFOs.'

Mrs Castle laughed. 'Did you see any little green men? Was it them chasing you?'

He didn't answer. Instead he asked, 'Can I get into the car? Please?'

She helped him into the car, keeping the weight off his feet, and told him to stay put while she went to get help. She told him that whatever her husband's faults, he would have made sure there were blankets in the boot, there would even be a shovel if she needed to dig them out of a snowdrift. Arnold would be safe. She put on her emergency lights and got out of the car, assuring Arnold that she'd be as quick as she could. Arnold ducked down, saying it was safest if he stayed out of sight.

Outside the car it was quiet. No wind. Calm.

Mrs Castle wondered if Arnold was all right in the head.

She looked up at the night's sky, and she thought it looked like a window. A window to a better place. Perhaps the UFO spotters were right: perhaps she would see something else up there tonight. The regulars at the Dragon thought the UFO spotters were nutters - and they did look like nutters. They talked like them, too - they told their stories with such authority, comparing notes, exchanging blurry photographs that could be of anything. But for the last few weeks they had congregated in Greyfrith, drawn there by tales of mysterious lights and even traces - they said - that the saucers had landed.

Mrs Castle knew what the UFO spotters wanted - they wanted there to be a better place. They wanted the world to be like it had been when they were children, when they had storybooks instead of *this*, when they'd welcomed the fall of snow. They wanted to fly, they wanted to travel to faraway places, they wanted there to be more to life than the human race had made of it. They wanted someone, anyone, to come to their rescue, and take them to a better life where cars didn't break down, where there weren't strikes and power cuts. Somewhere wives didn't hate their husbands so much they dreaded going home. Mrs Castle felt the same. She wanted to be swept up by the wind, or by a man on a white horse, or by the UFOs. She never wanted to go home: she wanted to go and live in outer space, or at least in London.

Deborah Castle looked down over the valley, and saw the air full of snow, and realised how much better life had been when she had been Debbie Gordon, and she cried.

You may feel like that, one day. I just hope that day doesn't come soon.

Chapter Two
The Doctor

Mrs Castle knew three miles was too far to walk in the dark, in this weather, on her own. There may be a late bus – in the early 1980s such things existed in England – but she couldn't depend on it. So that meant she knew she had to find someone nearby with a phone.

It didn't take her long to see a farmhouse in the valley below, a single light on downstairs, and smoke coming from one of the chimneys. It was about two hundred yards away, nestled among some dark trees. The path down wasn't obvious, but neither did it seem hazardous. She turned back to her car to tell Arnold that she would go down there and ask the owner if she could use his phone. Arnold agreed to stay put, and warned her to be on her guard.

Mrs Castle climbed over the locked iron gate. The snow had started to settle, it was quite a steep slope, and the ground was icy. Mrs Castle had lived in Greyfrith for most of her life, though, and she was more than capable of getting down to the farmhouse without injury.

From the road, the building had looked like every other farmhouse around here – a solid box with a high vaulted roof. There was a small barn to one side, but there didn't seem to be any sign of farming activity – no tractors or bales of hay. This was a house, not a working farm, and the barn was probably a garage now, or perhaps an artist's studio.

Between the barn and the house was an odd thing – a shed or… some kind of telephone box. It was dark blue, probably (it was difficult to say in this light, it could have been green or grey). It was a hut, with a stacked roof and little windows.

The sign over the doors said it was a police box.

What on earth was a police box?

There was a notice on one of the door panels:

> POLICE TELEPHONE
> FREE
> FOR USE OF
> **PUBLIC**
> ADVICE AND ASSISTANCE
> OBTAINABLE IMMEDIATELY
>
> OFFICERS AND CARS
> RESPOND TO
> URGENT CALLS
>
> PULL TO OPEN

This was just what she needed! It was a dream come true.

Mrs Castle pulled the handle, as the sign told her to, but the panel didn't budge. She could see that it was meant to. This was meant to be a little door, and behind it there would be a telephone and she'd pick it up and a policeman would come and sort everything out. He'd get Arnold to a hospital and take her home and arrange for the car to be towed to her house and everything would be all right.

But the little hatch didn't open, it was jammed shut. She tried pulling and pushing at the big door, trying to get inside, but that didn't budge either.

She put her head against the door and began crying again.

Mrs Castle didn't cry very often. Mrs Castle was brave, resourceful and intelligent: she knew that the problems in life weren't solved by men on white horses, or being swept away by the wind, or with a quick phone call. She knew she would have to solve her problems for herself. But knowing that isn't the same as having the solution. Knowing there was a way out, somewhere, only made her failure to find it more frustrating, and so sometimes, when no one else was looking, when it all got too much, she cried.

It was cold, and crying wouldn't change that. Mrs Castle pulled herself up and wiped her eyes. There was almost certainly a telephone in the house – that was why she had come down here. Now she looked, she couldn't see a telephone line leading down into the farmhouse. But they were bound to have one, living so far out here. She would knock on the door and ask to use the phone.

She walked up to the front door of the farmhouse and knocked on it. It was eight on a Saturday night, so she knew they may be out. She began thinking about what she would say: first, she would have to apologise for disturbing the house owners, most probably. But surely

they would let her use their telephone? It was an emergency, after all.

There was no answer. The snow was falling faster now, it was even beginning to drift up against the side of the police box. Despite her scarf and gloves, Mrs Castle was starting to get a little cold. More importantly, she knew Arnold could be seriously injured, and that she had to get help to him.

She tried the door handle, and was surprised when the door opened – she had expected it to be locked. The door was solid oak, and very heavy, but it opened silently and reassuringly. With a nervous look around, Mrs Castle stepped inside, out of the wind and the snow.

The hallway was dark. Some people have a telephone in the hall, but Mrs Castle was disappointed to discover that the owners of this house didn't. She stepped, ever so carefully, further along the long hallway. She felt very guilty, walking around someone else's house. Whatever the circumstances, it didn't feel right.

'Hello?' she called out, but there was no reply.

The carpet was thick, and quite old by the look of it. But the tables and picture frames were good quality. Mrs Castle wondered if she should take her boots off – she'd wiped her feet outside, but there would still be slush on them. She told herself off for being so silly – she was breaking and entering, after all. The owners wouldn't mind the dirty footprints – they'd mind the person who made them.

The front door closed behind her, the latch clicking.

Mrs Castle was worried that the owners of the house would find her. Out in the country, people had shotguns. She was an intruder, and the people here could be old, or scared of burglars. If they were in the habit of leaving their door unlocked in the night, then she wouldn't be surprised if there had been burglars here in the past.

'Hello?' she called again.

There was a long, carpeted staircase leading upstairs, and the hallway led through to a gloomy kitchen. There was one other door, down here, and as Mrs Castle approached she realised there was a light on.

She knocked on the door.

'Excuse me,' she said, as politely as she could manage.

No one answered. Mrs Castle was beginning to think the owners were out. When she went out she sometimes left a light on to fool burglars. Of course, if the people who lived here were that worried about burglars, she would have advised them to lock their front door.

She went into the room. The remains of a log fire were glowing in the fireplace at one end, and candlesticks were dotted about, casting warmth and shadowy light around the room.

The room was cluttered with old furniture, heavy-framed paintings of people and places, chunks of machinery and bits of scientific apparatus. There was an old microscope, and a very modern-looking telescope.

Next to a huge armchair in the middle of the room was a pile of books – all sorts of books: leather-bound hardbacks, cheap paperbacks, big textbooks, even a couple of *Blue Peter* annuals. All of them had bookmarks, and on top of the pile was a travel chess set, quite an old, battered one. There was a game in progress, and Mrs Castle (who was something of an expert) guessed that it had been under way for some time. Despite herself, Mrs Castle bent over to get a better look at the game.

It was then that she saw there was a man, fast asleep in the armchair.

He didn't look like a farmer – he looked like a poet. Mrs Castle knew, of course, that farmers didn't always look like farmers, and so some of them might look like poets. She knew a few poets from a local writing group, and they were scruffy enough to be farmers. But she knew what she meant.

He was not an old man, but not really a young man, either – he looked older than she was, but she was only twenty-six. His long face was oval, with an aristocratic nose and a full mouth. He had a high forehead, framed with long light-brown hair. He looked warm and peaceful, and his skin was milky pale. He wore a long, dark, velvet coat that spilled over the arms of his chair. He looked like a New Romantic, which was the fashion according to all the magazines, although living in Greyfrith Mrs Castle had never seen one in the flesh before, and it was like meeting a man from another world.

The man's eyes snapped open. Blue eyes, with traces of crows' feet around them.

'I-I'm sorry,' she found herself saying. 'The door was open. I've been in a car accident. My name's Deborah Castle.'

'I'm the Doctor,' he said, clearly a little bemused.

It wasn't a name at all, not a proper one, but for some reason Mrs Castle didn't think that, she just accepted it.

'I ran someone over. A UFO spotter.'

The Doctor frowned. 'Why?'

'Not deliberately,' she added hurriedly. 'He ran out in front of me. He's in my car at the moment. He's hurt his leg and can't walk.'

The Doctor showed her to the phone, hidden behind a pile of yellowing scientific journals in one corner of the room. Once she'd called an ambulance, the Doctor insisted on going back to her car with her. She didn't want to impose, and they didn't speak as they made their way back up the hill.

They arrived just before the ambulance did. Arnold was conscious, and lucid, and he and the Doctor exchanged a few words while Mrs Castle flagged the ambulance down. Arnold joked with the ambulancemen as they carried him into the back of their vehicle. Arnold seemed much more relaxed now, and didn't seem to bear Mrs Castle any ill will. The driver told Mrs Castle that they would need to check thoroughly, but that Arnold had escaped with a broken leg and some mild bruising. He took her details and reminded her that she would need to contact the police to report an accident.

He offered her a lift back into town, but she told him she was safe to drive, not too shaken – although the Cortina might not be up to it. The ambulance drove off, but without putting on its siren or even putting the blue lights on, which disappointed Mrs Castle a little.

The Doctor was already checking under the bonnet for signs of damage.

'Are you sure you can see?' Mrs Castle asked. 'Don't you need a torch?'

'Don't worry about that.' The Doctor said, peering into the depths of the engine. Mrs Castle could hardly see at all: just some dark shapes, connected together with a labyrinth of cables and pipes.

He fiddled around for a moment before putting the bonnet down, and then bent over the car, studying the panelwork.

'There's a slight dent on the bonnet,' he told her, 'but other than that, the car's fine, now. Were you having problems before the accident?'

Mrs Castle nodded. She had never owned a car of her own, and her husband had kept her away from the engine – he'd shown her how to open the bonnet and how to fill the screenwash bottle, but that was all. It felt odd seeing someone else closing up the Cortina's bonnet – particularly another man.

'Nothing major,' the Doctor announced. 'The radiator didn't like the cold weather. If it had been given a winter service, it would have been fine.'

Mrs Castle's spirits lifted. Not just because the problem with her car wasn't serious – although it is always good to hear news like that – but because it meant it wasn't her fault. More than that, it was Barry's – he'd talked about getting the car ready for the onset of the cold weather, but he'd never got around to it.

'Give it a go,' the Doctor prompted.

Mrs Castle got back into the car and turned the ignition key. It started immediately, and even she could tell the engine sounded perfectly healthy.

She wound down the window. 'Thank you so much,' she said. She took a deep breath. 'Time to get home.'

'You look shaken,' the Doctor told her. 'I'll make you some tea, let you calm down a bit.'

He unlocked the gate and pointed her towards his driveway, which was difficult to see under the snow, and they drove the short distance down to his house. The Doctor took her back inside, sat her down in his chair and then disappeared to make her a cup of tea.

Sitting here, in warmth and comfort, Mrs Castle couldn't argue with the Doctor's logic. Although it seemed a long time since the accident, her watch reassured her it was barely half an hour, and now the car was working again she probably wouldn't be any later home than she had told her husband. She was already more relaxed than she'd been all day.

The Doctor came in with a tray of tea things. He found a sofa under some boxes and cleared a space. As Mrs Castle watched him sit down, he yawned.

She felt guilty. 'I'm sorry to have woken you up.'

'I don't need much sleep,' he said wistfully. 'In fact, usually I can pretty well do without it.' Men always liked to boast how little sleep they needed. His voice was soft with an accent that was difficult to pin down.

'You seemed fast asleep when I came in,' Mrs Castle replied gently.

'I was dreaming,' he said, trying to remember. 'I was in a house, and it was my house but it wasn't. It went on for ever, and I kept finding new rooms. There were hundreds of bedrooms, a swimming pool, an art gallery and a library, even a greenhouse the size of Kew Gardens. I'm sure it means something.'

'It's a common dream,' Mrs Castle reassured him.

'It is?' He seemed disappointed.

'I've had the same dream. I'm sure you can find a book that will tell you what it means. When I have the dream it's an enormous empty school – classroom after classroom, corridor after corridor. But that's not a surprise.'

The man cocked his head to one side, confused.

'I'm a teacher,' she explained. 'Primary school.'

He nodded, as if he approved.

'Who are you playing chess with?' she asked. There was no one else in the house, she was sure of that. But some people conducted postal games, sending each move at the end of a letter.

'Oh, just against myself.' He seemed embarrassed by the admission.

'I do that,' Mrs Castle said brightly. 'I've played it since I was a little girl. My husband doesn't, neither do any of our friends.' For some reason, Mrs Castle was annoyed with herself for mentioning her husband. 'I run the chess club at school now, but they're only ten and eleven – they're still learning. Are you any good?'

'There's only one way to find out.' The Doctor was already setting up the pieces for a new game, starting to unpick the moves he'd made.

'No,' Mrs Castle said. 'I'm already late, and I'm sure I need to report the accident to the police.' She stood up, took a step back, almost standing on some apparatus.

The Doctor looked a little disappointed. To Mrs Castle, he looked a little like one of her pupils might when they were told to pack up their toys and get ready for school. She glanced back at what she'd almost stepped on. It consisted of a couple of car batteries lashed together with black tape, a TV aerial and a couple of old radios nestling in an old suitcase.

'Can you get Radio Two on that?' she asked.

'No, no. It's just something I'm working on. It generates soundwaves. Ultrasonics. When I get it working, it could be used to unfasten screws, maybe even open locks.'

Mrs Castle looked at the device, the size of a suitcase. 'Wouldn't it be easier just to use a screwdriver or a key?'

The Doctor looked deflated. 'Well, it's only a prototype,' he told her sulkily. 'The final version will be a lot smaller, I'm sure.'

'Do you live here alone?' she asked him, trying to lighten the mood.

The Doctor nodded.

'It must get lonely.'

'It's beautiful here,' he said softly. 'Peaceful.'

Mrs Castle had to agree.

'I've never seen you in town.' She was sure she would remember him.

'I go there from time to time,' he assured her. 'To pick up supplies: food, books, that sort of thing.'

'You've got a car?'

He nodded. 'A Trabant.'

'A what?'

The Doctor just laughed.

'And that police box out there? Is that yours? No, silly question – it belongs to the police.'

'It's mine,' the man said. When he saw her puzzled look he continued: 'It's a long story... at least I think it is. I found a book about police boxes once, in a library, but there weren't any clues in it.'

'I tried using the phone, but there isn't one.'

The Doctor frowned. 'Yes, I know. Odd, isn't it? I don't suppose you know why?'

Mrs Castle shook her head.

The Doctor looked disappointed again.

'Knights and castles,' she chuckled.

'Pardon?'

'My name's Castle, the man I ran over was Mr Knight. And you and I are both chess players. It's only a coincidence, but it's like something off *That's Life*.'

The Doctor was turning the white king over and over in his hand, watching it intently.

'The game's afoot,' he said. Then he looked up. 'At least, I think it is.' He studied the board.

Mrs Castle looked down at the board, at the remnants of the Doctor's game. A white queen, a few pawns, a couple of bishops, a couple of castles. Ranged against them were the black knights and castles, and the king. No pawns, at least few to speak of.

'What's that?' she asked. There was a large piece she didn't recognise, one that seemed to come from another set.

The Doctor picked it up, moved it, captured a white knight with it. 'I'm not sure,' he concluded.

He placed the white king firmly in the centre of the board.

'I'd better get going,' Mrs Castle said. 'Look, why don't you come to chess club on Tuesday night – four o'clock at the school? There's a team coming from Vale Mill. We'll play that game.'

The Doctor grinned. 'That would be good. I'll see you there.'

Chapter Three
The Girl with Two Hearts

Mrs Castle got home safely, and the snow kept falling for three more nights and days, but she didn't mind so much any more.

All that time, as she prepared and taught her lessons, she thought about the Doctor and how he had helped her. It was a simple, kind act, but the more Mrs Castle thought about it, the more complicated it became. Who was he? How long had he been living all alone in the farmhouse? How did he make a living? What did he do with himself all day?

She tried to work out how old the Doctor was. She could remember seeing the crows' feet around his eyes, and she thought he had a couple of grey hairs, but Mrs Castle found it very difficult to guess. She decided that he was older than he looked, but she couldn't decide *how* old he looked. She found herself looking forward to Tuesday night, and the chess club. The Doctor was a fascinating man, and she had the feeling that the answers to her questions would be even more intriguing than not knowing. Whatever the case, the answers were bound to be more interesting than her ordinary life, with its routine of schoolwork and living with Barry.

On Tuesday, around half three, as the sun set over the hills, and her pupils began packing up, she began to worry the Doctor wouldn't come. The snow was inches thick, now, and although the roads had been gritted it was still a hazardous journey. This time of the year, it was already night when the school day ended.

The school secretary put her head round the door and told Mrs Castle there was a phone call for her. Mrs Castle trudged over to the main building, leaving her class to pack up under the watchful eye of the secretary.

Mrs Castle thought the phone call must be from the police, wanting to talk to her yet again about the accident. The last time she'd been to the station, the desk sergeant, who had a couple of sons at the school, assured her that she wouldn't be charged: Arnold agreed that it was his fault for running out into the road. But that hadn't stopped an

endless pile of paperwork from mounting up.

But it wasn't the police: it was Mr Moxon, the teacher from Mill Vale Primary who ran their chess club. He told her the snow was coming down, and their team had been hit by the flu. He was sorry for the late notice, but he was going to have to cancel.

Mrs Castle put down the telephone, disappointed.

She walked back through the playground to her classroom block. Greyfrith Primary School was a collection of Portakabins huddled around a small playground. The only permanent structure was the Victorian main building she had just left, a wet, grey, slate-and-stone building which had the assembly hall, the headmaster's office and the small library. The cabins were meant to be a temporary solution to the expanding school roll, but they'd been saying that as long as Mrs Castle had been teaching here. The flat roofs leaked in this weather. The cabins were easy to heat – but there was no insulation, no double-glazing, and Mrs Castle could almost see the red arrows coming out of the doors and windows as the heat escaped, as they did on the public-information films.

The curtains for her classroom had been drawn – the first members of the chess club must have arrived. She could hear the scraping of tables and opening of cupboards. She knew she would have to break the news that the match that the club had been looking forward to for a week wasn't going to go ahead. She was disappointed for her pupils, but she knew that she was really disappointed because she wouldn't be seeing the Doctor this evening, if ever again.

There were a lot of parents around, picking up their children. Mrs Castle recognised a few of them, and stopped to say hello. The parents had heard about her car accident – word got around Greyfrith very quickly – and they all offered their sympathy and support.

Then Mrs Castle saw them: a man and a woman in their early twenties, looking more like a twin brother and sister than husband and wife. Mrs Castle remembered their piercing blue eyes, and their plastic mackintoshes. When she last saw them, they had been sitting down, so she didn't realise how tall and thin they were. They were standing right at the gates, looking at the children as they came out.

They watched her pass, in silence.

'Good evening,' she said, refusing to be cowed.

The two looked at each other.

'Good evening to you,' the woman said. Mrs Castle had forgotten

how deep the woman's voice had been. She was tall, with long thin legs like a fashion model's. Mrs Castle crossed her hands over her chest.

'Good evening,' the man echoed in his woman's voice.

'I've seen you before,' she said. She looked around for confirmation and - yes! - she saw their black Volkswagen Beetle parked over two spaces of the little school car park. 'You didn't stop for me on Saturday night, even though I told you there had been an accident.'

'We're not following you,' the man assured her. The woman glared at her... brother? 'I promise,' he added, insincerely.

'It's just that we've been taught not to talk to strangers,' the woman said smugly.

'What are your names?'

'Call us the Hunters,' the man suggested.

'You don't have a child here, do you, Mr and Mrs Hunter?'

The two smirked back at her.

'Then what are you doing, hanging around the school gates?'

'This and that,' the woman answered.

Mrs Castle dug her heels into the sludgy snow, and drew herself up to her full height and began telling them that she didn't care what they were doing, but they ought to leave, before she called the police.

But Mrs Castle realised the pair weren't listening at all: they were staring over her shoulder, the oddest expressions on their faces.

'Must be going,' the man announced.

Mrs Castle turned, and saw the Doctor sitting on the low stone wall, as if he had been there all the time.

'Are you having trouble?' the Doctor asked her.

Mrs Castle turned around, but the man and the woman had gone. She tried to see their car, but that had vanished, too.

'No,' Mrs Castle said, puzzled by the speed of their departure. 'Did you see them?'

'See who?'

'The...' She looked around. 'There was an odd couple. I saw them just after the accident on Saturday night. It doesn't matter. Er, hello. Bad news - the other team aren't coming, so I'm going to have to cancel.'

'Won't the children be disappointed?' he asked.

Mrs Castle sighed. 'Of course they will be, but what's the alternative?'

The Doctor frowned, unable to come up with the answer.

The school secretary was trudging towards them, arms crossed over

her chest. She looked very cold – her big glasses were almost misted over. 'Your Barry's on the phone,' she announced.

Mrs Castle rolled her eyes.

'I'll look after the chess club,' the Doctor offered.

Barry hadn't wanted anything in particular – he rarely did when he phoned his wife at work. He just did it to remind her who was boss. As she walked back to her classroom (along the path that the school caretaker had carefully cleared in the snow and ice), she was feeling very cross – it was cold and dark, and things weren't going the way they should be. She wasn't sure whether the world was whispering behind her back, or had forgotten that she was there altogether.

She went into the Portakabin, tutting at the slick of water in the corridor. The heating had been turned off, despite her asking the caretaker not to. Every week the caretaker forgot about the chess club and left them shivering. She wondered if the man genuinely forgot, or whether her constant requests and badgering had left him with some ill-formed grudge against her.

She braced herself to tell the children her bad news and opened the door.

The chess club were all sitting at their desks, heads down, trying to figure their next move. But they were all sitting on their own. The chair opposite each of them was empty.

The Doctor was sitting on the edge of her desk. He turned at the sound of her entering and beamed at her. Mrs Castle felt elated – she remembered what it was like when a teacher praised her work.

'I hope you don't mind. I came up with a little challenge of my own.'

She looked again and realised.

'You're playing all of them? Ten games at once?'

'Eleven,' the Doctor said simply, moving aside. There was another board set up on her desk. 'I hope you don't mind.'

Mrs Castle smiled, and picked up a white pawn and a black pawn, hiding one in each hand.

'Black,' the Doctor said, picking her left hand. His mouth twitched into a smile when she opened her hand to reveal the black pawn.

Mrs Castle put the pieces back and opened by moving her king's pawn.

'Be with you in a moment,' the Doctor said. He stood, and walked around the room. He stopped at the first board, made his move and

quickly moved on to the next one. He drummed his mouth with his fingers, then slid the castle up the board. Lee clearly hadn't expected the move, and it left him deep in thought. The Doctor was already up to the fifth board. Mrs Castle watched him scratch his head, purse his lips, strut about. He returned to her within a minute.

'Incredible,' she told him.

'Early days yet,' the Doctor told her. 'Anyone can do this and *lose* eleven games. A couple of them will give me a run for my money.'

'You can tell that already?'

'Oh yes.' He moved his king's pawn, nodded happily at some secret joke and began his circuit of the room.

'Check!' Stephen announced, delighted.

The Doctor sat down hard on the tiny chair opposite his opponent, shook his head, then took the offending piece with a pawn. 'Check!' he echoed. Stephen slumped.

'You're trying the king's gambit,' Daniel announced.

'Am I?' the Doctor said. Mrs Castle wasn't sure whether the surprise in his voice was feigned or not. He looked Daniel straight in the eye. 'So, what move should I make next?' he asked the young boy. Mrs Castle smiled – Daniel had ordered a book on chess openings for the school library, and had kept it out on permanent loan ever since it had arrived. He had it memorised, but couldn't always put what he had read into practice.

Daniel told him what he should do, and the Doctor obliged.

A few minutes and a few circuits later, the Doctor was at Mrs Castle's desk again.

He chuckled. 'Thought so,' he told her, 'you're castling early on. Quite apt, given your surname.'

'Gordon?' she asked, before remembering that her surname now was 'Castle'. 'Is there a Doctor's defence against it?' she asked.

He checked the board, a puzzled expression on his face.

'No need to pretend with me,' she assured him.

'Um...' the Doctor replied, feigning innocence.

'I can see what you're doing – you don't really need to think it through.'

'No?'

'No. I know you don't want to make beating the kids look too easy, and I appreciate it, but there's no need to spare *my* feelings. Especially not this early in the game.'

He moved a knight out.

Mrs Castle opened up the drawer in her desk and rummaged through the confiscated Smurfs for her packet of Polos. She offered them to the Doctor, who popped one his mouth, then asked her if she knew that the gelatin in them was made from melted bones.

Mrs Castle quickly swallowed her Polo and put the rest back in the drawer.

'So who's giving you trouble?' she asked, pushing out a pawn.

'Stephen, Daniel, Stacey and Rachel,' he replied without hesitation, moving his castle.

'You know their names?' she asked, moving her castle out.

'Of course.' Knight move to keep the castle in check.

'How?'

'They told me when I asked,' he replied, confused by the question.

Mrs Castle was impressed. Faced with a new class, it would often be a week before she could remember what they were all called.

She moved another pawn out. 'What about Miranda?'

The Doctor glanced over to the tiny blonde girl, sitting at the last table, deep in thought. 'Not really.'

'Watch out for her,' Mrs Castle warned. 'She's smart.'

The Doctor smiled. 'Thanks for the warning.'

He moved his castle's pawn forward two spaces and stood up to go about his rounds. Mrs Castle sipped at her coffee and looked down at the board, unable to believe what a poor position she was in already. She pulled herself away from the Doctor's theatrics and decided to concentrate on her game. It had been years since she'd had a proper opponent, and Mrs Castle was out of practice. The Doctor was back before Mrs Castle had put her coffee mug down.

'Not moved?' he asked.

'Thinking it through. How are you getting on?'

'Stephen's not planning far enough ahead, but he's good. Daniel... he's not seen my rook yet: he's too hung up on the theory. Stacey's being clever, playing a long game. Rachel can see what I'm doing, I'm not sure she knows how to stop it.'

'Miranda?'

He hesitated. 'I'm not sure. She doesn't look like a threat.'

Mrs Castle looked over. Miranda was an odd mix. She was small for her age – nearly eleven, but looked more like an eight- or nine-year-old – but was very confident: two things that rarely went together. But that was hardly the oddest thing about her.

Mrs Castle moved her castle, trying to press forward.

The Doctor took a pawn with his knight. 'Check.'

'So, did you ever play chess professionally?' she asked.

'No.'

'University team?'

'No.' She had hoped for a hint of his background – that was a clear invitation for him to discuss his past – but none was forthcoming. He wasn't being evasive: he just didn't take the hint. Mrs Castle took the castle back to take the Doctor's knight. The Doctor brought the other knight forward.

'Check. Mate in thirty-four,' the Doctor announced.

A couple of the other players looked up.

'You can't say that,' Daniel announced knowledgeably.

Mrs Castle wasn't so sure. She looked around the board. Everything seemed OK. There was the threat from the knight, but she could get that with her bishop.

She looked again.

'My God,' she said. Then, louder, 'Gather round, everyone.'

'Mrs Castle?'

'Look at this,' she told the children as they huddled around her desk. A couple of the brighter ones were already working out what would happen. It was a beautiful trap – sheer clockwork: to get out of check, she'd move a piece that would expose her king to further danger. But she wouldn't have a choice – the attacks would keep coming and coming, move after move, her pieces would swirl around the board, most of them falling into danger as they moved to defend. She couldn't see thirty-whatever moves ahead, but she could see far enough to recognise that the Doctor had her beaten.

Miranda and Stephen were looking at each other, unable to believe what they were watching.

Mrs Castle went through the motions for the others, let the Doctor spring his trap. She explained with every move that she didn't have a choice – a different move would place her in check or even checkmate. As the Doctor took her last castle and the game, there was even a small round of applause.

'Let's see if you lot can do any better,' Mrs Castle told them, ushering them back to their own tables.

The Doctor returned to the main task, working his way around the tables.

Three fell straightaway, including Stephen, who was clearly annoyed to be beaten. The rest fell more intently into their game, worried now they could see how good the Doctor was. This gave the Doctor an opportunity to return to Mrs Castle's desk.

'Tell me about Miranda,' he said.

'She's bright.'

'Right. Good at maths? A lot of chess players are.'

'Not quite top of her class, not far off. She's one of the candidates for extra tuition.'

The Doctor tapped his lips with his fingers.

'And –' Mrs Castle hesitated – 'she's got two hearts.'

The Doctor stared at her.

'Really,' Mrs Castle insisted. 'A birth defect. Well, not a defect at all, really. Both hearts are fully developed, one on each side. It means she's never out of breath, she's –'

'How do you know?' the Doctor asked levelly.

'Her parents have known since she was born. They didn't tell the school, but Miranda bruised a rib last year in PE and we had to take her to St Kitt's for an X-ray. They didn't give their consent to any other tests, which annoyed the doctors. The parents said they didn't want anyone to know she was different. That's fair enough: you know what kids are like. It doesn't bother Miranda, though.'

The Doctor was barely listening. 'Do her parents have –?'

Mrs Castle laughed. 'I've never asked. Why, do you think it runs in the family?' The Doctor didn't answer. He went back over to continue the games, more distracted than Mrs Castle would have thought.

Two more of his opponents fell, one of them resigning.

Daniel, Stacey, Rachel, Miranda and Paul were left. Stacey and Rachel were beaten quite quickly. Paul asked if he could have Stephen's help, which the Doctor allowed. The two boys conferred, but quickly agreed they were in a hopeless position. So the Doctor literally turned the tables and made a move. The two boys looked equally perplexed now they had command of the Doctor's old pieces.

Daniel almost beat him, then almost forced a draw, but the Doctor got him in the end.

Only Miranda was left now. The Doctor sat down opposite her – looking very silly in a chair designed for a ten-year-old – and began concentrating. The other children drew up their chairs, and Mrs Castle stood behind them, watching the game.

'Do you think that man was really chased by a space monster?' Miranda asked.

'Miranda,' Mrs Castle warned.

'What do you mean?' the Doctor asked.

'The UFO man.'

The Doctor looked up, stared at the girl.

'It's in the paper. A man ended up in hospital on Saturday night. He says he was chased by a monster.'

'St Kitt's?' the Doctor asked. Greyfrith had its own hospital in those days.

Mrs Castle shifted uncomfortably 'That's right. We shouldn't talk about it, and we shouldn't let it worry us,' she told Miranda, and the rest of the class.

Miranda grinned, showing a row of teeth that would have been perfect if one of the front ones hadn't been missing.

The Doctor leaned forward. 'Where was this?' He was talking to Miranda like an adult, and Miranda was happy to be treated that way.

'Cooper's Hill.'

'On Cooper's Farm?'

'Yeah,' said Stephen.

'Gosh.' The Doctor looked over at Mrs Castle. She nodded.

'There's no need to scare anyone,' Mrs Castle warned.

The Doctor nodded – thankfully understanding that there are some things you shouldn't say in front of children.

'So how long have you played chess?' the Doctor asked Miranda.

'Ages,' she said, suddenly a little shy.

'You're very good.'

'She's not,' Daniel snorted. 'I don't see why it's taking so long for you to beat her.'

Miranda looked over to the Doctor and they shared a smile. Daniel's jealousy was transparent.

The Doctor moved his queen into danger. Stephen and Mrs Castle exchanged a look – they'd noticed... but Miranda hadn't. She was at the other side of the board, faffing with her pawn structure.

The Doctor hesitated. 'You're letting me win,' he concluded.

Miranda looked up.

'I am,' she apologised.

'But why?'

She couldn't make eye contact with him. 'Well, if you lose, it's not as

big an achievement, is it? If you win ten games, but lose one, it's not as good.'

Mrs Castle gasped a laugh. She wasn't boasting, or being condescending.

The Doctor looked astounded. He moved his pawn to the eighth row, made it a queen. Checkmate.

There was a round of applause. The Doctor had won.

Miranda smiled.

'Why didn't you tell me that Arnold had seen a monster?' the Doctor asked Mrs Castle.

'I didn't think it was important,' she told him. 'Look, I've got a couple of things to do, then we can go down to the Dragon and I'll tell you everything he said.'

'Yes. I can't believe you didn't say anything before,' the Doctor repeated.

Mrs Castle smiled, pleased with herself. 'I thought you'd be less likely to help. After all, there are no such thing as monsters, are there?'

Chapter Four
Close Encounters

There was a couple on the swings where Daz Lewis was due to meet Julie.

She'd agreed to come here after she'd finished her shift at the Co-op, without changing. Daz had never told her, but he liked seeing her in her checked uniform and with her hair up. He unwrapped some gum and began chewing it. It was like Clark Kent and Superman, Daz thought. Julie could take off her glasses and suddenly she'd go from being plain to being dead beautiful. The uniform was dowdy, but when she took her hair down, suddenly she was the most beautiful woman in the world. He knew she had a good figure, but only *he* knew – the rest of the world saw only the buttoned-up old uniform.

Daz checked his watch – she was due in five minutes and the couple were still on the swings. He knew she'd see him, really, wherever he was in the small park. He knew they'd go and find somewhere else that was quiet. It was just that he'd planned this moment since Sunday, when they'd last seen each other. He wanted everything to be perfect. He'd even brought his Polaroid so he could take Julie's picture. There were a few more kids than Daz was expecting, and it was colder, but this was just how he'd pictured it. Apart from the couple on his swings.

Daz decided to ask the couple if they could move. He walked over. They were sitting with their backs to him, and didn't see him. He could see they were talking, and didn't want to interrupt.

They were about the same age as each other, and they looked like they were related. They were wearing plastic macs and odd-looking tracksuits.

'It was him,' the man insisted. He had a girlie voice, and Daz sniggered when he heard it. 'It's him, and that means this whole operation just got a hundred times more complicated.'

'Oh, it didn't look like him at all,' the woman said. Her voice sounded gruff, as if she smoked a lot of cigarettes. 'What are the odds of his just turning up here, of all the places he could turn up?'

The man sighed. 'Remember who we're talking about here. It's definitely him. Oh, come on, you must remember the last time...'

The woman rolled her eyes. 'It *had* to be the Doctor. Mr Gibson and he have history, too.'

'Mr Gibson?'

'That's what he's calling himself here – he says he wants to blend in.'

'Blend in?' he mimicked. 'I can't think of anywhere that he'd "blend in".'

'I'm just repeating what he told me. He's a psycho, you know that. I told you he would be trouble. I'm surprised he's managed to get this far without killing anyone.'

'Not for want of trying.'

Daz stopped in his tracks. These two were criminals, and they had an accomplice. They hadn't seen him yet, and he knew he should have got away, but instead he tried to keep very still and hear what they were saying, so he could tell the police, or at least his friends.

'I didn't want him along,' the woman said. 'The Prefect felt he was needed in case we ran into opposition.'

'To keep an eye on us, you mean.'

'I've asked him to keep a low profile from now on.'

'Well, hopefully he won't destroy this planet like he did his own.'

'Eh? But the reason he –'

'Oh, I know what he says, but that's not the whole story.'

Daz hesitated. Did the man just say their colleague had destroyed a planet? He couldn't have done. He must have said 'plant' or 'part', or something.

'But he said that it was destroyed by –'

'I've heard it enough times from him, I don't need to hear it again. All I'm saying is that he's not as innocent as he paints himself.'

The woman smiled and stroked the man's face. 'Who is?'

Irritated by the attention, the man pulled a small device that looked a bit like a calculator from his belt and swept it around. 'If we hadn't spent so much of our time looking after Mr Gibson, we'd have target acquisition by now. Trust us to land on the one part of Earth where everyone's looking out for aliens.'

'It might not be a coincidence. Our arrival would have created warping in space-time – the lights in the sky that these people have seen could be echoes of that.'

'Or it could be that everyone on this planet is just a stupid Joey who points up to the sky every time there's a funny light in it.'

'We're in the right area,' the woman assured him. 'We've done pretty well to narrow it down to this town in this time zone.'

The man frowned. 'Odd. I'm reading a life form just –'

He spun round, and leapt off his swing, landing just in front of Daz, glaring at him. The man seemed ready to pounce.

'I was just out… walking,' Daz stammered, suddenly afraid. He didn't want to put Julie in any danger by telling them about her.

'Walking? It's a very cold evening. Just walking? What's that in your hand?'

'Just a box of Milk Tray.' Daz held it out for the man to inspect. 'I… you can have them if you want.'

The man shook his head, scowling.

'You're from the UFO, aren't you?' Daz asked.

The man frowned. 'Youeffwhat?'

The woman had joined him. Despite himself, Daz thought she was quite a looker. She had great, long legs, and the top she was wearing was short, so you could see she had a flat stomach. She looked strong – stronger than her brother, or whatever he was.

'UFOs,' Daz said. 'Unidentified Flying Objects. Flying saucers. Aliens.'

Realisation dawned. 'Of course,' the man said. He pointed at the newspaper. 'Little green men.' He laughed, and looked up at the sky.

Daz forced himself to laugh with him.

The woman smiled encouragingly. 'Well – now we're here, what have you got to say to us?'

'I…' Daz didn't know what to say. He'd been watching *Buck Rogers* on Saturday night with his brother. There had been alien women in that – a whole planet of them, all wanting to go to bed with Buck Rogers. Daz and his brother had laughed about the UFO spotters – they'd agreed they wanted to meet aliens, too, if they were all like that. Daz had had a great dream that night about living on the planet Amazotica. Now he'd actually met some aliens, Daz wasn't so sure he liked it. There was something about the woman's eyes.

'You don't look like aliens,' he managed.

The man rolled his eyes. 'Please don't tell me I look like one of *you.*'

Daz looked at him. He didn't. He was too… elongated. His legs

were just a bit too long, his eyes a little too narrow, his hair swept back all wrong. Tiny differences, and he was sure this man could walk down Greyfrith high street without anyone noticing (he would have had to, to get to the park, Daz told himself, unless they'd beamed down like Captain Kirk) but this wasn't a human being.

'I didn't mean to offend you… or your… wife.'

'Wife?' The man looked over his shoulder at the woman. 'She's not my wife, she's… actually, I don't think there is a word for what she is in your primitive language.'

Daz tried to stay calm. 'Where are you from? I mean, what planet? Are you from Mars?'

'Xbike, no. That's even colder than it is here.'

'You could wear warmer clothes,' Daz suggested, looking over at the woman. She didn't seem impressed by his observation. She didn't look that cold, although she should do, dressed as she was.

The alien man bent down, a fluid motion, impossibly graceful. He smelled of… he didn't smell of human being. Some sort of flower. Not-quite-lavender. 'I'm from a planet you haven't heard of in the next galaxy over but five.'

'Oh, and we're also from a few million years in the future,' the woman added. Her smell was stronger, like Old Spice.

'Why are you here?' Daz asked, worried about the answer.

The man rolled his eyes. 'As if I'd tell you that.'

The woman frowned. 'Why can't we tell him?' The man couldn't think of a reason, so she continued. 'We're looking for a powerful alien being called the Last One. They've settled on Earth in this time zone, but we want to take them home.'

'You've not met anyone like that?' the man asked hopefully.

'No,' Daz admitted.

'Shame,' the man said. 'That would have made things a bit easier for us.'

The woman looked Daz up and down.

'What are you going to do to me?' he asked.

The woman looked puzzled. 'What would you like me to do?'

Daz considered his answer carefully, but decided not to push his luck. 'Just don't kill me.'

'Kill you?' The man looked almost offended. 'You're not important enough to kill. Just give us your camera and be on your way.'

'My camera?'

The alien woman pointed at the pouch strapped to Daz's belt. 'You did take photographs?'

Daz blinked. It hadn't occurred to him.

The alien man realised, and tutted. 'It speaks volumes about this planet that the dominant species are so –' He waved his hand as he searched for the word – 'rubbish.'

Daz handed over his camera. 'How can I be sure you won't kill me?'

'Because you're alive. Now go away.' The alien man looked away to examine the camera. He pointed it at Daz. 'Say cheese.'

The flash went off, which left Daz a little dazzled.

The alien man was already walking off, hand in hand with the woman.

Daz was still blinking when Julie arrived. She smelled of cigarettes, Daz noted, although she didn't smoke.

'Hi. Sorry I'm late. I stopped to buy a new blouse, then the Mini wouldn't start. Who were those people?'

Daz tried to smile, but he wanted to get as far away from here as possible. 'No one. Er… do you want to drive to Stockport and go to the pictures?'

Miranda put on her blue coat, wrapped herself up in a red scarf and gloves and went outside. All the other children had gone home now, but Miranda had to wait for her mum to pick her up. There were still a few lights on in the main building, and Miranda could see the caretaker gritting the steps. There was no sign of her mum yet, but Miranda was a few minutes early because chess club had finished sooner than usual.

The Doctor was standing in the middle of the playground, right in the football circle, staring up at the sky. He was wearing a black velvet coat, but he hadn't buttoned it up and it flapped around his knees. He didn't seem at all cold. It was a very clear night, which made it even colder.

'Hello,' he said, grinning, but not looking at Miranda.

'You can see his breath,' she said, pointing over to the caretaker. 'It's very cold.'

'Like a kettle,' the Doctor said.

'He's not a kettle,' said Miranda, because the caretaker wasn't.

'I mean it's the same principle. He's got water in his breath – when the air he breathes out is a lot hotter than the air around it, the water

condenses out. Like steam from a kettle. You do it,' he suggested.

Miranda agreed, and tried, but no breath came out. Puzzled, she tried again.

'You do it,' she said, frustrated.

The Doctor took a deep breath, then expelled it.

Miranda laughed at the Doctor's efforts. 'You can't do it either,' she chuckled.

'Why's that, do you think?' he asked.

Miranda thought about her answer, then said, 'Our breath must be colder than his.'

The Doctor nodded. 'Yes. Which is interesting.'

Miranda rubbed her hands together. 'This is the coldest place in the world. Why are you out here?'

'There are far colder places.'

Miranda found that hard to believe. 'Like out on the hills?'

'There, yes. This school is in a valley, and it's very cold, but up on a mountain it will be even colder, and exposed to the wind. The higher you go, the colder the air is.'

Miranda looked up. 'It must be very cold in outer space.'

'It is in most of space, it's almost as cold as cold can be.'

'That's a silly expression.'

'Yes, yes, it is, but there really is a temperature that's as cold as cold can be. Scientists call it absolute zero.'

'So cold all the water is frozen, even the boiling water?'

The Doctor smiled. 'So cold that the air itself becomes as hard as metal.'

'Is that why the UFOs are coming here? Because the space creatures want to get warm?'

'Possibly,' he said, and the way he said it made it impossible for Miranda to tell if he was being serious or not.

'My daddy and Mrs Castle told me that there's no such thing as space creatures.'

'Did they indeed? I wonder how they know.'

'Well,' Miranda said impatiently, stamping her feet a little to stay warm, 'are there or aren't there?'

The Doctor looked out into the night sky, lost in the stars and planets and constellations. He stood there for what seemed like several minutes, then squeezed his eyes shut.

'Doctor?'

'I don't know,' the Doctor said, his eyes still shut fast. 'I don't know, and I should, and –'

Miranda offered him her handkerchief, because he had started to cry. She didn't know why.

'Do you know the planets?' she asked him.

'Yes. There's Mercury, and Venus, and Earth, and the moon, and –' The Doctor counted them off on his fingers.

'The moon isn't a planet, it's a moon,' Miranda said primly. 'It's Earth's moon. Jupiter has twelve moons.'

'Thirteen, including Neophobus,' the Doctor said absently.

'They are discovering new moons all the time,' Miranda said. 'They sent a probe called *Voyager* and it took photographs.'

'Why don't you carry on with the list?' the Doctor suggested. 'After Earth and the moon...'

'Mars. Then the asteroid belt.'

'Which is?'

'Lumps of rock.'

'That's right, the remains of a planet that was pulled apart.'

Miranda shook her head. 'I've got a book at home that says that's wrong: it says some people used to think that, but the asteroid belt is really just what was left over when the planets had been made.'

The Doctor smiled benignly. 'I stand corrected. Then Jupiter.'

'Let me! Jupiter, then Saturn, then Uranus and Neptune and Pluto.'

'Very good. Now, point to Mars.'

Miranda looked up, then pointed.

'Don't guess,' the Doctor chided her. He held her wrist, moved it down until she was nearly pointing at the horizon.

'Which one's Mars?' she said. 'They all look like stars.'

'On a clear night like this, you can just about tell because it's red. If we stayed out here long enough, you'd be able to see it move across the sky. That's how people first saw there were planets out there. Stars stay fixed in place; the planets move.'

'I see Mars now.'

'Are you sure?'

'No,' Miranda admitted. 'Do you think the flying saucers come from Mars? What do you think Martians look like?'

The Doctor was rubbing his fingers together, trying to remember.

'Do you think they are green?' Miranda asked.

He glared at her, making her take a step back.

'I'm sorry,' she said, but she didn't understand what she had done to upset him.

'I thought I had it, then,' the Doctor said, not really talking to her at all. 'I'm sure I could remember. *Dass hunnar, ssli hoossurr.*' It was a strange, hissing sound, like gurgling pipes.

'Have you met a Martian?' Miranda asked. The Doctor was the only person she knew who might have done.

'Yes, yes, I feel sure of it. I've met lots of them.'

'What were their names?' said Miranda, giggling.

'I... can't really remember their names. I'm not very good with names. I can't even remember my own. Miranda means "to be wondered about", I know that. It was a Latin name originally.'

'There's a play by Shakespeare with a girl called Miranda,' she told him.

'Oh yes. *The Tempest*. She was the daughter of a powerful magician.'

'My dad's not a magician. He's an electrician.'

'Is he?'

'Here's my mum!' Miranda exclaimed. Her mother was walking over the ice towards them, desperately trying not to fall over.

The Doctor caught her just as she was about to slip. Miranda laughed out loud.

'Thank you,' her mum said and asked Miranda to introduce them.

'This is the Doctor,' Miranda said. 'He visited the chess club. He played us all, and he beat us. Even Mrs Castle.'

Her mum looked at the Doctor, and shared a smile with him. 'Did you really? He sounds like a clever man.'

'Oh, he is. He knows all about the stars and planets.'

'Your daughter is also very knowledgeable,' the Doctor said.

'Thank you. We do our best. Buy her books, encourage her.' Miranda wasn't sure she liked being talked about as if she wasn't there, but decided she didn't mind as long as they were nice about her. Besides, she was looking at the steam coming from her mother's mouth.

The Doctor nodded. 'Have you considered extra tuition?'

'We've not really thought about it, to be honest.'

'I really think Miranda would benefit. I'd be happy to volunteer some of my time.'

Miranda frowned. She didn't want to have extra lessons, but being with the Doctor wasn't at all like being at school.

'I'm not sure,' Miranda heard her mum saying.

'Muuuummm,' Miranda said, tugging her mum's sleeve. 'You've not asked me.'

Her mum smiled at the Doctor. 'It looks like I'll have to talk to my husband.'

The Doctor and Miranda grinned.

Chapter Five
Contact

There was music in the background. David Bowie.

'The Northwest has always been a nexus.'

'Sixty-seven.'

'Sixty-seven,' a number of the other UFO spotters echoed.

'Sixty-seven what?' George the barman asked, barely hiding a smirk.

'Nineteen sixty-seven,' one of them corrected, keen to have found an audience. 'There were sightings: Wilmslow, Glossop, St Helen's. Pilots and policemen saw them. Trained observers.'

'A policeman said he saw a cigar-shaped object, glowing at one end.'

'Is he sure it wasn't just a cigar?' the barman said, straight-faced. A few of the regulars laughed.

The spotters glared at him.

'The last few years, it's all shifted to the Southeast,' another piped up sagely, as if he was discussing regional investment. 'Have you seen the photos from Brentford?'

He rummaged in his bag and the others huddled together to look at photographs of an angular, blurry shape which the owner told them was a UFO that had been tracked on radar and landed in Brentford.

Mrs Castle gave the barman a knowing look.

'If I drank as much as they do, I'm sure I'd start seeing stuff,' he whispered.

'Not complaining, are you?'

'Not at all, not at all. Business is booming. These ones are on the house.'

Mrs Castle was puzzled. 'Why?'

'For running that bloke over. There were a fair few of 'em here before, but since the weekend you can't move for them.'

Mrs Castle knew the barman meant well. 'A gin and tonic and a water.'

The barman frowned. 'Water?'

'Mineral water, you know?'

'We've got some somewhere – your friend's a southerner, is he?' This was in the days before people drank water from bottles. Mrs Castle

had read about 'mineral water', but had never bought any.

Mrs Castle glanced over at the Doctor. 'I'm not sure what the Doctor is, to be honest.'

George looked thoughtful. 'Still, if someone wants to pay me for something that comes out a tap, I'll take their money. The customer is always right.'

'Perhaps there's money in it.' Mrs Castle chuckled. 'Charge five quid a pint and see what happens. After you've served me, of course. And if you make your fortune, then thank the Doctor.'

The Doctor had found a space in the corner, and was looking around as if this was the first time he'd ever been in a pub. He was watching the group of UFO spotters, fascinated by them.

'Does Barry know about him? Or does he spend too much time down the Co-op?'

'What?' Mrs Castle blushed. 'No. He's just a colleague.'

'Only teasing,' the barman told her.

'The Co-op?' Mrs Castle echoed as George went off to serve another UFO spotter. She remembered that she'd never really understood the barman's sense of humour, and went over to the Doctor. She squashed up in the seat next to him, then pulled away a little, in case anyone watching got the wrong idea.

'Are you sure you're all right with water?' Mrs Castle asked.

The Doctor held the water up, inspecting it. 'This should be fine,' he assured her.

'I'll stick to my gin and tonic,' she told him. 'Cigarette?'

The Doctor shook his head. Mrs Castle lit her cigarette and puffed on it.

'And it's not the regular army,' one of the UFO spotters said.

'I've got a friend in the army, and he says the United Nations have a unit operating in this country which covers up alien activity. The MOD know nothing about it, even though they recruit men from the regular army.'

Mrs Castle was surprised to see the Doctor spellbound.

'You're not listening to them, are you?'

The Doctor looked at her. 'Shouldn't I?'

'You don't believe in UFOs and little green men, do you?'

'Do you?'

'I asked first.'

The Doctor hesitated. 'I think it's good to have an open mind.'

'You can't always tell the difference between an open mind and an empty head.'

'No,' the Doctor agreed, 'no you can't.'

He stared into his mineral water, clearly disappointed with the world.

'Did I see you with Miranda?'

The Doctor nodded. 'I met her mother. A nice woman.'

'Happily married,' Mrs Castle said, perhaps a little too quickly.

'Good,' the Doctor said. 'I've offered to give Miranda some extra tuition.'

Mrs Castle raised an eyebrow. 'It's normal to talk to the school if you're going to do that.'

'Oh.' The Doctor didn't seemed unduly concerned about that. 'You were going to tell me about Mr Knight.'

Mrs Castle could almost hear the sound of three dozen UFO spotters' ears pricking up.

'We'd better go outside,' she suggested.

Mrs Castle had forgotten how cold it would be.

The burble of conversation drifted over from the pub, bringing some of its warmth with it. Mrs Castle tried to suck as much of the heat as she could from her cigarette.

The Doctor was sitting on the other side of the pub bench, looking at her expectantly.

'There's not much to tell,' she confessed. 'He said he was being chased.'

'By a monster?'

'That's what he said.'

'Did he describe it?'

'Describe it? Well…' She struggled to remember. 'He said it was metal. "A big metal alien".'

'And what did you do?'

'I didn't believe him!' She laughed. 'I'd just run him over – he must have hit his head.'

'Perhaps,' the Doctor said sadly.

She looked at the Doctor, sitting there, oblivious to the cold. She looked into his sad, blue eyes. 'Have you been crying?' she asked.

'Yes,' the Doctor admitted.

'Why?'

'I...' He stopped, then shook his head.

'Go on,' she prompted him.

'I get like this, from time to time,' the Doctor told her. 'I've lost... It's all right. I'll be all right.'

'You're lonely?' she guessed. 'Who have you lost?'

He didn't reply.

'There's no one else you can talk to, is there? I know we hardly know each other but –'

'You are the closest thing I have to a friend,' the Doctor said.

Mrs Castle sucked in a little more cigarette smoke than she'd bargained for. 'Really?'

'Really.'

'You're young, you're confident. I don't understand the problem.'

The words came slowly, as though the Doctor was having difficulty letting them out after so long. 'I'm... older than I look. And I don't understand the problem either. I just know that I'm... different. That I've lost a great many things and people and memories that were special to me.'

'Memories? There's nothing wrong with your memory: just look at the way you remembered everyone's name at the chess club.'

'I have a photographic memory,' the Doctor told her. 'Perfect pitch. A grasp of symbolic logic that put Alan Turing himself to shame. I can quote every line of Shakespeare, hum any song I've ever heard, speed-read... but my memories start with me waking in a railway carriage. There's nothing before that. Nothing except a sense that... that I was from a large family, that I travelled, and had friends everywhere I went, and that my life used to have a purpose, I used to make a difference.'

'Wow,' said Mrs Castle. 'Could the police help?'

'No. There are thousands of people reported missing every year. I'm not one of them.'

'What were you wearing? You could speak English?'

'I have thought about it. Too much, if anything. It's like trying to guess what the jigsaw is from only one piece. Have you ever had the sense you've been here before? That you *remember* the words that you're just hearing. A sense that everything is utterly familiar?'

'*Déjà vu*. Yeah. Everyone gets that.'

'I don't. I never have. Nothing ever seems quite right. There's never anything that feels ordinary, Debbie.'

It was the first time anyone had called her that since she had been

a child. And the name felt utterly familiar. It felt like she'd remembered her own name, after years of bafflement and defeat. And she looked at the Doctor, sitting on a pub bench, in his black coat and silk shirt, and suddenly he wasn't ordinary. He was... more than ordinary. More than human, but less than human at the same time.

He looked lonely.

Mrs Castle bent in and kissed him on the forehead, then leaned back, looked at his face.

He smiled down at her, calmer than he'd been.

'Thank you,' she told him.

The Doctor opened his mouth, and her husband's voice came out of it.

'Who's this?' Barry asked.

A heavy-set man in a tracksuit and parka was standing behind the Doctor, staring at them. He hadn't shaved, and his wiry, thinning hair hadn't been brushed.

He'd spoken before the Doctor could. And he hadn't seen her kiss him. It was an innocent kiss, not the sort of kiss that a wife gives a husband or a girlfriend gives a boyfriend, but she knew that Barry wouldn't have seen it that way.

'Hello, Barry,' Mrs Castle said. 'Doctor, this is my husband.'

'The bloke that fixed the Cortina?' Mr Castle asked.

'That's right.'

'You did a good job,' Mr Castle conceded grudgingly.

'Thank you.'

'Come inside. You play snooker?'

'Er...'

Mrs Castle and the Doctor followed him back in.

Mr Castle pointed over to the table. 'I'll set up.'

The Doctor's smile flickered.

'It's his way of saying thank you. But let him win,' Mrs Castle suggested. 'He likes to win. Thinks it's important.'

'Right,' the Doctor said, his mind elsewhere. He was watching the other snooker table.

'Looks easy enough,' he decided.

'You've never played before?'

'No. Have you?'

'Barry's got a table at home. He made me learn. I think he did it just so he could win all the time. Do you know the rules?'

'You hit the balls with that –'

'– cue,' she supplied.

'Cue. The object is to get the balls into the holes. Right. Sounds tricky.'

'It is. I keep potting the white by mistake.'

'Right. So the white ball has to stay on the table.'

The Doctor downed his mineral water in one and walked over to the table.

Barry had finished setting up. He ushered the Doctor over and handed him his cue.

The Doctor weighed it carefully, then paced around the table.

'Do you want to make it interesting?' Barry said.

The Doctor frowned. 'Is that actually possible?' he asked.

'Put a pound on it?' Barry suggested, holding up a pound note.

'Barry,' Mrs Castle objected, 'this isn't fair. The Doctor's never played before.'

'He can fix cars, can't he? He plays chess? Snooker's not going to be a challenge.'

'Yes, yes. All right.' The Doctor dug into his pockets and pulled out a pound in change. Barry put his pound note down on the cushion, and the Doctor piled his coins on top of it.

'You wanna break?' Barry asked. 'Go first,' he clarified, when the Doctor looked confused.

The Doctor nodded. Barry smirked.

The Doctor tapped the end of the cue with his finger.

'It's more complicated than it looks,' the Doctor confessed. 'On the face of it, this is a simple Newtonian system, but there are quite a few complicating factors. The felt isn't even, the balls have slight manufacturing defects, the tip of the cue isn't quite right.'

'You can chalk it if you want.' Barry handed the Doctor the cube of blue chalk.

The Doctor examined the chalk, then used it to smooth the tip a little.

'Hurry up, Doctor,' Barry said. 'It's not like chess where you spend ten hours on every move.'

The Doctor bent over, perched the cue on his left hand, and tapped the cue ball with it.

It rocketed forwards, breaking the reds, scattering them, sending them bouncing off every cushion.

'Whoa! Too hard,' Barry bellowed.

The first red ball fell into the pocket, followed by the yellow, another red and the black. The other red balls were ricocheting from cushion to cushion, catching the other balls as they went. Two more reds, the green, the pink and a few more reds rattled into the pockets. The initial momentum was dying down – the blue, brown and the rest of the reds merely rolled languidly into their pockets.

The last ball on the table, the white, tottered over the pocket nearest Barry. After a moment or two it fell in.

The Doctor's face fell. 'Ah well,' he said quietly, 'looks like you win.'

Barry took a moment to recover. 'Yeah. Yeah. You have to pocket them in order. Yellow, green, brown, blue, pink, then black.'

The Doctor looked back at the table. 'Really? I didn't know that. I was talking about the white ball. I'm not meant to pot it, am I? I tried not to, but…'

'Yeah,' Barry agreed eagerly. Barry wrapped the Doctor's coins up in his pound note and scooped the money up from the table. 'You're OK, right? Bit of practice and you'll be good. But you can't pot the white, yeah?'

'I see.' The Doctor handed the cue back to him. 'Ah well, I'll leave the game to the experts.'

'Well done, Doctor,' Mrs Castle said.

'Don't congratulate him,' Barry said. 'I won, love.'

Mrs Castle kissed her husband on the cheek, but she looked at the Doctor as she did it.

'Time to get going,' Barry said firmly.

'Bit early for you, isn't it?' Mrs Castle argued.

'I want an early night,' he told her. And with that, he dragged her away, but he looked at the Doctor as he did it.

Less than half an hour later, the Doctor was walking across the car park of the county hospital. The tarmac hadn't been gritted, but the Doctor didn't slip.

It was quite late in the evening, now, and the car park was almost empty.

Almost. In one corner, nestling under a large elm tree, there was a black Volkswagen Beetle.

The Doctor looked over his shoulder at it. The headlights were on, and they looked like eyes, watching him from the shadows. He wasn't

cold, but he shuddered anyway, and was glad to go through the sliding doors into the warmth and safety of the hospital.

As the Doctor arrived at Arnold Knight's room, a redheaded nurse was just leaving. The Doctor smiled at her, glad she wasn't asking him any awkward questions.

Arnold Knight was lying in bed. One of his legs was in traction, suspended at a forty-five-degree angle. He was in a room to himself, one that was full of get-well cards.

The Doctor introduced himself, and cleared up the confusion when Arnold assumed he meant that he was some sort of medical specialist.

'I've brought you some sweets,' the Doctor told him.

Arnold looked in the little paper bag the Doctor handed him. 'Jelly babies,' he said approvingly, and started tucking in.

The Doctor pointed at Arnold's leg. 'What are the doctors saying?'

'That I had a lucky escape,' Arnold told him.

The Doctor was checking the notes clipped to the end of the bed. 'Fibula broken in two places. Clean breaks, no sign of infection.'

'It could have been worse.'

The Doctor nodded, then asked, 'What were you running from, Arnold?'

'I told the police.'

'You said you were being chased by a bull.'

'Yes,' Arnold said, a trace of guilt in his voice.

'But that wasn't true, was it? For one thing, you came from Cooper's Farm, and George Cooper only keeps sheep and chickens.'

'No,' Arnold admitted. 'I lied.'

'Why did you tell Deborah Castle that you were being chased by a monster?'

Arnold Knight was suddenly suspicious. 'Who are you?'

'Someone who believes you.'

'You wouldn't.'

'You went looking for little green men and flying saucers and you found them.'

Arnold blinked. 'How?' he asked.

'How did I know?' The Doctor shrugged. 'Call it an instinct. There's something going on, Arnold, something that's quite out of the ordinary.'

'It was a robot. A big robot.'

The Doctor bit his lip. 'Where was it?'

'Cooper's Woods. There were lights down there, and then it came for me.'

'Describe it.'

'About ten feet tall. Bulky. Chunky, but it could move gracefully – you know, not like robots are meant to. It was humanoid – two arms, two legs and a head.'

'Did it say anything?'

'No, it just came for me.'

'Did you try to talk to it?'

'No – I was scared.' Arnold looked at the Doctor: he believed him. It was such a relief.

The Doctor paced around the room for a moment.

Then he smiled.

'There is nothing to discuss,' Mr Gibson told them in that too-calm voice of his. 'Arnold Knight must die.'

The Hunters glanced at each other, but didn't move from their seats. The inside of the Volkswagen suddenly felt claustrophobic.

'We are not killers, Mr Gibson,' the woman said.

'Not professionally,' the man added.

Mr Gibson gave a low rumbling noise, like a disapproving grunt. 'Arnold Knight has seen too much. The Doctor is in contact with the woman who ran him over. She did not believe Knight, but the Doctor will. Knight must be eliminated before the Doctor and Knight make contact. The Prefect's mission must not be compromised.'

'We are not sure that it *is* the Doctor,' the man reminded Mr Gibson.

'I know him of old,' Mr Gibson said softly, but with a snarl in his voice. 'It's him.'

'If you're that convinced, then why bother with Knight, why not just kill the Doctor?' the woman suggested.

'Yeah – do your own dirty work.'

Mr Gibson laughed – an unpleasant sound like a motorbike engine revving.

'I will kill the Doctor, when the time is right,' Mr Gibson vowed. 'You have your orders – now go!'

'Excuse me, nurse?'

Nurse Collins looked up, and was glad she had. A handsome man

with long light-brown hair was looking over at her, fixing her with the most beautiful blue eyes.

'How can I help?' she asked, looking for his wedding ring. Nurse Collins wasn't married herself, and often checked to see whether men she met were or not. It was a habit she had.

'Arnold Knight, the man in traction, is after a glass of water. And I'm looking for the medical records.'

She was on the alert. 'Who are you?'

'I'm the Doctor,' he said disarmingly.

'Dr Hennessy?' she asked. 'I didn't think you were starting until next week.'

The doctor smiled amiably.

'Any record in particular?'

'Yes. Dawkins. Miranda Dawkins. She's ten, so it's probably a paediatric record.'

'I'll help you look. This way.'

They weren't far from the records room. He was lucky that one of her duties involved some clerical work in here, so she had the key.

The room was small and dusty, full of old filing cabinets. Despite that, the staff knew their way around, and she quickly located the file and handed it over. The man opened up the folder, took out the sheaves of paper and flicked through them, pausing only a couple of times. After only a few seconds, he stuffed them back in the folder.

'That was quick,' she remarked.

'I'm a fast reader,' he assured her.

'Are you this fast at everything?' she asked, leaning in. His skin was milky-pale, and flawless. He wasn't wearing aftershave, but she could catch the scent of his hair.

'No,' he said, laughter in his voice. 'If only. Thanks for showing me this, and don't forget Arnold Knight's glass of water.'

He handed the folder back to her and strode out of the door.

'Good evening, Arnold,' a strange voice called out. It was a woman's voice, but it was deep. The woman was tall, angular, and she had such a good figure and bone structure that she should have been beautiful, but she wasn't.

'Hope we find you well,' said a man with a high-pitched voice. He looked like her twin brother.

'Who are you?'

'Oh, that doesn't matter,' the woman said.

'We're not killers,' the man said. 'I think we should make that clear from the start. I don't want you to think that we are killers.'

Arnold reached for his alarm button. 'It was you in the car. It was you that didn't stop to help when I was run over.'

The man saw what he was doing, and grabbed his wrist, twisting it. 'Now, Arnold, just because you're scared doesn't mean you have to act like a complete spaz.'

'I-I'm not scared,' Arnold stammered.

The woman shook her head. 'You are.'

Arnold nodded.

'You're right to be,' the man told him. 'You've seen all sorts of things you're not meant to have.'

'We weren't going to kill you,' the woman added. 'We didn't think anyone would believe your stupid stories. We know the police didn't. But then the Doctor turned up.'

'The Doctor?'

'Yes. He knows the woman, the fat cow who ran you over. He'll be looking for you, and when he finds you, he'll believe you. Then he'll get involved and he'll interfere with our employer's plans.'

The man had pulled a device from his belt – it looked like a wand.

The woman kissed Arnold on the forehead. 'We don't want to kill you, but Mr Gibson insists.' She drew back.

'Don't worry,' the man assured Arnold, pointing the wand at him. 'This won't hurt.'

The man lunged forward, stabbing the wand down through Arnold's forehead where the woman had just kissed it. Arnold heard the bone splitting, but didn't feel any pain. There was a low hum, then a jolt down his back, like an electric shock, then it felt as if his stomach had caught fire. Arnold tried to move, but he couldn't. He was being surrounded in a green aura, he could see his nerves and bones. He was being eaten away.

He had only two thoughts. Indignation. Indignation that this man had told him it wouldn't hurt and it was absolute searing agony. And serenity. A calmness that came from knowing he was right, that he'd found the extraordinary proof that he had been looking for, that he was right and everyone else had been wrong.

Arnold screamed.

Chapter Six
Talking to Strangers

Miranda sat at her desk, waiting for the Doctor to start the lesson.

The Doctor was at the back wall, examining the pictures.

'With it being so cold and wet at the moment, we spend a lot of playtime in here, drawing.'

The Doctor nodded. The back wall was covered in old squares of computer paper, Blu-Tacked up. Almost every picture was of spaceships and alien monsters, vividly brought to life in crayons and paint.

'What's that?' the Doctor asked.

Miranda wasn't sure. 'I think that's Metal Mickey – it's a robot on telly.'

The Doctor nodded, and moved on to the next picture. 'It's fascinating that they all come up with the same images: flying discs, death rays, green monsters.'

'They're just copying off the TV,' Miranda told him. 'They see that sort of stuff in cartoons and comics, that's all. Or they just copy off each other.'

'But all of them drawing spaceships and monsters.'

'That one's Monkey and Pigsy.'

The Doctor peered at it. 'But all the others...'

'It's the UFO. All the boys think they're Luke Skywalker or Flash Gordon.'

'What about the girls?'

'We have to make do with being Princess Leia.'

The Doctor raised an eyebrow. 'Make do with being a princess?'

'She doesn't do anything. Just gets captured and waits for the boys to rescue her. That's all women do in that sort of thing. I'd rather be Luke. Or Darth Vader.'

Miranda wondered where the Doctor had gone to school. She just couldn't see him running around a playground – she couldn't imagine his school days at all. It was always odd to think that teachers had once been boys and girls, but it was impossible with the Doctor.

'Why do you think the UFOs are coming here?' he asked.

'They could be here because they want to conquer Earth,' Miranda suggested.

'What makes you say that?' the Doctor asked, genuinely wanting to know.

'Well, that's what they do in films. There's that one with the flying saucer that lands outside the White House, and the army surrounds it with tanks and guns and then a giant robot comes out and blasts them.' Miranda hesitated. 'I don't know why they'd start by conquering Greyfrith, though.'

'Perhaps they are here to help,' the Doctor suggested.

'Help what?'

'Tell us where people are going wrong. Stop pollution, end wars.'

Miranda looked thoughtful. 'That would be much better,' she concluded.

The Doctor shook his head. 'If they were going to do that, they'd have landed, surely? They've not tried to make contact with us. It's almost as if they are monitoring us, or searching for something.' A thought struck him. 'Perhaps they are UFO-spotter spotters.'

Miranda giggled.

The phone rang, but the girl on the other end had dialled the wrong number.

Debbie put the phone down and went back to giving Barry his tea: bacon, eggs and chips. She sat opposite him. He had his copy of the *Star*, she had her book. She didn't like reading at the table, but it was better than talking sometimes. Their house was very cold, because Barry didn't like wasting money.

'What's that book?' Barry asked.

'I got it from the library. It's about chess. I'm looking for hints. I need to get into practice again if I've got any chance of beating the Doctor.'

'I don't want you to see him again,' Barry told her flatly.

'He's teaching Miranda Dawkins. I'll have to see him.'

'He's weird. I bet he listens to Kate Bush.' He held up his paper to show what had led him to that conclusion. It was a picture of a young woman with staring eyes and not much on.

'Instead of ogling her, you mean?'

'Yeah. If you want to put it like that, yeah. There's something wrong with him. I mean, look at that.' He decided to follow his own advice and returned his attention to his newspaper.

Debbie felt a little sad. Barry didn't know it, but he was right. There was something wrong with the Doctor, or rather the world he'd found himself in. A place, where if you were different, or if you showed just the slightest imagination or kindness, people looked at you suspiciously and... she'd kissed him, and just for a moment, both their problems had gone away.

She looked at a photo of the chess game. It was an old photograph, colour, but that odd, watery colour that old photos have, as though they weren't sure whether to be black-and-white or not. Two men, bending over a chessboard, surrounded by people in fifties suits, and women in those tailored dresses and hats they used to wear. It reminded her of her childhood, just a few years after this photo had been taken.

Debbie looked again.

One of the men was wearing a long black frock coat. He had a mane of dark hair, and sad-looking eyes, and seemed to be looking straight at her.

She checked the date of the photograph. The caption said it had been taken in Stalingrad in 1951. Four years before she had been born, and on the other side of the Iron Curtain.

And if it wasn't the Doctor... then why was he wearing the Doctor's coat?

Mr Cosmo welcomed the Doctor as he entered the newsagent's. A couple of the children recognised him and said hello.

'The usual, Doctor?' he asked.

The Doctor nodded, handing over his money. 'Make it half a pound, would you – I'm running a bit low.'

Mr Cosmo smiled, and shook a few more jelly babies out of their jar.

The Doctor was looking down at the *Evening News* laid out on the counter.

'Are you reading about that man at the hospital? A very strange business.'

A man with a broken leg had vanished from his hospital bed – and had managed to get out of his plastercast. There was a photo of the empty bed on the front page, the plastercast hanging from the traction gear.

'You seem a bit down today,' Mr Cosmo told the Doctor. 'Is it the weather?'

The Doctor seemed to force himself to smile. 'No, I like the snow. Those two, out there, do you recognise them?'

Mr Cosmo peered out of the window into the gloomy evening. A young man and woman were sitting on the wall on the other side of the road. They wore similar modern clothes, and Mr Cosmo thought there was something sinister about them. The young man seemed to be playing with a camera – not taking photographs, just checking the back and fiddling with it.

'They were there yesterday,' one of the boys told the Doctor.

The Doctor didn't seem surprised.

'Are you sure, Daniel?' Mr Cosmo asked. 'I don't remember them.'

'They were,' Daniel insisted.

'And they were in the park yesterday,' Stephanie piped up. 'They were on the swings and wouldn't let us on.'

Mr Cosmo looked over to the Doctor. 'They could be tourists, Doctor. There are quite a lot of people in the village at the moment. They may be here because of the UFOs.'

The Doctor hadn't taken his eyes off them. 'They may indeed.'

The children started looking out of the window. 'We could ask them,' one suggested.

'No. Remember, don't talk to strange men,' Mr Cosmo advised.

The boys and girls all nodded or voiced their agreement.

The Doctor was heading for the door.

'Where are you going?' Mr Cosmo asked

'To talk to them,' the Doctor said firmly.

'This is hopeless. We can't just expect the Last One to –'

'Hello there,' the Doctor said. 'I'm the Doctor.'

The strange man and woman looked nervously at each other.

'Hello,' they chorused back, finally.

The strange man stood up, the strange woman stayed where she was.

'Don't you have names?' the Doctor asked.

The woman's smile flickered. 'That's Rum.'

The man waved weakly at him. 'This is Thélash.'

'Delighted to meet you,' the Doctor said. He looked Rum up and down. 'Are you waiting for someone?' he asked.

'Just enjoying the view,' the man assured him, digging his hands in his trouser pockets and circling round the Doctor.

The Doctor turned his back on Rum and faced his partner. 'Have you come far to be here?' he asked.

Rum couldn't help sniggering, until a glare from Thélash silenced him.

'Not really,' she replied curtly. 'Yourself?'

The Doctor's expression didn't change for a moment, then he broke into a smile. 'You tell me.'

'We're just seeing the sights,' Rum told him.

The Doctor waved his hand at Rum's camera. 'And taking some pictures?'

'That's right,' he said. 'Can we take yours?'

The Doctor straightened up, turned his head. 'This is my best side,' he told them. 'You know, on some places on this planet, the people think that taking a photograph captures someone's soul.'

'Is that right?' Thélash asked.

There was a flash of light, and a whirr as the instant camera expelled the picture.

Rum shook the picture to dry it. 'An excellent likeness,' he declared, flashing it at the Doctor.

The Doctor checked his pocket watch. 'I'm afraid I've got to be going.'

'I hope we'll see each other again soon,' Thélash said, holding out her hand.

'Thank you.' The Doctor shook her hand, but watched her suspiciously.

'I told you it was him,' Rum hissed when the Doctor had gone. 'He's rumbled us. I'm sure he recognised us.'

'I knew it was,' Thélash agreed. 'This changes things.'

He gave a nervous moan.

'There's no need to be such a coward,' she announced. 'He didn't try to stop us.'

'You still think it's a coincidence he's here?'

Thélash considered her answer. 'Yes. Perhaps he's just following up the UFO reports.'

'But what do we do?'

'We'll have to tell the Prefect.'

Rum thought for a moment. 'We could just send Mr Gibson after the Doctor. He's dying to kill him, you can tell.'

'Absolutely not.'

'Why not?'

Thélash spelled it out slowly, as if she was talking to a stupid child. 'Because Mr Gibson is not subtle in his methods. He's going to kill the Doctor for what he did, and there's bound to be collateral damage.'

'What did the Doctor do?'

'It doesn't matter – but we have to keep those two apart.'

'Whatever you say.' Rum broke into a grin.

'I don't know what you've got to smile about,' she told him.

He rooted in his trouser pocket and pulled out a small plastic case. He opened it up. Inside were three cubes, each a little bit bigger than a sugar cube, with space for another.

'These,' he announced, 'are nukes.'

Thélash's eyes were wide open.

'Relax,' he said, stretching the word out. 'They're only little nukes. Mini-nukes. Enough to atomise a building, but that's all. Not that it matters to us, but there would only be minimal fallout.'

He turned the plastic case over and tapped the back.

A display panel lit up, a network of red circuitry with a large red dot in the middle.

'Press this, and boom! It's so clever – the bomb reads out the five-second countdown, but there's nothing you can do if you hear it, unless you've got this box. It's war surplus. Genuine antiques. I forget the name of the race that used them. Those chaps with all the tentacles.'

'Ingenious, I'm sure. What has this got to do with the Doctor?'

Rum smiled. 'Well, while you were dazzling him with your charms and sparkling conversation, I slipped one of the nukes into his coat pocket.'

Thélash looked over at the receding figure of the Doctor.

'Press it!' she ordered. 'We're out of range.'

'No way!' Rum shouted. 'We'll use it if we have to, and only if we have to.'

'He could find it. You've just handed the Doctor a nuclear weapon. He'll find a way to use it against us. He does that sort of thing.'

'Oh, he's so overrated.' The man tapped at the control box. 'It's got a light sensor on it. I've set it so if he takes the bomb out of his pocket, it'll blow up.'

Thélash bit her lip. 'I'm still not sure.'

He kissed her on the forehead. 'What can possibly go wrong? Now,

we need to get back to Mr Gibson and make contact with our employer.' He reached for his belt. 'I've left my communicator behind,' he said. 'You'd better make that call.'

Debbie answered the door and was astonished to see the Doctor standing there.

She looked around nervously.

'What are you doing tonight?' the Doctor asked, so abruptly that Debbie lost her breath.

'Barry's out at the pub with some friends. A darts tournament or something.'

'But what are *you* doing? Are you going?'

'He wouldn't want me there.'

'Good, good, then you're free. Come on.'

Debbie found herself agreeing, then hesitated. 'Where are we going?'

The Doctor smiled. 'That would be telling. Wrap up warm, though.'

'Right. I'll… just get changed.' She hurried upstairs, and it was only when she was on the landing that she realised she'd left the Doctor standing on the doorstep.

Debbie checked her hair in the mirror, changed her sweater and, after a moment's thought, sprayed a little perfume on. That done, she dashed back downstairs, almost tripping over herself. She locked up, and joined the Doctor as he walked down her drive. He was grinning, and swept out a hand to indicate his car.

'Our carriage awaits,' he told her.

He opened the passenger door for her.

Inside, the car was a bit scruffy. The Doctor had to move a pile of books on to the back seat to make room for his passenger.

He pulled out the choke, tried the ignition, then tried it again.

'What sort of car is this again?' she asked.

'A Trabant. I picked it up in East Germany.'

'You were in East Germany?'

'Yes.' The engine turned over, but didn't fire.

'When?'

The Doctor rubbed his lip with his finger. 'A while ago, now.'

She remembered the photograph in her book, and looked back over at him. He didn't look a day older. But it had been almost thirty years.

'What do you think about *Close Encounters*?' the Doctor said.

Debbie blinked. 'Pardon?'

'The film. It's just that I'm planning to re-enact it tonight.'

'I... think it's romantic.'

The Doctor looked a little taken aback. 'You do?'

'Yes.' Debbie closed her eyes. 'Strangers waiting for a train. A married woman, who knows nothing about a man. All that steam and clinking crockery.'

'*Close Encounters* is the one where the big UFO comes down and they play that music at it to communicate. You know...' And he hummed five notes.

Debbie blushed. Barry had taken her to see it, and he'd come out deeply unimpressed.

'We're going UFO spotting?' she asked.

'We're going to make contact with aliens,' the Doctor corrected her.

'Aliens?'

'Yes.' He saw her sceptical expression. 'It's not that difficult. I did it by accident this morning.'

Debbie looked over at him. 'You did?'

'Yes. Two of them, in the High Street.'

A few days ago, she'd have thought anyone who talked about aliens and UFOs was mad. A few days ago, she *had* thought that, she'd doubted Arnold's story.

Now it all seemed perfectly normal.

The Doctor turned on his car radio. There was a steady bleeping, like an electronic heartbeat. 'I've modified this so that it only receives high-energy pulses. That's how the aliens communicate with each other.'

'How?' Debbie asked. 'I mean, how do you know that?'

He held up a small silver box which was covered in little black knobbles, and which was plugged into the car's radio. 'I borrowed this from a chap called Rum. The technology is straightforward enough.'

'That's an alien CB radio?'

The Doctor handed it to her and tried to start the car again. 'That's right. And we can use it to follow them.'

'Wow.' It was light, and looked ugly.

The engine spluttered a little, but only a tiny amount.

'Almost there,' the Doctor assured her.

Debbie remembered something about the film. 'Doesn't Richard Dreyfuss have trouble starting his car in that one because there are UFOs around?'

'That's right.' The Doctor beamed. 'Sure sign we're on the right trail. Er... can we take your car?'

'Here we are,' the Doctor announced. The bleeping from the device he'd plugged into Barry's car radio was insistent now. The Doctor turned it off and disconnected it.

Debbie could just about see the Hunters' black Volkswagen parked in a lay-by. She parked the Cortina alongside it.

Over a dry-stone wall was a dark wood. The bare trees stood out against the snow.

'Do you know the area?' the Doctor asked as he got out.

Debbie locked the driver's door and shook her head. 'I think that's Cooper's Wood. A lot of couples come here. I've never been.'

'Well, it's definitely the right place.' He pointed at the Beetle. The Doctor was already strolling off down the footpath.

Debbie caught up with him, doing up her coat buttons and tying her coat belt. 'Is this wise?'

'I think so.'

'Arnold was scared. I bet he'd tell you not to come here.'

The Doctor stopped in his tracks. 'Arnold Knight is dead,' he told her. 'Murdered last night in hospital.'

Debbie suddenly felt terribly sick, terribly out of her depth.

'The Hunters – do you think they're involved?'

The Doctor shook his head. 'There's a connection, I'm sure. Everything here is connected.'

Debbie shivered. Even the first time she'd met them the Hunters had scared her – and they'd been hanging around the playground a few nights later. The Hunters had been following her around.

'I don't understand what we're meant to be doing here. Shouldn't we call the police?'

'They wouldn't listen. Wait!'

Debbie froze in place.

'Down!' the Doctor hissed.

As they took position behind a bush, Debbie caught sight of the strange man and woman. Mr Hunter was leaning against a tree. His wife, or sister, or whatever she was, had knelt down, and was playing with what looked like a camper stove. She seemed to be trying to encourage it to work by talking to it.

Debbie knew she should be getting cold, but she was excited, and

the adrenaline seemed to be keeping her warm. This was an adventure for her – she was sure the man and the woman were up to no good. They looked like criminals, she decided – there was just something shifty about them.

The woman said something to the man. The Doctor looked over to Debbie hopefully, but she shrugged: they were too far away to hear anything.

Mr Hunter was clearly restless, and it was getting infectious – the woman began pacing about. She pulled something from her belt and checked it: Debbie recognised it as a communicator, just like the one the Doctor had.

There was a flash of light. It took Debbie a moment to realise that it was the man, taking a photograph of the woman. It was a Polaroid, and the little square picture emerged. The man looked confused by the fact that the picture hadn't quite developed yet.

'They could pass for human, don't you think?' the Doctor asked softly.

Debbie looked at the two people standing in the clearing, then back at the Doctor. 'No,' the Doctor said, answering the question she hadn't asked. 'I don't think they are.'

'They're the aliens,' she whispered.

'Yes.'

Debbie was almost disappointed they didn't look like the monsters in her pupils' drawings. Where was their robot? Why couldn't they be lizard people, or have blue skin or tails, or something? They drove around in a *Volkswagen*, for God's sake. But she realised she didn't doubt what the Doctor was saying.

'We have to make contact,' the Doctor said, the words hanging in the air.

Debbie realised she must have looked horrified at the thought, because before she'd had the chance to say anything, the Doctor continued: 'No, no, don't worry. It has to be on our terms. And we have something they want.'

'We do?' Debbie asked puzzled.

'Yes. They're very, very unlikely to kill us.'

Debbie imagined that the Doctor thought he was being reassuring, but she didn't feel reassured.

There was another flash. The man playing with his camera, Debbie thought, but she was wrong.

The man and the woman were now both looking up at the sky.

The Doctor and Debbie stared up, trying to see what they were looking at.

And the clouds parted, billowing back like a theatre curtain, to reveal a metal disc, fifty feet in diameter. There were no lights on it, no markings, no breaks in the perfect steel surface. It was almost invisible, and silent.

It drifted down towards them.

The Doctor was mumbling something under his breath. 'It's not spinning, or firing rocket blasts, there aren't any visible energy fields. Something exotic, something far beyond the state of the art of the human race at this time.'

Down in the clearing, the man and the woman watched the disc descend the same way Debbie would have watched a train coming into a station. They had been expecting this, obviously. Debbie wondered if the device Mrs Hunter had been using had summoned it somehow.

The Doctor nodded over at the odd couple. 'They don't look happy.'

'They seem a little tense,' Debbie managed to agree.

The saucer stopped around ten feet above the ground and just sat in the air for a moment. Then the underside opened, and a ramp slid smoothly open.

'There's someone else there,' Debbie told the Doctor. She could see a small figure silhouetted in the light at the top of the ramp. Smaller than either of the couple, almost squat alongside them.

The man and the woman straightened themselves up, as if they were standing to attention. Although they were nervous, they looked at home... *in context*... standing at the bottom of the ramp of a UFO.

There was a second figure at the top of the ramp. Taller and broader than the first. Together the two men – they were men, there was no doubt about it – began striding down the ramp.

The two alien men stopped in front of the Hunters.

They were both in what looked like military uniform. The shorter of the two men was powerfully built, and wore black combat gear, like a futuristic version of SAS gear. He was old, or in late middle age at least. He was almost bald, but what hair he had was white, and closely cropped.

'Where is Mr Gibson?' he barked.

'He's guarding the exit,' the woman replied.

The other man – and Debbie was sure he was their leader – wasn't as tall as the Hunters, but he was an imposing figure – broad-shouldered, muscular. He wore a green tunic, and a long fur-trimmed greatcoat, and his black boots almost came up to his knees.

Debbie looked back at the Doctor, to see what his reaction was, only to realise that the Doctor was moving forward. She tried to grab his sleeve to stop him, but the Doctor was already too far away.

'Stick close,' he suggested. Despite herself, Debbie found that she was following him. The ground was uneven, and she could hear every crunch as she and the Doctor moved across the snow. They were less than fifteen feet away, now. There was a faint hum in the air, like standing near an electricity pylon.

The aliens watched the Doctor approach, clearly caught out by his sudden appearance.

'Good evening,' the Doctor declared. 'I am the Doctor. I come in peace. Take me to your leader. That sort of thing.'

The Hunters and the man in the black coveralls tensed, and seemed ready for a fight. The man in the green tunic was more calm. He turned, and stepped forward. He had wiry hair, steel-grey and tightly curled.

'I know why you are here,' the Doctor announced. 'I know why you are here on Earth.'

The leader stood silently, not giving anything away.

'You're here for the girl,' the Doctor told them. 'You are here for Miranda.'

If the leader replied, Debbie didn't hear him.

Chapter Seven
Inside the Spaceship

Miranda didn't need much sleep, indeed she could do without it.

She knew this made her different but, usually, it didn't bother her. She sat at her desk and read. Sometimes she would play with her toys. She didn't like to make too much noise, in case she woke her parents, so if she did put the radio or a tape on, then she always used earphones.

It was nice. It was a time to be quiet, a time to be alone. She never got scared in the dark, as children were meant to. She didn't like to sleep. She didn't like her dreams. She dreamed of fog and rocky, broken ground. She dreamed of screaming and fire. Monsters, but not furry, scaly, giant monsters as in *Where the Wild Things Are* or *The Muppet Show*, but monsters that looked like people on the outside. There were silver palaces full of servants in her dreams. But everyone was running from something. They were running away from her because anyone who knew her was being killed where they stood. They didn't want to die, so they ran. It was always the same dream, and she seemed trapped in it. It scared her.

So Miranda didn't sleep.

But tonight was different. Tonight she wanted to sleep, but she couldn't. She lay on her bed, staring up at the ceiling. She was tired, but a part of her mind was telling her that she couldn't go to sleep, or she'd never wake up. She'd be trapped in her scary dream.

Miranda realised she was crying, and she was lonely.

She went up to her parents' door, and then into their bedroom.

Her dad had woken up. She heard him shift around, then turn on his bedside light.

Mum was awake now. She looked at Dad to see what was wrong, then saw Miranda. Her mum didn't say anything, just pulled her up on to the bed and hugged her. She was so warm and big and comforting.

'It's the UFOs,' Miranda explained.

'What do you mean?' her mother asked.

'The Doctor was telling me about them. And he says they are real.'

Her dad looked angry. 'He has no right to. Look, he's scared you.'

Mum was pulling on her dressing gown. 'Let's get you some cocoa.'
'Are they real?' she asked.
'I'm going to have words with that Doctor,' Dad said angrily.
Miranda looked over at him. 'But are they real?'

They were right underneath the disc now. It was *wrong* that it was hanging there, Debbie decided. It was bigger than a house, and it was made from solid metal, but it hung there like a hot-air balloon.

And there were four aliens standing there, leaving footprints in the Derbyshire snow.

The Hunters, standing together at the back, keeping out of the way but looking down their noses at her. The balding man in SAS gear, standing to one side, clearly ready to fight. And, at the head of the group, the imposing figure with curly steel-grey hair and a green military tunic.

'Doctor,' this man said, his voice deep and full of authority. 'I'm afraid I don't recognise your charming companion.' He was their leader – that was obvious from the way he stood, the tone of his voice. A born leader.

'I'm not his companion,' Debbie said quietly. 'We're just friends.'
The Doctor frowned. 'You know me?'
The man hesitated. 'Of course. You don't know me?'
The Doctor gave a slight shake of his head.
The leader exchanged a quick look with the bald man.
The Doctor smiled helplessly. 'Have we met?'
'You don't remember?' the bald man asked, and Debbie was sure he was fingering the scar that ran down his cheek.
'No. I've... forgotten a great deal. I remember Rum and Thélash, of course, from our little chat today, but I'm afraid I don't remember you.'

Debbie was nervous of the whole situation, but the little bald man in particular scared her. His combat gear was practical, and had obviously seen use. She had no doubt at all that the pouches contained all sorts of weapons and lethal devices. 'You don't remember Galspar, or Falkus?' he asked, oozing suspicion.

'Those are your names?' the Doctor asked.
Mr Hunter burst into laughter. The bald man spun to face him, silencing him.
'Places?' the Doctor guessed.
'Planets,' the leader confirmed. He was stern, but seemed more

amiable than his colleague. 'But you don't remember them, do you?'

'No. I'm sorry, but you have me at a disadvantage.'

Debbie was sure that the bald man smiled at that prospect.

'I am Prefect Zevron, this is my Deputy, Sallak.'

The word 'prefect' summoned up for Debbie images of little badges and looking after dinner queues, but she knew that it had been what the Romans had called their military commanders. 'We are time travellers, like yourself.'

Debbie and the Doctor looked at each other. 'Time travellers?' they asked, together.

'You know about Miranda?' the Prefect asked, seemingly pleased that he had managed to surprise the Doctor.

'Yes.'

'Then it seems we have something we could learn from one another. Please... step inside.'

The Doctor peered up the ramp, then turned to Debbie, grinned and began bounding up into the spacecraft.

They walked through a small garage, or hangar, into a central landing sort of area, with doors leading off in all directions. All the doors were closed but one, which they passed through. The room they found themselves in was opulent, with heavy metal sculptures mounted on the walls and on small plinths. The floor was thickly carpeted, or perhaps it was fur of some kind. It was warm, there was a thick, musky smell and a regular electronic burble in the air.

Debbie wanted to get out.

The door hissed shut behind them, sliding up from the floor.

'We're trapped,' she said, panicking.

'Stay calm,' the Doctor told her. He was stepping further into the room, with the same expression on his face kids have in toy shops.

'But what if we take off?' she asked. 'They could be going back to their planet.'

'That's out of our hands,' the Doctor said. 'If they were going to be hostile, they could have thrown us into a cell, or a torture chamber, or just had us killed outside.'

She wanted to go back the way they had come, open up the ramp and run as far and as fast as she could. She wanted this ship to go away, and she wanted to go back to her life, her stupid, normal life with her stupid, normal husband and his darts and his police record and his

Ford Cortina and his mortgage arrears.

Debbie forced herself to stand still. 'I can't hear an engine. I don't think we're moving.'

'Relax,' the Doctor suggested.

'There's something wrong,' she said, looking over to the Doctor for reassurance.

'No,' he whispered.

'There is,' she insisted.

The Doctor shook his head. 'It's a natural reaction to this object and the almost imperceptible differences that come from materials that weren't mined, refined or synthesised on Earth.'

Debbie realised he must be right. This place wasn't *shocking*: it was perfectly within the realm of human imagination. But there were tiny things, things that she didn't notice until she looked for them, but they unnerved her all the same – the devil in the detail. There weren't any screws or rivets. The furniture seemed to be made out of metal, not wood, but it felt like plastic.

'You don't feel it?' Debbie asked.

'I feel it,' the Doctor said softly. 'I've felt it for as long as I can remember. Every morning, when I wake up in a world with buttons, green leaves, paper money and traces of argon in the air I breathe.'

Debbie rooted in her pocket for her cigarettes.

'We all get like that. Everyone feels like they are on the outside looking in from time to time,' Debbie told him. 'Most of us get over it by the time we've done our A-levels.'

The Doctor glared at her. He had been deadly serious. He turned his back on her, busied himself trying to open the door.

At least it was warm, and Debbie was glad to be given the chance to sit down. The chairs were simple padded stools. The Doctor paced around the room, his brow furrowed. He looked so at home here, surrounded by machines and ornaments quite unlike anything Debbie had seen before. She lit her cigarette, and took a deep breath, pleased to smell something familiar.

Debbie wondered why the Doctor wasn't as scared as she was.

'Passing for human,' she said under her breath, looking at him again.

Nothing about him had changed. He was wearing the same black velvet coat, the same boots, a shirt that was identical to the one he'd been wearing in the photograph.

But everything had changed. He looked perfectly at home here,

standing in a chamber in a UFO.

He wasn't human.

The Doctor looked over at her and smiled.

He wasn't human.

She looked at him. She looked at the time traveller, the man without a past.

Before she could say anything, the hatch had opened again.

A young woman walked in, someone they'd not seen before. She was wearing a grey tunic and veil, her long skirt made it look as if she was gliding. The woman took their coats away and served them each a glass of dark-blue liquid from one of the sculptures, which turned out to be a dispenser of some kind.

'Thank you,' the Doctor said, sniffing the drink, then tasting it. The servant left, the door sliding up behind her.

Debbie put her drink down on a low table, untouched.

'Slaves?' the Doctor asked Debbie. 'Servants at the very least. Not the mark of a civilised society... by modern standards, at any rate. I suppose *historically*...'

'I don't trust them,' she confessed.

The Doctor turned to look at her, disappointed. 'Why ever not?'

'I –' But Debbie was unable to put it into words.

'They are clearly very advanced,' the Doctor said. He motioned around the room. 'Capable of producing some striking art, and maintaining a galactic empire. That fact alone implies a great deal about the state of their communications, their transport and their logistical skill. They could teach us a great deal.'

'Are they your people?' she asked, almost under her breath.

The Doctor stopped what he was doing.

'That had occurred to me,' he admitted.

'You're not a human being, are you?'

The Doctor couldn't look her in the eye. 'I'm not sure.'

'No?'

'No.'

'I know *I'm* human,' she said, surprised how angry she was. 'Why aren't you sure?'

'How do you know?' the Doctor replied gently. 'You only think you know. I thought I was human – of course I did. I thought I was like everyone else, that everyone else's life was like mine. I learned that was not the case.'

Debbie took a deep breath. 'And you travel through time?' Realisation dawned. 'Of course! I saw a photograph of you at a chess game in the fifties. You didn't look any younger. But you were just visiting the past.'

'I don't travel through time,' the Doctor said, 'well, I do, but only in the same way you do. I don't age.'

'But...' That was worse, Debbie thought.

'I told you I woke up in a train carriage. What I didn't tell you was that it happened over a century ago. In that time... well, I look a couple of years older now than I did then, no more.'

Debbie wanted this to stop, but it didn't.

The Doctor was deep in thought. 'Now, I've no idea what my lifespan is. I could live long enough to see time travel invented. How long could that be? I've lived over a hundred years, I'd only have to live a couple more centuries – less, if mankind makes contact with a people who have already got the technology.'

'Shut up...' Debbie said, very softly.

But the Doctor continued, enthusiastically. 'Like... like the Prefect and his people. Maybe I don't remember meeting them because it hasn't happened yet. Perhaps this is where it starts – now I know time travel is a scientific possibility, I'll dedicate myself to building a time machine of my own.' He hesitated, looking around. 'Or maybe I could skip all that by stealing one.' He looked thoughtful. 'Perhaps even this one.'

The Deputy bowed his head as he entered the Prefect's chamber.

'You sent for me?' he asked.

The Prefect was sitting on an austere, low chair. He said nothing, nor did he need to.

'You are worried by the Doctor's presence,' the Deputy told him. 'We know that this era was monitored and protected, and the –'

'I know my history,' the Prefect snapped.

The Deputy tried to keep his master calm. 'We also know that Earth in this period is one of the Doctor's favourites, and is a major nexus. But the strategy computers discounted the probability of his intervention.'

'Computers,' the Prefect spat. 'If we'd trusted ourselves to computers, we'd have been dead a long time ago.'

'We registered no time travel to or from this zone except our own

time corridor. He's got in under our detectors. He has also managed to find the Last One before the Hunters have.'

The Prefect looked dangerously close to panic. 'This cannot be a coincidence.'

'The Doctor claims not to recognise us. As far as he is concerned, this might be before Last Contact.'

The Prefect was intrigued. 'Is that possible?'

'I will have to check the files,' the Deputy admitted, 'but time travel throws up these possibilities. He may be lying, but if he doesn't remember us, it gives us a great advantage. We have him and his companion where we can see them. This situation is far from lost.'

The Prefect nodded. 'We need to hear the Hunters' report before deciding on a course of action.' He pressed a control on the arm of his chair and a door slid open.

Rum and Thélash entered and stood to attention in front of the Prefect's chair. The Deputy took his place behind his leader and looked at the sorry couple in front of him. Everything about them looked unprofessional – their clothes were flashy, impractical, in stark contrast to his own combat gear. The man in particular stood sloppily. The woman showed more potential, not to mention better muscle tone, but there was insolence there, mixed with complacency.

Were these really the best Hunters in the galaxy?

'Report,' the Deputy ordered.

'The Doctor is here,' Thélash said.

'Evidently. So?' the Deputy asked.

'So,' Thélash snapped, 'we should get out of here before he thwarts our plans, uses our own weapons against us, blows up our home planets and gives you another scar... *sir*.'

His partner's defiance had made Rum bold. 'Our contract says nothing about *intervention*. The Doctor has contacted the Last One and...'

'Your mission has not changed,' the Deputy told them. 'We are very concerned with your performance. The Prefect is not pleased.'

'Isn't he?' Thélash began, glaring down at the Prefect. 'He's keeping very quiet. Are you as scared as I am, Prefect Zevron?'

The Deputy moved forward, ready to kill her for her insolence.

The Prefect held up his hand, stopping the Deputy in his tracks. Then he stood and stepped forward. Now he was right in front of the

woman, one hand resting on the curved dagger that hung from his belt. He wasn't as tall as she was, but that didn't matter – she looked small, like a tiny child alongside him. He smiled, and it was the sort of smile that made the woman take a step back.

'My colleague and I mean no disrespect,' the woman insisted quietly, her head bowed.

The Prefect reached out to stroke her face. She tried hard not to flinch.

'I'll deal with the Doctor,' the Prefect assured her. 'But I need to know where I stand. He has located the Last One.' He turned to her partner. 'Have you?'

'Our search continues,' Rum admitted, his voice trembling.

'You have already taken longer than you said you would. Doctor or not, the timegate reopens tomorrow night. We only have until then.'

'We are aware of the deadline,' Thélash said firmly, in her mannish voice. 'The delays were forced upon us – our *colleague* attacked a native, and as a result the local authorities are being more vigilant. We've had to keep a low profile, and spend time covering our tracks.'

'We operate better alone,' Rum added. 'If you hadn't insisted Mr Gibson came with us, we could have operated more openly.'

The Prefect nodded. 'That is regrettable,' he agreed. 'But at the same time, this is a primitive civilisation. Are they really so much of a match for you?'

'I know we're being well paid,' Rum replied. 'We appreciate that you want a return on your investment.'

The Prefect turned to him. 'Your mission is a simple one,' he reminded them.

'We have made progress,' Thélash said.

'Progress?' the Deputy asked sceptically.

'Sir, we have familiarised ourselves with the area.'

'This was meant to be a snatch-and-grab operation, not a sightseeing one,' the Deputy reminded them.

Thélash glared at the Prefect. 'There has always been the chance of hostilities, and the need to prepare for them. The Doctor's arrival proves we were right to take such precautionary measures. Sir, we have been aware of the Doctor's presence since yesterday and have monitored him. It is clear that he is still investigating this situation, sir.'

The Prefect nodded. 'I have heard enough. We can find out from the

Doctor where the Last One is hiding.'

The Deputy began to usher the Hunters from the room.

'Hey!' Rum objected. 'What happens now?'

'Your services are no longer required.'

Thélash dug her heels in. 'When do we get paid?'

'We will review that shortly,' the Prefect promised.

'What does that mean?'

The Deputy smiled. 'It means if you behave, we'll pay you. If you cause any more trouble, then we'll slit your throats.'

The Doctor and Debbie were sitting in silence when the door slid open and the Prefect and the Deputy entered the reception chamber.

The Doctor raised his glass. 'Thank you for the drink.'

The Deputy smiled, his earlier gruffness replaced with an amiability that Debbie found at least as disturbing.

'No doubt you have many questions,' the Prefect deduced. He was talking to the Doctor, and barely seemed to notice her. She wondered if the women on his planet were second-class citizens, or whether it was a more personal snub.

The Doctor nodded. 'Where are you from?'

'You said you were time travellers,' Debbie reminded him.

'We are from your future.'

'When, precisely?' the Doctor asked, businesslike.

'The exact figure is difficult to calculate,' the Deputy told them. 'But it is several million years hence.'

Debbie was looking over at the Doctor. 'And that is where the Doctor is from?'

The Doctor was already shaking his head. He may not know what he was, but he did seem to have some sense of what he wasn't.

'The Doctor has visited our time zone on a few occasions, but is not a native. Now, if I may: where is the Last One?'

'Who?'

'Miranda,' the Prefect explained.

The Doctor sat back in his chair. 'Last One? Last *what*, precisely?'

'The last empress of the most corrupt regime the universe has ever seen,' the Prefect said, letting the words hang in the air.

'Miranda's not an empress,' Debbie said, laughing. 'She's just a girl. I remember her starting at the school.'

The Doctor winced, and put a finger to his lips.

'So you know her as well?' the Deputy asked.

'I know her,' Debbie said, defying the Doctor's silent attempts to shut her up. 'And she's not some evil space queen.'

The Prefect nodded, but didn't look at her. 'She is not what she seems. She contains the seeds of evil. It is her genetic destiny.'

The Doctor snorted. 'Nonsense.'

'She is not human, Doctor. She is the last of her kind. Power corrupted them – they became decadent, sadistic. They believed themselves to be above all other life forms. The lesser races were… *playthings* to them. Their powers were unrivalled. They started a sequence of events that led to whole galaxies being evacuated, whole sections of the timeline being erased. When that was done, when most of space and time was left broken and dead, they imposed their regime on the survivors, exterminated any opposition.'

The Prefect paused.

'And so it was for a thousand years. The Imperial Family, rulers of the universe, answerable to no one but themselves. Millions died through their neglect, their cruelty, or just for their sport. There was a Senate, but it was powerless: it lived in fear of the Emperor.'

'You were a Senator?' the Doctor guessed.

The Prefect smiled. 'Yes. There were powerful and influential factions within the Senate. I am the ruler of Faction Klade. The Imperial family let us fight among ourselves for scraps of power and wealth. But then we stopped fighting. Secret meetings were held, alliances forged. A revolution was hatched. The leader of this insurrection was my mother, a powerful Senator. And when the conspiracy was discovered, and my mother was dragged from her home and murdered in the street, that was when the revolution started. Fifteen years ago. I was made to watch, holding my infant brother in my arms.'

Debbie tried to smile sympathetically. The Prefect must have been about her age when it happened.

'The civil war was brutal, but it was short. The Imperial Family were wiped out, many by my own hand. A new regime rose, a more democratic system is now in place.'

'I like a happy ending,' the Doctor informed him.

'It isn't over, yet,' the Deputy snarled at him. 'There's still much rebuilding to be done, there are still many wounds that must heal. The Prefect is a key figure in the reconstruction.'

'If that's keeping you busy, then why leave there to come here?' Debbie asked.

The Prefect looked at her for the first time. 'An intelligent question,' he commended her.

'And the answer?' the Doctor asked.

The Prefect smiled. 'The war, as with all wars, saw refugees. Even before that, to escape the political purges instigated by the Imperial Family, many people fled into the depths of space or –'

'The depths of time,' the Doctor completed. 'People used time machines to hide in the safety of the past.'

Debbie wondered what the Doctor could be running from.

'As their palaces and fortresses fell, some members of the Imperial Family fled into time. With her dying breath, my mother declared a blood feud on the Emperor and all his line...'

The Prefect drew a knife from his belt. It had a six-inch blade, slightly curved, with an ebony handle. The blade was rusted. It looked very old, but also very sharp.

'A ceremonial weapon,' the Doctor guessed. 'You've tracked the Imperial Family. Hunted them down.'

There was a glint in the Prefect's eye. 'It was a system instigated by the Imperial Family themselves. The terms of the feud and the rules of engagement are clear – everyone of his blood is to die by that knife. Miranda is the Last One. The last of her race.'

Debbie gasped. 'You want to kill her? You want to kill Miranda?'

'I will cut her hearts from her chest as I did with the others. And then it will be over.' There was a hint of regret in his voice, but not a flicker of doubt. He would do it, given the chance.

'Hearts?' the Doctor echoed.

'Members of the Imperial Family have two hearts,' the Deputy explained. 'It's how you tell their kind apart.'

The Doctor shook his head. 'She's a girl.'

'Now, yes. But she will be a tyrant. It is inevitable, as inevitable as an acorn becoming an oak. You must help me find her and stop her.'

'You're asking me to tell you how to find a ten-year-old girl so you can go round and butcher her?'

The Prefect nodded earnestly. 'For the sake of the universe. To put things right.'

'Whatever crimes her family committed, whatever wrong they did you, Miranda is innocent.'

'I remember her starting school,' Debbie told him. 'I've watched her grow up. She's never harmed anyone. She's kind, and funny and clever and...'

'She is evil,' the Deputy stated simply.

The Doctor stood. 'Can we have our coats back, please? This discussion is over. I will not be party to the death of a ten-year-old girl, whatever her destiny, however inevitable it is.' The Doctor hesitated. 'I will do everything in my power to stop you,' he vowed.

The Prefect nodded. But not at the Doctor's request – he was giving a signal to his Deputy. Debbie glanced over her shoulder, and saw that the bald man had moved behind the Doctor. There was something in his hand. Something metal. He raised his arm.

'Doctor!' she screamed. 'Look out!'

But it was too late. The Deputy stabbed down at the Doctor's head, slapping something to it.

The Doctor's legs buckled and he fell over, a glistening metal slug attached to his scalp. It wriggled into his hair.

He scrambled, trying to get it off. He fell to his knees, his arms swiping spastically.

When it started to bury itself in his head, the Doctor started to scream.

Chapter Eight
Prefect Timing

The Doctor's body lay on the floor.

Debbie tried to revive him, but the Deputy pushed her away, then bent down to recover the metal thing that was attached to the Doctor's head. He pulled it free of the long hair.

'What have you done?' she asked. She was shaking.

The Prefect was calm, clinical. He held up the metal slug, which wriggled. 'This device is a mindeater. It extracts memories. If the Doctor knows where the Last One is, now we do, too.'

'Extracts memories?'

The Deputy looked over at her. She could tell what this military man was thinking: that he wasn't impressed by her. Why should he be? She was young, but overweight and unfit, pretty much his exact opposite. 'It is far beyond your technology,' he said.

He activated the device. The Doctor's memories appeared in the air in front of him in a ghostly bubble, one after the other, arranged into a semblance of order. Fire and madness and bombing and cobbled streets, and colour and a succession of faces. Debbie saw herself as the Doctor saw her. She was surprised how pretty she looked.

The Prefect was behind him, impatient for the answer.

'The Doctor didn't offer any defence to the mindeater,' the Prefect said, a little surprised. 'Not like last time.'

Once again the Prefect was ignoring her.

'I don't think he has been to Falkus yet,' the Deputy said. 'He has clearly not mastered the psychic defence techniques he demonstrated there or he would have used them.'

'Then…' The Prefect leaned over the Doctor's inert body. 'Then we have destroyed him before our first meeting?' He looked up. 'Is that possible?'

The Deputy nodded. 'Most temporal theory was lost, but such things appear in some of the apocryphal records.'

She understood the words they were saying, but found it difficult to piece everything together. She knew what 'destroyed' meant, though. 'The Doctor's dead?'

The Prefect shook his head. 'Merely braindead. His memory has been wiped.'

'Is that... is that what happened to him before?' she asked.

'Before?' the Deputy asked, checking the data.

'A hundred years ago. He lost his memory.'

'No... oh, I see.' The Deputy stared at the display for a moment. 'That was quite a different process.'

'But he'll be all right?' Debbie asked.

'No,' the Prefect told her, pulling himself away. 'He will remain like this –' he tapped the Doctor with his foot again – 'for the rest of his life. If you don't feed him, that shouldn't be more than a few weeks.'

Debbie was too shocked to reply.

The Deputy turned to the Prefect. 'I have the information.' He squeezed a control on the device and the image of a typed form appeared. 'He consulted her medical record yesterday. The address appears on it. Note that it confirms she has two hearts.' The Doctor had been in a storeroom, Debbie saw. With a pretty nurse who was making eyes at him.

The Prefect nodded, pleased. 'Let us end this,' he said.

The Deputy followed his leader from the room, the door swishing shut behind them.

Debbie knelt over the Doctor. He looked peaceful.

She wondered what would happen to her. The Prefect seemed utterly indifferent to her. If they were going to kill her, they had just missed the perfect opportunity. Perhaps they'd take her back to their time, make her a servant, give her the veil and the long skirt.

Or perhaps they'd just push her down the ramp and abandon her to Barry.

One thing was for certain – the Doctor wasn't going to help her escape.

The Doctor's eyes snapped open.

'I thought they'd never go,' he said cheerfully. 'Shall we escape?'

The Prefect watched the Deputy making his preparations.

He was a craftsman, a connoisseur. Every weapon he selected was a replica of a human device from this century, reconstructed from historical records and stored here in the ship's armoury. They would do this properly: they wouldn't dishonour the warriors of this time by using weapons a million years more advanced than those of their enemies.

The Deputy meticulously removed the weapons from their storage compartments and found a place for them on his body. A spring-loaded knife concealed up his sleeve, a larger blade in a sheath in his boot, a pair of throwing knives on his belt, alongside a samurai sword. Knuckledusters, a garrotte, a cosh, half a dozen grenades, all finding places in pouches on his flak jacket. Then the guns: a pair of automatic pistols on his belt, one on a leg holster, one tucked into the small of his back, and spare clips for each of them. Finally, a stubby machine pistol, which hung from its shoulder strap, and a bandoleer that contained the rounds of ammunition. That done, the Deputy put his gloves on, and stood to attention.

The Prefect took a smaller pistol and a shoulder holster – the Deputy helped him strap it on, then passed him his greatcoat and gloves.

They each took a mindeater, in case they needed to extract further information from the populace.

The Prefect drew his knife, held it up.

'Tonight,' he vowed.

The Doctor tapped another combination into the door controls. Once again, it squawked back at him, but the door didn't open.

'How many potential combinations are there?' Debbie asked.

He sighed. 'I thought you were a teacher. Each digit can be one of ten, there are eight digits. Ten times ten times ten times ten times ten times ten times ten times ten. One hundred million combinations. Who knows? I may live long enough to try them all.'

Squawk.

'You've really been alive for the whole twentieth century.' Debbie didn't doubt it any more. It seemed straightforward compared with the rest of her day.

Squawk.

'Yes.'

'That is so... incredible,' Debbie told him. 'Where were you when Kennedy died?'

'Pardon?'

'President Kennedy – 1963. I was eight, and it was snowing, and the radio was on.'

Squawk.

'I didn't know he was dead,' the Doctor admitted. 'I spent most of

the sixties and seventies travelling.'

Debbie wasn't sure whether he was joking. 'So where were you on the twenty-eighth of May 1976?'

'An odd date to pick.'

Squawk.

'My wedding day,' Debbie said. 'It seemed like the best day of my life at the time. It seemed like everything was going to work out.'

The Doctor stopped what he was doing and grinned to himself. 'I was in England. Spending some time with a... friend. A young widow named Claudia.'

Debbie looked away. 'So, what *do* you know about yourself?' she asked him, changing the subject, half hoping that the mindeater had shaken a few of his memories to the surface. 'Before you woke up on that train? Anything at all?'

'Nothing,' the Doctor said, frowning as the door squawked at him again. 'There was the police box... well, it didn't look like a police box then, that's a more recent development. I've really no idea what's going on with that, but I wish it would hurry up. And there was a note.'

Squawk.

'A note?'

'Yes. Yellow paper, of a type common in this century. Handwritten, but not by me. "Meet me in St Louis', February 8th 2001. Fitz." If it was meant to be helpful it's been more than a little counterproductive.'

Squawk.

'Someone arranged to meet you, but gave you over a hundred years' notice?'

'Yes. Perhaps this Fitz thought it would take me a hundred years to work out what on Earth he was talking about. He may well be right. It's already the nineteen eighties and I'm no nearer. A phone number would have been nice.'

'How do you know it's a "he"?'

'I don't. In fact, one graphologist I showed it to says it's a woman's handwriting.'

'Isn't there a place in America called –'

Squawk.

'Yes,' the Doctor said wearily. 'In Missouri. I've been there. I've been there three times, in three different decades, looking for some hint. The note says "St Louis'" anyway. I've also looked for as many people called Fitz as I could. I've tried to work out the significance of the date

February the eighth. Once fingerprinting had been developed I checked for fingerprints, but only found mine. I once spent two years trying to see if it was in code or there was some hidden meaning in there.'

Squawk.

'You must have come to some conclusions.'

'I'm trying not to. I don't have enough evidence.'

Squawk.

'But you must have some guesses.'

The Doctor didn't tear himself away from the door control. 'If Fitz put that note in my pocket, inviting me to meet him over a century later, then Fitz is obviously an immortal like me. A product of the same experiment, or bloodline, or evolutionary breakthrough or... well, I suppose, the same sort of alien.'

'And Miranda is, too?'

Squawk.

'Yes. She must be. Two hearts, a lower body temperature. Like me. She's the only other person I've ever met like that. But she's ageing at a normal rate, her parents, or at least her mother, is perfectly normal and now the Prefect tells me she's from a million years in the future. It's so frustrating.' *Squawk.* 'I have the horrible feeling this is all some elaborate joke at my expense.'

'Time travel,' Debbie said, everything suddenly clear.

Squawk.

'What about it?' the Doctor said, clearly irritated by his failure to open the door.

'Well... what if this Fitz *knows* you meet him in 2001? What if he's a time traveller? He could have written the note *after* you met, then travelled back in time to deliver it. You'll meet because... well, it's already happened.'

The Doctor stopped what he was doing and turned to stare at her.

'That... works,' he said. 'Wait! Why just the note? If you were this Fitz person, wouldn't you just wake me up and talk to me in the past?'

'Well... if he's met you in the future, he knows that he didn't do that. That's all history as far as he's concerned. It's like I know you don't build a time machine and go back to my wedding and tell me I needn't go through with it, I'm going to have a misca-'

'That's brilliant!' the Doctor said, grabbing Debbie and almost dancing around the room with her.

He leapt back to the control panel, slapping in a new combination.
And Debbie wasn't remotely surprised when the door slid open.

The Deputy activated two hoverdiscs from their wall-mounted control panel.

They rose a few centimetres from the metal floor of the hangar. The ramp set into the floor began sliding silently open.

'I have the co-ordinates,' he told the Prefect.

The Prefect climbed on to his hoverdisc, took hold of the handrail. The Deputy did the same.

'Hold it there!' a voice shouted.

The Deputy turned. It was the Doctor, framed in the doorway to the hangar, the human woman behind him.

Without thinking, the Deputy spun round and aimed his machine pistol. Even as he squeezed the trigger, he cursed himself for giving the Doctor enough time to slam his fist down on the door control. The metal door slid up in front of the Doctor as the bullets arrived, and they just bounced off.

Only then did he allow himself the luxury of wondering how the Doctor had escaped.

'Leave him,' the Prefect ordered, ducking to avoid one of the ricochets.

The Deputy shot out the door control, to be on the safe side, then keyed the launch sequence.

The discs lurched forward, then sped down the ramp, out into the winter evening.

The Doctor flinched as the bullets rained into the door in front of his face, but none of them got through the thick metal.

Once the sound had died down, he tried the controls again.

'You can't go back in there,' Debbie bawled at him.

A door behind them and to the right slid open.

Thélash stood there, annoyed. 'What the cruk is that noise?' she asked, addressing the question at no one in particular.

She saw the Doctor and Debbie and dived back behind the doorframe.

It was an act that could have been mistaken for cowardice, but a moment later she reappeared, a bulbous gun in her hand.

There was a sound like a whipcrack as she fired.

The wall behind the Doctor and Debbie exploded into a shower of sparks. Rum was behind Thélash now, trying to get a clear shot with an identical weapon.

Thélash's second shot hit the locked door, blowing it open.

'Run!' the Doctor told Debbie, pushing her through.

Barry squirmed to get comfortable in the passenger seat of the Mini. He was too big to be in such a small car.

When he looked over at the driver it reminded him why he was here. She was wearing a cheap silk blouse and tight jeans. She was smiling, and had too much make-up on, because she wanted to look older than she was. The cigarette in her mouth was meant to have the same effect. Barry smiled back at her, because he thought that seventeen was just the right age. 'Nearly there,' he told her.

'This is a long way to go for a walk,' she said, and the way she said 'walk' made them both laugh. 'It's going to be dead cold. Why can't we go to your house, like last time?'

'I'll keep you warm,' Barry chuckled.

As the Mini approached the lay-by, it became clear that there was a problem. Two cars were parked there.

'I thought you said it would be quiet here,' she said, annoyed with Barry. 'There's more people here than at a City match.'

But Barry didn't care about that.

'Stop the car!' he shouted.

'Here? No. We'll find somewhere else.'

Barry glared at the girl, and she stopped the car.

'That's my Cortina!' Barry told her, pointing to it.

She laughed. 'Perhaps your wife's gone for a walk up here.'

This time, the way she said 'walk' made Barry very angry. He got out of the Mini and strode over to his Cortina. It was empty, and so was the black Beetle parked next to it.

The girl had followed him out. She had her hands crossed over her chest, and was shivering, but the temperature wasn't what was bothering Barry.

'I'll kill her,' he snarled.

'For what?' she shouted back. 'For doing what you were planning to do?'

Barry told her that was precisely why.

The girl was about to say more when something shot out of the woods and over their heads. An aircraft. No – too small for that.

'What was that?' she asked.

Before they could decide, another one came straight for them. Lower this time. It was a man standing on a disc. The disc was flying – about six feet off the ground and at about sixty miles an hour. Barry barely had time to register that the man was wearing a green jacket before the disc had vanished over the hill.

Barry looked around.

'You saw that?' the girl asked.

Barry nodded, but he wasn't sure he had. It didn't seem like the sort of thing he would see.

'Someone's coming,' she warned him.

Barry could hear footsteps, crunching through the snow. There were people running towards them.

The Hunters stopped at the foot of the ramp.

'Wait. We shouldn't be chasing after them,' Thélash declared.

Rum stopped peering out into the winter's night and lowered his neutron gun. 'You're right. This isn't part of our mission. You heard the Deputy: our mission hasn't changed.' He hesitated. 'But if we do capture the Doctor, it'll look good when it comes to our pay negotiations.'

Thélash shook her head. 'They'll just say we shouldn't have let him escape in the first place.'

Rum was convinced.

'Besides,' Thélash reminded him, 'the Doctor won't get past Mr Gibson.' She smiled. 'Let's watch from the comfort of our chamber.'

Debbie and the Doctor came running out of the wood.

Barry let them get to the car. Both of them were out of breath, red-faced. He shook his head very slowly at his wife.

'Barry, not now,' Debbie told him. She looked over at his friend. 'Who are you? Hang on – don't you work at the Co-op?'

The Doctor stepped between them. 'Did either of you see… discs? Flying platforms made of metal, with people standing on them?'

Barry grabbed the Doctor's shirt. 'Look, mate, that's not your biggest problem right now.'

There was a clunk to their right. From the Beetle.

They all turned to look at it.

'I think you're right,' the Doctor said softly.

Barry let go of him and took two steps over to the car. He peered in.

'There's no one in the car,' he concluded, standing up.

'Stay back!' the Doctor warned.

The car was matt black, almost invisible in the failing evening light. It had fat sports tyres on it, and Barry was sure he'd find a great big chrome exhaust round the back.

The Doctor was scowling at him, but followed him over. 'We're in the gravest danger.'

'From someone that drives a VW? Doubt it. Nice bodykit on it – *très* sporty.' He turned back to the Doctor. 'You're right about you being in trouble, though.'

Barry slapped his hand down on the Beetle's roof, to prove his point.

'Get your hands off,' a deep, almost musical voice said calmly.

Barry looked around, but there was no one around. There was definitely no one in the car. He turned to face the Doctor. 'Here, are you throwing your voice or something?'

The Doctor shook his head. He pointed back to the car. There was a strange noise, like a hydraulic piston.

Barry turned, and saw the Beetle standing up.

It was an odd sight. It bent in the middle, the fat sports wheels sliding to the back of the car. The side panels opened up and slid out, almost like arms, but with massive biceps like Popeye. They propped the car up. Now it looked like a man on all fours – pushing itself up. The bonnet slid down to become a chest plate, the chrome bumper was now slung at the thing's waist, like a belt. It stood upright, legs forming from the rear of the car, giving it feet like moon boots. Hands like boxing gloves slid out of housings. Finally, a boxlike head swung up and out, locking into place. Its headlamp eyes blinked, it flexed its arms and made a hesitant step forward.

The Volkswagen had become a robot. It was around twelve feet tall, and was a bulky, solid thing.

'Cease and desist,' it ordered in a megaphone voice.

The Doctor stepped in front of Barry. 'Of course. Which would you like me to do first?'

The giant robot bent down, peering at the man he so easily dwarfed.

The Doctor smiled. 'Good evening. You, I presume, are the elusive Mr Gibson.'

'Indeed. Greetings.'

'Eh?' said Barry, thoroughly confused.

'Barry Castle, Mr Gibson; Mr Gibson, Barry Castle. Your wife ran over a UFO spotter who was running away from this chap.'

'He's a robot.'

The Doctor had a big grin on his face. 'Well, yes.'

Mr Dawkins looked over at his wife, although he wasn't really Mr Dawkins, and they weren't married.

Kim smiled at him, an encouraging smile, one to disguise what they both knew she was really thinking. She had been so brave.

Mr Dawkins laid the time detector down on the table. 'I didn't check. For the first week in ten years, I didn't check.'

'It's not your fault,' Kim told him.

'A time corridor. Four nanoseconds' duration, ten thousand miles directly above our heads. It opened on Saturday. A saucer came through it. A small one, but...'

He couldn't see Miranda. She was in the front room, drinking her cocoa.

'I'll get a sleeping draught ready,' Kim said. 'Miranda will sleep through this, whatever.' She squeezed his arm. 'We knew this could happen. We've done what we could for her. This isn't over yet.'

He nodded, and started to head for the garage.

Debbie couldn't move. It felt as if her feet had got stuck in the ice.

The woman – girl – Barry had had with him didn't have the same problem. She was already halfway to her Mini.

The robot towered over them all. It was enormous. It looked vicious and practical, the way military equipment often did. It looked like a tank or an armoured car.

'Doctor?' it asked. 'You don't recognise me?'

The Doctor shook his head. 'Does everyone in the universe know me?' he asked, sounding more than a little exasperated.

'Don't you *remember*?' Debbie hissed.

The robot made a noise somewhere between a growl and an engine revving. 'You don't, do you? You merely add insult to injury.'

The Doctor stepped forward, holding his hands out in a conciliatory gesture. 'If I've ever done anything to insult you, then I –'

'*Insult me!*' the robot bellowed. 'You destroyed my world.'

The Doctor stopped in his tracks.

'You let my palace fall, killing my queen.' The robot hesitated, and there was a burst of electronic squealing. 'The most exquisite mechanism in the cosmos. Helpless, I watched my cities burn, one after the other. All because of you.'

The Doctor hesitated. 'Me?'

The robot raised its arm, and some sort of weapon popped from a compartment on its wrist.

Debbie grabbed his sleeve. 'Come on!'

The Doctor was jerked from his reverie.

'Run!' Debbie told him.

The Doctor was heading for the Cortina.

'Here!' Barry objected. 'What are you doing?'

The Doctor was in the car, and he'd somehow got the engine going without the key.

Debbie pulled open the passenger door and got in beside him.

'Debbie, this isn't your fight,' the Doctor insisted.

Barry had got into the back. 'It's my car,' Barry grunted. 'Drive it carefully.'

The Doctor slammed his foot down, and the Cortina pitched forwards with a squeal of tyres.

Mr Dawkins was ready for them as they came.

Hoverdiscs, flying low over the houses, barely high enough to clear the telephone lines. He thought it would be Zevron who would come for him, and he was right. Behind him, as ever, was his Deputy, Sallak.

Dawkins's first shot went clean between them, off into the night. Both discs swerved to avoid it, and shot over his house without getting in an attack.

He heard the car start and opened up the garage door with one hand, keeping a firm grip on the neutron rifle with the other. The door was stiff, but swung up. Kim was in the car, ready to go.

Faster than he'd been expecting, the Deputy appeared above him, swooping low, firing a machine pistol, blowing chips from his driveway. Dawkins stood his ground, as the cold air gusted past him, but his shot went wide, blasting a hole in the roof of his house.

Prefect Zevron had always been a little slower. As his disc appeared over the rooftop, Dawkins got a shot in. It hit the disc, not the man, but it was enough. The disc was knocked off course, and Zevron

tumbled off, down the roof, and into a pile of snow in the front garden. One more shot disintegrated the disc before it could hit anything else.

There wasn't any more time. Dawkins threw the garage door open. His wife drove the car out. Miranda slept under a blanket on the back seat. He tried to get in, but the passenger door was locked.

His wife leaned over, fumbled for the lock.

He could hear the Deputy's hoverdisc coming back towards him. 'Go!' he shouted. The Talbot surged down the drive and smacked into the gate, throwing it open. It was already through, turning on to the road.

The Prefect was on his feet, but too dazed to do anything about the car's escape.

Dawkins turned to face the hoverdisc.

It was coming for him at sixty miles an hour.

The Deputy had a sword in his hand, held horizontal at his waist. His eyes were cold, grey, full of malice.

The blade was coming straight for Dawkins, and there was nothing he could do.

Chapter Nine
The Last Battle

The Doctor wasn't stopping at the junctions. The car sped along the hillside path, passed snowbound fields and dark woodland.

'We have to get to the Dawkinses' house.'

Helpless, Barry looked out of the back window. The robot was chasing them, catching them up with each step. It had one arm raised, and there was a rocket launcher on its wrist. It flashed, and he actually saw the missile heading straight for them. But the Doctor put on another burst of speed, and accelerated away. The blast lifted up the back of the car for a moment. When they'd slammed back down, Barry turned back to check the speedo. One hundred and twenty miles an hour. He could hear the engine straining.

'What have the Dawkinses got to do with anything?' Barry asked. He'd met John Dawkins once – he'd come round to fix their wiring.

His wife looked over her shoulder at him. 'They're here to kill Miranda Dawkins.'

'What? A kid? A little girl?'

'A ten-year-old girl,' Deborah confirmed. 'There are two men – those two that you saw flying past.'

'They won't stop until they've killed her,' the Doctor said, almost matter-of-factly.

'Then we go there and we stop them,' Barry told them. 'That's what we do.'

'We have to keep that robot away from populated areas,' the Doctor said.

'No,' said Barry. 'We save the girl.'

His wife gave a laugh, her looking-down-at-him laugh. 'Aren't you even going to ask who they are?'

Barry smiled back. 'No. I don't care who they are. I just want to stop them killing a little girl. If you've chickened out, you take me there, and I'll stop them.'

He could see the Doctor looking at him in the rear-view mirror.

'You're right,' the Doctor said, turning the car around.

The road ahead of them exploded in a cloud of black rubble. The

Doctor yanked the steering wheel to the right, swerving to avoid it, then pulled the car left.

'Excuse me,' the Doctor called, as the Cortina swerved past the robot.

Deborah glanced back. 'You'll damage the engine,' she squealed.

'So will Herbie there,' Barry reminded her, jabbing a thumb over his shoulder.

The Doctor threw the car around a corner, making the tyres smoke. Out of the corner of his eye, Barry saw the robot carry on the way they'd been going, unable to fight its own momentum. It used its hand to brake, ploughing a swathe from the tarmac. The Doctor had bought them a few seconds.

'You're a good driver.'

'Thanks.' There was a straight stretch of road. They were heading out of town. 'I'm still going the right way?'

Deborah nodded. 'Keep on this road,' she told him.

'Good. Yes.'

The road here wound around the hill. There were a lot of blind bends, a lot of corners where there was nothing but a crash barrier between you and a one-hundred-foot drop. People who lived in Greyfrith could always tell if they were behind someone who wasn't from the village – everyone else took them nice and slowly.

But not even Barry would drive as fast around these corners as the Doctor did.

The back window was suddenly full of bright white light.

He looked back. The robot had become a Volkswagen again, and was haring towards them, travelling even faster than the Doctor could get the Cortina to go. It was half a dozen car lengths away now.

The Doctor was biting his lip, one hand slapping against the steering wheel.

'It's going to catch us,' Deborah warned.

He nodded, then slammed the brakes on, just as they reached a bend.

The robot didn't have time to stop – it carried on, finding itself tearing through the crash barriers. Somehow it managed to transform to its original form in midair, but was still unable to stop itself falling.

The Doctor drove forward, parking right at the lip of the drop. Together the three of them watched the robot as it crashed down the hillside, tumbling over itself, limbs flailing as they tried to find some

purchase. But its weight was just too much, and it crushed everything in its path. Barry saw it grab at a tree, only to pull it out at the roots. It rolled through a stone wall. The noise was like a train crash.

Their car started reversing, and the burning robot disappeared from sight. Barry looked ahead at the Doctor, who was looking over his shoulder, steering the car back as far as it would go.

'We've damaged it,' the Doctor said. 'But we haven't destroyed it.'

He closed his eyes, seemed to be counting under his breath.

'Get out of the car,' the Doctor told them.

'Eh?'

'Out! Both of you.'

Barry and his wife found themselves getting out. 'Aren't you coming?' Deborah asked as she was about to close the passenger door.

The Doctor shook his head.

Barry stepped forward. 'Hang on, what are you planning?'

The robot began rising over the edge of the hill. First its head, then its torso. One of its eyes was smashed, and it was badly dented and scratched. It looked angry.

Barry stood his ground, waited for the robot to come to him.

The Cortina's tyres started squealing, then it leapt forwards, heading straight towards the gap in the crash barriers and the robot. Barry was frozen to the spot, and saw it all happen.

The robot raised an arm, but the missile launcher wasn't there, it must have been broken off in the fall. It hesitated, momentarily surprised by the exposed wires and cables on its wrist.

The Cortina was heading towards it.

The driver's door suddenly opened, and the Doctor flew from the car, his head and arms tucked close to his body. He hit the ground hard, rolling ten or twenty feet.

The Cortina kept going, clearing the edge of the hill, heading straight into the robot's torso like a missile.

The robot registered the threat and tried to swipe at the car with its hand.

The Cortina hit it in the midriff, then pivoted up, the roof smashing the robot square in the face.

The robot staggered back, losing its footing.

Then the petrol tank in the Cortina went up. The robot was briefly visible, silhouetted in the fireball before it starting falling backwards.

Barry hurried to the edge. He watched the burning robot fall,

following the furrow it had carved on its first descent. There was a trail of thick black smoke marking its progress. This time, there were smaller explosions rocking it, deflecting its course. By the time it had come to rest, there was very little left. There was no sign of the Cortina.

His wife hurried over to the Doctor. He was on his side, rubbing his face. There was blood on his shirt.

'You're cut,' she told him. 'Don't worry, it doesn't look serious. Can you move?'

The Doctor nodded, wincing a little as he sat upright. 'The robot?'

'In pieces.'

The Doctor nodded. 'Just as well – I'd just run out of ideas on how else I could beat it.'

He stood, a little shakily at first, and Deborah helped him over to the hillside. The Doctor peered down into the gloom, watched the column of black smoke rising over the burning remains. 'Shame. I would have liked to study it.'

'Do you think it will be able to repair itself?'

The Doctor bit his lip and looked over the edge again. There were still small explosions starting up. Barry imagined that all the missiles and bombs the robot was armed with were going off.

'Not in the short term,' the Doctor assured her.

'That Cortina was my pride and joy,' Barry told them. 'I'm going to kill you.' But he wasn't thinking about that yet: he was too busy watching the explosions.

'There's a queue,' the Doctor told him. He grinned, but the effort made him wince, which saved Barry the bother of punching him.

In their chamber the Hunters squirmed as they saw Dawkins's head lopped from his body, which just keeled over. The dark, hot blood and the cold, white snow did not go well together.

'I wouldn't want to get on the wrong side of that Deputy,' Rum told his partner.

'We *are* on the wrong side of him,' Thélash reminded him. She pointed back into the hologlobe at a figure in a green uniform standing up. 'I thought the Prefect was a goner.'

The Deputy was brushing off the snow and helping the Prefect on to the remaining hoverdisc. The two sped off.

'Keep up with them, you flid!' Rum shouted.

Thélash struggled with the controls. 'Oh... I'll switch to Mr Gibson for a moment, let's see him tear that Doctor's head off.'

The image switched to a pile of burning metal, hissing and popping in a pile of snow and churned earth.

'When Mr Gibson gets going, he does some serious damage,' Rum laughed. 'It's a real grudge match.'

'Because the Doctor destroyed his planet?'

'No,' Rum laughed. 'Mr Gibson *blames* the Doctor, but that's not the same thing at all. The Doctor helped free the slaves on Mr Gibson's planet, he ended Mr Gibson's practice of throwing all his political opponents into the volcano he just happened to have under his palace.'

'Why?' Thélash asked. 'What did the Doctor have to gain from doing that?'

Rum shrugged. 'Mr Gibson started to panic and set the volcano off by dropping a nuke down it. But he didn't check where Mrs Gibson was first.'

'Mrs Gibson?'

'She wasn't called that, I admit. It doesn't matter. His queen, his mate, the mother of his little metal children. She, they, all his allies were wiped out when the volcano erupted. The rebels won. It's a story with a clear moral: don't be such a psycho.'

Thélash nodded. 'Or if you are, then don't build your palace on an active volcano.' She looked back at the hologlobe and all the scrap metal. 'Is the Doctor under all that, do you think?'

Rum was pale. He'd just seen a pair of shattered headlights staring blindly into the camera. 'Thélash... that *is* Mr Gibson.'

Thélash looked at him. 'This is not good,' she concluded.

'Sit down,' Debbie ordered the Doctor.

The Doctor found a section of crash barrier that hadn't been twisted out of shape or hurled off the hillside and did as he was told. Debbie leaned in alongside him. Barry was still staring down into the valley, transfixed by the rising column of black smoke.

'It's a cold night,' the Doctor said, looking up at the stars. 'A clear sky.'

'Doctor...' she began.

'I can't remember,' he replied quickly. Then more slowly, 'There's obviously a lot I can't remember.'

'That robot said you destroyed its planet.'

'Yes.'

'You can't remember?'

'No.'

Debbie sighed. 'Does destroying planets sound like the sort of thing you do?'

The Doctor shook his head. 'How are we going to get back into town?' he asked. 'We need to get to Miranda.'

Barry had come over. 'Too right. Or at least get to a phone to warn them.'

There was a car coming. Debbie found herself flinching.

'It's a Sunbeam,' Barry said, exercising his talent for identifying cars from their headlights.

The three of them stood in the road, waving their arms and hoping it wasn't so dark the driver wouldn't see them.

The car slowed down, and Debbie was surprised to recognise the owner.

'It's Kim Dawkins,' she said.

The Doctor was scanning the horizon. Barry was opening up the car door.

'What's going on here?' Mrs Dawkins asked. She had seen the column of smoke and the wrecked crash barrier. She looked haunted.

'We've run into some friends of yours,' Debbie said.

'They... they killed John,' Mrs Dawkins said softly. Debbie wondered if she was in the early stages of shock. It didn't look like she was safe to drive any more.

'Miranda?' the Doctor asked, coming over.

Kim looked at the blanket on the back seat. 'I drugged her. They're following me on discs.'

'I've got a good view, and there's no sign of them yet.'

'John hit one of the hoverdiscs. That will slow them down.'

Barry looked around. 'I'll keep watch,' he said.

'We know everything,' Debbie said. 'We've been aboard their ship.'

'We don't know everything,' the Doctor cautioned. 'We know one person's version of events. I doubt the Imperial Family were really as bad as Zevron painted them.'

Mrs Dawkins sighed. 'I imagine everything they told you was true. Miranda's people abused their genetic privileges. Their birthright gave them great powers and potential. To a man, every member of the Family used those gifts to satisfy their own lust for power. For

centuries, every one was a sadist, a pervert, a mass murderer –' She started to choke.

The Doctor was trying to keep her talking, trying to keep her focused. 'You're not her real parents, but you were on the Emperor's side during the civil war?'

Mrs Dawkins nodded. 'I was part of the Emperor's household, a wet nurse. John was a bodyguard. Miranda is the Emperor's granddaughter, last of that line. She was two months old when Zevron came for her. We couldn't let her die.'

'They're here!' Barry shouted, running over.

The hoverdisc was arcing towards them, barely visible in the night sky.

Mrs Dawkins had a gun in her hand. 'Take Miranda, Doctor. Keep her safe.'

Debbie opened the back door of the car and lifted Miranda out, keeping her wrapped in her blanket. She was surprisingly light.

Debbie ran for cover. Behind her, Mrs Dawkins was firing into the night, using the same sort of weapon the Hunters had had on the ship. She pulled herself down into a ditch at the side of the road. She had a good view out, but was well hidden.

The Doctor and Barry were shoulder to shoulder, waiting for the hoverdisc to arrive.

It was moving slowly, weighed down by having two men on it. The Deputy was piloting, the Prefect had something in his hand. As it swept past the car, barely four feet above it, something fell from the hoverdisc and clanked against the roof.

The Doctor shouted something and pulled Barry and Kim away.

The Talbot exploded. Before tonight, Debbie had never seen a car explode. Now she knew just what to expect – tiny explosions, followed by a big *whump* as the petrol tank went up.

The hoverdisc came in to land. The Prefect disembarked, but the Deputy stayed put. Once the Prefect was on the ground, the disc was airborne again, and was much faster. The Deputy was swooping around, keeping Kim Dawkins and her ray gun away from the Prefect.

'Where's the girl?' the Prefect shouted at the Doctor and Barry.

Debbie ducked her head down, shielding Miranda from view.

'Stay where you are, Doctor,' the Prefect ordered. He was tall, powerfully built, but he was practically middle-aged.

The Doctor stood his ground.

'Here!' Barry objected, shoving himself in front of the Doctor.

'Mr Castle, don't,' the Doctor warned. 'The Prefect is –'

Barry turned. 'Don't think I've forgotten what you were doing with my wife. I'll deal with you in a minute, once I've got rid of this –'

The Prefect gave him a swift chop to the shoulder, and Barry sank to the floor.

'Now, Doctor,' the Prefect said, 'where is the Last One?'

Barry pulled himself up, pushed his way between them.

The Prefect elbowed him in the stomach, Barry doubled up.

Barry grabbed the man's shoulder, and pulled himself upright.

The Prefect turned to face him. 'The capacity for learning is clearly not one of your attributes.'

'You sound like *her*,' Barry said, cocking his head towards Debbie.

The Prefect smiled, and starting heading towards her.

'Oh, well done,' the Doctor said scornfully. 'You've led him right to –'

Barry headbutted the Doctor, left him lying where he fell and ran up to the 'Prefect'.

Barry lunged to punch him, but his opponent was too fast, stepping out of the way and delivering a blow to Barry's shoulder as he went past.

'You're asking for it, now,' Barry warned him. 'You want a go? You want a go?'

The Prefect frowned at Barry, then lashed out. Barry fell to the ground, and this time had the sense to stay down.

The Deputy swung the hoverdisc around, increased the speed.

Another neutron blast whizzed past. His opponent was a nurse, not a fighter. She'd fired a gun before, but the Deputy doubted she had ever managed to hit a target, let alone a moving one.

Nevertheless, she was the main threat at the moment: a single stray shot from her would be enough to kill either him or the Prefect.

The Deputy set a course towards the woman, steadied the disc and unslung his machine pistol.

Barry watched, helpless, as Kim Dawkins was torn apart by machine-gun fire.

He'd seen pictures, he'd heard about it from mates who'd been in

the army. But this was different. One minute she was a person, a good-looking woman, the next she wasn't anything.

Barry felt sick. He pulled himself upright. These people, whoever they were, wherever they got their flying machine and that walking robot thing (Barry reckoned it was probably the army - they had all sorts of secret weapons), they were trying to kill a ten-year-old girl.

Barry wouldn't let them.

He tried to get up, but couldn't.

His side ached. Broken ribs - he'd had a broken rib before, and recognised it.

The man who'd done it - the Prefect, the Doctor had called him - was striding up to his wife, who, true to form, was just cowering there. This lot were soldiers - he should have realised before. As with policemen and ex-policemen, you could always tell if someone had ever been a soldier. Both were too old now, but they'd kept fit.

They had twenty years on him. The little guy on the flying thing looked old enough to be his dad.

Barry forced himself up on to his knees.

It didn't matter how good their training was. It didn't matter how fit they'd kept themselves. Barry was in good shape himself: he was thirty years old, at his peak. He lifted weights. These people knew the theory, but he'd put what he knew into practice, on the football terraces, and round the back of the Dragon. He didn't need any Bruce Lee stuff, just his fists.

He stood, took a deep breath. The rib may not be broken - just bruised.

The Prefect was only a few feet from his wife.

Barry took a couple of steps forward, and, encouraged by how easy that had been, took a few steps more.

The Prefect saw Barry coming, but did nothing - he underestimated his opponent.

Barry grabbed the man's shoulder - barely registering that it was almost solid muscle - and pulled him round, punching him just above his stomach. He was wearing a bulletproof vest underneath his green jacket, but he'd still hurt him. Barry had the advantage, and used it to pull the man down, bringing his knee up to meet the man's nose. The man couldn't get much grip in the ice, and was sliding about. There wasn't much hair to grab, so Barry just balled his fist and hammered it down at the base of his skull.

Barry should have felt the man's legs give way, but the man just broke away and headbutted him. Barry could feel his nose getting warmer. Blood.

He took a deep breath through his mouth.

The Prefect drew a pistol and pointed it at Barry's head. An automatic. A VP70.

It was the first time Barry had seen a gun. A real gun.

He recognised it from one of his magazines.

And while part of his mind was telling him that it was a Heckler & Koch 9mm semi-automatic pistol, how many rounds it carried and that it was a must-buy item in its category, he was really thinking that this man could have killed him at any time since they'd met, that his being alive was just a privilege this man had granted him.

Deborah was screaming, the stupid fat cow.

'Go,' the Prefect said to them. He had a deep voice, like an actor's. 'This isn't your fight. I'll kill you both if you stay.'

Deborah was crying, but she was also standing up, letting go of the girl.

'I'm sorry,' she said to her, and also to Barry.

Barry grabbed her hand and pulled his wife away from this madman.

The Prefect laid the girl down in the snow.

It was better, he thought, that she wouldn't wake to see this.

He unbuttoned her pyjama top, trying not to think about what he was doing. He had not relished this moment, and the sight of her torso, still that of a child, did not make him proud of what he was about to do. This could be his younger brother's chest. Ferran had been born the same year as Miranda. They were both still smooth-skinned children. Then he remembered that two hearts beat there, and which blood was in her veins. She was nothing like Ferran, she mustn't be allowed to live.

He mentally rehearsed the two swift strikes that would end this.

He raised the knife.

'Ahem, aren't you forgetting someone?'

It was the Doctor, standing firmly in the snow.

'You won't be able to stop me, Doctor,' the Prefect said wearily.

'Not with weapons or fists, no. I don't want to fight, Prefect: I want to talk.'

'This isn't your concern, Doctor,' the Prefect spat.

'It is. You want to kill an innocent –'

'No!' the Prefect spat. 'If this creature lives, a lot more than one child will die. Her kind have killed untold numbers. This is not an innocent.'

'She's a girl. She's not killed anyone. Look at her, Zevron – is killing a *child* really the only way this can end? Is this really how the ruler of a galactic empire acts?'

The Prefect felt his arm lowering. This was madness. Miranda was just a girl.

The Deputy swept past on the hoverdisc, forcing the Doctor to take a step back.

'You know I'm right,' the Doctor shouted across.

The hoverdisc dived back towards the Doctor, who stood his ground until the last moment. The Doctor soon broke for cover when the Deputy started firing at him.

The Prefect had regrets. The universe just didn't work in the way the Doctor said it did. There had been a time when there was order in the universe, a time when not everything ended in blood and fire. That had been before the Last One's ancestors had spoiled everything. Kill her, he told himself, and those times would return.

Perhaps there had never been order. Just the illusion of order.

Kill her.

He raised the knife again.

Someone barged into him, pushing him over.

'Barry!' the Doctor's companion shouted.

It was the woman's husband, the fighter. Straddling him, pummelling him. No subtlety, no elegance. But he didn't need those things. He was strong, each punch connected. The Prefect was already blind in one eye, he already could taste his own blood on his lips. The man's fists were large, brutal weapons.

The man was shouting at the Prefect, but the words reaching him were slurred, incoherent, full of profanity. He could guess what the man was saying.

The Prefect tried to find some purchase on the icy ground, but couldn't. He felt his opponent tearing at his hand, tugging his gun away, taking it for himself. The Prefect reached down, tried to stop him, but it was too late. There was a moment of darkness and disorientation. The human had broken his neck, the Prefect thought. He was already dead.

The human loomed over him, the gun in his hand.

The Prefect tensed, his hand closing around a pouch on his belt.

The human hesitated.

And the Prefect's arm swung up, clapped the mindeater to the side of the human's head, then flopped away uselessly.

'Barry, no!' Debbie shouted, at the sound of the shot.

As she reached her husband, she saw something was wrong. He was straddling the Prefect's body, but he was swaying, as if he was the one who had been shot in the head.

Then she saw the metal glisten on his temple and she understood.

He keeled over into the snow. The mindeater fell off, its work done.

And Debbie stood there for a moment, unsure whether or not to cry.

The Doctor darted past her, past the Prefect and Barry. He knelt over Miranda, checked her pulse.

'She's alive!' he called out, lifting her out of the snow.

And the ground around him erupted into plumes of snow and mud and there was a second's delay as the sound of the bullets and the hoverdisc making its pass caught up with the bullets themselves.

The hoverdisc was already swinging around for a second pass, the snow parting like a cloud of flies. Debbie could see the Deputy, a gun in one hand, the other gripping the handrail of the hoverdisc.

The Hunters watched the events, safe in a chamber deep within the Prefect's ship.

'This is not going well,' Rum noted to the maidservant as she poured him another drink.

Thélash glared at him, then returned her attention to the holographic globe in the centre of the room.

'Staring at it won't make it any better,' he added. 'Our employer is dead. All we can do now is go home and put in a claim for our money.'

'Shut up. I'm thinking.' She looked up. 'There's no option: it's time to use the bomb we planted on the Doctor.'

'*We* planted?' the man asked archly.

'All right: *you*. Hurry, before the Doctor comes for us.'

'It'll kill the Deputy,' Rum objected.

His partner raised her eyebrow.

Rum took the black control box from his pocket and tapped it a couple of times. He held it up, showing his partner the spidery red display. 'OK, OK. Detonation sequence activated. Ten-second

countdown. It's done.'

Thélash leaned in, until her nose was practically dipped in the hologram. 'Any second now...'

The Doctor was standing his ground, nobly remaining in front of his fat little friend as the Deputy's hoverdisc swung around for a final attack run. The Doctor looked desperate. They were putting him out of his misery, really. They felt a twinge of regret – anyone that had wiped out Mr Gibson and his entire race couldn't be all bad.

'Wait!' Rum squeaked. 'He's not wearing his coat!'

'Where's the coat?' Thélash demanded.

The maidservant bowed. 'Pardon me, sir and madam, but I took the Doctor's coat from him when he and the human woman came on board. I believe it is in the reception chamber. Would you like me to fetch it?'

Rum and Thélash stared at each other.

Neither the Doctor nor the Deputy was looking towards Cooper's Wood, so they didn't see the fireball blossoming. A couple of seconds later, though, they heard it: a crack, then a great rolling, rumbling sound.

The Doctor knew exactly what it was.

The hoverdisc stalled, almost throwing the Deputy. Suddenly he was using both hands to cling to the handrail, trying to keep standing. The disc was still hurling forward, but now it was merely following its momentum – it had lost all power.

The Doctor pushed Debbie out of the way, then dived down. The disc sliced the air above his head, but it was falling. Now it hit the ground and tumbled over. The Deputy was flung from it.

What happened next was inevitable and inexorable. The hoverdisc came down on top of its pilot, crushing him underneath it. The force of impact was enough to churn up the snow and the ground beneath it, to smash the disc in two, and mangle the handrail. Exposed circuitry plopped from the cracks, fizzing and crackling to itself.

The Doctor ran towards the wreckage, keeping back until he was sure it was safe. Something had caught fire, and there was a terrible smell of burning plastic.

The Deputy's legs lay under the pile of scrap metal. They could have been crushed, or perhaps only pinned. Either way, the Deputy was clearly in agony, and unable to move.

'Your disc drew its power from your spacecraft, didn't it?' the Doctor said softly. 'It's over: you're marooned here, the Prefect is dead. There's nothing left to fight over.'

The Deputy still had a knife in his hand. He waved it at the Doctor, but the effort was almost too much for him.

The Doctor prised his fingers apart, took the knife from him.

'Fighting isn't the answer. And even if it was, this isn't your fight. Save your strength.'

'Blood feud on you and all your kin,' the Deputy spat.

'No,' the Doctor said. 'Not today, thank you.'

The Deputy glared at him, but then his eyes glazed over, as if just staring was too much effort. The Deputy's head lolled.

Debbie helped the Doctor to his feet. He squeezed her hand.

'I'm OK,' she told him. 'Barry's...'

The Doctor nodded. 'This one is unconscious, but he'll live.'

They heard Miranda groan.

'Check her,' the Doctor ordered, searching the pockets on the Deputy's flak jacket. He found what he was looking for in a side pouch – simple wrist restraints, which he used to bind the Deputy's hands behind his back. There was no anachronistic technology that the Doctor could find, apart from a wrist communicator, which he removed.

'Miranda's OK,' Debbie called over. She was doing up Miranda's pyjama top.

The girl was rubbing her eyes. 'What's happened? Why am I outside?'

The Doctor moved over to her and knelt down, so he could make better eye contact.

'Something terrible has happened,' Debbie said calmly, as her teacher training said she should.

There were police and ambulance sirens now, but they seemed so distant. Like the fire and the snow, they seemed to be happening elsewhere.

The Doctor clutched Miranda's hand. It was warm, tiny next to his own.

'I'll protect you,' he told her, tears in his eyes. 'I'll look after you.'

Part Two

'Masters of the Universe'

The Mid-1980s

Chapter Ten
Eighties' Child

Rex saw the young woman on the way to pick up a fax.

She was sitting on the leather sofa outside the interview room. She was a teenager, permed blonde, with long legs. She was wearing Levi 501s, a baggy white shirt and a tapestry waistcoat. If she was here for an interview, she wasn't dressed for it. But if Rex had been doing the interview, she'd definitely have got the job.

Rex straightened his tie and went over.

'Hi,' he said. 'Are you OK there?'

'There's nothing to read,' she complained. Her accent was difficult to place, but vaguely northern. She sounded younger than she looked.

'Can't help you there,' Rex replied. 'Do you want a drink?'

'Water?' she suggested.

Rex smiled and pointed to the fridge. 'No one ever sees it,' he reassured her, opening up the panel on the wall. 'Good, eh? This whole reception area was designed by Imojagi.'

She nodded, but clearly hadn't heard of Imojagi. Well, that was good: not many people had yet.

He handed her a bottle of Dragonwater. 'Nothing but the best here,' he assured her.

'Wow! Dragon,' she said, and Rex was exhilarated by her enthusiasm. 'I come from Greyfrith, where this is bottled. Do you have a glass?'

Rex sat down beside her. 'Drink it from the bottle,' he told her.

The young woman did, a little awkwardly at first. She had to lower the bottle for a moment to giggle at herself. Rex laughed along with her.

'What's your name?' he asked.

'Miranda,' the young woman said.

'Miranda. Miranda Who?'

She laughed, a lovely, musical sound.

'I'm Rex,' he said, although she hadn't asked.

'And what do you do, Rex?'

'I'm on the board,' he said, although that wasn't enough to impress

her. 'I'm here today because...' He lowered his voice. 'Because in there,' Rex began, 'is the genius behind Dragonwater. Five years ago, hardly anyone drank bottled water. Since then, there have been a couple of safety scares. People don't trust what comes out of a tap. And nowadays people like labels. They don't want to settle for second best: they want designer stuff. He saw all that. Legend has it, he was in a pub and he told the barman to sell his pub and buy a bottling plant, start selling water from a local spring for five quid a bottle. Now Dragonwater's worth twenty mil a year.'

The girl raised an eyebrow and took another swig from the bottle.

Rex pointed to the door. 'He's the best. He charges ten K a day, and he's worth every penny. He's a genius. He's been here three days and he's already completely restructured this company. I was in one of his meetings this morning. Incredible speaker, cuts through the crap. He's Thatcherism personified.'

The door to the boardroom opened and a man emerged. A young forty-something, his long light-brown hair tied back in a ponytail. He was wearing an Armani frock coat, had bright-red braces and was carrying a leather briefcase.

'Doctor!' Rex said, delighted.

The Doctor smiled. 'I'm done here. It was good to meet you, Rex. I've tinkered a little with the company structure, but it should be right as rain now.'

'Any redundancies?'

The Doctor looked at him as though he'd never heard the word before. 'No,' he said, puzzled. 'Why would there be?'

'Well, you know: cutting out the fat.'

'You're businessmen, Rex, not butchers.'

'"Businessmen not butchers", I'll remember that.' Rex turned to the girl. 'I told you he was good.'

She grinned. 'You did.'

'Are you drinking that from the bottle?' the Doctor asked the girl sternly.

'You know her?' Rex asked, already knowing the answer. Of course – ten thou a day and the Doctor would have blonde teenagers all over him. God only knew what he drove – a different 924 for every day of the week, probably.

The girl stood up and pecked him on the cheek. 'Rex told me it was the in thing, Dad.'

The Doctor smiled down at Rex. 'Is it? Interesting.'
But all Rex could answer was: 'Dad!?'

The Deputy sat in his cell, reading the newspaper.

He'd learned a lot about Earth in the last five years. Living among their criminally insane was an education in itself. There were men like this in his own time, but the Factions used them, they had a part to play. Rum and Thélash would have been locked away – but how much better to utilise their talents. The whole system here was wasteful – mines and shipyards and steelyards closing every day. Resources wasted in competition and 'advertising' and holding elections only to see the same leader returned, time after time.

His cellmate slept on the top bunk. Joel was a man of little conversation, a thief with a penchant for arson, but he'd taught the Deputy some useful techniques for dealing with the mechanical locks and crude security systems of this time.

The Deputy coughed. The medical facilities on this planet – or at least in this institution – were primitive. Hygiene was a matter of crude disinfectants and chemical compounds. But he was being better treated than the prisoners he had taken in his time, and the humans of this island didn't have the death penalty.

The Deputy started to read the financial section, a story about corporate restructuring. The people of Earth were obsessed with money. One man was causing a stir in the business world, his consultations leading to what the paper called 'a revolution'. These humans had never seen a real revolution.

He saw the man in the photograph, he saw that his company's phone number was listed.

The Doctor.

'I knew you'd show your face sooner or later, Doctor.'

He woke Joel, and asked to borrow his Walkman.

Debbie Castle held Barry's hand.

'Eileen Lewis has started school. She's got your eyes. You probably don't even remember Julie, do you? Her husband doesn't suspect a thing, but I know. They got married very quickly when Julie got pregnant. Sound familiar?'

Barry didn't respond. He lay there, the machine at the side of the bed beeping away to itself. Thinking about it, he probably would

remember Julie. If he woke up now, the events of five years ago would just be like yesterday to him. Not that he would be waking up. The doctors insisted that there was no point talking to him, he couldn't hear. It had been four years now since they'd decided to call his condition a 'persistent vegetative state' instead of a 'coma'. Debbie had read up on the subject, but still couldn't tell the difference.

The mindeater had lived up to its name. Barry was still alive, still breathing without help, his body doing all the things you didn't need to think about. But there was nothing in his mind. He'd been asleep for five years. He looked peaceful. After all this time without exercise, his muscles had atrophied; he had lost several stone.

Well, Debbie thought, she'd lost weight, too.

She loved him. It was ridiculous, but she still wore her wedding ring, and Barry still wore his. She couldn't even think of looking for someone else. She dreaded the day that they withdrew treatment. The law seemed so inadequate here. They couldn't give him a quick injection to put him down, but they could stop feeding him and let him starve to death over a few weeks. He wouldn't feel it, but it seemed cruel.

But a long time ago Debbie had realised she wanted him to stay like this. She wanted to visit him twice a week, tell him her news. She wanted to be stronger and healthier than he was, she wanted to have the upper hand. She finally had him where she wanted him.

She thought about her life. Still teaching Class Six, still living in the same house, still playing chess on Tuesdays and attending the local poetry group. What had changed? She didn't drive any more; she hadn't gone to the Dragon since it was renamed the Flying Saucer. She'd cut down on smoking; she'd started doing aerobics.

She'd met a time traveller, she'd been aboard a UFO, run away from a giant robot, nearly been killed by an alien king.

And it hadn't changed her life.

She looked down at Barry's pale, wasted face.

Living death.

'So how did he escape?' Anderson asked. Sallak's cell was empty, except for a couple of telltale signs on the table – tiny screws and clipped lengths of wire.

'One of the warders let him and his cellmate out.'

Anderson looked up. 'What?'

'He doesn't know what happened. He led them straight to the car park and handed over the keys to his Rover. He thinks he was hypnotised.'

'You believe that?'

'It was Sutherland, Dr Anderson, he's got ten years' experience. He says Sallak had a device in his hand.'

'A hypnotic ray?' Anderson laughed. 'Check out Sutherland. Sallak paid him off, blackmailed him, threatened him.'

The prison officer was shaking his head.

'Do it!' Anderson insisted.

Dr Anderson had the psychiatric report on Sallak in his hand, but he didn't need to refer to it.

'John Sallak,' he said out loud. The subject that had taken up so much of his time in the last five years.

Sallak was a genuine mystery. He'd appeared one day, killed a married couple – the husband by beheading him with a samurai sword, the woman with a machine gun. He'd had a colleague whom a member of the public had shot and killed. The police also suspected he was linked to two big explosions in the area that night, but had been unable to prove anything.

That was when Anderson had been called in. The judicial process needed to assess Sallak's psychological state to know whether he'd spend the rest of his life in prison or in a secure hospital. Interviewing Sallak, running every test in the book, getting other specialists in to discuss his case – none of it had helped. Sallak was disciplined, intense. He'd killed two people, but he'd done it like a soldier, not a psychopath. His motive was unclear, but all the psychological tests suggested that Sallak was goal-orientated, focused on the mission at hand. Unlike a lot of killers, he didn't have any cranky religious beliefs to justify what he did. He had a high IQ, but not one so high that it gave him a sense of superiority or invincibility. While on remand – and subsequently in prison – he'd fitted easily into the hierarchical system, seemed almost at home. That suggested he was used to institutions – children's homes, the army, prison. He respected the authority of his warders, but wasn't easily led or particularly suggestible. He interacted normally with the other inmates and the guards – but he'd never given anything about himself away to them.

Anderson had recommended that Sallak was fit for criminal trial. Sallak had pleaded guilty, denying anyone the chance to cross-examine

him in court. It was a move that also minimised publicity. Sallak had earned a few tabloid headlines, but there weren't any photos of him - the whole story was that there wasn't a story. The newspapers drifted away, occasionally referring to him whenever they wanted to whip up some fervour for the return of the death penalty.

Anderson had stayed with the case, keen to find at least some answers. Sallak looked and acted like a soldier, but the police, army, MI5, MI6, Interpol, the United Nations, the CIA and God knew who else had no record of him. The best theory Anderson had heard was that this was an intelligence officer, abandoned by his government - of course no one would admit that they'd sent a spy to kill a civilian couple. Which government? He just didn't look American, he didn't seem to know any French, German or Russian. The British? Anderson doubted he would ever know.

Then there was the Doctor... or at least that's what he called himself. For the first two years after Sallak's arrest, the Doctor had been a thorn in the side of the authorities. He had been one of the witnesses to the murders, and he demanded to be allowed to question Sallak. The Doctor had been persistent, until Sallak's lawyers put an injunction on him, one that prevented any contact between the Doctor and the people treating their client. Anderson hadn't heard from the Doctor in three years.

He remembered the Doctor's last words, as a security guard led him out of the building: 'Test his blood. The Deputy's not human. Just test him.'

After objections from the lawyers had been overruled, they had tested his blood, and it was perfectly normal. And Sallak... Sallak had looked shocked at the news, repulsed by the idea that he might be a human being.

None of this had solved any of the mystery surrounding the man.

And now John Sallak had walked out of a bolted cell, taking his cellmate with him.

'How long has he been gone?'

'No more than twenty minutes. We've alerted all ports and airports, set up roadblocks.'

'He'll get past them.' Anderson hesitated. 'I need to make a phone call.'

The Doctor handed over some money to the man who'd washed his

windscreen while his car was stuck at traffic lights. Miranda had been a little worried that the vigorous sponging would be enough to push the Trabant's windscreen in, but it had held.

The Doctor wound up his window. 'Kind chap,' he concluded. He turned to her, not looking as he set off from the lights. 'So what do you make of Rex?'

'I think Dinah would call him Yuppie scum. Then sleep with him.'

'But you weren't tempted?'

Miranda looked over at her father. He'd never asked about her love life before. There was nothing to tell, of course, but she was surprised he was asking. 'No,' she said.

The Doctor smiled. It was clearly the right answer.

She decided to try her luck. 'Is it the thought of me having a sex life, or the thought of Rex in particular?' she asked.

The telephone rang, and her father tapped the button for a hands-free call, grinning that he'd been saved by the bell. She switched the radio off and kept quiet while her dad went about his business. Some oil company wanted his expertise, by the sound of it. She'd never worked out exactly what her father did – the explanation from Rex had actually clarified a few things. He went into companies and, in the space of a week of tinkering and rallying cries, he'd overthrown the old ideas, revolutionised their business practice, set them on course for the future. Or sometimes there would be a specific problem that he'd sort out, or he'd arbitrate between companies that had a dispute.

The traffic in central London was notorious, and Miranda guessed her father had insisted on driving in only to make some obscure point to his City clients about status. The Trabant had been parked in a row of Porsches and BMWs, like an old drunk uncle at a wedding.

When her dad finished his call, he put the radio back on for Miranda. The news on Radio Four. The first item was about an IRA bomb scare on the Tube that had closed the Central Line. So it was a good job they'd brought the car.

'Are we going abroad?' she asked. The oil company wanted some help with some African operation. Half-term was coming, and she'd often accompany her father abroad if it didn't interfere with her schoolwork.

'No, I wouldn't miss running the Marathon, not after last year,' he assured her. 'I have to defend my title. And I've got dinner with Clive Sinclair on the fifteenth.' He smiled. 'You're a grown-up, Miranda, I trust

you. If you want to keep some things private, then I respect that.'

'Well, don't worry, I don't have any secrets.' Miranda giggled. 'Least of all a secret lover.'

Her father nodded, pleased with the answer.

The car phone rang again.

'Doctor? This is Phillip Anderson.'

Miranda looked over at her father, who had the oddest look on his face.

He picked up the handset and listened for a few moments.

'Are you going to make this public?' he asked, then visibly relaxed at the answer. 'I can't talk now,' the Doctor told Anderson. 'But thank you for the warning.'

He replaced the handset.

'Who was that?' Miranda asked.

'Nothing.' But her father looked distracted.

'Come on,' she prompted.

'Anderson works with the police,' the Doctor said. 'He was warning me that an old enemy is around.'

'An old enemy?' Miranda repeated. 'You have enemies?'

The Doctor gave a wry smile. 'A few. It's probably nothing.' He hesitated.

'Now who's got secrets?' she chuckled.

'No secrets,' he said quickly. 'Just be careful, keep an eye out for strangers hanging around the house, that sort of thing.'

Miranda was tempted to laugh it off, but her dad sounded worried.

'Are we going to get police protection?' she asked.

'I'm not sure that would help,' the Doctor admitted.

Miranda was confused. 'Wait: who is this?'

'A man called Sallak. Also known as John Sallak. A dangerous man who's escaped from prison. I've got a photograph of him at home, so you know who to look out for. Now, he's got no idea where we live, so I wouldn't worry too much. Just stay alert for a while.'

He smiled, and Miranda knew she was safe.

Chapter Eleven
UFO Detected

Miranda plunged into the pool, ready for the cold water.

She was three or four strokes along already, dimly aware that some of the others were only just hitting the water. She was at an advantage, not having to worry too much about her breathing. She wasn't racing *them*, anyway: she was racing the clock. Dinah was close, but nowhere near close enough.

Miranda reached the other end, flipped over and launched herself back. As her head broke the surface, she saw Dinah almost at the end, and the others about three-quarters of the way there. She made the same even, measured strokes, but increased the pace a little. She already knew she wasn't going to beat her personal best. She increased her pace again, but lost her rhythm a little.

She reached the end, grabbed the rail, annoyed with herself.

Miss Andrews was leaning over with a stopwatch. 'Nearly,' she told her. 'That was very good going.'

Miranda didn't think so. She pulled herself out of the water, sat on the edge and wrapped a towel round herself as the others finished and bobbed around catching their breath.

She shook her head at Dinah, who was looking red-faced.

'You're just getting *better*,' Dinah complained, half jokingly. 'I don't mind being second if it's a close second.'

'The record is under twenty-four seconds,' Miranda told her.

Dinah laughed, 'The *Olympic* record is, yeah. The county under-seventeens one isn't.' She pulled herself out of the water.

'Aren't you cold?' Miranda asked.

The others started to troop through into the changing rooms.

'I thought you were from oop North,' Dinah said lightly. 'Don't you lot think it's warm if it's not actually snowing?'

'I'm not cold, I just wondered if you were.'

The bell went. Miranda walked through the showers, just enough to get the chlorine out of her hair. Dinah stepped round them.

'Are you OK?' Dinah asked.

Miranda frowned as she retrieved her bag. 'Yeah.'

'Worried about getting old?'

'Sixteen,' Miranda said. 'It's ancient, isn't it?'

'Old enough to smoke, old enough to –'

'Shush,' Miranda said, blushing all over. 'It's too old to be in the under-sixteens swimming team.'

'And so you've ended up in the under-seventeens... strange that. I can't wait to be sixteen.'

'So I heard,' someone called from across the changing room.

The changing room was little more than benches and hooks, and it was always far too cold. Even though spring was well under way outside, in here it was still winter. The girls had got the knack of dressing quickly and silently. Dinah's technique was typical – she yanked off her swimming costume, dabbed herself with a towel, then seemed to be in a race to get dressed.

Miranda was a little less efficient, trying to protect her modesty with her towel, and also making more of an effort to get dry.

'Hurry up,' Dinah moaned, buttoning up a white shirt over a black bra. 'We'll miss half of lunchtime. It's nothing we haven't seen before.'

'You get my watch when you go to get yours,' Miranda suggested, self-consciously.

Dinah sighed. 'Yes, your majesty.' She stomped off to the valuables drawer on the other side of the room.

Human civilisation did not extend as far as this.

The roads were cracked, the windows of the crumbling high-rise accommodation blocks were broken, covered with metal grilles or, in the majority of cases, both. Every wall bore obscenities or tribal territorial claims disguised as support for the national ball game.

As the Deputy walked across the wasteland (that was the locals' own name for it), he passed a burned-out car. He didn't recognise the marque, but could tell that it was an old vehicle. Locals stealing from locals, rather than crossing into the more prosperous suburbs, only a few miles away. Sensible criminals, then, ones who knew that a local crime wouldn't even be investigated, but an attack on the rich would lead to persecution and imprisonment.

The employers who had once flourished here had retreated, leaving behind burned-out and boarded-up shops. The people who eked out a living on this estate did so by exploiting 'the system', state-welfare payments. The Deputy couldn't help but think that the system was

exploiting them – removing all forms of income, police coverage and public transport, failing to maintain communal property and facilities. Closing every factory, car plant, shipyard, coal mine, steelworks and textile mill for a hundred miles around, and offering nothing in its place.

In the centre of the wasteland was the Tower. There had been three here once, full of young families, full of life and hope. But there was no hope here now, and the Tower's companions had been demolished late last year. The Tower had been spared, so the local legend went, because the local authority had run out of money. It was deserted now, officially at least.

A couple of youths were circling around him, at a distance, trying to work out whether the contents of his carrier bag were worth stealing. The young preyed on the old, lurking in broken lifts and stairwells, behind collapsed walls and demolition sites. The youths' calculations weren't based on the risk of capture, simply whether it would be any less boring than what they were doing already. They made no effort to hide their presence – indeed, they had a music player nearby, hurling out repetitive thumping sounds and screeching, incoherent vocals.

The Deputy was an oddity to them – not a victim, like most of the people here. An old man, but not one who was wasting away on a tiny pension and an indifferent medical-care regime. They could see he was a strong man; their hunters' senses were probably attuned enough to tell them he'd spent time in prison and served with the military.

They edged towards him.

'Geezer!' one of them shouted.

The Deputy stopped and turned, and they laughed at him for doing that.

He said nothing as they came over. If they'd seen him as a threat, or they'd had an ounce of wit, then one of them would have got into a defensive position, tried to get behind him. They didn't, they just stood there.

'Give us some money,' one of them said, boldly.

'You have money,' the Deputy told him. The beer can in their hands, the other two by their radio, told him as much.

'We've got money. Loadsamoney,' the youth gargled. 'We want more.'

The other just swore, struggling to even pronounce the monosyllable.

The Deputy took a step forward, broke the boy's leg in two places, and watched his face as he realised he was in terrible pain.

The other one, the one who could speak, hesitated. The Deputy turned, cupped his hands and clouted the youth's ears. Done properly, as here, it was a move that would burst an opponent's eardrums. The youth was reeling. The Deputy pushed him over and knelt down to reach into his leather jacket. He removed a wad of small-denomination notes. There was the equivalent of six months' pension here. Indeed, judging by their mode of operation, this probably *was* pension money.

The Deputy could not be concerned with the inequalities on this planet in this time zone. He needed the money.

The Deputy left them to their agony, pulled down one of the boards that allowed access to the Tower, then began climbing the anonymous stairs, passing rows upon rows of identical doors. This wasn't so different from prison, but it was a prison where people didn't know where the next meal was coming from, a prison without warders or hope of release.

There were worse places than this on Earth, the Deputy realised. Places where the crops failed year after year, and the people died in their millions. Places where the nuclear reactors exploded, where hurricanes, earthquakes and floods devastated whole cities.

Joel and Kirst lived on the top floor of the Tower.

The Deputy took the key from his pocket, opened the door.

Joel was in the front room with Kirst, his woman, on his knee, both of them in a haze of narcotic smoke. The television sat in the corner, hypnotically relaying pictures of a brighter, more beautiful planet quite unlike this one.

'Get what you want?' Kirst asked, getting up to make a drink for them all.

'I did.'

He handed her most of the money he'd taken from the youths. The look on her face suggested she thought this was the end to all her problems.

'I like your friend,' Kirst told Joel. 'Pays his rent.'

The Deputy opened up the bag, took out the components he had bought one after the other, laying them out on the table. That done, he went into his room to retrieve the device.

'It's a radio?' Joel asked as he returned.

'It's the only way of contacting my people.'

Joel had shown little curiosity about who the Deputy's people were. After sharing a cell for a few months, Joel knew he wasn't 'working for the police', and that seemed to be the only possibility that he would find unacceptable.

The Deputy fitted the new parts into place.

'It's just bits of old carpet on a turntable,' Joel said, not for the first time.

'It's a static-electricity generator,' the Deputy told him. He pointed at a small plastic vial. 'The static charge is stored here in that mercury, which converts it into magnetic energy.'

Kirst had come back with mugs of coffee. 'I did science at school, you know,' she said. 'This is all a load of rubbish.'

The Deputy spun the turntable, flicked a switch, and the device began to hum. The turntable picked up speed as it began creating energy.

'How's it doing that?' Kirst asked.

Joel was looking proud. 'Hey, this man turned my Walkman into a mind-control thing,' he said. 'This is no problem.'

'I need silence,' the Deputy told them. 'I need to concentrate.'

He stared into the spinning disc, let himself be mesmerised, brought the mantra up from within himself and focused it at the device.

Kirst found herself shaking her head. She was getting dizzy. What was going on?

'Miranda, are you OK?'

Dinah was bent over her.

'You fainted,' Miss Andrews told her.

Miranda shook her head to clear away the fuzziness in there. 'I'm fine,' she said.

Dinah handed Miranda her Swatch. Miranda was relieved that she'd finished getting dressed before it had happened. She scolded herself: her main concern should be why she had fainted.

'Get some fresh air,' Miss Andrews suggested. 'See the nurse if you need to.'

Miranda nodded, a little worried.

The Doctor screwed his eyes shut, then snapped them open to clear his head.

He'd fainted. He couldn't remember ever fainting before. He hadn't

been overcome by fumes – that was difficult, because of the way he was made, and anyway the air in his laboratory was clear and clean. He went over to the window and opened it, just in case.

There was something around him. Like a stone being dropped in a pond. Like ripples.

But ripples in what?

He struggled to put what he was thinking into words. He paced over to the blackboard, wiped clean one of the corners and started to scratch in a few equations he thought might express it.

He looked at his work, but it still felt not quite right. 'No...' he murmured. 'No. No.'

The Doctor pulled aside a framed copy of the periodic table, revealing a safe with a combination lock. He twisted the dial a couple of times.

There had been precious little evidence left by the Prefect's people. The saucer was completely atomised. Mr Gibson must have had some sort of self-destruct mechanism, too – there was nothing useful left of him. All the Doctor had were these trinkets.

He lifted down a tray containing odds and ends: the communicator he'd adapted to track the Hunters, a futuristic-looking wristwatch, a dead mindeater. There were also components that looked like fancy silicon chips. Pride of place was given to a large instrument he'd found in the Dawkinses' house.

He'd seen straight away that it wasn't just part of John Dawkins's electrician's gear. It had taken a while for him to work it out, but finally he'd realised it was an early-warning system. These time machines moved by warping space, and this device registered that warping effect. The Dawkinses must have had it so they'd know if anyone was coming for them.

Much good it did them, the Doctor thought.

There had been no activity for the last five years. He'd checked it every day. Every day, he reviewed the last twenty-four hours of activity, and found that there was nothing to review.

The Doctor flicked a switch on the detector. It began beeping.

A screen on the side lit up, like an oscilloscope.

'There's a source,' the Doctor told himself.

An object travelling through time – or rather the ripples of that object. But it wasn't as large as a saucer. And it was happening now.

The Doctor peered into the display, adjusted settings like a radio

ham desperate not to lose a signal.

The screen flared.

It's coming this way, the Doctor realised.

He couldn't stop himself looking up at the ceiling.

Kirst shook her head. Joel was staring open-mouthed at his friend Sallak, in exactly the same way he'd just been staring open-mouthed at *Anne and Nick* on the telly.

There were veins pulsing on the old man's bald head. It looked like he was about to burst a blood vessel.

'Hey, cool it, Sallak,' Kirst said, putting a soothing hand on his shoulder.

The air in front of them burst open like a water balloon.

As it sloshed back into place, there was a silver figure in the middle of the room. A slim shape in a gleaming silver metal space suit. Its head was covered with a black insectile helmet. It seemed to be glowing.

Kirst saw her own astonished face reflected in the shining metal. It was like an angel, it was like a knight in shining armour.

'Help!' it cried, its voice a harsh electronic bark.

The figure collapsed.

There was a park behind the school, one that you could sneak out to during lunchtime. It was frowned on, but on a warm day like this over a hundred pupils made their way out on to the grass to sunbathe and chat. As long as they didn't smoke, or stray from the park, or the girls didn't try to tan too much of themselves, no one seemed to mind. A couple of teachers sat around the grass, trying so very hard not to look like playground monitors.

Dinah and Miranda met Bob and Alex there.

Alex was Dinah's current boyfriend. They gave each other a chaste kiss, acutely conscious that they were being watched. Miranda knew far more than she needed to about what they got up to when they had some privacy. As it was, all they did here was share a can of Quattro and a bit of furtive hair-stroking.

Bob was Bob. Alex's friend, brought along – as Miranda was – because girls weren't meant to go out to meet boys on their own. As Dinah and Alex nuzzled together and started discreet snogging and whispering, Miranda opened up her book, *A Tale of Two Cities*, one of her O-level set texts. Bob had the latest *Batman* comic.

Bob smiled weakly at her. 'You've been swimming,' he told her.

'I know.'

'I can tell from your hair. It's wet.'

'Thanks.' Miranda shifted her legs, just in case Bob could see up her skirt.

'She fainted,' Dinah said. 'You OK now?'

'I was then,' Miranda said. 'I don't know what came over me.'

Alex and Dinah started sniggering.

Bob was embarrassed, too. He decided to change the subject and started looking around. 'It's spring,' he said finally.

Miranda saw what had attracted his attention – a couple of white butterflies, circling round each other, completely oblivious to the human world, or indeed anything but each other. There was an ant clambering over her hand. There were far more insects in this park than people, she thought, trying to imagine the park as the vast jungle the ant must see it as. The whole world was different to the ant: it would see it as chemicals and vibration, not colours and sound. Ants didn't worry about money, or falling in love, or how big their car was or how much more their house was worth this month. Their senses were entirely different, and of course everything operated on a different scale.

'There's a planet where the moths and the ants are at war,' she said absently.

'What?' Bob asked.

'She gets like this, Bob,' Dinah assured him, taking a break from Alex's attentions. 'She's weird.'

'It's something my dad told me, once,' Miranda said, turning her hand over to make it easier for the ant. 'When I was little, he used to tell me stories. About places where the anthills were the size of mountains, there were men made of Liquorice Allsorts and there was an empress who lived in a big jam jar.'

'Science fiction?' said Bob, his interest piqued.

'I suppose.'

'Cool. Is he a writer or something?'

'No. He's a business consultant.'

Bob was clearly a little disappointed. 'What's your mum do?'

Miranda took a deep breath. 'My mum died. So did my real dad.'

'Oh, wow. I'm sorry, I didn't mean to...'

She saw his embarrassment. 'In a car accident when I was ten. Don't

worry. I know people don't really know what to say.'

Bob's mouth flickered. 'My mum died when I was six. It's OK, I understand.'

Miranda smiled back at him.

The boy lay on Joel and Kirst's bed, wearing a pair of Joel's old pyjamas. He was eighteen, nineteen at most, and although he obviously worked out, he wasn't Kirst's type and he was far too young.

His armour lay spread out on the bedroom floor, and Kirst and Joel were staying away from it, just like Sallak had told them.

'Who is he?' Joel asked.

'His name is Ferran. He is the younger brother of my employer, Prefect Zevron. As Zevron is dead, Ferran should have inherited his rank and title. We have not been in contact for some time.'

It wasn't much of an explanation. Kirst tried again. 'And... and why did he beam down into our living room?'

'The device I built was a distress signal. He came to rescue me.'

'This is a rescue?'

'Sallak?' the boy said weakly.

'I'm here.'

The boy sat upright. 'This is Earth?'

'It is.'

'The time journey... without a transmat at this end, it was difficult.'

'We will need to build one,' Sallak agreed. 'Get a transmuter here, and more men. Why didn't you send a saucer?'

Kirst looked over at Joel for some reassurance that this was insane. But he was lapping up every word, with that same zeal on his face he had when they rented a sci-fi film.

Ferran smiled, leaning up on his elbows. He was gaining strength fast.

'We cannot spare the resources,' he said. 'Things have changed since your time.'

'Civil war?' Sallak asked.

'Not yet.' Ferran took a deep breath. 'The Factions observe an uneasy truce. There have been a few atrocities, but no one wants a return to the Imperial system. Most feel it is only a matter of time before the truce collapses and one of the Factions makes a play for dominance.'

'And are we ready? We have ships?'

'We are as ready as anyone else. But we need men like you there, Sallak. Leaders. Soldiers. We need an advantage.'

'You have grown to become a fine leader, Prefect. You have a lot of your brother about you.'

Ferran shook his head. 'You are not the only reason we came here: I have another mission.'

'The blood feud.'

'The feud. You have located the Last One?'

'I was captured by the humans. They were aided by the Doctor.' Ferran's eyes were wide open at that news. 'Your brother was killed by a man called Barry Castle.'

Joel was hanging on every word. 'You're time-travellers, yeah? So how come they didn't send a rescue party straightaway? I mean, like to ten minutes ago? Or before you were arrested?'

Ferran smiled at him, the sort of smile a teacher gave a bright pupil. 'We have only recently acquired time travel. We still have much to learn about its mysteries.' He turned back to Sallak. 'Deputy, three people must die: Barry Castle, the Doctor and the Last One.' Kirst was a little shocked how easily those words came to the young man's lips. He was already plotting how he'd do it.

'We will start as soon as you are strong enough,' the Deputy vowed.

Chapter Twelve
Voices from the Past

Dinah sat in Miranda's huge back garden, looking back at her huge house. Miranda's dad had brought them a jug of lemonade, which Dinah steadfastly refused to believe he had made himself. Then he disappeared back into the house, claiming he had some work to do in his laboratory.

Dinah was always impressed by Miranda's house, and had no doubt at all that there was a laboratory in it somewhere – it seemed bigger on the inside than the outside. That in itself was quite an achievement – it was a large house, which had probably once been a vicarage, maybe even a schoolhouse.

The gardens were beautifully tended. Roses, old statues, even a couple of beehives. 'Any idea why you've got a police box in your garden yet?' she asked.

'None whatsoever,' Miranda admitted cheerfully.

'Your dad's gorgeous,' Dinah said, once he'd gone.

'Dinah!' Miranda said, genuinely shocked.

'Oh, I'm not going to ask him out or anything.'

Miranda was shaking her head. 'I take that for granted.'

Dinah grinned. 'Who are you bringing to my party, then?'

'Everyone I know is invited anyway,' Miranda replied. She hadn't got all that many friends. She wasn't *shy*, but she was hardly a social animal, either.

'Bob likes you,' Dinah said, trying to provoke a response.

'No, he doesn't.'

'Oh come on, Rand, don't do this again: I'm fed up of blokes coming over to me and looking lovestruck, then me getting my hopes up and then it turning out that they want to know if you've got a boyfriend. Just get one, so I can tell them you have and they can go away.'

Miranda gave her a withering look. 'That's not what happens. Besides, you've got Alex.'

'And he spends half his time looking at you.'

'He doesn't. He thinks I'm a bit strange.'

'Let's go through the list: you're tall, long legs, blonde hair, great tits,

athletic, a bit strange. Yes, I can see why he's ignoring you.'

Miranda was blushing. 'I'm not into all that, you know that.'

'Into what? Boys?'

'Sex,' Miranda said, clearly shocking herself by saying the word.

Dinah grinned. 'You don't smoke, swear, drink, sweat or belch. You ought to do something, Rand. Even the law says you're old enough.'

'I do lots of things,' she said, not taking the slightest offence. 'I just don't feel that way.'

'You're missing out,' Dinah said.

'I'm not,' Miranda insisted. 'You know I'm not. I spend every summer abroad, I've got my swimming, my chess, friends, schoolwork. Plenty of things. You'll be telling me to start smoking next.'

Dinah was jealous. Her parents were well off, but Miranda's dad was a millionaire – money just wasn't a problem. Despite that, or perhaps because of it, Miranda wasn't at all acquisitive. She dressed smartly, and quite fashionably, but she didn't know any of the labels, and didn't seem to care. It was the same with boys: Miranda had beauty, but didn't use it. It was a waste, Dinah thought. She'd never come up with a good theory why.

'Are you worried what your dad would think?'

Miranda frowned. 'No. Should I be?'

'Put it this way – if my parents ask, I've been round to your house loads recently, and as far as you know, I've only ever held hands with Alex.'

'I don't think the Doctor would care.'

'The Doctor?'

'My dad. You know that's what he's called.'

'I know that's what you call him, it doesn't stop it being strange.'

'I don't think he'd mind me having a boyfriend. If he noticed.'

'Well, do you mind him having girlfriends?'

Miranda laughed. 'He doesn't.'

'It's not that ridiculous.'

'My dad's never had a girlfriend.'

'What?'

'Not since I've known him, as far as I know. Certainly not since he adopted me.'

'Oh, come on, you're just being naïve. I know it can be pretty horrifying to think that your parents do it, but he must do.'

'No.'

'Never had a woman round to stay? A "friend"?'

Miranda smiled. 'Once. About a year ago. She said she was an old friend, although Dad couldn't remember her. She stayed here. Don't look at me like that: she slept in a spare bedroom. Her name was Iris. Dad got on with her, but... no, he got all embarrassed when he accidentally caught her in the bath. She said she'd come to help sort things out and explain a few things, but she just ended up confusing us, to be honest. She left in a huff after a day or two.'

'He goes on loads of business trips, though, yeah?'

'Yes.'

'There you go. A girl in every port, he wants to keep them secret.'

'From who?'

'Er... he's so hunky, though. It's a waste.'

'Hunky?'

'Does he go for the schoolgirl type, do you think?'

'Dinah, that's my dad you're talking about.'

'Well, what's his type?'

'Is there something wrong with your hormones, Dinah?'

'Something wrong with yours. Ask Bob. Bob's nice. I should know, I used to go out with him.'

'For five minutes.'

'Three dates,' Dinah corrected her. 'And he was the perfect gentleman. That's one of the reasons he had to go. Look. You don't have to... y'know. Get to know Bob, as a friend, then see what happens from there. You might surprise yourself.'

Miranda considered the idea.

'Follow your heart,' Dinah urged.

'Which one?' Miranda asked her.

'Either of them. Both. Come on...'

Miranda smiled. 'If it'll shut you up...'

Debbie arrived at the hospital, waving at Nurse Collins, the duty nurse.

She knew all the nurses by name, knew their shifts better than they did themselves. Walking to Barry's room was something she did without needing to think where she was going. She'd often end up at his room surprised she was there already – she just hadn't needed to switch her brain on.

This morning, something was different. There was someone in the room.

An old man in a white coat. He had his back to her, and was bent over Barry. He was helping him to sit up.

Barry was awake.

Debbie couldn't move her feet.

Barry was awake.

He was trying to speak. The sounds were incoherent – brain damage, perhaps, or lack of practice. Perhaps just a dry mouth.

Debbie made her decision, and stepped into the room.

'Barry,' she said, ever so softly.

He looked round at her, recognised her.

Then the older doctor turned around, and she recognised him.

Sallak.

He was five years older than the man whom she'd seen gun down Miranda's mother, the man who had stood in the dock and pleaded guilty, without an ounce of emotion. His face was a little more lined, his short hair was thinner.

'Mrs Castle... Debbie. You came,' the Deputy said, and it was clear from his voice that he had expected nothing else.

Debbie had to get help. She turned on her heel – and came face to face with a young man with spiky blond hair and piercing blue eyes. He wore a glossy black suit, and carried a small object that didn't quite look like a pistol.

'Stay where you are,' he recommended. 'We want you to see this.'

He closed the door, leaned against it so no one else could get in.

The Deputy turned back to Barry.

'Do you know who I am?' he asked.

'Bazz-dud,' Barry managed. The effort of sitting up was too much for someone who'd literally not moved a muscle in five years.

The Deputy pulled out a long knife, waved it in front of Barry's face.

'I want you to know who I am. So you know who has killed you. There's no sport in killing a man in a coma.'

And Sallak was swinging his arm round, and there was a long, curved knife in it, and he was stabbing Barry through the chest.

Barry tried to reach for his chest, tried to breathe. He coughed up blood.

Debbie screamed.

The young man smacked her down on to the floor. She sat sprawled there, holding her jaw.

The three of them watched Barry die, choking on his own blood.

Debbie couldn't believe it was real. It felt like watching a video nasty, not like she was in the room. Her husband had little strength; finally he collapsed. A minute later, the Deputy checked his pulse.

'Dead,' he announced, unnecessarily.

'One of our enemies dead. And another delivered to us.' He looked down at Debbie.

'You woke him up,' she told the Deputy. 'You could have told the hospital how to do it at any point, but you didn't.'

The Deputy smiled. 'Revenge,' he said simply. 'He killed the Prefect, this man's brother.'

Debbie looked up at the young man. She could see the family resemblance. But this was a young man, almost young enough to be the Prefect's son.

'Where is the Last One?' he asked.

'Miranda?' she said, before clamming up.

The Deputy took something from his pocket. One of the little devices that had turned Barry into a vegetable, that had threatened to do the same to the Doctor. A mindeater.

'She lives with the Doctor,' Debbie told him quickly.

'Where?'

'I don't know. We… we lost touch. He moved down South.'

The Deputy seemed to know she was telling the truth.

The young man fished a newspaper cutting from his jacket pocket. 'We know what he is doing. But we want his address. It is not a matter of public record.'

'I can't help you.'

The Deputy sneered at her. 'Oh, I think you can.'

Bob was standing by the drinks machine, trying to get his money out, when Miranda came over. She was a tiny bit shorter than he was, but because she was a girl, she looked taller. She was, by common consent, very good-looking, but no one who'd ever asked her out had got anywhere. There was something odd about her. She was attractive, but asexual. She just didn't give out the vibes. Bob didn't, either, it seemed, but with Miranda it seemed to be out of choice.

'Hello, Bob.'

Bob liked Miranda. He liked anyone who called him 'Bob' without doing a Rowan Atkinson impersonation.

'It's stuck,' he told her. 'It says it's giving change but it isn't.'

'I wanted some orange juice,' Miranda told him.

'Stick with the coffee,' Bob advised. 'The orange juice is called that because of the colour, not the flavour.'

A plastic cup popped out and started filling with orange juice. 'Oh, I don't believe this,' Bob moaned. 'I press the buttons and nothing happens, I say "orange juice" and it can't stop itself dispensing.'

He reached in for the orange juice. Before he'd finished taking the cup away, another one popped out and started filling.

'Coffee!' he yelled, yanking his hand away.

'Bob,' Miranda said gently, taking the orange juice from him, 'do you want to go out sometime?'

It took a moment for the question to sink in. Bob spent the time sucking juice off his fingers. 'Me and you?'

'As friends. I mean just the two of us, see how it goes?' He must have had the oddest expression on his face, because Miranda said, 'You look horrified.'

'No,' Bob said, very quickly. 'No. Yes.'

Miranda looked puzzled as she sipped her drink.

'I'd love to,' Bob confirmed. 'Er... so, do you want to go to Dinah's party with me?'

Miranda looked very determined. 'Yes.'

Bob grinned, unable to believe his luck. On the one hand Miranda had just asked him out. On the other hand... boiling coffee.

He let Miranda disappear before he squealed with pain.

Miranda got off the bus, smiling to herself.

She hadn't expected Bob to turn her down, but she was relieved that the process had been completed smoothly. It was something of a relief that she would be going to the party with someone. She'd reached the age when everyone seemed to be paired off when they went out, and she ended up in a corner, cogitating about the anthropology of the situation.

The sun was shining, too. Spring was under way, the trees beginning to bud.

The iron gates swung open automatically at her presence. Actually, the presence of a gizmo she had on her keyring, but the effect was the same.

Dad was home – the Trabant sat incongruously on the gravel drive.

She let herself in and called out that she was back.

There was no answer, so she made a couple of mugs of coffee and took them through to the lab.

Her father was there, in his shirtsleeves, rifling through a pile of handwritten notes. She glanced at them.

'Five-dimensional vectors,' she said. Looking over at the blackboard, she saw a string of equations. She crossed over, tried to work her way through them. 'This is a bit beyond O-level maths,' she said.

'So are you,' the Doctor reminded her. She knew what he was really telling her: you can work it out for yourself.

She had another look.

'Co-ordinates,' she said. 'It's the description of the path of an object. But it's travelling in five dimensions. Then... this bit is... That's notation I'm not sure about.'

'Ordnance Survey grid references,' the Doctor said, without looking up.

He'd taken the road atlas out of the Trabant. It was sitting on the workbench by the jar he kept her milk teeth in. Miranda thumbed through it.

'Oh, I see. Northern England.'

The Doctor looked up. 'What do you mean Northern England? Great Britain, yes, well done, but it's impossible to pinpoint it closer than about a thousand kilometres.'

'You've made a mistake,' she told him, tapping the blackboard. 'You've missed out...'

He was already alongside her. 'Of course, of course.' He crossed out the offending symbols and replaced them with the right ones. 'And the implication is that the exact co-ordinates can be narrowed further. Down to –'

'To within a metre and a second,' Miranda guessed.

'Perhaps not that far.'

Miranda smiled. She found it funny that the Doctor could get so worked up about a theoretical problem.

The phone in the hall started ringing.

'Could you get that?' he asked. 'It's probably for you.'

Miranda scowled. She thought she'd proved beyond all statistical doubt, and despite her dad's insistence, that when the phone rang, it was almost always for him.

She trudged out into the hall, leaving him to his scribblings.

'I'm coming, I'm coming,' she told the phone.

She picked up the handset.

'Hello?'

A terse man on the other end asked if she had a pen. She had. He asked her to write down an address, then told her to take it to the Doctor and tell him that was where he would find Debbie Castle. Then he hung up.

Miranda was annoyed with the rude behaviour. So annoyed, that she was halfway back to the lab before she remembered who Debbie Castle was.

She handed her dad the address.

He was almost out of the room, grabbing his coat from the hook on the door.

'I've got to go somewhere,' he said. 'You look after yourself.'

Miranda was surprised, to say the least. 'Where are you going?'

'North.' He smiled.

Chapter Thirteen
The Black Tower

Night was falling as the Doctor drove into the city.

The motorway came in over the hills, and he saw the city laid out before him, a murky orange starscape that stretched to the horizon in three directions. It was a magnificent sight, like a living organism with the lights of the cars as corpuscles on the arterial roads. There were aircraft overhead, and smoke drifted from the few factories and mills that had yet to close.

As he drove along the flyover, the buildings began getting taller. He wasn't heading into the city centre, with its brightly lit concrete shopping areas and office blocks, or the new canal development, where the old warehouses and mills had been converted into smart new flats and all-night cafes and clubs and multiscreen cinemas.

He came off the flyover just before either of those.

The buildings here were falling into ruin, even though they were barely older than Miranda. The skyline was dominated by grey tower blocks that looked like all the Coronation Street terraces they had replaced piled up on top of each other and covered in pebble-dashed concrete. It was difficult to believe that anyone had thought this was the best solution to urban overcrowding – unless it had been designed to drive people away from the city. It was almost deserted here, even at eight in the evening. Thick metal shutters over every shop window, nothing but piles of litter to suggest anyone had been here recently. There were a few people, huddling like moths around the warm light of the takeaways and the taxi offices.

His car passed a couple of men pushing each other around on the pavement. The Doctor couldn't tell if they were playing around, or really starting a fight. He was itching to intervene, but remembered that he was here for Debbie, and drove past.

Why had Sallak come here? Perhaps he had made local contacts while he was in prison. Perhaps he had come to a place where crime was commonplace and there was little in the way of police presence.

The Doctor didn't need to check the address: the Tower stood out,

a monolithic structure in the middle of a building site that was gradually becoming a garden for weeds and grasses. The ground was dark, deserted. There were no street lights, no source of light for a hundred yards.

There was a road encircling the waste ground, and the Doctor drove the Trabant all the way around it to get a better idea of the lie of the land. There were lights on at the top of the tower. Thirty or forty storeys up, it was difficult to be more precise.

That was where Sallak was keeping Debbie.

The Deputy would have a commanding view. If he had binoculars – and the Doctor didn't doubt that he would – he could very well already have seen the Trabant and recognised it from their last encounter.

The Doctor found a well-lit street to park in – not that there was much danger of anyone stealing a Trabant. He stowed the carphone in the boot, took his briefcase out and locked the car. He started heading for the Tower, hoping he'd come up with some sort of strategy en route.

It was as though a patch of an alien planet had been imposed on the city. All around the edges of the wasteland life went on as normal: late buses, street lamps, sloping roofs. But here was a no-man's-land of burned-out garages and sheds, overgrown paths and bare trees that had failed to bud this spring.

And, overshadowing it all, the Tower itself.

The Doctor picked his way across the ground. It was dark, but also quite open. He could hear things scrabbling around twenty feet to his left: dogs, perhaps even foxes. On the other side of the Tower there was a small campfire. Children, intravenous drug users, the homeless or perhaps a combination of the three. He could hear them talking, laughing, trying to sound tough.

But no one approached him and there was no sign of activity from the Tower.

The Deputy wanted him dead, the Doctor had no doubt about that. But most of all he wanted to watch the Doctor die – and seeing it through the sights of a sniper's rifle wouldn't satisfy that desire.

The Doctor had reached the base of the Tower. The first four floors were all boarded up. 'Condemned' notices were plastered all over the place. The place smelled of urine and ash.

There was movement inside.

The Doctor ducked out of sight, hiding behind a burned-out car.

At first the Doctor didn't think it was human. It was humanoid, dressed in matt black that made it difficult to see in the gloom. It wore a helmet that was part cockroach, part gas mask, and carried a long, sleek rifle. As the Doctor watched, it became clear it was a man in a uniform. A tall man, but essentially just a man.

One of the Deputy's people, but too tall to be the Deputy.

So, he'd managed to get reinforcements into this time zone. Reinforcements and hardware.

The guard hadn't seen him.

The Doctor looked at the tower block, let his eye travel up to the lights on the top three floors. That guard wouldn't be the only one: the Doctor may have to get past a squad of them on each of thirty floors to get where he wanted.

He squatted down behind the car, confident they hadn't seen him yet, and that he was hidden where he was. He needed a plan.

'So what's so great about the Teen Titans?' Miranda asked Bob.

Bob was a little self-conscious at first, but it was a fair question: after all, he had insisted on walking Miranda home, before realising he wouldn't be able to get back to LV426, the comic shop, in time, and so he'd contrived a detour for them.

Miranda had been surprisingly good about it, genuinely interested. Now they were back on course for her house.

'The Perez art,' he said. 'Look.'

'Glossy paper,' she noted, flicking through.

'It's called Baxter paper. It's so popular they bring it out in two editions. Er... careful with that.'

'You know the name of the paper it's printed on?'

'Er... yes. That's a bit tragic, isn't it?'

She smiled at him. 'No. Having knowledge and enthusiasm is never a bad thing.'

Bob decided not to demonstrate quite how much knowledge he really had about comics. He suspected that Miranda's admiration might become pity.

'They live in a big tower, shaped like a T,' Miranda giggled. 'T for Titans.'

'It's... you'll have to read it. It's good.'

'There are a lot of scantily-clad women in this,' she noted, a little

archly. 'Apart from this one. "Raven, conceived in another dimension, born on Azarath, died on Earth".'

'She's a sort of witch. That demon's her dad, but she fought against her evil nature and became a good guy. And she formed the New Teen Titans to fight him. Er... don't bend it back like that.'

'Why not?'

'Well, they're worth more if they're mint condition.'

Miranda handed the comic back to him, smiling.

'It's wish fulfilment, really,' Bob said.

'What do you mean?'

'Superheroes and stuff. I mean, everyone wishes at some point that their parents aren't their real parents.' He clammed up, realising what he was saying. 'I didn't mean...'

Miranda smiled generously. 'Don't worry. I know what you mean.'

'I bet you've sat at home wishing you were really a princess from space, with a load of special powers, and the fate of the galaxy in your hands.'

Miranda laughed. 'No,' she said. 'Is that really what you spend your time thinking?'

'Er, well, no,' Bob lied.

Miranda looked very knowingly at him. 'Perhaps I don't read enough comics.'

'You can borrow it if you want.'

Miranda thought about it. 'OK,' she said, finally. He handed it to her, and she placed it carefully in her bag, keeping it flat in the folds of a textbook.

'Thanks for coming with me,' he said, feeling that he ought to.

She smiled. 'Thank you for taking me.'

'Are you looking forward to the party tomorrow?'

'I'm not really comfortable at parties,' she admitted.

'I'll look after you,' he assured her.

Miranda smiled. 'Thank you, Bob.'

She paused at a set of iron gates. 'I'm home,' she said.

Bob laughed and looked through the gates at the perfect driveway, the manicured lawns and the huge house in the middle of it all. 'Good one. Whoever lives in there must be loaded. Must have millions.'

Miranda said nothing.

'I wonder if he's got a daughter,' Bob joked, oblivious. 'I'd go after her for her money... I'd keep you as my bit on the side.'

Miranda opened the gates. 'There wouldn't be any need to do that,' she told him.

'Miranda, what are you doing? There will probably be guard dogs and all sorts. Oh, I see...'

'Night, Bob!' she called back, laughing.

The rough concrete was pitted, so there were plenty of footholds.

The Doctor had circled round to one of the sides of the Tower that didn't have an entranceway. Then he'd started to climb, as swiftly and silently as he could. He'd counted thirty-three storeys. He wasn't going to ascend quite that far – he was just looking for the right place.

He peered into the fifth-storey window. A deserted flat.

The window was on a latch, but it was pitifully easy to dislodge it. Evidently, the designers of the building hadn't thought that anyone would try to force an entry.

The Doctor eased himself through the window, dropped to the floor, as carefully as he could. That done, he tugged the string he'd looped around his wrist, hauling his briefcase up from the ground floor. Once that was safely inside, he slid the window shut.

The room smelled of damp, cigarettes and chip fat. It had been stripped bare by the council, and no squatters had found a use for it since. The Doctor wouldn't be staying long.

The Doctor put his briefcase down, opened the door a crack and looked out on to the landing. As he suspected, there was a single guard, in the same uniform as the one on the ground floor. This one was facing away from him, peering (a little half-heartedly, the Doctor thought) down the stairs.

The Doctor crept out, up behind the guard, put his neck in an armlock, and kept it there for not a second longer than he had to.

The guard was unconscious.

The Doctor dragged him into the room to strip him of his uniform. At first, he was worried the man was too heavy and it would make too much noise, but it was easier than he'd thought.

The Doctor slipped his own coat off, undid the guard's uniform (an odd type of fastener, a lot like the one some freezer bags had, he noted), and pulled it off. He yanked the helmet off. The guard was a young man, blond.

The Doctor put the uniform and helmet on. There was a belt, too –

it had useful things on it like a radio and what looked like a Psion organiser.

He propped up the man by the window, draping his coat over him to keep him warm.

Stepping back on to the landing, the Doctor checked the settings on the guard's rifle, then fired it a couple of times into the air. As the energy bolts were flying he was already shouting.

'The Doctor! He's here! Intruder on the fifth floor!' The helmet turned his voice into a shrill electronic bark.

He fired a couple more times, then started running around, stomping his feet.

The speed of response was impressive: a guard came running up the stairs, just as another appeared from the floor above.

'In there!' the Doctor shouted, 'I heard him climb in.'

'You've seen him?'

'I've got him pinned down. He's through that door.'

The two guards levelled their guns and fired. The door burst into splintering slats.

'He's there!' one of the guards shouted, before the dust had settled.

The Doctor winced as they both opened fire on the guard. They sprayed the room, not just the man. The wall behind him cracked and blew out, the window frame crashing down to the ground below. The guard fared no better – three shots to the chest, at least one to the head. The force of the barrage pushed him out of the hole in the wall.

He always seemed to lose his best coats fighting these people.

The Doctor had a momentary panic, but a tap to his trouser pocket assured him that he hadn't left his car keys in his coat.

Before the guard had hit the ground, the Doctor was already climbing the stairs, two or three at a time. Other guards were coming, paying him little attention as they clambered downstairs, eager to be in on the kill.

An earpiece in his helmet that he hadn't known was there started to bark instructions at him, helpfully telling him exactly where all the guards were going or heading. The Doctor was sure it was the Deputy giving the orders.

It was a long climb, but he went unchallenged. The upper floors weren't as well guarded – from the tenth to the twenty-fifth, there was no one. The Doctor guessed there had been about a dozen guards. All military men, all trained to use their equipment. This wasn't a gang of

mercenaries from this time – the Deputy had obviously managed to get through to his own people. They could have hoverdiscs or even things like Mr Gibson at their disposal. In here, those two weapons wouldn't be much use to them, but they had had time to prepare this place – he couldn't take anything for granted.

The Doctor hadn't quite worked out yet how he would escape: he was still concentrating on finding Debbie.

There was a door ahead. Two guards, watching him. But the door itself fascinated the Doctor. It was solid metal, the same stuff the Prefect's saucer had been made from.

The Doctor lifted up his briefcase. 'The Doctor was carrying this, I've brought it for the Deputy to inspect.'

They let him through, both of them having to key a control on their wrists to unlock the door.

This was the original structure of the building, but on the upper floors, things had been altered. They'd renovated the place for their own purposes, built themselves a base of operations. The floors and ceilings were solid metal, the walls were thick plastic. There was no obvious source of light, but there was a harsh glare, like standing out in the desert sun. All around was the familiar electronic pulsing sound that had permeated the saucer, a sound the Doctor had completely forgotten about.

A woman in long grey robes walked past, bowing her head as she did.

A thought struck the Doctor.

'Excuse me,' he asked the woman – suddenly worrying he was being too polite – 'where is the female prisoner?'

'We've just moved her to Room Twelve-Kappa. Fourth door on the left,' she replied, her voice without emotion. Perhaps she was a robot, he thought as she drifted away.

That would make her easier to kill, wouldn't it?

The Doctor sighed. He'd let a man die in his place. Not a nice man, in all probability, but just a man doing his job. Perhaps it was the uniform. Wearing this sleek, imposing uniform, with a helmet that hid his face, and a heavy rifle in his hand, the Doctor didn't feel as accountable. No one would know who he was in this.

Disgusted with himself, the Doctor dropped the rifle, pulled the helmet off, shook his head until his hair was loose.

He had reached the fourth door on the left. There wasn't even a

guard on it. There was a touch control. As he tapped it, a box on his belt buzzed – some sort of electronic key, proving he was authorised? Whatever the case, the door slid open.

The Doctor stepped in, cautious, checking his blind spots.

The room was little more than bare metal. Debbie was lying on the bed, a handcuff on each wrist, splaying her into a Y shape. She had a piece of duct tape over her mouth.

The Doctor hurried over, sat down on the bed, put the briefcase down on the floor and carefully eased the tape off.

'We must stop meeting like this,' he told her softly.

Debbie had been crying. 'They killed Barry,' she told him.

The Doctor held her. 'I'm sorry.' He paused, then, 'I'll get you free with the sonic suitcase.'

He pulled the briefcase up on to the bed, opened it up, flicked a switch. There was an ultrasonic screech and the handcuffs fell away.

'It works,' Debbie said, grabbing the Doctor, hugging him. She was shaking, and started sobbing.

'We've got to get out of here,' he told her, doing up the case.

He stood, went over to the door and opened it.

The Deputy was standing there, a gun in his hand.

'I thought you'd want to deal with me personally, not leave it to your guards,' the Doctor said levelly, taking a step back. 'You can let Debbie go, you have me now.'

Sallak shot him.

Chapter Fourteen
The Interrogation Game

Ferran watched, unmoved, as two guards dumped the Doctor on the interrogation table. This was the first time he'd seen his brother's enemy.

The Time Lord was unconscious, corpselike and blindfolded. They strapped him into the restraints without his so much as stirring.

The interrogation chamber had been grown quickly in one of the rooms on the top floor of the Tower. Its size meant it should be an intimate space, but the white-tiled walls, the stainless-steel surfaces, the harsh light gave it the ambience of an abattoir.

'We should kill the woman,' he told the Deputy.

'She could still be useful.'

'The Doctor's our prisoner. He's not going anywhere.'

'You have never faced him in battle, My Lord. We should keep the girl alive, as a possible hostage. If he escapes, rescuing her will be his priority.'

Ferran nodded. He'd read enough of the archives to know the Deputy was right. He thought about killing the Doctor while he had the chance, finding the Last One for himself, but accepted that this was the most efficient way to obtain her location. 'As you wish. Begin the mind probe.'

The Interrogator stepped to the control box. He was a small man who looked like a toad. He began turning dials with clear relish for the task ahead.

'The Doctor possesses a great many mental techniques and defences,' the Deputy told the Interrogator. 'I suggest you concentrate on the mental link between the Doctor and his TARDIS.'

Ferran frowned. 'What good will that do us?'

The Deputy smiled. 'The Doctor is never far from his police box, you can't imagine him without it. But it's not within a hundred miles of here, or we would have detected it. So the Doctor is based elsewhere.'

'Find the TARDIS and we find the Last One?'

'That is the theory, My Lord. He and the TARDIS have a symbiotic link. Logically, the TARDIS will provide the safest place to secure the Last One.'

The Interrogator bent over the controls. 'We should be able to follow that link, My Lords.' He took a circlet from its compartment on the console and placed it on the Doctor's head. The Interrogator was already wearing the matching one.

As the Interrogator set about his work, the Deputy began examining the case the Doctor had brought with him. Ferran looked over his shoulder. Half the case was taken up with a bulky piece of equipment, the other half was packed with odds and ends.

'Components salvaged from the saucer,' the Deputy said. He took a few items out, then something caught his eye.

He pulled it out, brandished it.

Ferran snatched it from him.

This was the knife, blessed by his brother, imbued with his sacred duty. This was the knife with which he would carve out the Last One's hearts.

'The instrument of his destruction,' he laughed. 'He kept it. He didn't understand what it symbolised.'

The Deputy was watching him, silently pleading for his master to show more reverence.

'It is destiny,' Ferran hissed.

Joel lay back on his silk sheets. He was full of champagne and amphetamines.

Kirst lay alongside him, smelling of perfume, diamond earrings hanging from her ears like bunches of grapes catching the candlelight.

'Can't beat going straight,' he said.

Kirst was worried, he could tell.

'We've not stolen anything,' he reminded her. 'It's that transmuter they've got.'

'They've got a girl tied up downstairs,' she reminded him. 'It says on the news that the police are looking for her; they say she's a teacher and her husband was stabbed to death.'

'You heard what they said, Kirst: that's why they're here. Three people. That's all they want. The bloke they've killed, the Doctor, that Last One they keep going on about.'

'Do you know who that is? I asked Sallak. It's the Doctor's daughter. They want to kill a sixteen-year-old girl.'

'We don't know what she's done.'

Kirst slammed her hand down on to Joel's chest, squeezing the air out. 'Sixteen,' she repeated. 'What *could* she have done?'

Joel sat up. 'What do you want to do, then?' he asked. 'In two or three days, Sallak and Ferran go back to outer space, we get to keep all this.' He reached out to the fruit bowl, dug his hand into the pile of gemstones and let them trickle through his fingers.

'If we're not caught.'

'I keep telling you: we've not done anything wrong.'

Kirst leaned over, took a ruby from the bowl. 'So we buy things with these from now on – we go into a shop and hand over a ruby and ask for our change in emeralds?'

'No, we sell them.'

'Where?'

'Jewellers,' he said, annoyed. 'OK – we fence them. I know people.'

'Yeah, criminals. Your big plan is that you tell a bunch of criminals that we've got a house full of gold and jewels and would they like to buy them off us, at the market rates?'

Joel glared at her, but he knew she had a point.

'Look, we'll worry about the details later,' he assured her.

She rolled her eyes.

'Look, we're better off than we were. I'm not totally happy with this, but Sallak's not a monster.'

That was when the man they had imprisoned upstairs started screaming.

The Doctor's mouth was wide open, but it was silent now.

The Interrogator was motionless, lapping up every moment. He was in direct control of the Doctor's mind. The Doctor's thoughts were his thoughts. His face twitched as each agony he was inflicting on the Doctor fed back to him.

'So much,' the Interrogator breathed. Every thought and memory would take a little prising out of the Doctor's mind.

'Focus,' the Deputy ordered.

The screen on the Interrogator's console was showing a blue box. An image of the Doctor's TARDIS, taken by one of Sallak's robot marines on Falkus. The Doctor was standing to one side, along with two young people: a tall man and a dark-skinned woman. This would act as a trigger image – the Interrogator would search the Doctor's mind for it.

The Interrogator gleefully pulled levers, as if he was operating a rack. Each adjustment brought a new type of scream from the Doctor. Each agony was mirrored on the Interrogator's face.

Finally a new image swam into view. The same police box, sitting on a lawn.

'There,' he gasped.

'Where?' the Deputy demanded.

But the image had gone.

Ferran watched the Interrogator, who was swaying slightly. 'He has a powerful mind.'

'Your address,' the Deputy said. 'What is your home address?'

Instinctively, the Doctor remembered. The address appeared on the screen, but the words were blurred.

'He's too powerful,' the Interrogator said. He stared ahead, he started clutching his chest.

'What's happening?' Ferran demanded to know.

The Interrogator lunged for the console, started scrabbling around it.

'He's trying to release the Doctor,' Ferran realised. It took both him and the Deputy to pull the Interrogator away from the control panel.

'Why?' the Deputy asked.

The Interrogator opened his mouth, but no sound came out. Then he keeled over.

'Oh dear,' the Doctor said from the table. 'It looks like the poor chap forgot how to keep his heart beating.'

Ferran and the Deputy turned to the Doctor. The Time Lord was smiling, undeterred by being blindfolded.

'I saw inside his mind,' the Doctor said. 'And I have no doubt that he deserved that. Now, let me out, and we'll discuss this rationally.'

The Deputy drew his pistol, pointed it at the Doctor and fired.

Ferran shoved into him just in time. The energy bolt exploded against the back wall, shaking the room.

'There's a better way,' Ferran told him, pulling the circlet from the Interrogator's head and placing it on his own.

He felt the Doctor's thoughts.

'My Lord, this is most dangerous,' he heard Sallak say, through two sets of ears.

Ferran narrowed his eyes, focused on his hatred for the Last One.

'Miranda,' the Doctor echoed, weakly.

The image on the screen changed. Now there was a girl with frizzy blonde hair, standing at a window.

Ferran smiled.

Miranda didn't need much sleep, indeed she could do without it.

Tonight she had wanted to doze and dream, but the weather conspired against her. The rain was clattering against the roof, the wind was shaking the trees as if they were rattles. She was also buzzing from asking Bob out, with her father's absence, with his warning her to be on her guard. She was drowsy and warm.

She'd read and reread the comic she'd borrowed from Bob, and was sure she was missing the point.

The grandfather clock had tocked its way past midnight. It could be set to chime the hour, but Miranda and her father both agreed that was merely irritating.

The television sat unwatched in the corner, there to provide illumination as much as anything else. Miranda was dimly aware that it was the weather forecast, and that there was a severe-weather warning in force across the whole country.

Miranda went over to the window, drew the thick velvet curtain back a little, and watched the rain. The garden was walled off from the rest of the world, the house was set back from the road. It was like her own private kingdom. Very safe: the walls were lined with infrared sensors, there were security cameras around. A burglar, intruder or her father's 'enemy' could get into the grounds, with difficulty, but Miranda would know they were there. They couldn't get into the house, she was sure of that. The doors looked like wood, but underneath were made of thick steel plate. The windows all had locks, and were double-glazed. Her father had insisted on the best when they'd moved in. It had sounded paranoid, as though he had been expecting trouble, but Miranda was grateful for it.

There was a light in the garden. Either a flashing light, or one that was being continuously obscured by branches as they swayed in the wind. She tried to work out which.

There was a distant crack of thunder. She hadn't seen the lightning; perhaps that had been before she'd gone to the window. In which case the storm was still a long way away. She wondered how far.

There was the light again, a regular pulsing light. It was like a signal, the sort of beacon a secret lover would use to signal across the moor

to his lady, or that a spy on a clifftop would send out to a submarine.

She dismissed the idea that it was Bob. He was possibly capable of a romantic gesture, but it wouldn't be something so cryptic.

She saw the lightning this time, or thought she did. Automatically, she began counting under her breath. Six seconds later there was a roll of thunder.

The flashing light was calling to her: she felt it drawing her towards it.

No, that was silly. She tried to analyse the thought, but it remained out of reach, as though it belonged in a primal part of her brain. The nearest she got was that it was calling her home.

Miranda went to the front door, opened it.

The rain was coming down in sheets, all beautifully lit by the security light above the door that had flicked on automatically as it sensed her presence. Another sign that there wasn't an intruder – he'd have triggered it.

The beacon was still there, winking on and off lazily.

Miranda decided to investigate. She took her raincoat down from the hatstand that stood in the hall and put it on over her pyjamas. She took her slippers off, though – she didn't want to get them wet.

She stepped out of the house. It was impossible to lock yourself out, so that didn't worry her.

Her feet were already very wet.

She stepped briskly forward, on to the lawn, which was half an inch deep in water. She walked towards the light.

When she was halfway across the garden, the security light went off, plunging the garden into darkness. Now there was only the beacon. Miranda followed it.

When she realised it was the lantern on the top of the police box, she was almost disappointed. Miranda couldn't remember it ever flashing before. Her father had never come up with an adequate reason why he would have such a thing in his garden. There was a trend for people having the old-style red phone boxes as garden furniture, but he'd had the police box back in Greyfrith, and he'd insisted it come with them when they moved down South.

The rain was getting heavier, and was beginning to penetrate her raincoat. Cold water was seeping over the collar, beginning to squeeze down her back. She pulled herself close to the police box, which at least provided some shelter.

It was warm. Warm and humming, as though there was a generator in there. Or as if it was alive.

Miranda found herself holding her palm flat to its surface.

It *was* alive.

It reminded Miranda of something – she tried to remember what. That was it: it reminded her of when she had bad dreams and her mother had to hug her and hold her and tell her that there weren't any monsters here, all the monsters were a long, long way away.

She tried to remember what had scared her so much.

It had been a recurring dream, and it had terrified her. Given her an aversion to sleep that she'd never quite lost, she realised. But she couldn't remember the nightmare, now, only the emotions it induced.

Fire, she thought. Fire and corridors and screaming people.

She shivered.

The lightning cracked right overhead, and the thunder had already caught up with it.

There was a man in the garden with her, standing perfectly still in the rain.

She jumped, but felt strangely abstracted from it all. As if this was a dream.

He was young, but older than she was. Seventeen? Eighteen? But the details were vague, as if they hadn't quite been finalised. She couldn't see his face.

The lightning cracked again, and he had vanished.

Miranda shook herself.

She'd seen him.

She took a step forward, not in the least bit scared. The grass squelched underfoot, and something suddenly occurred to her. She went over to where the man had been standing, only about six feet away from the police box. She knelt to check, but she could already see that he'd left no footprints.

She looked around, trying to work out what had come together to make the optical illusion of a young man. Her mind worked through absurdities: that it was tree branches and a bin bag, or that it was her own shadow, cast by the police-box light.

She was getting soaked. The raincoat must have trebled in weight, and she'd just got cold mud on one of her knees.

Miranda hurried back inside, and was very careful to lock the door behind her.

* * *

Ferran pulled the circlet off his head, panting, exhausted.

'You've beaten him,' the Deputy said, proud of the boy.

'I know where she is,' he said. 'For a moment I was there. I saw her.'

He was at the table, leaning over the Doctor, who was on the brink of unconsciousness.

'I was stronger than him,' Ferran said, gasping for air. 'I saw everything. He's adopted her, he's pledged to protect her. He loves her, more than he's ever loved anyone.'

He held the knife close to the Doctor's face. For a moment, the Deputy thought Ferran would whip the blindfold off and carve a scar in the Doctor's skin.

'Was that all you saw?' the Doctor asked.

Ferran looked at him, then away, ashamed.

'I know you, now, Ferran. It's not your fault you were born when you were, into that family. Since your cradle, since before you can remember, all you've been taught is revenge. Vengeance and blood and blood feuds and a sacred duty of vendetta.'

'There is nothing else,' the Deputy said.

'There is,' the Doctor insisted. 'It's like an addiction, Ferran. You can help yourself. I know that deep down, below all those layers of hatred that others have filled you with, that you're a decent man. You know me now, you've seen almost a century of humanity.'

Ferran smirked. 'Oh, yes. The human race shows great potential.' He seemed almost drunk, the Deputy thought, a little out of his depth as he assimilated the Doctor's memories. 'I see a column of tanks rolling past a ruined cathedral; I see napalm and rape and crippled workers and flooding mines and mushroom clouds and border guards shooting those who would escape.'

'Is that all you saw?' the Doctor asked again.

'Rockets,' Ferran said. 'AIDS, stock-market crashes, Red Indians and Jews and Kulaks and Gypsies and embryos being led to their deaths like cattle. Anthrax and agent orange.'

'There was so much else,' the Doctor said softly. 'It wasn't like that at all. It happened, but that wasn't all that happened. Is that really all you remember?'

Ferran leered at him. 'I'm going to kill your daughter, Doctor. You've told me where she is, and now I'm going to kill her.'

Chapter Fifteen
Target Acquisition

The Doctor woke to find Debbie Castle leaning over him with a sponge full of cold water.

'He was too strong,' the Doctor said. 'The Interrogator weakened me. But Ferran was fresh to the fight. He was stronger than me.'

'You have to rest,' Debbie told him.

'No. I have to stop Ferran before he leaves. He knows where Miranda is. He'll kill her.'

Debbie sighed, too exhausted to cry or shake any more.

'What is it?' the Doctor asked.

'You've been unconscious for almost a day,' she told him. 'Ferran's had plenty of time to get to her. Doctor, there's a good chance she's already dead.'

'Check him out,' Dinah said breathlessly.

There was a boy they'd never seen before emerging from the changing rooms. Tall, lightly muscled, tanned. He had cropped blond hair, piercing blue eyes. He walked around the pool, towards them and the deep end.

'Wow,' Dinah said.

'Look at those eyes.'

'I wasn't looking at his eyes.'

'Dinah!' Miranda said, shocked. 'Don't let him hear you.'

'He looks like he should be in the Hitler Youth,' Dinah said.

'Will you shut up?'

He looked over at them, his expression giving nothing away.

'He's looking at you. He wants Aryan babies.' Dinah was running towards him. 'Fiver says you can't beat Miranda,' she blurted.

The new boy looked over at Miranda. From his expression, it was clear he resented the idea of racing with girls. Disdain, bordering on pity. He was in for a surprise.

'I will race you,' he said. The words were slightly stilted, he seemed a little awkward.

Miranda smiled back at him.

Dinah nodded. 'I'll clap my hands to start, yeah?'

Miranda and the young man both nodded, and Dinah got out of their way. Miranda wasn't listening any more: she was focusing on her swimming, preparing herself. She concentrated: increased the supplies of adrenaline and sugar in her bloodstream, her heartsrate and the level of oxygen carried by her respiratory system. Ordinary people couldn't do it, apparently. Her dad could – he'd taught her the mantras she needed. She'd tried teaching Dinah once, but her friend couldn't get it to work, and just accused Miranda of making it up.

Her body was buzzing, ready for the race. This was one time she wanted to be different. One time she liked having two hearts. She had a competitive streak, she always had, and this gave her the edge.

They lined up. The boy would have stood next to her, but Dinah bustled her way between them. The boy ignored Dinah, looking into the face of his opponent. Miranda found herself staring back. He was handsome, but he knew it, which wasn't at all attractive.

They stood in place, limbering up.

'Two lengths. Ready? OK. Marks. Set.' *Clap!*

Miranda dived into the water, powering away. A clean start. Practised strokes, measured. But he was alongside her. Miranda picked up the pace a little, but now he was ahead of her.

He was flipping over as she reached the far end. She caught up with him now, pushing away powerfully. The race back was a matter of power, and the boy had plenty of that. It felt like he was miles ahead of her. Really, she was doing well, only a head or so behind him.

Enough for him to win. Miranda looked over at him, angry. He was staring straight at her again, but now he was grinning. An expression of triumph, a sentiment that bordered on gloating. Miranda felt a sudden urge to wipe the smile off his face.

'He beat you!' Dinah giggled. 'But I think you beat your personal best.'

Miranda glared up at her, then pulled herself out of the water, and stomped off into the changing room, tried to collect her thoughts. Dinah was right: she'd shaved a little from her own record for the fifty-metres, a record that had held since before Christmas. But she was a sore loser, a trait made worse by the fact she rarely lost.

She stuck her head under the shower, just enough to get the chlorine out of her hair. She went to her locker, unlocked it and retrieved her kitbag.

When she turned around, the young man was standing there, staring at her.

'This is the girls' changing room,' said Miranda.

This changing room was like the one he had used – an area with a number of empty cubicles. The same tangy disinfectant had been used, the floor had the same slimy tiles.

The Last One was towelling her hair. Ferran felt a thrill to finally see her. Since before he could remember, he'd been told about this creature, the last of the line that had humiliated his people, driven his genetic line to the brink of extinction.

'You did very well,' he told her.

'Not well enough. Look, did you hear me?'

Ferran reached into the towel bundled under his arm. He felt the hilt of the knife. She was clearly not armed, or wearing armour. Even alone in the women's quarters with a strange man, her guard was down. It would cost her her life and birthright. He went through his strategy, checked his escape route. A double-blow to the chest, as he had practised so many times, then a swift escape. The blood on the blade would suffice as proof of the kill.

The door swung open. It was a hefty-looking woman in purple loose-fitting clothes, like the man at the reception desk. An employee here.

She was obviously shocked by his presence. 'What are you doing in here?' she demanded to know. 'The men's changing rooms are next door.' She turned to the Last One. 'Is he bothering you?'

'No,' the Last One replied, laughing.

'He's a friend of yours?' the woman asked. 'I don't care what you get up to at home, but –'

'I have made a mistake,' Ferran said, keeping his hand on the concealed knife. 'It's my first time here, I took a wrong turning.'

The woman looked him up and down. 'OK,' she said eventually. 'Go now, though.'

Ferran nodded and left. The Last One was grinning at him. Mocking him.

He could not have killed her like that. Her last thought would have been of his humiliation, not of his triumph.

Ferran returned to the men's changing room, showered, dried

himself, dressed. He kept looking at the back wall. Behind that whitewashed brick was the Last One, alone, unarmed, vulnerable. The thought sent a thrill down Ferran's spine. He could kill her at any time. He had absolute power over her.

The Doctor was at the door, still searching for a control.

'It's solid metal,' Debbie told him. She'd done it herself, gone round the room, discovered that the room they had been locked in was a metal tank, seemingly cast in one piece. There weren't joins, welds, or anything of the sort. The room was bare, apart from the old bed, the space-potty thing in the corner, and the chess set she'd been given when she'd asked the Deputy for one.

The Doctor slammed his fists against the door, knowing it was futile.

'She's not dead,' he said.

'Doctor, I know this isn't easy for you –'

'She's not dead,' he snarled, 'or the Deputy would have come in here to tell me. That could happen at any moment, but it hasn't happened yet, so there is still hope.'

'Come and sit down,' she said.

'You look worn out,' he said, apologetically. 'I know the last few days haven't been easy for you.'

Debbie patted the bed, and he sat down next to her.

'I'm not sad,' she said. 'I'm shocked. I saw a man killed, and... well, I've seen that before, and it's upsetting.'

'Of course it is,' the Doctor said.

'But I'm not... in mourning. Is it terrible to admit I'm glad that Barry's dead?'

The Doctor looked startled. 'I thought you loved him.'

'I did. I did, but I don't think I liked him. All I can think of, really, is that a terrible weight has been lifted.'

The Doctor looked at her for a moment, unsure what to say.

'I understand,' he said finally.

Debbie remembered Mr Gibson towering over them, blaming the Doctor for the death of his beloved queen and the death of a whole planet. Physically, the Doctor didn't look a day older, but he carried that weight with him, she could see that, now.

She held out her hand. 'All of us carry the weight of the past, even if we don't know what that past is.'

* * *

Dinah and Miranda walked into the reception area of the swimming baths.

Dinah couldn't believe what Miranda had just told her. 'He went into the ladies' changing room? Did you see him in the shower?'

'No!' Miranda laughed.

'Didn't you want to? God, if I'd been there I'd have got in with him.'

'I've asked Bob out, now, Dinah. You should be happy with that, not trying to turn me into a bigamist. Besides, you said he looked like a Nazi.'

Dinah smiled.

The young man was sitting in reception, watching them.

Miranda was hesitating. 'Dinah...'

But Dinah couldn't believe her luck. She tried to imagine him without his shirt and jeans on... then she remembered she'd already seen that, and it hadn't been a disappointment. 'Hi!' she said, surprised at how shy she felt.

'Hello,' he said. His accent was odd, difficult to place. A bit like Miranda's.

'Well done at beating Miranda,' Dinah said. 'Not many people do. I used to be able to.'

'Thank you,' he said, noncommittally.

Dinah realised her charm offensive wasn't working.

'I'm Dinah, by the way. I'm having a party tonight,' Dinah told him. 'You can come if you want.'

'Will the La– Will Miranda be there?' he asked, looking straight through Dinah and at her friend.

Dinah felt her shoulders sag. 'Yes.'

'I'll be there. Where is it?'

'Hang on, I've got some invites in my bag.' She rummaged around for them, already wishing she hadn't bothered to ask him.

He studied the card. 'Thank you,' he said again.

Dinah rejoined Miranda. 'You're in there,' Dinah grumbled.

Ferran watched them go.

The Last One was in his power. He closed his eyes, inhaled, felt some of the Doctor's memories of her wash over him. They were fading now, like dreams, but he could still catch the sense of them, the emotions evoked. The love the Doctor felt for her, his pride in how she was growing up into a beautiful, talented young woman

with the world as her oyster.

To have killed her just then would have been anticlimactic.

For so long he'd been picturing the death of the Last One. He'd thought it would take place in the desert, in warsuits, hydraulic limbs tearing away at the plate armour until she was exposed. Or in a burning building, with the two of them exchanging shouts and screams.

He could kill her at any moment, whenever and however he wanted. To have struck then would have been to slurp down a vintage wine. He would savour this, take his time, make it perfect.

He reread the invitation.

He wouldn't have to wait long.

Bob and Alex arrived five minutes early, and Miranda was running five minutes late.

They looked very smart. She was still in her dressing gown, waiting for her nails to dry. She'd worn nail varnish a few times before, but still wasn't used to it. She rarely wore make-up, but had dabbed on some blue eyeshadow. Bob just gawped at her, clearly astonished and delighted to see her bare legs and a flash of collarbone.

She got them to sit in the front room, telling them that her dad was away. Alex nudged Bob at the news, which made Bob blush. Miranda went back upstairs and got dressed. She'd bought matching white underwear that afternoon when she'd bought Dinah's present. She put it on, then found jeans and a white shirt to go over it.

Where was her dad? He'd often go shooting off for days at a time, especially now she was old enough to be left by herself, but he was always meticulously precise about when he would return. Miranda wasn't worried – his absence made a few things she was planning a little easier – but she was curious as to what he was getting up to.

She dabbed on some White Musk, put on her waistcoat and went downstairs.

Bob had brought a camera, and he got Alex to take their picture together, from a number of different angles. There was, Miranda thought, an abstract thrill about the whole situation. But she still felt distanced from it all – like someone looking at the pictures, not the girl in them. Whatever she felt for Bob, and she did have feelings, it wasn't love or lust.

She tried to analyse it. Power. She had power over him. He'd turn up

when she said, he'd phone her up, follow her around, do whatever she said. All because he wanted a glimpse of her body, with the prospect of more glimpses to come. She wondered whether she ought to be worried that the level of control she had over him seemed to be his main attraction.

When the last photo was developed, it would show her grinning a little more broadly than on the others.

Alex handed Bob's camera back to its owner. 'We ought to get going.'

'I'll just get my bag,' Miranda told them.

'Girls can't go anywhere without a handbag,' Alex said. 'Dinah's the same. I mean, it's not like they keep anything in them. They just cart old receipts and tissues around.'

'You must spend a lot of time rooting through girls' bags,' Miranda noted as she came back into the room, hefting her overnight bag.

'Going on holiday?' Bob joked.

'Staying overnight at Dinah's.'

'Wish I'd have known. I'd have asked and brought my pyjamas.'

Miranda leaned in. 'Ask me nicely and you might not need them.'

His face did odd things. Miranda smiled. Power.

Ferran looked at the invitation again.

He had already checked the route, scouted the area. He had half a dozen possible escape routes from Dinah's house ready. The knife was heavy in his jacket pocket, but it didn't show.

He parked his car a hundred yards down the road, checked he hadn't been seen, and got out. The weather this evening was calm, not like the storms of the night before. The clothes of the era still seemed absurd, like theatrical costumes rather than anything someone would really wear.

He could hear the party from here – a faint thumping, music familiar to him from the crash course Joel had given him in the indigenous culture. Humans, particularly young humans seeking a partner, set great store by knowledge of the fashions. Joel had ensured that the right labels and symbols appeared on Ferran's clothing and footwear. Ferran had studied periodicals on the subject: *New Musical Express* and *Smash Hits*. He'd memorised the contents of one of Kirst's compilation tapes, songs she had recorded from the radio on to magnetic tape.

He saw the Last One heading down the street, accompanied by two

men. He hoped that the two men would leave her side for a moment, because a moment was all he needed. But they stayed with her, one either side.

Ferran remained out of sight, which was easy enough in the twisting streets and evening gloom. Out of necessity, he was out of earshot for much of the time. When he did hear the conversation, it was banal: one of the men complained that they should have got a taxi. The Last One told him not to be so pathetic.

They soon reached their objective: the house that was the location of the party. The front door was open, Dinah was there, welcoming people in.

Ferran hung back, tried to see what would happen next.

Chapter Sixteen
The Party of Doom

The door slid open.

Debbie felt sick. The Doctor looked like a condemned man, about to be led away to the gallows. She knew this would be the Deputy, come here to tell the Doctor that his daughter was dead.

Instead, it was a young West Indian couple. He wore a sharp suit and a Rolex, she was in a T-shirt and jeans. The woman seemed far more comfortable to be here. Behind them was a guard in black uniform and full helmet. Without, as far as Debbie could tell, touching anything, he managed to get the door to shut, sealing the four of them in.

'I'm Kirst,' the woman said. 'This is Joel.'

The Doctor said nothing, but brooded in the corner, watching them. Debbie stayed on the bed, let them say what they had to.

'We heard you screaming last night. We want to check you're OK. Sallak let us.'

'They want to kill my daughter,' the Doctor told them.

'You're the Doctor,' Joel said.

The Doctor nodded. 'This is Debbie,' he added.

'Debbie Castle...' Kirst said. 'Sallak's talked about you.'

'He killed my husband,' Debbie told her.

'Yeah, we know,' Joel said. 'We're sorry about that.'

'Are you prisoners, too?' Debbie asked. There was an edge in her voice. Almost hysteria. She tried to get a grip.

Kirst didn't know where to look. 'No, we're... Joel was Sallak's cellmate. He promised to help us out.'

'You're working for them?' Debbie said, horrified.

The young man brushed his hands against his lapels. 'He's looked after us.'

'He's not human,' the Doctor said. His voice was quiet, but insistent. Like a teacher. Debbie realised it reminded her a little of her dad's voice. She'd not noticed that before.

'We know that. But it's not like they want to invade Earth or anything.' But Kirst clearly felt uneasy even as she was saying it.

'No,' Debbie said bitterly, 'they just want us dead.'

'I don't know what you did to them,' Joel said, 'but they're well unhappy with you.'

'They want us dead,' she repeated. 'They want to kill the Doctor's daughter.'

Joel jabbed a finger at her. 'Tough break, but you think I was wearing Sergio Tachinni a week ago?'

Kirst smiled, trying to be more conciliatory. 'They let us come in here to check on you. They aren't monsters.'

The Doctor stood up slowly and looked Kirst in the eye.

'Do you think they'll honour their promises?' he asked.

'No,' Kirst said quietly.

'Of course they will,' Joel interrupted. 'Why wouldn't they? What's it to them?'

'What have they promised you?' the Doctor asked.

'That we get to keep this,' Joel told them proudly, looking around.

'This tower block?' the Doctor said. 'Is it theirs to give you?'

'Not the building. Just what's in it. They've got a machine. It just turns ordinary stuff into anything you want. We've got a bowl full of gemstones, we've got gold.'

'The Doctor can give you money,' Debbie told them. 'Help us get out of here, he'll give you money. It won't be stolen, it'll be a gift. You can stick it in the bank, spend it on whatever you want. If anyone asks any questions, the Doctor will vouch for you.'

'And if that Rolex was really made by Ferran's machine, it's a fake anyway,' the Doctor pointed out.

Joel shook his wrist, irritated.

Kirst looked at the Doctor, who was smiling at her. 'I'm game if you are,' he said.

'A million,' Joel said. Kirst was going to turn around and tell him to shut up, but before she could –

'Agreed!' the Doctor said cheerfully.

Joel clearly rather wished he'd asked for more.

'You've got a million?' Kirst asked.

The Doctor nodded, and that seemed to be good enough for her.

Joel was looking nervous. 'I don't know about this,' he said.

Kirst grabbed his fancy lapels. 'Real money, no strings, no hassle. A million quid. Given to us by nice people, real human beings who will get us out of here before Sallak and that little psycho decide to kill us.'

Joel nodded. 'OK, what do we do?'

'Get us out of here,' Debbie said. 'We need to save Miranda.'
'No,' the Doctor interrupted. 'Take us to this machine first.'

'I thought you'd never get here,' Dinah moaned as she let Miranda, Alex and Bob in.

They'd heard the music from halfway up the street. Now it was almost deafening. Miranda identified it as Marillion, before filtering it down until she could hear conversations a little better. In the front room, everyone was shouting at each other, trying to get drinks of lager or cadge a cigarette.

Dinah was wearing a new skirt and a red-and-black jumper.

'Are these ribbons OK?' she asked, tugging at her hair.

'You look very vivid,' Miranda assured her, handing over her present, which she had carefully wrapped in dinosaur wrapping paper.

Dinah began pawing at it, eventually reaching the box inside.

'A gold necklace,' she said. She pulled it out and – with a little difficulty – put it on. She kissed Miranda on the cheek. 'It's beautiful,' she said.

Alex was staring out across the street. 'There's someone on the other side of the road.'

Miranda turned. 'The boy from the swimming baths.'

'The one that beat you?' Bob asked, tactlessly.

Dinah was already strolling out. 'Hi, there!'

The boy looked startled, but came forward.

'It's OK, you've found us. Come in.'

He came over. He looked at Miranda, who felt Bob's arm around her.

'It's chilly out here,' Bob told her, by way of explanation.

The room they were looking for was right at the top of the restructured part of the Tower, although all the windows had been sealed over. It was circular, with consoles dotted around which hummed with power. There were also bins, full of builders' waste and other scrap, looking very out of place in such a futuristic environment.

The sonic suitcase was sitting by one of the consoles. The Doctor opened it up, and checked everything was in order. 'A couple of things are missing,' he noted.

At the centre of the room was a raised area about five metres in diameter.

'You should see this thing,' Joel said. 'It can make anything. You just put stuff on the platform and it turns it into other stuff. And that thing –' He pointed at a device that looked like a petrol pump, which sat on a trolley – 'That's like the portable version. You point it at stuff and it transforms it.'

'That's how they've redecorated,' Debbie said.

'More than redecorated,' the Doctor said. 'Restructured it all at the molecular – even atomic – level. This is incredible technology. I'm not even sure how it could work.' He turned to Joel. 'And it can reproduce anything? Not just raw materials, but complex items?'

'Watch,' Joel said, proudly. 'Sallak showed me how to do a few things.'

He went over to one of the bins, then threw a few bricks on to the platform. Then he crossed to one of the consoles and pressed a combination of buttons.

The console hummed, and the bricks shimmered and vanished. A few seconds later, the humming stopped, and there were half a dozen red roses there instead.

The Doctor went over and picked them up, sniffing them.

'Incredible. Smell these.' He passed a handful over to Debbie. 'These are all identical,' he noted. 'It's like a three-dimensional photocopier.'

'It's a big machine, it's fixed in place. We can't take it with us.'

The Doctor shook his head. 'I don't want to. It's a very useful machine, but it's far too advanced for this time zone. Imagine if this fell into the hands of someone who wanted unlimited plutonium, or guns. Even if they only wanted gold or coins, this thing could destroy the world's economy with just a few days of production.'

'So what are we going to do?'

'Stand away from that!' an electronic voice barked.

One of the guards had entered, he was aiming his rifle at the Doctor. He moved forward warily. His helmet hid his expression, but Debbie doubted that it was anything other than grim determination.

'Sallak will be angry if you shoot me,' the Doctor assured the guard. 'He wants that honour for himself.' He turned his back on the guard and began examining the machine on the trolley. He picked up the nozzle.

'Put that down!' the guard ordered.

The Doctor tapped a control on the console with one hand and jammed the nozzle of the device over the rifle barrel with the other.

The rifle became several dozen identical roses, which fell into a pile on the floor. But it didn't stop there. The roses spread, carried on up the guard's arms, over his shoulders and down his back. Debbie glimpsed the man underneath, pale and muscular, then all that skin and muscle began changing, too.

The process was fascinating to watch. Even the guard himself seemed to think so. He didn't scream, or cry out, or even look worried: he just watched his metamorphosis until he had no eyes left to watch with.

For a moment, the pile of flowers was roughly the shape of the man it had replaced, but there was nothing holding them together, and they just fell away.

The Doctor looked sadly down at the pile.

'I've just had an idea,' he told them.

'Do you like Guns 'N Roses?' Dinah asked.

It was half an hour after he'd arrived before Dinah had a chance to go up to the blond guy, but that was still the best opening line she could come up with.

He was sitting on his own, seemingly happy to let the party lap up around him, rather than to be any great part of it. He had a bottle of lager in his hand, but had barely touched it. His leather jacket, torn jeans and Adidas trainers looked brand-new.

'I think Axl Rose is the ultimate rock frontman.'

'That's an anagram, you know.'

'His real name is William Bailey.' He recited it as if it was French vocab.

'What's your name?'

'Ferdy,' he replied. Then, 'Happy birthday.'

'Sweet sixteen,' she said. 'How old are you?'

'Nineteen,' he said. That looked about right – he looked mature for his age, but was also quite fresh-faced.

'N-n-n-nineteen, eh?' she joked.

Ferdy looked at her in a very odd way. She decided to stay away from pop music from now on.

'What do you do?' she asked instead.

He seemed puzzled by the question.

'For a living?' she elaborated.

'I work as a yuppie,' he told her, after a short pause.

Dinah laughed. 'That's funny.'

He smiled back, a little uncertainly. 'Thank you.'

* * *

The Doctor checked the connection between the sonic suitcase and the transmutation machine, then flicked a couple of switches.

A humming noise, quite a low, ominous sound.

The Doctor snapped the briefcase shut and checked the readings.

'We've got two minutes,' he told them. 'So let's make the most of them.'

'You've set it to blow up?' Joel asked, worried.

The Doctor smiled and ushered them towards the door.

'But all our stuff!' he complained.

Kirst grabbed him. 'The Doctor's going to give us a million quid. It's not like you've got anything worth saving.'

'The telly...'

'The telly is from Rumbelows,' she reminded him. '*Nicked* from Rumbelows.'

They hurried out of the door, into the corridor.

The metal door stood between them and the unrenovated lower storeys of the Tower.

'How are we going to open the door and get past the guards?' Debbie asked.

'I'll use the sonic suitcase,' the Doctor said, ushering them out of the way. He had opened it up, balanced it on one knee. He pressed something and the door slid smoothly open. The Doctor closed the briefcase and waited.

The guards on the other side clearly hadn't been expecting the door to open. They turned and edged forwards.

'Halt!' they said.

'Not even the sonic suitcase can get us out of this one,' Debbie whispered.

The Doctor smiled, then, without warning, he charged forward, holding the briefcase out in front of him. Before the guards had time to raise their rifles, he'd swung the case around, smashing both of their helmets with enough force to crack them.

The guards fell to the floor, out cold.

'It's a very versatile tool,' the Doctor noted.

Behind them, the humming of the transmutation machinery was reaching a crescendo.

'Run!' he ordered.

'God, Alex is going to punch that bloke if Dinah doesn't cool off a bit.'

'Oh, you know what Dinah's like: "Ooh, look at his muscles. He looks like a Nazi. I want to shag him."'

Bob looked at Miranda.

'That's brilliant,' Bob told her.

'What?'

'That impersonation. It sounded just like Dinah.'

'Oh, yeah, it's a trick my dad taught me.'

'Your dad taught you to do impressions?'

'Well, yes. "Hello, I'm Bob."'

'I don't sound like that.'

'You do.'

'Oh. You should be on *Spitting Image*.'

'Why, thanks.'

'As a voice, I mean, not a puppet. Can you do Maggie Thatcher?'

'Yes, I can,' Miranda said, then, in her best Thatcher voice: 'It's not that difficult to mimic someone.'

'I can only do Rik Mayall,' Bob confessed. 'Right on, Vyv. Oh wonderful. Give money to tramps, Thatcher out, anarchy rules.'

Miranda smiled generously.

The Doctor threw himself down the stairs, two, three, even four at a time. His hand was clamped around Debbie's. She was already out of breath, her feet barely touching the steps as they went. Joel and Kirst were behind them, right at their backs.

The guards they passed were far more worried by the wave of roses that was surging after them than the escapees themselves. The guards seemed unsure what to do – most seemed to think the best strategy was to fire their rifles at the mass of rose petals and wait for the transmutation effect to wash over them.

So the Doctor and his companions hadn't had to worry too much about the guards.

Now, though, the tidal wave of roses had almost caught up with them.

'Don't look back!' the Doctor shouted.

They piled down another set of stairs, stray roses falling down ahead of them.

Dinah's front room was full of people, smoke and sound. Only five or six people were up on their feet, the others sitting back, trying to talk

and pull. There were a lot of boys here – about two boys to each girl. It meant that a lot of hopeful glances were aimed Miranda's way.

Miranda tried to teach Bob how to dance, but early on she realised it was a lost cause. Instead, she just pulled him in close, let them be alone together in the crowd. The song was about a group of people building a city on rock and roll, but Miranda couldn't identify it.

'Lager?' Bob asked.

Miranda shook her head. 'Alcohol doesn't affect me,' she said.

'Yeah, yeah,' Bob said drunkenly.

'It's true, I just don't metabolise it.'

Dinah was talking to Ferdy, who had been sitting all on his own nursing a fruit juice. Alex was at Dinah's side, impatient.

When Phil Collins came on and started singing about his two hearts, it reminded Bob of something.

'Dinah says you've got two hearts.'

Miranda glared over at Dinah, but she was still too busy with Ferdy. 'It's meant to be a secret. Dinah only found out accidentally.'

'It's true? I thought it was a joke.'

'It's true.'

'Nah. Prove it.'

There was a discreet way she could have done so – if he'd touched her wrist, Bob would have felt a double pulse. But she'd thought of a better way.

Miranda gently led Bob out of the back door, into the garden, round the side of the house where no one could see them.

'It's cold,' he noted.

Miranda leaned against the wall, pulled her shirt up and took Bob's hands in hers.

'Here,' she said, guiding him up beneath her shirt. She let go of his wrists.

'Put your hands on my ribcage – and I *mean* my ribcage,' she warned him.

Bob gulped, his hands sliding up her stomach. They were warm, a little ticklish. He stopped with his first fingers brushing the base of her bra, his thumbs between her breasts. He was trying his luck just a little. It was a nice sensation, so Miranda let it pass.

Bob was grinning like a kid with a new toy. 'Two hearts!' he whispered. And, gentleman that he was, he withdrew his hands, slipped them easily into place around her waist.

The moment where Miranda realised they were about to kiss elided with the kiss itself.

Her first kiss, not his. Miranda was surprised how pleasant she found an experience she'd had down as just another thing she ought to have done by her age.

Confident now, Bob slid his hands up a little, under her shirt, and was stroking bare skin at the small of her back. She put her arms around his neck, stroking it. They were still kissing, and Miranda felt strange: not entirely in control of herself. She brought her heartsrate back under control, started tinkering with her hormone and pheromone production.

'What's wrong?' Bob asked.

'Nothing.'

'You tensed up a bit. Was that your first kiss?'

'You could tell?'

'Well, yes, you know, I'm not the world expert, but I could tell.' She must have looked distraught, because he immediately continued. 'It was great. It's just, y'know, the first time's always going to be a bit awkward.'

There was silence, broken only by the Communards.

Bob stroked Miranda's face, but the spell was broken. It was a cold night, and Bob was a drunk sixteen-year-old lad with too much of his dad's aftershave on.

'I'm sorry it wasn't what you were expecting.' She wondered about his first kiss. Had it been Dinah? She couldn't remember what her friend had told her.

'Miranda,' Bob pleaded.

She toyed with the idea of raising her pulse and the supply of blood to the skin surface, and wondered if it would be cheating. Judging by his blushes, Bob's blood supply was working without conscious help. She looked at him. She was different. He had only one heart, he was beginning to get tired, he was shivering a little in the spring night air.

It all seemed so unreal.

Chapter Seventeen
Urban Regeneration

'The door's been barricaded!' Joel said as they reached the ground floor.

Their way was blocked. Rose blossom was drifting down. Above them it sounded as if a tidal wave was about to break. Debbie saw the Doctor glance up nervously, knowing they hadn't got long before the transmutation wave caught up with them.

The Doctor kicked the plywood board down, grabbed Debbie's hand and pulled her after him, out into the night. Joel and Kirst were right behind.

'Keep going!' he shouted.

It was dangerous ground to run over, tiny potholes and fragments threatening unwary feet and ankles. Behind them, there was a sound unlike anything Debbie had ever heard – a cracking and rustling, getting louder and louder. It sounded like a tree being felled, she decided.

Halfway across the wasteland, the Doctor stopped running and turned.

'We're safe, now,' he told them.

Debbie looked back. The light streaming from the floors at the top of the Tower were blood-red. Rose petals, filtering the light from the windows.

Then, the windows became roses. Some petals drifted away, but most were caught in waves that poured down the side of the building like waterfalls. The window frames followed, the walls after that. The whole building became a cascade of roses, floor after floor bursting and throwing out a plume of red petals.

They saw one of the guards leaping from a twenty-something-storey window. But it was too late: he was already changing. As he hit the ground, he billowed out into a cloud of flowers.

'Will it stop?' Kirst asked, and the way she asked it suggested she wouldn't mind if it never did.

'I'm afraid so,' the Doctor said. 'The transmuter will burn itself out.'

It happened before it ran out of building. The noise died down and

it was obvious the pile of roses wasn't getting any larger. It was impossible to tell how many floors had survived. Everything was under the heap, which was a rough pyramid, around a hundred feet high.

The scent began to drift over. Beautiful, but almost overpowering.

'Never say I don't get you flowers,' Joel said.

'Are they dead?' Kirst asked.

The Doctor nodded. 'All but Ferran. Which reminds me: we have to be going, Debbie.'

Joel grabbed his hand. 'You promised us money.'

'Would it surprise you to learn that I don't have a million pounds in cash on my person?'

'We'll go to a cash machine,' Joel suggested.

The Doctor laughed. 'I'll write you a cheque.'

Joel looked unconvinced. Kirst stepped between them. 'That will do nicely,' she said.

The Doctor laid his briefcase on the ground and opened it up. He rummaged through the stuff and found his chequebook and a pen.

A moment later he rose and handed a cheque to Kirst. 'Don't spend it all at once,' he advised, as they stared at it, scarcely believing what they were looking at. Then the Doctor grabbed Debbie's hand. 'Come on!'

Ferran looked around the room, and realised that he hadn't seen the Last One for several minutes. The crowd was thinning a little; a few of the weak-hearted had bowed out for the night. Was she one of them?

'Where is Miranda?' he asked Dinah, as casually as he could.

'Gone outside with Bob, I think.'

'Her boyfriend?'

'That's right.'

He tried to get up, but Dinah stopped him. 'I don't think they want to be disturbed, you know what I mean?'

Before she had finished saying it, the Last One had entered the room. She came over, looming over them in their armchair.

'Can I have a word, Dinah?' she asked.

Dinah detached herself from Ferran. 'Sure,' she said.

Ferran looked around. He realised he was not going to get his opportunity to strike, at least not here. 'I have to go,' he said.

Dinah looked disappointed.

Ferran excused himself again and stood up.

* * *

In the time it had taken the Doctor and Debbie to cross the wasteland, curtains had twitched, word had spread, and the streets had started to fill up. Men and women, children fetched from their beds, Asians and skinheads, police and dealers, all standing shoulder to shoulder and looking out at the tower of roses, breathing in the perfume that was filling the city air. No one - apart from a few kids - had crossed the threshold yet, stepped on to the broken ground, reclaimed the wasteland, but they would.

The Trabant sat, untouched, in the street where the Doctor had parked it. Debbie was amazed that it was still going, and told the Doctor as much.

'It costs quite a lot to keep on the road,' the Doctor admitted, 'but I'm quite attached to the old girl.'

Debbie took a last look back at the roses, growing where there had been only the dark Tower.

The Doctor was already in the driver's seat of the car, reconnecting the carphone.

The almost musical autodial was followed by the ringing tone.

'Come on,' the Doctor said.

The phone continued to ring. After a moment, an answering machine kicked in, and Debbie heard the Doctor's voice. But only for a moment. The Doctor hung up and immediately redialled.

With the other hand, he was starting the ignition.

As the phone rang again, he was parping the car horn, trying to negotiate the crowds.

'This isn't like Miranda,' he said.

'It'll be hours before we get to your house,' Debbie said quietly. 'We should call the police, get them looking.'

The Doctor hung up the phone. He hesitated. 'If she's not at home, where is she?'

Alex had gone home.

Dinah claimed she didn't have a row with him, but Miranda knew she'd been planning to spend the night with him. She had found that shocking, in a rather abstract way. Thinking about it, though, it was only because it wasn't the sort of thing she would ever do.

Dinah claimed Alex was ill, and 'too drunk, anyway'.

So there were just the three of them. Bob was hanging around, trying to get back into Miranda's good books. She was suddenly very

self-conscious around him. Miranda had told Dinah what had happened, and Dinah agreed to have a chat with Bob. After that, they agreed to clear up in the morning, and went their separate ways. Dinah was in her parents' room, Bob in her little brother's. Miranda got Dinah's bed.

Miranda didn't need much sleep, indeed she could do without it.

Bob and Dinah both seemed exhausted. Minutes after they'd gone to bed, the house was silent.

Miranda lay on the bed, staring up at the ceiling. Dinah's room was odd. There were posters all over the walls. Posters of Tom Cruise and a-ha, all the pop stars and film stars Dinah had a crush on. Dinah had a record player, and a stack of albums and tapes. At the foot of the bed was a menagerie of toy animals. She wondered where Dinah kept her chemistry set or her encyclopedias.

All so unreal.

Perhaps the alcohol had affected her a little, after all. She felt a little giddy.

She'd just had her first kiss, she reminded herself.

And then all this *thinking* had spoiled it. Her endless analysis, her constant need to sit back and mentally write up what had just happened to her. Treating the world as though it was an experiment and she was the neutral observer.

She was doing it now.

Miranda wondered what the solution was. By definition, a display of spontaneity now wouldn't be a true display of spontaneity, but a calculated act.

And she was doing it again.

She liked Bob, she had liked having a boyfriend. It was... virgin territory for her, but she didn't feel nervous. She trusted him.

Miranda made her decision: to go to Bob, slip into bed beside him and see what happened. No plans beyond that. She asked herself where she would draw the line, doubting that Bob would, and surprised herself by not knowing the answer. That clinched it as the right course of action.

She checked herself in the dressing-table mirror, took a deep breath, and then sneaked out on to the landing, tiptoeing so that she didn't wake anyone up or let anyone know what she was doing.

Bob was in Dinah's brother's room. Miranda knew which door that was. She decided not to knock. She'd sneak in, get into bed beside him.

The door was a little ajar. She went in, closing it behind her.

The room was cluttered, full of toys belonging to Dinah's little brother.

The bed was empty. It had been slept in, but now it was empty.

Miranda was baffled, but only for a moment. She stepped back on to the landing. The next door along was Dinah's parents' room. The door was closed, so she opened it, ever so carefully, just in case, as she hoped against hope, she was wrong.

She was right: there were two people on the bed.

It was dark, but Miranda could see in the dark.

Dinah was straddling Bob, wearing nothing but a gold necklace. Bob had his skinny legs together, his arms around Dinah's neck and his eyes closed.

Dinah turned her head and saw Miranda. Her face was expressionless, dead, as though it didn't know where to start.

And the only thing Miranda could bring herself to think was, I bought her that necklace.

Bob was perfectly placed to tell there was something wrong with Dinah. He turned to see what she was looking at. He was wide-eyed, startled to be caught out.

'Rand...' Dinah began.

Miranda was already on the landing. She could hear Dinah following, the bedsprings creaking guiltily, Dinah's whispered command telling Bob to stay where he was.

Miranda was back in Dinah's room, pulling her clothes on. The house and all its contents seemed a long way away.

Dinah came in, turned on the light. She'd pulled on a dressing gown, but looked bedraggled. There were tears in her eyes.

'Rand...' she said again. She didn't seem to sense the *rage* Miranda felt. Right now, she could have taken Dinah and broken her in half. Miranda realised she wasn't exaggerating. She really did want to kill her.

Miranda pushed past Dinah, but had to steady herself on the handrail before she could go downstairs.

Dinah was calling after her. Miranda ignored her.

She opened the front door – Dinah hadn't even locked it; how irresponsible could she be? – and walked out into the night.

It was cold.

* * *

Ferran had found the perfect place to conceal himself, across the road from Dinah's house. One by one, all the guests began drifting out and away into the night. He'd been watching them all night, counting them, memorising their faces.

Twenty-eight guests, not counting himself or Dinah. Now, twenty-six had gone. Only Dinah, Miranda and Bob remained in there.

Ferran had managed to get a good look around the house, inside and out. He watched the house lights as they went through a predictable sequence – the lights downstairs going off, the lights in the two upstairs bedrooms visible from the front going on briefly. Now all three were in bed.

Bob wasn't a threat. Even if he shared the Last One's bed, Ferran knew he could get to her and kill her. He would kill her as she slept, he decided. No doubt she would wake up at some point during the process; she'd know why she had to die.

Ferran dug his hand into the pocket of his leather jacket. His brother's knife was there.

And the door opened, and the Last One just stepped out, alone, into the night with him.

Dinah was at the door, shouting something after her, but the Last One wasn't listening. She walked out on to the pavement, started looking across the road.

Dinah went back inside, closed the door.

The Last One was alone.

She started to cross the road. She was heading straight towards him.

She could see in the dark. All her kind could see in the dark.

Was she coming for him? She looked tense, ready to lash out. Had she seen him? Was this the final confrontation he had dreamed of?

She was ten metres away, but hadn't seen him.

He felt distanced from it all – as if it was happening to someone else, and he was just watching.

The reason for that was simple – he was acting automatically: he'd practised for this moment until, having drawn the blade, bringing it down was as easy as catching a ball or opening a door.

She turned and saw him. 'Ferdy?' she said. And she broke into a smile.

A car drove up, its horn parping.

The Doctor.

The Last One turned to see her father. 'Dad?' she said, baffled.

He'd escaped Sallak. He'd managed to escape.

The Last One had her back to him. Ferran stayed down, out of the Doctor's sight.

'Get in the car!' the Doctor shouted.

She hurried towards her father, out of his reach.

Ferran felt the knife in his hand, but all the certainties of the moment had dissipated.

The Last One waved goodbye to him as she got into the back of the Doctor's car.

And to his disgust, all Ferran found himself doing was waving back.

Chapter Eighteen
Escape to Destiny

Debbie wasn't surprised that the Doctor was already up and about, fully dressed, when she came downstairs, or that he'd found himself a new coat.

'Morning,' she said, watching him as he busied himself with a coffee maker.

He smiled over at her. 'You slept well?'

She nodded. Debbie had spent the day here yesterday and felt safe here. The house was vast, but she didn't feel intimidated by it, or that she could ever get lost in it. The feeling of security wasn't just a fancy of hers: there was also an elaborate CCTV system. The Doctor glanced from time to time at the tiny monitor mounted on the wall by the toaster and kettle. At the moment, it was showing him the front gates.

'You like the house?' the Doctor asked. '*Interiors* keep asking me to do a photoshoot.'

'You've moved up in the world since I first met you,' she told him. 'Remember that farmhouse?' They'd arrived here having driven through leafy, prosperous suburbs. Flat countryside, with money almost growing from the trees – the pavements and driveways were lined with new BMWs and Mercedes Benzes.

'I need to look after Miranda,' the Doctor said. 'My priorities have changed. I need to make sure she has a good start in life, that she isn't denied any opportunities.'

'But where did you get all that money?' Debbie asked.

'Oh, it's absurdly easy if you know how. I'll explain later.'

'It's nothing like Greyfrith,' Debbie noted. 'Does Miranda even remember who I am?'

'Oh, yes,' the Doctor said.

'She didn't seem very chatty yesterday.'

The Doctor nodded thoughtfully. The drive home from Dinah's had passed in silence – the Doctor so relieved to see his daughter alive that he hadn't asked her why she seemed so upset. 'She's safe, that's the important thing.'

'And she's in the fifth form?' Debbie asked.

'That's right.'

'Does Miranda remember anything about her home? Her *real* home?' Even in the privacy of the Doctor's kitchen, she couldn't help but speak cryptically.

'Her real home is here,' the Doctor said firmly. 'But, no: remember, she was only a month or two old when she came here. She doesn't need to know. I want her to have a normal upbringing.'

'She doesn't know she's an alien?'

'She doesn't need to know,' the Doctor repeated.

'OK. So I'll be careful what I say. What have you told her?'

'I've told her everything about me. Well, nearly everything. She knows I'm older than I look; she knows I don't know who I am. She doesn't know anything about time travel; I didn't tell her anything Zevron told me.'

'What have you told Miranda about *her*?'

The Doctor smiled over at her. 'Well, you know she thinks her parents died in a car accident. That's it, really. She knows she's different. I've helped her come to terms with that, taught her some tricks – holding her breath for a long time, a bit of self-hypnosis.'

'When are you going to tell her?'

He looked at her, puzzled.

'You'll have to,' Debbie insisted. 'She must be nearly old enough to know.'

'The Dawkinses wanted her to have a normal life. We find Ferran, we stop him, then everything gets back to normal.'

The Doctor returned his attention to the coffee maker, the conversation over.

There was a creak on the stairs, and a moment later Miranda entered the kitchen.

'Morning.'

Miranda had been quite a late developer, but she'd made up for it now. She had a fantastic figure (she'd been a keen swimmer, Debbie remembered), she'd got a loose perm. In her school blazer, with a big grin on her face, she reminded Debbie of the Doctor. She had the same confidence, the same slightly otherworldly air. And she clutched her lapels as he was wont to do when he was particularly pleased with himself.

'Good morning, Mrs Castle.'

'You can call me Debbie.'

'You look well.'

A twinge of guilt... Her husband, the man she'd been married to, had been butchered, just a couple of days ago, but she felt better than she had in years. The last time Miranda had seen her, she'd been the dumpy, put-upon housewife. Now she was free. A horrible slogan on one of those posters in the sports centre came to mind: TODAY IS THE FIRST DAY OF THE REST OF YOUR LIFE.

'Thank you,' she said.

'You're going to school today?' the Doctor asked.

Miranda looked a little confused. 'I didn't realise it was optional.'

The Doctor nodded his head, clearly worried, but not saying anything. Surely not telling Miranda about Ferran would put her in more jeopardy? Debbie quickly suppressed the urge to tell Miranda everything – that there was an alien prince on her trail, out to assassinate her. Where would she start? As a teacher, she'd got used to respecting parents' wishes, however misguided and dangerous she thought they were.

The Doctor had kept Miranda virtually housebound yesterday. He'd even been nervous when she'd gone out into the garden. But, of course, he wasn't telling her the reason for her house arrest, and his daughter was getting a little jittery.

It was also clear that something had upset her at the party she'd been to. The Doctor, bless him, didn't have the radar to spot boyfriend trouble, but Debbie could tell. She didn't know Miranda anything like well enough to talk to her about it, though.

'Just be careful,' the Doctor told his daughter, glancing at the security monitor. 'There's someone out there,' he said. 'Wait here.'

Bob gazed through the gates.

It was a huge house, and there was no sign of Miranda. But he knew which bus she caught, and he knew roughly what time she would have to leave the house to catch it.

Suddenly there was a man standing there. He was about forty, with long light-brown hair and a long black coat.

'What are you doing here?' he asked.

'I'm waiting for Miranda,' Bob said.

The man stared at him, watching him for something.

'I'm... you know, a friend. I'm not a stalker or a murderer or anything.'

The man's eyes narrowed. 'I didn't say you were. Why are you waiting for my daughter?'

Daughter?

'You're the Doctor, yeah?'

'Don't you recognise me?'

'We've never met, have we?'

Bob was surprised how young Miranda's dad was. Forty wasn't too implausible: he'd have been twenty-four when Miranda was born; so he'd have been right in the middle of his doctorate. Then Bob remembered: Miranda was adopted, so he could be even younger.

If he hadn't known she was adopted, he'd never have guessed. She looked just like her stepfather – same height, they stood the same way, very upright. They had the same blue eyes and pale skin. The Doctor also had that same unnerving stare. Miranda could look into his eyes and it was as if she was staring into his soul.

Bob wriggled, a little uncomfortable under the Doctor's scrutiny, and tried desperately to think pure thoughts.

'I'm Bob. Miranda might have mentioned me,' Bob said, wincing a little: this was the point where he was castrated for betraying this man's daughter. 'I'm her boyfriend,' he added, when it became clear that her dad didn't know him from Adam.

'Miranda doesn't have a boyfriend,' the Doctor stated, with absolute certainty.

'It's OK, it's just Bob.'

They both turned to see Miranda standing there with her schoolbag slung over her shoulder.

'Can we talk?' Bob pleaded.

The Doctor looked at them, from one to the other.

'Your boyfriend?' he asked.

Miranda bit her lip, obviously unwilling to explain. 'A friend who's a boy.'

The Doctor was grinning, mistaking her reticence for coyness. 'Splendid! Bob, I was going to give Miranda a lift to school. Why don't you come with us?'

Bob agreed. Miranda glared at him. The Doctor opened up the gates and let him in.

The Doctor's car looked like the poor cousin of a Lada, Bob thought.

'You get in the front, Bob,' the Doctor suggested.

Miranda took her place in the back. Bob wriggled to get comfortable

in the passenger seat, but he could sense the hostility boring into the back of his head.

The Doctor seemed totally oblivious to it.

Bob had hoped that he could talk Miranda round. Five minutes after Miranda had stormed out of the house, it had occurred to Dinah why she'd been sneaking around in the first place. Dinah and Bob had felt very guilty – they'd even cried as they realised what they'd done. They'd got up, talked, and Dinah – who knew Miranda better than anyone – had convinced him that he could make amends. Bob had gone back to bed, alone, kicking himself. Dinah was a friend, a comfort. Miranda… Miranda was perfect. If he'd gone to Miranda, not Dinah. If he'd just stayed in his own damn bed, then…

'What do you see yourself doing, Bob?' the Doctor asked brightly.

Bob gulped, then realised he was talking about his life.

'I'm only sixteen, I've not really decided.'

'Quite right,' the Doctor said. 'I'm over a hundred years old, and I've got no idea yet, either.'

'He's not really over a hundred years old,' Miranda said quickly. 'He's –'

'Thirty-six,' the Doctor said.

'Forty-one,' Miranda finished.

Bob forced himself to laugh. 'Nice one.'

'Miranda hasn't had a boyfriend before,' the Doctor declared. Bob could feel her skin burn red. 'How many girlfriends have you had?'

'A few,' Bob admitted. 'Two,' he conceded, finally.

The Doctor looked over at him.

'Two isn't that many,' Bob said awkwardly. It was an embarrassingly low total, he'd always thought. 'And we only kissed, yeah?' Not strictly true, but near enough.

'He stays in touch with them, don't you, Bob?' Miranda said, with a voice that would freeze nitrogen.

'That's good,' said the Doctor.

They had, mercifully, arrived at the school.

The Doctor parked just outside the gate, blocking it. 'Here we are,' he said joyfully. 'Enjoy yourself at school. But not too much!'

Miranda was already out of the car.

Bob was about to skulk away.

'No, stay there Bob,' she said sweetly.

He rooted himself to the spot. This was his chance to set things straight.

The Trabant whizzed away, the Doctor waving as he went.

Once the car had turned the corner, Bob leapt into action. 'I'm so sorry,' he said.

Miranda crossed her arms.

Bob was very conscious that he was getting an audience: a group of giggling third-years, a couple of wryly amused sixth-formers.

'I... I made a mistake. I really like you, and I was drunk, and just give me another chance, and I know I don't deserve it.'

Miranda smiled.

Then she swung around, putting her whole weight behind a punch to his face.

At an earlier age, Bob would probably have imagined a large '*Ka-pow!*' over his head. Now it was a pale-blue caption, describing how he felt one knuckle crunch into his nose, then the others rolling into it. He heard something crack between his eyes, and felt a rush of warm liquid.

The shock alone would have been enough to bowl him off his feet, but the force of the impact did it anyway. Bob's hands were too busy instinctively grabbing up at his nose to cushion his fall. So hitting the tarmac drive hurt far more than it should have done.

He looked up at Miranda, certain that she'd broken his nose. She was looking down at him, and her expression made it very clear that if he tried to stand up again she'd put him back on the floor, and this time he wouldn't be getting up.

In later years, when Bob came to recall the moment, he would tell people that he'd put a brave face on it, even managed to get a great quip in. 'I said, "I'll take that as a no",' he would claim, and his mates would laugh, and he'd feel the pang of regret that would never quite go away.

The dozen or so people who were there heard only a slight yelp.

Sallak stepped from the train, looking exhausted.

Ferran was waiting for him in the car park. The Deputy had barely escaped the Tower, and everything there was lost. A dozen men, a lot of equipment that could have been useful.

Sallak was limping a little, he looked almost shell-shocked.

Ferran's bracelet had enough charge left for one recall signal. The only other object from his own time he had now was his brother's knife. Those were not his only resources, of course – he had the car he'd bought, clothes, a bag of money, some tools and a handgun.

But he'd run out of luxuries, now – the death of the Last One was a

necessity, the only thing that could save this mission from the ignominy of total defeat.

The Deputy got into the car.

'I'm sorry, My Lord,' he said. 'We should have killed the Doctor when we had the chance.'

The loss of the Tower was Sallak's fault, of course. As was keeping the Doctor alive so that Sallak could tell him his daughter was dead. No wonder the Doctor had survived so long with enemies so vainglorious.

'We still have that chance,' Ferran said. 'The death of the Last One is still our destiny. I've searched the Archive, and beyond this year there was absolutely no record of her.'

'The Archive is incomplete,' Sallak reminded him. 'An absence of evidence proves very little.'

'He's broken your spirit,' Ferran snapped. 'The Doctor is our arch enemy. He has been since the genesis of our race. We knew that. But if we kill his daughter, we will inflict the greatest defeat he has ever suffered. Think about that.'

The Deputy looked chastened. 'You are right, of course, My Lord.'

Ferran wished he could be so certain.

The laboratory was three doors down a narrow corridor. Debbie was a little disappointed by it: it was light and airy, not the Frankenstein's lab she had been expecting.

The Doctor was in his shirtsleeves and bent over the time detector. 'There,' he said. 'That burst there is the equipment in the Tower going up. We've trapped Ferran here.'

Debbie wasn't really listening. She'd picked up a little glass jar full of tiny white nuggets. The label read MILK TEETH.

'You've collected Miranda's teeth?'

The Doctor nodded. 'A useful source of data. I've got to be careful, of course: I don't have the proper equipment for analysis here, and the big labs would be more than a little interested in how I got hold of extraterrestrial biological samples.'

Debbie shivered, but decided not to say anything.

The Doctor had lost the signal, and couldn't find it, however busily he twisted dials and flicked switches.

'There's been no more time-travel activity?' Debbie asked.

'There was the original source, which must have been Ferran arriving,' the Doctor said, pointing it out. 'Then two more trips: the

guards and equipment arriving at the Tower, I imagine. Nothing since then, not even radio signals. So Ferran is trapped here with us.'

Debbie took a deep breath. 'Or vice versa,' she pointed out. 'We need to call the police.'

The Doctor shook his head. 'The last battle was fought on his territory. Now, he's got to come here. I'm ready for him.'

Miranda sat in the park. It was the first time she could remember going there on her own. Dinah, Alex and Bob were nowhere to be seen.

She felt like crying. She wasn't crying, but Dinah and Bob had betrayed her, her father was acting strangely, and having another woman in the house – even someone as lovely as Mrs Castle – was affecting her, changing the subtle territoriality of her home.

There was a line in an Eliot poem, about a man who wouldn't change his routine because he dare not disturb the universe. That was what had happened to Miranda: her world, which had all seemed so cosy and stable just a couple a days ago, had now lurched into uncomfortable and unfamiliar territory.

She had no feelings for Bob – she never had had, and what relationship they'd had had fizzled out after their kiss. Dinah and Bob were free to do what they wanted, by any of the rules of engagement she'd read about in Dinah's women's magazines. Miranda now knew that she would have regretted it if her plan to sleep with Bob had worked out.

But she was still angry.

A shadow fell over her.

She looked up.

'Ferdy?'

He smiled down at her. 'I'm glad I've caught up with you,' he said. He had his hands stuffed into the pockets of his leather jacket. 'You look upset.'

Miranda nodded.

'How about you come with me?'

'The bell goes in five minutes – I'll have to get back.'

The young man smiled. 'Come on, be a rebel,' he said, 'for once in your life.'

Chapter Nineteen
Date with Death

Debbie had convinced the Doctor that they had to tell the police.

'We have to be careful what we tell them,' she said as the Trabant arrived at the police station.

'We shouldn't tell them anything at all,' the Doctor grumbled. Debbie thought he was going to sulk, but instead he considered the situation. 'We tell them about Sallak, we tell them that we're worried that he's got accomplices. That Miranda is at risk.'

'They will be looking for you,' the Doctor said.

It hadn't occurred to Debbie, but of course he was right: Barry was dead, she was missing from her home and job. She shook herself – she'd not even *thought* about her job. What would her class think about their teacher missing on Friday and today?

Greyfrith seemed like another world. It seemed so far away, so irrelevant. Without realising it, she'd decided she wouldn't be going back there. What she'd do instead, she wasn't sure.

She glanced over at the Doctor.

Ferran watched the Last One from across the table.

'I don't usually come to pubs,' she told him. Her mastery of the human language was impressive, he thought, although her species had always had a gift for translation. As he thought that, he remembered that she had come to Earth as an infant. English was her first language. He wondered if the Doctor had taught her the language of their own people.

She was smiling. She was an attractive woman, Ferran could admit that. From the outside, she was a young woman with a fine figure and a nice smile. But that had always been the way of her family: they looked like ordinary people, but inside that chest beat two hearts, and the blood in her veins wasn't really blood: the genetic material twisted and writhed and re-formed the whole time. There were legends on many worlds of creatures who wore human form, but who were really demons, shapeshifters. That is what this 'woman' in front of him was.

She must die, and now.

'What would you like to drink?' he asked.

'Er... Pernod and black?' she said, asking him, rather than deciding for herself. She was weak. Where was the fire in her blood that had made her family rulers of the universe?

Ferran nodded, and went to order the drink. He walked up to the bar, tried to accost the serving maid, but the more obvious he made his impatience, the more the girl seemed to ignore him.

'Fetch your master!' he demanded.

The woman glared at him. 'I beg your pardon?'

'Not granted,' Ferran told her. 'Fetch your master.'

She called out, 'Vic.' This human was fat, jolly.

'Can I help you, sir?'

'Yes. A Pernod, a black, a lager. And I want to see this wench punished.'

Vic laughed. 'Pernod and black and a lager. A pint?'

'A pint of each,' Ferran confirmed. The innkeeper chuckled again.

'Is that your lady?' he asked, indicating the Last One with a nudge of his head.

Ferran's stomach lurched at the idea. 'No,' he said.

'Your sister?' he asked.

Ferran glared at him. 'I want your wench punished.'

The barman looked at him. 'Now, that joke was funny the first time, but I don't think it's funny now.' He placed the two drinks down.

Ferran threw him a fifty-pound note, and while the man checked it – such insolence! – Ferran slipped a capsule from his pocket. A nanotoxin, tailored to the Last One's species. Death would be instantaneous. He dropped it into the drink. Ferran watched, quietly fascinated as it dissolved.

The wench coughed. Ferran looked up, about to reprimand her for her poor hygiene. She had a collection of notes and coins in her hand.

'Your change,' she explained.

'How dare you!' Ferran snapped.

The barman was heading back over. 'That's it, young man.' He opened up the till, pulled out the fifty-pound note. 'Get out!'

Ferran glared at him.

The barmaid delighted in snatching the drinks back off the bar, and pouring them away.

The Last One was behind him. 'Is everything all right?'

'Get out, the pair of you.'

She grabbed Ferran's arm.

He recoiled, instinctively.

She pulled away. 'I'm sorry,' she said, hurrying off.

'Wait!' Ferran called, running after her.

The Last One hesitated at the doorway, then stepped out.

Ferran followed her into the street. 'I apologise,' he said, the words coming more easily than he'd thought possible. 'I was tense. I meant no offence.'

She smiled. 'You're forgiven. Where should we go now?'

Ferran stayed silent.

'All alone,' she said, smiling. 'I think this is the first time we've been alone together.'

'It is,' he assured her.

'Someone always seems to interrupt,' she continued.

'I had noticed that, too,' he admitted.

Ferran toyed with the idea of killing her here: the knife was in his coat pocket. A group of office workers bustled past, ending that idea there and then. The road was busy, there would be a lot of witnesses, and Ferran knew he wasn't sure of his escape routes. He needed to get her alone. He led her to the side of the building. It was early afternoon. The car park was virtually empty of cars, and there weren't any people.

'Not that way.' She laughed and skipped out into the road.

He could feel the knife weighing down his jacket pocket. He slipped his hand down, so casually she didn't even register it.

He looked over at her, thinking how she was oblivious to her fate, oblivious to the danger she was in.

There was a car.

She was perched on the kerb, but she lost her footing.

Her eyes went wide as she began slipping back.

The car sounded its horn, started skidding to a halt.

It was going to hit her.

Ferran leapt forward, grabbed her arm, pulled her upright.

She hugged him, out of breath. He could feel her chest heaving on his, her breath on his neck.

'You saved my life,' Miranda said. She leaned in. Her eyes peered into him. It was one of her kind's tricks. She was inside his mind, she knew him.

'What's the matter?' she asked.

Ferran hesitated. She didn't know. He blinked, sighed a little in relief.

Miranda slumped back, exasperated. 'What?' she asked, irritated.

He stared at her.

One swift stroke and this would be over.

He leaned in, imagining that he could hear and feel her hearts beating, faster than they should have been. His hand reached for the knife again. He felt his fingers tighten on the hilt.

He could feel the cool warmth of her body.

She looked him in the eye.

Her lips brushed his.

They were kissing.

And it was only when they broke away from each other, some time later, that Miranda realised she hadn't been *thinking* for a while.

Ferdy was watching her, confused.

Bob had done the same after they'd kissed. But all Bob had done was realise she was kissing him as part of some experiment, not out of any passion. Bob had sensed her coldness towards him. With Ferdy everything had been different.

'If you don't want to…' she began.

Ferdy looked into her eyes, which made her feel exposed. Then he moved forward, kissed her again, held her tight to him.

'I want to,' he said, sounding surprised at his decision.

They kissed, and Miranda found her hands were all over the place. Ferdy's were, too, but she didn't mind that at all.

'Not here,' she said, knowing they were getting carried away. 'Do you have your own place?'

'No,' Ferdy admitted. 'I have a car.'

She knew very little about him, Miranda realised. She wanted to. She corrected herself: she wanted to, but not yet.

Miranda looked deep into his eyes. 'Why don't we go to my place?'

Miranda lay on her bed, Ferdy leaning over her, kissing her, stroking her side.

They were taking their time, they'd agreed there was no rush.

Her dad and Mrs Castle were out. She'd known that as soon as she'd seen that the Trabant was missing from the driveway, but she'd done a sweep-search of the house, keeping Ferdy close by, anyway. Knowing

they were alone, she'd led him upstairs.

They'd stood there, kissing, holding each other, in no doubt at all what they'd do next. A moment later they'd been on the bed, unable to keep their hands off each other.

Ferdy broke away from her mouth, and began to nuzzle her neck and collarbone. He loosened her tie and undid the top couple of buttons of her blouse to make it easier. She undid a couple more. Ferdy was confident, and that was steadying her own nerves a little. They shifted around a little, and the weight of him beside her on the bed felt normal, relaxing.

'I love you,' he told her, looking very intently at her.

'No you don't,' she said, laughing.

He paused.

She strained to get a look at his face. 'I'm sure you like me, I'm sure we'll love each other. But we only met a few days ago. It's not like it's our destiny to be together. I don't know anything about you, I don't know where you're from, whether you've done this sort of thing before.' He looked worried. 'There will be time for all that,' she reassured him, hugging him.

Ferdy was looking down at her. Miranda didn't feel at all shy: she felt more comfortable than she ever had, even getting changed in front of Dinah. It was as if she'd known him for a long time.

'Miranda,' he said, very seriously. He was clearly going to say something very important. For a terrible moment, Miranda thought he was going to propose to her. 'Miranda, I –'

She realised he was going to tell her he had a girlfriend.

Downstairs, the front door opened.

Ferdy's head snapped around. He looked terribly panicked.

'Miranda! We're back!' a voice called.

She began buttoning up her blouse, doing it so fast she got it muddled and had to start again. 'It's Dad,' she told him. But he had already relaxed at the voice. 'Were you expecting someone else?' she asked lightly.

Ferdy forced himself to chuckle. 'No.'

She kissed him on the forehead. 'Do I look OK?' she asked him. 'I mean, it's not *too* obvious.'

Ferdy shook his head. 'You look fine.'

'Stay here,' she told him, heading for the door.

* * *

The Doctor was peering up the stairs. He'd seen Miranda's coat the moment he'd entered the house. He had run out of patience half an hour ago, at the police station, when the desk sergeant's best suggestion had been that the Doctor make sure he set his burglar alarm. Finally, the police had agreed that if the alarm went off, they'd treat it as their top priority.

Miranda was coming downstairs. Debbie looked over at her while the Doctor and his daughter hugged each other. Her school shirt wasn't very well tucked in, and she'd not checked her tie.

'Is there anything wrong?' the Doctor asked.

'No,' Miranda replied quickly. 'I was just playing a CD,' she lied badly. 'I didn't hear you.'

'Why aren't you at school?' he asked.

'I felt a bit faint again,' she said.

'Tell you what,' the Doctor suggested, 'I'll make a pot of tea and see if that helps clear away the cobwebs.'

Miranda started to say something. Debbie decided to intervene.

'You'd rather listen to that CD?' she asked Miranda.

'Yes,' she said, relieved.

The Doctor looked a little deflated. 'Oh. Well, come down when you're ready.'

He disappeared off to the kitchen.

Debbie stayed where she was. 'A CD?' she said, a little archly.

Miranda blushed. 'I've not even got a player.'

'Bob?' Debbie asked.

Miranda went a deeper shade of red. 'No. Someone else.'

Debbie chuckled. 'I was young once,' she said. 'Unlike your father.'

'I don't think Dad would understand,' Miranda told her.

'No... no, I doubt that he would.'

'But you understand what I'm going through?' Miranda seemed sceptical.

'Not all of it. But I know enough to keep your father out of your way,' she promised. 'Come down when you're ready.'

Miranda was still blushing. 'Thanks.'

Miranda closed her bedroom door, leaned on it for a few seconds, superstitiously, as if it would help jam it in place.

Ferdy was standing in the middle of the room. He was tall, but not broad-shouldered. He was about the same height as Bob, but looked

like he came from a different species. Ferdy could be a model, she thought, or a sports star.

'Where were we?' she asked, a little mischievously. The thought that her dad or Debbie might accidentally come in amused rather than worried her. This was a big house, they had as much privacy as they needed.

Ferdy was looking very serious. 'I was about to tell you something.'

She went over to him, hugged him, felt all those muscles. He didn't budge.

'Something important?' she asked.

'Yes,' he said. He broke away from her, indicated that she should sit on the bed.

She did, puzzled. Perhaps he's *married*, Miranda thought, as she sat on the edge of the mattress. He sat alongside her. Or he had some terrible illness, or he was an escaped criminal.

'What?' she asked, a little exasperated.

'You are different from other people,' he began, choosing his words carefully.

'Flatterer.'

'No. I mean I know you are different. You have two hearts, you're stronger and fitter than other people, you've got greater mental capacity: better memory, faster responses. Have you ever wondered why you are different?'

He wasn't proposing to her.

'Of course,' she said, leaving aside how he knew all this about her for the moment – that information was obviously on its way. 'But my dad's the same. There are probably lots of us – it's just we don't talk about it. It's not like it's a problem, like some disease or syndrome or anything.'

'There are two of you,' Ferdy said. 'Two of you on this entire planet. You and the Doctor.'

'Oh, there can't be.' She laughed. 'What would be the odds of that? It's rare, I know it's rare, but –'

'Two of you,' Ferdy insisted.

'You can't possibly know that,' she told him, still not angry with him. 'You've been round and checked, have you?'

'I know because I know that you are not of this world, you are not of this time.'

Miranda frowned.

'You are not human. You and the Doctor are two of a kind: time-travellers. You have a unique destiny.'

Miranda looked around, wondering why she wasn't getting the joke. 'You don't read Teen Titans comics by any chance?'

'Miranda, you are the last of your race,' Ferdy continued, 'and you alone –'

'Wait a minute.' She laughed, a little nervously. 'You said Dad was one, too. And he's not even my real dad – my parents didn't have two hearts. What are you on?' She didn't understand why Ferdy was doing this. She waited for the punchline. She wanted him to get whatever it was off his chest, so they could get back to –

'Those weren't your real parents.'

'They were.' She stood up, annoyed now. 'Ferdy, where are you getting this from?'

'The Librarinth. It's a place where all the records are stored, along with art treasures, blueprints, genetic codes. Most of it is still out of bounds, but my family have limited access.'

'I think you ought to go.' She didn't know what he was doing this for, and it was beginning to scare her. She'd invited a maniac into her house. Into her *bed*. She started heading towards the door.

Ferdy grabbed her arm. 'I have travelled more than a million years into the past to avenge the death of my brother,' he told her. 'I came here to kill you.'

And then he pulled a long, curved knife from his jacket pocket.

Chapter Twenty
Don't Leave Me This Way

Miranda listened as Ferdy told her. The knife stayed in his hand the whole time.

He told her about the far future. He told her that in the future the universe had been devastated, drained of energy, with whole galaxies uninhabited and uninhabitable. Somehow - no one was quite sure how - this was the fault of her people, the last remnants of which imposed their rule on the other survivors.

Ferdy - Ferran - was the ruler of one of these other groups. From his description, his civilisation sounded like a fascist dictatorship, although he seemed proud of that. There were many other groups, including - from what Miranda could put together - a group of goblin shapeshifters and a race of robot gangsters. These huddled on their shattered planets, eking out what they could with whatever resources were left. They had advanced science, but precious few resources to apply that science in a practical form.

For a thousand years, the tyrant Emperor had controlled all time and space travels, and operated a secret police force that ruthlessly crushed all dissent before it had even happened, using arcane technologies.

Ferdy's mother, then later his elder brother, had led a revolution. They had stormed the Emperor's palace, butchered most of his family, scattered the rest. Ferdy's brother had tracked the Imperial Family down through time and space, killed them where he found them.

Miranda had pieced together the next part. She was the Last One. She was the daughter and heir of the Emperor, and the last survivor of her entire race. Her stepfather, the Doctor, was one too, but one from an earlier period. He was a war criminal, a man who'd destroyed whole planets.

He didn't need to show her the strange (*alien*) bracelet he wore on his left wrist. He said it was a time machine, with just enough power for a recall signal. Somehow, just looking at it, she knew he was telling her the truth. It was the same feeling she'd had just before she'd fainted a week ago. 'Time sensitivity', Ferdy called it, and it made her sick.

When he told her how John and Kim Dawkins had died, how the Doctor had known all this, she really was sick, into the wastepaper bin. Ferdy watched her, impassively.

Once she had mopped her mouth with a tissue, Ferdy handed her the knife. It was ceremonial, he said, sanctified by the Gods of War and Legacy. He was meant to kill her with it, he couldn't rest until her blood dried on it, as the blood of her family had. She saw the pitted blade, covered in what looked like rust.

'So, you are going to kill me?' she said, feeling nothing.

Ferdy shook his head. 'I love you,' he said. 'I want you to marry me.'

The Deputy edged around the police box, sneaked a glance at the Doctor's house.

The Doctor's car was on the driveway. It was a warm day, so the Doctor and his companion could be in the back garden. He took the detector from his belt. Ferran was inside, upstairs – or at least his time bracelet was.

He saw movement in the house. The Doctor and the woman in the lounge downstairs. No sign of his daughter.

There was a flurry of movement, and the Last One was there with them.

Where had Ferran got to?

'Why didn't you tell me?'

The Doctor looked taken aback. He stood in the front room, feigning innocence. 'Tell you what?' he asked.

Miranda clearly wasn't fooled. 'Time travel, that we are aliens.'

The Doctor blanched. 'How?' he asked.

'You did know,' she shouted. 'My parents were murdered, and you didn't even tell me?'

Debbie held out a hand, tried to sound soothing. 'He was always going to tell you when –'

'You knew?' she said quietly. 'He told you?'

'I was there,' Debbie said, helplessly.

'Who told you?' the Doctor asked, his voice low.

'I did.'

Ferran was standing in the doorway, just as he had stood while Sallak butchered her husband, Debbie noted. He was wearing a leather jacket and jeans. His expression wasn't the sneer she had

been expecting: it was almost apologetic.

'She had the right to know,' he said, and this time there was more than a hint of malice in his voice.

'Did he also tell you that he came here to kill you?' Debbie asked.

Miranda nodded. 'He's been completely honest.'

'Stay away from her,' the Doctor ordered Ferran.

Miranda held out the knife. 'He's not going to kill me.'

'She's going to come back with me,' Ferran said, taking the knife back.

Debbie stared at the pair of them.

The Doctor was open-mouthed.

'No, I'm not,' Miranda said.

It was Ferran's turn to look shocked. 'It's your genetic destiny,' he told her.

She was shaking her head, backing towards the door. 'My destiny is to do A-levels, to go to university. To see the world.'

Ferran edged towards her. 'Those were lies: I can show you *worlds*. You can rule those worlds. We can rule the universe.'

Miranda looked stricken.

'It's your duty,' Ferran told her. 'I told you about the Factions. If we ruled together we could unite those Factions under us.'

'You don't have to do anything you don't want to,' the Doctor insisted. 'There's no such thing as genetic destiny: you can find your own fate.'

'Is that why you didn't tell her, Doctor?' Ferran asked. 'You'll let her come to her own choice, but you won't mention that she's not even human? You won't tell her who and what she is? Were you ever going to tell her? How can she make a choice if she doesn't know all the facts?'

Miranda was staring at her father, daring him to answer.

'You needed to be protected,' the Doctor insisted. 'Protected from things like him. He'll destroy you, or use you for his own ends. If you don't do what he wants, he'll destroy you.'

Miranda stood perfectly still, came to a decision.

'I'm leaving,' she announced.

'You're coming with me?' Ferran said, the relief evident in his voice.

'I'm leaving,' Miranda repeated. 'I don't want this. I don't want any of it.'

Ferran tried to block her. 'You're not going anywhere.'

She tried to struggle free. 'Stay away from me!'

Ferran grabbed her arm. 'Listen to me, I love you. I know you love me.'

The Doctor and Debbie looked at each other.

'I barely know you,' Miranda insisted. She looked back at her father. 'I don't know anyone any more.'

'Miranda,' the Doctor began, edging forward.

'Stay away,' she told him. She shrugged Ferran off her. 'And you get off me, too.'

Ferran was following her into the hallway. The Doctor hurried after them, and Debbie tagged along. 'It's fate,' Ferran called after her. 'It's in your blood. It's who you are.'

Miranda shook her head. 'I don't want any of this.' She unlocked the front door and opened it.

Ferran grabbed at her as she stepped over the threshold, catching the scruff of her shirt. 'You're not going anywhere. I'm right. I'll make you see that I'm right.'

Miranda turned and punched him in the face.

Caught out, he reeled, but he recovered quickly. He drew a knife – *the knife*, Debbie thought – and lurched towards Miranda.

Debbie had time only to register the knife (another part of her brain seeing that the Doctor was already moving to help). Miranda's eyes were wide.

But the Doctor had been expecting the attack, and caught his wrist. He pulled him over, and Ferran lost his balance as he stumbled over the doorstep.

Ferran tried to pull free, but the Doctor squeezed his wrist. Ferran was wearing a bangle, which was covered in what looked like buttons and lights.

There was an electronic sound, which built and built to a crescendo.

'Wait!' Ferran shouted, 'the co-ordinates aren't set!'

Miranda stood back. The Doctor let go.

Ferran was surrounded by a shimmering blue aura. He was sprawled over the doorstep, holding his hands up as though it was trapping him and he could use the knife to cut himself free. Already he wasn't quite there. Debbie couldn't describe where he was: there just wasn't the vocabulary for it, at least not in English. An instant later, he had gone completely.

The Doctor was heading towards his daughter. 'You're safe now,' he said, the relief obvious. 'We're safe.'

Miranda backed away. 'No,' she said. She stayed outside, in the sunshine. 'You lied to me. You… I can't stay here.' She hesitated for a moment, then turned on her heels, started running up the drive.

'Miranda!' the Doctor pleaded, but she didn't even look back.

And then the Deputy was blocking Miranda's way, aiming a pistol at her chest. He'd been hiding in the bushes.

The Doctor's eyes were wide. 'Keep away from her!'

The Deputy smiled. 'So, Ferran failed in his mission?' Miranda was slowly backing away: he was still at point-blank range.

'Your dispute is with me,' the Doctor said.

'My duty is to kill the Last One.'

The Doctor smiled, relaxed. 'Zevron and Ferran called blood feud on her, not you. You're just working for them. But you declared blood feud on me. Remember? Just after you watched your Prefect die, just after I'd beaten you.'

Sallak stepped out of Miranda's way, to get a clearer view of the Doctor. Miranda hurried past him.

'I'll come for you, girl.' He aimed his gun squarely at the Doctor.

Miranda stopped about ten yards away from the Deputy, looking back, seeing how she could help.

'Go,' the Doctor said softly.

The Deputy smiled at the Doctor.

'The universe will thank me for this, Doctor.'

'Will it, now?' the Doctor spat. 'It'll send you a card, will it? A thank-you note? Don't flatter me, Deputy, and don't flatter yourself.'

There were sirens. The police were coming.

'It's over, Sallak,' the Doctor said. 'You must have tripped an alarm when you came over the wall.'

The Deputy ignored him.

'Your line ends here,' the Deputy spat. 'I'll kill you, then I'll kill your daughter.'

The Doctor cast a worried glance towards Miranda, who was shifting her weight from one foot to the other, unsure what to do next. Debbie entertained the idea of throwing herself between the Deputy and the Doctor. Taking the bullet for him, like a minor character in a cop video.

The Deputy took a step forward, his face like that of a predator

waiting to pounce: weighing up his options, deciding how to do it. In the films, gunmen like this held their pistols at arm's length, and all the hero had to do was bat it out of their hand, but the Deputy held his gun close to his body. Debbie had the feeling that she ought to be running for cover.

There was a flurry of movement behind the Deputy. The gun was being wrestled from him.

Miranda, with a look in her eyes... Debbie had never seen anything like it. Even in films, all those stories about soldiers out to avenge their brothers' or their fathers' deaths, there had been nothing to hint at the intensity.

'She'll kill him,' Debbie whispered.

If Miranda turned her back on this man she'd get a bullet in it. If she stopped for a moment, he would take advantage. He was ancient – a pensioner, shorter, older, less fit than she was. But she didn't feel like she was any better. He still had the gun, and every iota of his effort was dedicated to keeping it there.

His arm was high in the air, trying to keep the pistol out of her reach. As she jumped to grab it, and he ducked out her way, it struck her what this reminded her of. *Netball*. It must have looked like netball.

She had the height advantage. She clutched his wrist, tried to squeeze it, reminding herself that the tactic had worked with Ferdy. Unfortunately, the Deputy didn't just disappear in a blue swirl.

So the Deputy was trapped here. He had nothing to lose.

Miranda was vaguely aware of her father edging forward. She wanted his help, she needed it, but she didn't want to see him shot.

Her elbow came down to break the Deputy's nose, but he was already sinking his teeth into her arm.

She shrieked – half pain, half battle cry – and the sound terrified her.

This wasn't the way.

What would her father do?

Which one? The Doctor? John Dawkins? Whatever alien warlord it was that had butchered this man's people?

Her father... the Doctor... he'd try to talk the Deputy out of it. He'd use reason. Show him the error of his ways, do the unexpected. But the Deputy was a fanatic – he'd travelled all this way, endured so much, simply to see her dead.

So she hesitated just for a moment, and the Deputy broke free, pushed her out of the way and levelled the gun at her.

The Doctor had been edging towards them. Now he stopped abruptly, the gravel of the driveway skittering.

'Too analytical,' she said quietly. 'Too much thinking.'

She was still doing it. Wondering what the bullet would feel like. It would kill her – the Deputy would see to that – but would it hurt? The bullet would be hot, she thought, a piece of metal travelling that fast would generate friction. That had never occurred to her when she'd seen bullets fired on *The A-Team*. Would she be dead before her body hit the ground?

The Deputy smiled, knowing it was over.

The unexpected. It was her way out of this.

She screamed, the same scream she'd made when he'd bitten her. She leapt straight at him.

For an instant, the gun wasn't where he needed it to be. She shoved into his shoulder. She'd always been stronger than she looked. She had the advantage, but she knew she could lose it in a fraction of a second.

She grabbed his hand, squeezed it against the gun he was holding in it until she heard bones crack, but didn't let go, even when the gun was on the floor and the Deputy was crying out.

She put a leg on the ground between his legs and tripped him over, bent down for the pistol, brought it level with his head.

The Deputy's eyes were wide.

'Do it!' he spat.

'Don't do it, Miranda,' the Doctor shouted. 'He's beaten. Can you hear that? Sirens. The police are here.'

She could hear them. The new sirens, the American-style ones, not the old-fashioned waa-waa sirens. Her father was coming over.

'I'm not a killer,' she told the Deputy.

Her father was behind her, now. Debbie Castle was staying back.

'The Doctor has taught you well – he's kept you from your nature. You're a monster. Your kind laid waste to the universe. You destroy worlds, you drain the life from whole galaxies. You can't escape who you are. Kill me. Kill me, or I'll kill you – it's the only way this can end. Let me live and I'll hunt you down.'

She shot him, twice, in the chest.

The Doctor couldn't believe it. He tried to work out what had really

happened. Miranda's hand had slipped, or the gun had gone off by itself.

But he knew.

'I had to do it,' she told him. 'He was right: this was the only way to end it.'

Not a hint of doubt in her voice. The same cruelty and cowardice that he'd heard from Zevron, Ferran and Sallak.

They could hear the police cars screeching to a halt. Shots had been fired, so the police would keep back for a minute or so while they assessed the situation. The Doctor had no idea where the nearest armed unit would be – there almost certainly weren't any locally.

'Hand me the gun,' he told her, 'then go.'

'I'm willing to take the consequences,' his daughter told him.

'You won't have to,' he told her.

She handed him the gun. 'You lied to me. All this time, and you were lying to me.'

The gun was warm in the Doctor's hand. Miranda showed no remorse. She'd just killed someone, but didn't seem even slightly disturbed by that. 'The police haven't had time to get round to the back of the house. They'll be there in a minute, maybe less,' he said. 'Find your own destiny.'

She looked at him, fixed him with those blue eyes of hers. 'I love you,' she told him. 'You know that, don't you?'

He couldn't reply.

He watched her hurry away, through the house, stopping only to grab her coat from its hook in the hall.

'Police!' a megaphone voice shouted. 'Drop your weapon!'

The Doctor held his arms out, then tossed the gun over on to the lawn.

The Deputy was staring at him, defiant even in death.

'Let them in, would you, Debbie?' he asked.

Part Three

'Defenders of the Earth'

The Late 1980s

Chapter Twenty-one
All Around the World

A clear November night, a little cold, but the crowds out on the streets didn't care.

There were fireworks, now. Western camera crews at every vantage point. Men in bright jackets and designer jeans helping their countrymen up on to the Wall, or even through the gaps that had begun to emerge in it. They looked like lifeguards, pulling shipwrecked survivors out of the sea. There were men and women swarming across the abandoned checkpoints. The border guards and their guns had just melted away.

You could feel history changing around you, the Doctor thought. The Cold War that had defined history and humanity for half of even his lifetime was over. But the details were what made this special – the people who had clearly dressed quickly to be here, the smiles, the fact that no one could quite believe what was happening and needed to be here to make sure it was true.

Everything had changed tonight.

'Here, here,' Dieter Steinmann was telling him, urging the Doctor to take a sledgehammer.

The Doctor held up his hands. 'This is your moment,' he told the young man.

'But you –'

'My contribution was nothing,' the Doctor insisted. 'And whatever I achieved here, it wasn't really what I came to Berlin for.'

Dieter lowered the sledgehammer. 'Miranda. She is not here. I am sorry. You have helped us, but we have not been able to help you find your daughter.'

The Doctor nodded sadly. 'I have to get back to England. There may have been other leads.'

He walked away, through the Brandenburg Gate, against the flow of the crowd.

An hour after dawn, the day was already hot, and smelled of spice and dried flowers. Miranda's companion was fast asleep beside her, worn

out from the night before. He smelled of pot and cheap beer. It wasn't too difficult to extricate herself from him.

Miranda stood and stretched, smiling with the body-memory of the night before.

She saw his rucksack at the foot of the bed. Perhaps if she searched it, she'd find some ID. He'd told her his name at the beginning of the evening, but she had been distracted by the TV. He was West German. No, news update: last night he'd been West German, but this morning he'd wake up – assuming he did ever wake up – a German. They'd watched satellite TV in the hotel bar, seen crowds surging through Checkpoint Charlie, scaling the Wall, attacking it with sledgehammers. Unable to speak Hindi, he'd relied on Miranda's running commentary. Neither of them could believe it was happening. It had been a full hour before they'd been sure it wasn't some sort of science-fiction film.

And they'd drunk – although only he had *got* drunk – and he'd smoked – which hadn't appealed at all – and they'd gone up to her room and spent the night celebrating. She'd laughed when he'd asked if it was her first time, and she'd surprised him, and then they'd made sure they were safe, then they hadn't needed to speak any more.

She found her Batman T-shirt in her bag and put it on, before opening up the shutters and stepping out on to the balcony.

So hot and so light! So colourful!

Below, in the courtyard, the crowds were swarming. There were so many people here. People to carry your bags, people to open the doors, people to serve your drinks, people to *bring* you the drinks. That was the division between East and West, she decided – here the cheapest part of any process was the cost of labour. Here perfectly ordinary houses had half a dozen servants, or staff, or whatever you wanted to call them.

Miranda hadn't yet discovered the history of the hotel, but it had plainly been a palace once, and no doubt its staff had been even more numerous than the army currently working here. It was a vast building, with blue minarets and a vast golden dome. It didn't seem to belong on the same planet as the filthy, congested, thrown-together streets that surrounded it.

There were vultures circling overhead. When she'd first arrived in the country, that had seemed ominous. When she realised they nested in the eaves of the hotel, as doves would have done in England, it had

seemed absurd, Pythonesque. A month on, and it seemed the most natural thing in the world.

So why had the crowds stopped to stare up at them?

For a moment, Miranda thought they were looking at her. A few years ago, she'd have been absurdly self-conscious in just a T-shirt, but now she quite enjoyed the idea of standing on a balcony while a crowd below hung on her every move.

Then she looked up, back over her shoulder.

A silver disc, hanging above the hotel like a couple of extra storeys.

It was the size of a house. For a moment, it didn't strike Miranda as odd: there were things she'd seen in India that were far more alien.

Then she realised what it was, that it didn't *belong* and that it had come for her.

But by then she couldn't move. She was surrounded by a blue haze, and the world around her evaporated.

Her eyes were the same.

Her face was a latex mask. Her skin looked as if it had been bathed in something corrosive, something that had scored lines into it while also loosening it from her skull and making it melt a little. Her hair was white, now, and wispy, contrasting with the dark Terylene of her nightdress.

She looked into his eyes, and didn't say anything. It wasn't difficult to know what she was thinking: that he barely looked a day older than the last time she'd seen him, that he'd looked the same since they'd first met. Now she was in an old people's home, her life nearly spent.

'Betty,' the Doctor said.

She smiled, the effort almost visibly draining her. She seemed to draw strength from the beautiful roses in their vases and the flickering light of the television screen playing on her face.

'Have you found her?' she asked.

He shook his head. 'I thought she was in Berlin. I went there, but no one had seen her. I've just come from there.'

'I didn't see you on the telly. They had a newsflash during the break on *Coronation Street*. Show me the photo again.'

The Doctor took the photo of Miranda he kept in his coat pocket, apologised that it was a couple of years out of date. She would be nineteen now.

'I love her,' the Doctor said.

'Of course you do, she's your daughter. She's very pretty,' Betty said. 'I can see the resemblance.'

The Doctor nodded. 'Everyone said that. We weren't related – I adopted her.'

'You never could do things the easy way, could you?' She chuckled, admiring the photo. The Doctor looked at the picture frames lined up on Betty's shelf – children, grandchildren, even a great-grandchild now. All that history, all those connections. Betty belonged here: her life, her history, her genes, all weaving and interweaving across more than a century. Now the century was about to enter its final decade, and his friends had started dying, one by one: Salvador, Irving, Larry and Graham just this year. They'd left so much behind; they'd contributed to the planet they'd found themselves on. In that same time, what had he done? He'd known he was different, but had always thought that meant he should lie low – keep himself out of the history books. If he went tomorrow, what would he leave behind? He could have made a difference, in this of all centuries. He could have made things better.

'Do you want a handkerchief?' Betty asked, handing the picture back.

He shook his head. Then he looked at the photograph in his hand and he knew. Wherever Miranda was, whatever she thought of him, he knew that he'd achieved at least one thing.

'She's a good girl,' the Doctor said quietly. 'I'm so proud of her.'

'Nineteen?' Betty said. She hadn't heard the last thing he'd said. The Doctor realised with a start that Betty was going a little deaf. 'I wasn't that much younger when we first met. Things have changed, though. Kids grow up so much faster. I've got grandchildren Miranda's age, and... oh, the things they get up to.'

'You were engaged at Miranda's age,' the Doctor reminded her.

'We didn't have teenagers when I was a teenager,' Betty chortled. 'You never really grew up, did you? You're like Peter Pan. You don't change.'

'The world's changed around me,' the Doctor said. 'Remember when I talked about the future? Well, it's starting to happen. Things have changed, and usually for the better. There's mass production, but mankind isn't the slave of machines. We treat the mentally ill like people now, we don't just lock them away. Computers are everywhere. And now, now the Cold War's over. The world's a better

place than it could have been. But a lot of things have changed since I first went to Middletown.'

'You always were ahead of your time,' Betty said, laughing.

'I tried to give her a normal upbringing,' the Doctor told her. 'Sometimes, I know I was a bit of a Victorian parent, but –'

Betty laughed, and the Doctor realised why. 'No offence,' he chuckled.

'Maggie's always going on about Victorian values,' Betty said. 'I was there. The life we have today, it's better.'

The Doctor's portable phone rang. He took it out of his briefcase.

Betty clapped her hands together. 'That's so clever,' she said.

'Debbie?' the Doctor said into the phone. 'Isn't it past your bedtime?'

Miranda woke, surrounded by the unfamiliar.

The room was circular, as was the bed. There was a metal structure hanging over it, giving the impression that it was a four-poster. The wall looked like plastic, and had little niches and backlit computer panels set along it.

There was a pulsing in the background, an electronic sound. Beneath that a humming, like a generator, or engines.

She was still wearing just her Batman T-shirt.

There was a woman standing at the foot of the bed. She was tall, wearing a form-fitting black outfit in what looked like sculpted rubber. She was in her mid-thirties, Miranda guessed. Her dark hair had been scraped back and gelled to her scalp. He lips were painted a vivid scarlet. There was something familiar about her that Miranda couldn't place.

'I have clothes for you,' the woman said. The voice was a trained monotone, clearly how the formalities dictated she should speak, but there was more warmth in her eyes.

Miranda stood, stretched a little to ease some of the cramp in her legs and arms.

The woman held up a one-piece undergarment, rather like a silk swimming costume, and swept her free hand to indicate the rest of the clothes: a polo-necked top that Miranda could tell would be a tight fit, a stiff-collared, shoulder-padded tunic in very dark green, baggy trousers that looked as if they'd been borrowed from an aviatrix, and heavy-duty-looking boots.

Miranda tugged her T-shirt off and started to put the ensemble on.

The woman helped, sensing that Miranda didn't want any more assistance than was absolutely necessary. She threaded the belt, buckled the shoes, adjusted the buttoning on the tunic to make it fit better.

The clothes felt good, comfortable, made-to-measure.

Another Miranda appeared in front of the original, startling them both. This one was smartly dressed in odd clothes. She looked like Miranda from some parallel universe where she ruled over Earth. Miranda held up her hand, as did her double.

'A mirror,' she said, her double silently mouthing the same words.

'A hologram,' the woman confirmed, slightly disdainful. Clearly holograms were common in these parts.

Miranda looked at the woman again, then back at the hologram.

'Do you have a brush?' she asked, unsure what was nagging at her.

'And cosmetics.'

'I don't wear them,' Miranda told her. 'I just want to brush my hair out.'

The woman nodded and walked over to one of the niches in the wall.

'I'm on the flying saucer, aren't I?' Miranda asked.

'You are aboard the *Supremacy*. The flying saucer brought you here.'

'A mothership.'

The woman sat her down and began brushing the knots from her hair. The brush was gentle, and the bristles seemed to be moving independently, but the woman's technique was rather brusque.

'What is your name?' Miranda asked.

'I am the Deputy.'

'That's your title, but what's your name?'

No answer.

'Where are we? I mean, where is the ship?'

'Earth orbit,' a man's voice said.

Miranda whirled. It was a stocky man in a green uniform. He was in early middle age, but had seemingly made no effort to keep fit. His jowls hung down, his arms were almost flabby. He was wearing a cloak, which disguised some of his bulk.

And she recognised him.

'Ferran?' Miranda asked, standing up.

He stepped forward, arms outstretched. 'I've come back for you.'

* * *

Debbie was sitting up in bed, all four pillows propping her up.

'I'm watching *News at Ten*. Put it on. Be quick.'

'OK. Hang on.'

There was a pause; she heard him putting the phone down. Debbie took the opportunity to find a cigarette and light it.

'What am I looking –' He stopped mid-sentence.

Trevor McDonald was reading out the final item, but the Doctor would barely be listening: he'd be looking at the accompanying pictures.

A large silver disc, hovering over an exotic Indian building.

Cut to an excited Indian man. 'It was UFO ship. It was there for just a minute, just a minute, then it went straight up, up into star.'

An image of a silver disc was being shown – hurriedly (and amateurishly) captured on some tourist's cine camera – and Trevor McDonald was saying, 'Scientists insist that the UFO is really a common cloud formation in the area, which is prone to monsoons.'

'Where exactly?' the Doctor was already saying.

'They only said "Northern India". I'll phone Reuters, get them to pin it down.'

'Good. Have you checked the –'

'I've only just seen the report. I'll go downstairs.' She got out of the bed, found her slippers on the other side. The phone was cordless – she leaned her head against her shoulder to pin it to her ear. The heating hadn't gone off yet, but it was starting to get chilly.

'It was them,' Debbie said. 'It looked like the ship from Greyfrith.'

He didn't pause for a moment. 'Of course it was them, but whatever they were doing in India, they've finished doing it.'

'You think Miranda was in India?'

She went into the lab, moved aside the poster with the periodic table on it.

'There are only two people on this planet in this time that Ferran is remotely interested in – he didn't come for me.'

'But how would he know that Miranda was there if you didn't?'

'I don't know.'

'You've spent enough time trying to find her. None of the leads we've had said India.'

None of the leads had actually led anywhere, though, she reminded herself. She activated the time detector, let it warm up.

'It's on the student trail,' he said thoughtfully. 'We never went there

together, so she might want to see it. It's a beautiful country – I've not been there for... twenty-seven years. Heavens, how time flies. What's the detector saying?'

Debbie was already leaning over the display.

'A source, two hours ago. It arrived in space, er, and it went back up to the same point. It...'

'Just read it out,' he suggested.

She read out the numbers the display was showing. She could hear the Doctor scratching them down.

'It's still there,' the Doctor said, puzzled.

'How many years has it been?' Miranda asked.

The woman in black, the Deputy, had taken her place behind her master. Miranda studied Ferran's face. It was covered in lines now, and those cheekbones of his had given way to fat. She glanced at his wrist. He was still wearing his computer bracelet, but even that was looking past its best now.

'Twenty,' he snapped. 'Three for you, twenty for me. You have aged rather better than I have. You knew I'd come, didn't you?'

'No. I thought I was rid of you.' Ferran looked confused. 'You must have known,' Miranda said.

'We were lovers,' Ferran told her.

Miranda chuckled. 'We *nearly* were,' she corrected him. 'But so what?'

Ferran's face twitched, as if he was desperately trying to keep control. 'I travelled a million years to see you again.'

'You must have known I wouldn't have come willingly. Otherwise why would you have abducted me instead of just talking to me?'

'I thought you would be pleased,' Ferran insisted, his voice almost a whine.

Miranda realised she should have been angry, but she had no feelings at all, just a blank where her feelings should have been. She looked at the Deputy – who wore the same dead expression Miranda's face must have. 'We're heading back to your time, aren't we?'

'Not yet. This ship is magnificent, but we've developed a fault in the time engine. The self-repair circuits have it under control. We will return to our native time in three Earth days. You are probably wondering how I tracked you down.'

Miranda was a little embarrassed to realise it hadn't even occurred to her.

'Cate,' Ferran prompted. So the Deputy's name was Cate.

The Deputy stepped forward and handed Miranda a golden circlet, indicating that she should put it on her head.

Miranda slid it into place, and felt whispering in her mind.

'What does this do?' she asked.

'Enhances natural telepathy – allows you to operate some of our machines.'

The wall behind him became a writhing mass. A man and a woman in bed. There was an earnest voiceover, a man speaking German.

She watched for a moment, wondering why he was showing her this, until she realised the woman looked like her – or had been made to: the blonde hair was a wig, the face was slightly more angular. The man was her German tourist, or – again – an actor who looked like an idealised version of him. The room was his hotel room, the one she'd just left. But the layout was all wrong, the decoration too elaborate, too ethnic, too beautifully lit. There hadn't been the sitar playing when she'd been there.

'That's not me,' she said.

It was the night the Berlin Wall fell, the voiceover was saying.

Ferran watched the couple, spellbound. Cate had her back to the screen. 'Your friend won the Best Foreign Non-Interactive Film Oscar for this in 2017. He wrote and directed it. It's autobiographical, about how the major events of his life happened on historically significant dates. He was born the day the Beatles split up. It ends with him marrying his wife on the day Princess Diana died.'

'Is that Jodie Foster?' Miranda asked. A number of people had said she looked a bit like her.

'It's her daughter,' the Deputy replied without hesitating.

The narrator never saw Miranda again, he told his audience, as, on the screen, they held each other close, radiant, trying to catch their breath. He had looked for her, he said, but all anyone would talk about was the flying saucer the locals said they'd seen that morning. And she was gone from his life, but he would never forget her.

'The director died,' Ferran said, without any sense of regret. 'He left a wife and three sons. Nothing of any historical significance happened that day.' He paused. 'Some of his work was preserved in the Librarinth. It's the only trace you've left on history. After the police

reports on Sallak's death, that's it.'

'I tried to lie low.'

'You did, but you couldn't hide from me. I've had a team of researchers looking for records of you for fifteen years. That's all they could find, but that was enough. The Doctor made more of an impact, of course. The Lloyds building, Baghdad, Waco, the Martian invasion, that business with the Kulan... but I'm getting ahead of myself.'

'I've not seen him for years.'

'I've traced his every movement, every credit-card transaction, every official record. He wasn't punished for Sallak's murder. He claimed self-defence. When that matter was settled, he dedicated all his time and effort trying to find you.' He smiled, checking a timepiece sewn into the cuff of his tunic. 'At the moment he's on the M25. In five minutes he buys petrol from a Shell garage near Junction 19 and makes a substantial cash withdrawal from the cash machine there.'

The Doctor hurtled along the M25.

'Meet me at Heathrow as soon as you can,' he told Debbie over the crackle of the line. Glancing down at the petrol gauge, he realised there wasn't going to be enough petrol to get him there.

'Heathrow?'

'You know, the big airpor–'

'OK, OK, I'll be there in an hour.' He could hear her moving around, opening up the wardrobe.

'We're going to India. Bring your passport.'

'But the saucer's long gone from there. It's pointless. And don't we need visas, or at least some jabs?'

The Doctor looked down at the phone, angry that Debbie, of all people, didn't understand.

When he looked up again, Miranda was in the road ahead of him. Standing there in the fast lane.

He slammed the brakes on, but there wasn't enough time.

No.

The car screeched through her. He hadn't stopped in time, but neither had he hit her.

He looked back in the mirror – she was still there.

'Doctor, Doctor!' Debbie was calling. He killed the phone.

The Doctor yanked on the handbrake and got out of the car. Miranda stayed where she was, facing away from him. There were

headlights coming towards her.

He called out to her, then, when she didn't hear, he ran up to her, tried to grab her, tried to shield her.

A car swerved into the middle lane, honking furiously, barely missing him.

This wasn't the safest place to stay. But for the moment there was nothing else coming.

She wasn't here, not really. The light was wrong – like a crude fake photo, she was in good light, everything around her was in darkness.

Another car swerved, the driver shouting obscenities.

'Miranda?' the Doctor asked, trying to touch her. She was older. Her hair was straight, and so long. She was more beautiful than he remembered. She was wearing... It wasn't clear what she was wearing. It kept changing.

The carphone was ringing.

Her lips were moving. He tried to read them.

Concentrate.

He did, closing his eyes, clearing his mind, not even seeing or hearing the lorry until it had gone past. Her lips weren't moving, now. Whole concepts were flooding into his mind at once, and unravelling, blossoming like flowers.

I can't be long/(Jodie-Foster's-daughter/me/Cate) eyes squeezed closed, mouth wide open/I'm (secretly) using (telepathic circuits) to find (you-father)/(Tiny part of mind) only/(Ferran-Ferdy) found me and captured me/Till receipt (Shell station) (Junction 19 of the M25)/Deputy Cate looks familiar/He must have married late – (Princess Diana) only twenty-eight/(Three days)/The time engines will take three days/He's tracking you – (knows you buy petrol) – how I found you/I love you/I don't know what he's going to do to me/(Safe for the moment)/I won't see you again/Goodbye

And she was gone.

'I love you,' the Doctor called after her, but there was nothing there.

The carphone was ringing.

'Maniac,' someone shouted as they sped past him.

The Doctor hurried back to the car, started the engine and answered the phone.

'Change of plan,' he said, without waiting for Debbie to start speaking. 'We're getting the next Concorde to New York, then Florida.'

'Why Flo–'

'Because the saucer's in space. Because my daughter's up there, but only until they've repaired their time engines. We've got three days to get to them. The *Atlantis* is due to launch tomorrow evening, and it's the only way I can reach her in time.'

'The space shuttle?'

'That's right.'

'Doctor, they won't just let us hitch a ride on the space shuttle.'

The Doctor smiled, and slammed his foot on the Trabant's accelerator, astonishing the owners of the Audi he cruised past.

'Then we'll just have to steal it.'

Chapter Twenty-two
Today America, Tomorrow the World

Debbie had accompanied the Doctor on American business trips a few times: a couple of trips to Berkeley, a weekend in New York, a week in Texas. But it was still enough of a novelty to have some value. She was never going to persuade the Doctor to give up his window seat, but she got occasional glimpses of the sea beneath them, patches of land that may – or, indeed, may not – have been the coast of Greenland or Newfoundland.

The Doctor kept asking for napkins. It had got to the stage where the stewardess had one in her hand as she came over, instead of having to ask what he wanted.

Concorde was far smaller than Debbie had expected, and – in first class at least – rather overcrowded with all the stewardesses and their trolleys. But it was phenomenally fast. They would be in New York in less time than it took getting from the Doctor's house to Greyfrith by British Rail. There was no sense of that in the plane itself: they weren't pinned to their seats, despite the fact they could outrun a bullet, despite the fact that no air force in the world had an interceptor fast enough to intercept them.

Their problem was not of this world, anyway. Neither was their eventual destination.

'How much faster is the space shuttle than Concorde?' she asked the Doctor.

He smiled and, without hesitating, replied. 'Concorde can cross the Atlantic in three hours; the shuttle orbits the Earth in ninety minutes. Concorde can fly just over twice the speed of sound –' He pointed at the digital display at the front of the first-class compartment, which indicated that was precisely what they were doing – 'during launch, the shuttle peaks at about Mach fifteen.'

'We're really going to steal it?'

'Borrow it,' he assured her. The Doctor handed her one of the napkins, with his spidery handwriting and incomprehensible doodles over it. At the top of the napkin, neatly underlined, was How to Steal a Space Shuttle: Part 1. 'Tell me when you've read it. I'll hand you the rest.'

Around then, the stewardesses brought round the customs forms and immigration cards. Debbie leaned over to see what the Doctor was putting under 'Purpose of Visit'.

'Family Reunion', he'd written.

She began studying her napkin.

Ferran looked at the hologlobe, leaned forward, peered through the steam coming from his bathwater, watched Miranda pacing around her stateroom.

'She's magnificent. Like her father. They are like the tigers of Earth… superb creatures, beautiful and powerful. But when man came along, they were suddenly nothing but trophies for hunters.'

'Do you love her?' Cate asked, leaning over, sloshing water, but not daring to block his view.

Ferran looked his Deputy in the eye.

'Once I did. But now I have you.' He sponged her collarbone.

'She doesn't suspect, does she?'

'About us?'

Cate was suddenly self-conscious, almost shy. 'About *me*.'

Ferran dabbed at her neck. His hand was lobster-red, almost scalded by the hot water. Cate's skin stayed as milky-pale as ever, just as it had been designed to.

'No.'

She stood, let the water run off her, then stepped from the bath.

As she started to towel herself down, Ferran turned back to the hologlobe. He leaned back, letting the hot water soak away the pain in his shoulder and into the welts on his back.

'Will you marry her?'

He smiled. 'I thought you were above jealousy, my dear.'

'And when you need an heir?'

Ferran looked into the globe. 'Miranda and I will come to an arrangement. If she will not bear me one, there are other ways of going about it. You would make the perfect surrogate.'

She looked at him levelly.

'Is that emotion, Cate?' he asked, 'I thought your kind were above such things.'

'As your Deputy, I have to raise my concerns about your strategy. I am just doing my job.'

Ferran smiled. 'Of course you are. Now get dressed and go to our guest.'

* * *

Miranda thought about her father, and the message she had sent. She *thought* she had seen him standing in the road, looking just the same – except for a few grey hairs – but she had no way of knowing whether she'd just imagined it. Ferran had taken the circlet away with him, ushered the Deputy out and left Miranda alone for several hours.

She'd paced the room, discovered a bathroom (and worked out, she hoped, which one was the toilet and which one was the shower), the wardrobes full of clothes that had been tailored to fit her, and which items mounted on the walls were functional and which were decorative.

And she still didn't have a plan.

She had three days. Three days minus however many hours it had been. She'd left her watch – a fifteenth birthday present from her father – on the bedside table of her German friend's hotel room. Normally she had a good sense of what the time was, even without a watch, but she was obviously suffering from space lag, or whatever.

The sense of the time machine getting ready to depart was almost palpable to her. She could feel it, somewhere deep within the ship. A weird sense, vaguely familiar to her, comforting and primal as being held in a mother's arms. Salmon must feel like this when they start swimming home.

What was Ferran planning?

He hadn't said. He wasn't planning to kill her, at least not *just* that – he could have done that hours ago. Or on the balcony of the hotel. Perhaps there was a state execution planned at the other end. A public occasion with ceremony and baying crowds. But that hadn't been his style last time they'd met. Last time they'd met, of course, he'd gone from being Gold Blend bloke to intergalactic Nazi assassin and back again in the space of a day.

Finding herself. As the stock-market boom and property boom and credit boom all came to an end with the decade, a lot of the City types had been forced to give up their excesses and ambitions and optimism and to look within. Miranda had met a few of them in India, following the brand name and designer label as always, looking for the hippie trail and trying to pay for everything with a Gold Amex.

But she'd been looking within for over three years for some answers.

In a cave in Greece, a mystic had told her – for five dollars – that she was her father's daughter and the answers lay within her.

That hadn't helped in the slightest.

And she'd gone to India and found nothing. Now, of course, she'd been reminded exactly what she was – that she had two hearts, a blood type that wasn't even blood, and one of the two highest IQs on the planet.

Miranda sat on the edge of the bed, trying to form a plan. But she couldn't escape – even if she could reach a flying saucer, she couldn't fly one. For the moment, her fate was in Ferran's hands. The door hissed open without warning, and the Deputy, Cate, entered.

'You are rested?' she asked, with all the concern of a speak-your-weight machine.

'What will happen to me?'

'It is not my place to say.'

'Well, what *can* you tell me?' Miranda asked. 'Are there just the three of us on this ship?'

Cate glared at her, with a loathing it took a moment for Miranda to rationalise. Three's a crowd, Miranda realised.

'Prefect Ferran has a whole legion on this ship, and support staff and slaves. But, even then, we've not explored the whole ship.'

'Explored the ship? Didn't you build it?'

'No, My Lady. It was a shipwreck.'

'And it's big. How big?' Miranda asked.

'The size of a city.'

Miranda shrugged. 'What does that mean?'

'Four kilometres long, a kilometre in diameter at either end. A thousand levels.'

'Levels?'

'Storeys. Floors.'

Miranda gulped. Finding the hangar, or wherever it was you keep a flying saucer would be virtually impossible, especially with a legion of soldiers looking for her and blocking her way.

Not without recruiting some help.

'Where are you from?' Miranda asked.

Cate lowered her head.

'Don't you have parents? A family?'

'No,' she said, simply.

'You and Ferran are lovers?'

Cate's lip curled. 'After a fashion,' she said.

Miranda decided to change the subject.

'What's it like where we are going?'

Cate looked up. She seemed to be asking herself whether she should answer. She was glancing up, as though she might be overheard. Was the room bugged? Miranda wondered, kicking herself for not even considering the possibility.

'I'm going there anyway,' Miranda reminded her.

'Ruins,' the Deputy said quickly, so quickly it took Miranda a second or two to be sure what she had said. 'The palace is all that's left. That and a few shelters. For generations, that is all there has been.'

'Because of the war?'

Cate nodded. 'It's the same everywhere. Everything is rationed, reused, but everything breaks down. There's no law. Only people doing what they want and imposing their will on others. Without the Empire there would be anarchy.'

'Do you know who I am?' Miranda asked.

Cate nodded. 'I know who you are. Everyone knows who you are. You are the Last One.'

Miranda put her hand on Cate's shoulder. 'I don't remember anything. I was a baby. I only know what Ferran told me. I know my family did terrible things, but I never knew them. What does Ferran want from me?'

Cate shook her head. She wasn't going to answer.

'He wants me alive. Why? What does he want?'

'What do *you* want?' the Deputy asked.

Miranda sighed. 'That's a very good question. I really don't know.'

Florida was hot and humid, even in November.

The Doctor had mislaid the sonic suitcase, and they'd spent an hour trying to find it. Debbie suspected someone had snatched it while he'd been buying local guidebooks at the airport Waldenbooks and she'd been buying them doughnuts and coffee. The Doctor's faith in human nature meant he couldn't accept that explanation.

'I feel like I've just lost an old friend,' he had told her. Then, as they were about to give up looking, they'd found it just where the Doctor had left it – in the bookstore.

They hired a car and drove down to Cape Canaveral, making three stops on the way, and booked themselves – with a fair amount of difficulty, since shuttle launches always attracted the crowds – into a motel room in Titusville. To Debbie it looked like every motel room

in every American movie she'd ever watched.

They could see the shuttle through the window, sitting on the horizon, the size of a skyscraper, in an otherwise perfectly flat landscape. According to the space-shuttle book the Doctor had bought Debbie on one of their stops, it was fifteen storeys high. They sat together at the window, just looking at it.

And playing chess. Debbie had beaten the Doctor on the flight over, for the first time in months. Characteristically, he'd blamed the travel chess set, and the tiny pieces, which he claimed all looked the same – but after sulking for a couple of minutes, he'd congratulated her.

'No clouds,' the Doctor said. 'The launch should go ahead tomorrow as planned.'

'Why would clouds make any difference?' Debbie asked. 'It's not as if the shuttle couldn't fly through them.'

'Clouds carry an electric charge. The shuttle could be hit by lightning as it passes through them, it could damage electrical equipment aboard. They discovered that during the Apollo missions.'

'The... shuttle is safe now, isn't it? I mean, one blew up.'

'There's a one-in-a-hundred chance of a major problem,' the Doctor said. 'NASA official figures. Of course before *Challenger*, they said one in a hundred *thousand*, but that's neither here nor there. If it launches, it'll be safe. The last thing NASA want is another disaster. We have to hope they don't err on the side of caution and postpone the launch. If it goes ahead then there's a ninety-second window at launch when it's really dangerous. After that we'll have got away with it.'

'Why ninety seconds?' Debbie asked, wondering whether she really wanted to know.

The Doctor tapped a sheaf of papers marked Ascent Pkt Checklist. 'Once they light the engines, they can't turn them off, they have to use up all their fuel. Solid rocket fuel is dangerous stuff. Looks like putty, but, of course, it's highly explosive – wouldn't be much use if it wasn't. If there's a problem with one of the solid rocket boosters then the mechanical stresses would almost certainly just pull everything apart. You can't eject them; a detached orbiter wouldn't be able to outrun them.'

'We'd have a crash-landing.'

'Oh no,' the Doctor said wickedly, 'Mission Control would self-destruct us – you wouldn't want us crashing in an inhabited area. So, the solid fuel burns out after two minutes, and then those two tanks

detach. The liquid fuel in the middle tank's burning at about three thousand three hundred degrees, of course, but most of it's burned off by then. That's when we hit Mach fifteen. Ninety seconds.'

Debbie must have looked very pale, because the Doctor leaned over her. 'You don't have to come if you don't want to.'

'I'm coming with you,' she insisted.

'Good.' He handed her a security badge with her name on it. 'I used some of my business connections,' he explained vaguely.

'How can this work?' Debbie asked him.

'A shuttle launch runs to a timetable. A totally predictable and controlled sequence of events,' the Doctor said. 'If you know the process, it's easy to exploit that knowledge.'

'They must have security.'

'They do – and I know the precise location of each guard, fence and camera. They don't even know we're here, let alone what we're planning to do. Even if they did, I doubt they'd believe we could achieve it.' He smiled. 'We have the advantage here. I almost feel sorry for them.'

Miranda was getting the guided tour, but Ferran was keeping the details vague.

Miranda was starting to piece things together, though. The ship was cylindrical, or something like that, with the living quarters and control rooms and recreation areas at one end, the hangars and things in the middle and the engines at the rear.

A ship this vast was a community, not just a warship. The corridors had soldiers – blond and blonde; servants in the drab robes; but other people too. Guessing from the costumes, there were entertainers, technicians, minor noblemen, chefs... and many other types besides.

There were search parties, fanning their way through the ship, taking pictures, drawing up maps and technical diagrams.

They were all Ferran's people. There were no robots, no monsters, no mutants. No black faces, either, or Chinese ones, only a few female soldiers. Racial purity. She shuddered.

Studying Ferran and Cate together worried her, too. He showed concern about her, appreciation – but only the concern a man might have for a sports car, or a particularly stylish music centre. She was property.

The flight deck was a short lift journey from her own quarters.

Miranda stepped in behind Ferran. Cate followed.

The room was hexagonal, with a high vaulted ceiling. They came out on to a raised walkway. The lighting was soft, throwing shadows everywhere. The walls were dark – glossy black metal and gold trim. There were a number of ramps down towards the centre itself, where six high seats all faced towards the centre of the room, each with computer panels set into the armrests.

In the centre of the vaulted ceiling, hanging down like a chandelier, was a pyramid full of swirling lights.

Her bedchamber had been an exercise in steel and plastic minimalism. This was more ornate, and as architecturally striking as it was functional.

Each seat had one of Ferran's men in it. All wore smart green uniforms, all were blond, a variety of ages, but otherwise with little to distinguish them from one another.

'What is our status?' Ferran asked.

The reply came from all around: a woman's voice with a slight electronic distortion.

'Ship is in class-three orbit above planet Earth, all ship systems are operating at full capacity, with the exception of the time engine, which is repairing in line with previous estimates.'

Miranda pointed up at the pyramid. 'That was speaking?'

'That's Computer,' Ferran told her. 'It controls the ship. And I control it.'

'Where did you find the ship?' Miranda asked.

Ferran turned, looked at Cate carefully. 'How did you know?'

Cate's face gave nothing away.

Miranda had no intention of betraying a confidence or losing a valuable source of information. 'If you had built this ship, it wouldn't look like this. You'd have your own chair, for a start, and it would be in the middle of the room.'

Ferran narrowed his eyes, but broke into a grin. 'It crashed near the Librarinth, a very long time ago. One of my teams there recovered it.'

'Who are the original owners? My people?'

He shook his head. 'People who have long since gone. Nothing to do with you. This is a relic of an earlier time. A time that may not even have happened.'

She looked down at the activity. The people looked out of place here, like schoolboys allowed to drive their dad's company Merc.

'It's impressive.'

'*Supremacy* is beyond the state of the art. Its weapons, its defences, its time travel. It's the advantage I need to win the war.'

'The war?'

Ferran turned to her. 'The Factions and Houses are at open war with each other, now. No one is strong enough to take it too far. The whole system is on the brink of collapse – everything from the economy, the military, communications, transport… But during my long years at the Archive I discovered far more than how you spent your teenage years. I've found maps, histories, secrets. Enough to unite the Factions under me, and the force to impose my will.'

Miranda looked him in the eye. 'All the things you called "atrocities" when my family did them to you.'

Ferran gave a cruel smile. 'But then, my dear, the Imperial Family had the biggest guns. Now I do. That's all there is: power. Have that, and ethics and morality bend to your will.'

'"Might makes right",' Miranda said, disgusted.

'That's all there is. Justice will be my justice, law will be my law. When I've uncovered all the secrets of this ship I'll build a fleet of them. Nothing will stand against me.' He paused, enjoying the theatricality of it all. 'And you have your part to play.'

Miranda laughed out loud. 'If you think I will do anything to help your –'

'You will,' Ferran said with absolute certainty. 'You will, because I have all this, and you have nothing except that which I grant you.'

Chapter Twenty-three
Escape Velocity

A pair of white-suited technicians, the pad team, checked Commander Fairchild, and one led him inside. The other crewmen remained waiting in the White Room, the area hundreds of metres up the launch gantry that was level with the entry hatch on the side of *Atlantis*.

It was a laborious process. Each astronaut in turn would be taken to their seat, manoeuvred into it, facing up, then packed and strapped into place. Fairchild, the commander, went in first. He'd be followed by Beale, who'd be sitting to the commander's right and would act as pilot. Then Kim Sawyer, the flight engineer, who'd go in behind the commander. Then, set back a little, Mather, the mission specialist, would go in last.

All following procedure, laid down years ago, with little significant variation. There were no short cuts here. Before every launch, every single component was checked and rechecked. The shuttle was taken apart and rebuilt – making a mockery of the claim that it was reusable, of course. Below them, at Mission Control, hundreds of techies and scientists were running diagnostics, monitoring everything to the slightest degree.

And despite all that, seventy-three seconds after take-off, on 28 January 1986, a shuttle had exploded. That thought was all around them. No one ever quite admitted it, but the loss of *Challenger* informed everything that was said and done, even for Mather, a military man only seconded to NASA.

It was clearly uppermost on the mind of the female technician who stayed in the White Room with the crew. Mather didn't recognise her. She was in her mid-thirties, white, with the first hints of grey in her black hair.

'You look more nervous that I do,' Mather joked. 'Anyone would think it was you going into space.'

'Anything goes wrong,' she said, in a British accent, 'and it's me that gets in trouble.'

'I've been training two years for this,' he said. 'This is my big moment.'

'Two years?'

'Sure, that's just the standard training period.'

The other member of the pad team, a man with long light-brown hair poking out of his cap, emerged and ushered the pilot and flight engineer aboard.

All around them were clanking, whooshing noises. The liquid-hydrogen fuel being pumped into the fuel tanks.

A couple of minutes later, the man re-emerged. 'Last but not least,' he said, leading Mather inside.

'Everyone around here's British,' Mather noted.

Five minutes after he'd led the mission specialist aboard, the Doctor came out and told Debbie the astronauts were all safely strapped in up on the flight deck, and the trapdoor hatch to the lower deck had been closed and locked down.

Debbie attached a gizmo the Doctor had built over breakfast to the elevator control. The Doctor recovered the sonic suitcase and the travel bag from where they had concealed them.

'What if someone finds that cupboard in the visitors' centre where we locked the real pad technicians?'

'Then they'll abort the launch and we'll be found and arrested,' he said cheerfully. 'Here we go,' the Doctor said.

He bowed, sweeping his arm around like the owner of a fairground ride. 'Step aboard.'

Debbie did as she was told.

The hatch looked a bit like the door on Concorde. Past it was cramped, functional – what she was expecting, really. Again, it looked like an airliner's galley. It looked a bit old-fashioned, to be honest – a bit *seventies*. Everything was battened down for launch. And everything was at a ninety-degree angle, of course, as the orbiter had its nose pointed up at the sky. The ship was designed for zero gravity, so there wasn't the rigid distinction between up and down that there was in every other aircraft ever built. They pulled themselves in using the handrails attached to every surface. The Doctor, with some difficulty, managed to shut the hatch and used the sonic suitcase to lock it, a task impossible from the inside without the device.

Debbie clambered towards the spare seats. On other missions, the mission specialists and scientists would sit here, strapped in for launch. This was only a four-man mission, and all the crew were

upstairs. The ladder to the flight deck was dead ahead, reminding her she couldn't make too much noise. The astronauts wouldn't get out of their seats now, not unless there was an emergency, but they were in radio contact with mission control, and could easily call security.

'The external hatch is sealed,' the Doctor told his radio.

'Roger that. Exit White Room, pad team.'

The Doctor wiggled his eyebrows to prompt Debbie. She squeezed the remote control. Outside, she could hear the elevator start its descent.

The Doctor checked his pocket watch, eventually reporting that they were clear of the gantry.

'Roger that.' The woman at Mission Control sounded a little confused – she hadn't seen them come out of the tower, but the instruments were telling her the hatch was closed, and they couldn't have locked themselves in.

The Doctor and Debbie grinned at each other. It wasn't over yet, but they were aboard, and, so far, no one had stopped them. The Doctor strapped Debbie into one of the spare seats. Underneath her technician's one-piece suit was another one – a simple pressure suit, like those that fighter pilots wore, bought by the Doctor over the phone at Heathrow, and waiting for them in Titusville. They wouldn't have helmets. If there was an emergency after launch, a loss of cabin pressure, anything like that, then they would be in serious trouble. There were, the Doctor claimed, ways to evacuate if necessary, but he didn't elaborate.

The Doctor strapped himself in, looking confident.

'How can you be so calm?' she whispered.

He just grinned and held his finger up to shush her.

All they could do now was wait.

For nearly two and a half hours.

A long time to wait as, above them, they could hear the astronauts making pre-flight checks. All around was the creaking and clanking of gantries being retracted, fuel being loaded. It wasn't long before Debbie wished she'd brought a book. After about an hour Debbie realised she'd nodded off for a moment. She admonished herself for not being as nervous or excited as she should be, but this was a bit like wearing a seat belt while being stuck in the waiting room at Stockport station.

The Doctor looked serene, which was astonishing in itself. Usually he was a fidgety, awkward passenger.

After a very long time there were some very final-sounding clanks from outside.

'Here we go,' the Doctor whispered.

The astronauts were talking again; little warning bleeps were going off all over the place up there. It was warm, a little dark. It was noisy, too – fans and pumps, like on an aircraft, but with no concession to the comfort of civilian passengers.

Debbie thought she heard someone upstairs say, 'T minus four.'

'That's the fuel purge,' the Doctor said under his breath. 'They've not found any malfunctions. Step by step, control of the shuttle is switching over to us instead of the ground.'

He was a little more tense now.

Then there was a bang, a long way away.

Debbie turned to the Doctor, who shook his head. 'Nothing to worry about,' he said. 'Just the opposite, in fact.'

The cabin was shuddering, just ever so slightly.

Activity upstairs, astronauts with raised voices.

Ignition.

Debbie felt the exact moment.

Then a sense of power, a sense of movement. She was pushed back into her seat, but not violently. They were moving. The shuttle was launching.

The cabin was starting to shake.

The noise.

It filled the room like choking smog. It prevented thoughts from forming, it...

She closed her eyes, lost in the moment. There was nothing else. To die like this... it didn't seem wrong. She felt safe, more safe than most of her time on Earth.

It sounded like bits of gravel or something were cascading down the outside of the shuttle. But that was nothing compared with the sound of the engines. The *roar* of the engines.

She was suddenly anxious again.

The Doctor was counting under his breath.

'Eight,' he said.

Eight? Eight seconds? Was that *all*? It felt like she had been here as long as she'd been married to Barry.

The whole shuttle lurched and rolled, like the Corkscrew at Alton Towers.

The Doctor was still calmly counting, 'Twelve.'

They were upside down.

They cruised for long seconds, hanging in their chairs as if they'd been strung up.

'Just about to break the sound barrier,' said the Doctor.

Somewhere, possibly, there was a sonic boom.

'This is the dangerous bit,' the Doctor said matter-of-factly. 'They're going for throttle up.'

Now even he was looking pale.

She was pushed back in her seat as there was another burst of speed. Just as she thought they couldn't go any faster, the speed increased again, incrementally.

There was a moment where she thought they'd died. Just for a second, as the Doctor's countdown, or countup, was somewhere in the one hundred and twenties, the rockets seemed to have died.

Then there was a *crump*, and the ride became much smoother.

'There go the SRBs,' the Doctor said, visibly relaxing. 'Mach four.'

Debbie tried to picture what had happened. The two 'little' side rockets (forty-five metres long, four metres in diameter) had been jettisoned. The big rocket was still there, powering them up into space.

It was a smooth climb. There was still a roar, but even that was dying away a little (as the air outside thinned? she wondered). She felt relaxed now. Not in control of the situation, not by any means, but she knew now that Florida policemen couldn't drag them away, that the engines weren't going to explode.

And she was in outer space.

Commander Fairchild ran through the procedures, not even having to think about them.

'OMS cut out, we are in orbit.'

A moment of elation and relief.

'What does OMS stand for?' an English woman's voice asked him.

'Orbital Manoeuvring Syst–'

Fairchild tried to jerk his head around. There were two of them, right behind Sawyer. A woman with short black hair and a man with light brown hair and blue eyes.

'What the – You're the technicians. How did –'

The man was staring out of the pilot's window at the Earth above

them. The soft blue light suffused the cabin. The weather over the equator was good for the time of year, but you could see the remnants of hurricanes, see the sea glittering in the evening light.

'Beautiful,' the man said.

'Who?' Beale asked helplessly.

'I'm the Doctor, this is Debbie.'

'Hello,' the woman said, holding on to the engineer's seat for dear life.

'We need a lift,' the Doctor said. 'Is that OK?'

'A lift?'

'A ride,' the Doctor clarified. 'What is it with you Americans and the word "lift"? We need a ride.'

Debbie looked out of the window.

All the clichés were true: from this height, there were no national boundaries, the grey of the cities merged into the landscape. There were signs of human endeavour – electric lights of the large cities, neat, square cultivated areas and canals breaking up the ground. Everything that had happened to the human race had happened down there, apart from the efforts of the astronauts.

And there was something unnatural about being up here, even the basics went against all her instincts. Moving in zero gravity was a bit like swimming, but without the purchase water gave you, or the resistance. If you pushed away from the side, you kept going until you hit something else – you had to grab on to the rails and pull yourself around.

The other astronauts managed it. The Doctor, of course, seemed perfectly at home.

'It's so strange, isn't it?'

The Doctor shook his head. 'No.'

Debbie should have known.

The Doctor wasn't smiling. Now they were up here, now they stood a real chance of finding Miranda, some of the pent-up anger and frustration was starting to surface.

Debbie decided to leave him alone for a moment or two and turned her attention to the front of the cabin, where the commander and pilot were in negotiations with Houston. Their presence was a *fait accompli*. Debbie and the Doctor had submitted to a search, the astronauts had checked the cabin. They'd found the sonic suitcase, but

not the guns and Semtex they'd expected to find. The Doctor had explained why he was here, and with all the fervour (and persuasiveness) of a man recently rereleased into the community, had shown them his tiny collection of broken alien artefacts.

NASA and the shuttle crew seemed to have agreed that the Doctor and Debbie weren't dangerous – they didn't represent an immediate physical threat to *Atlantis*, and they weren't on a suicide mission.

Mather and Sawyer were watching over them. The crew were keeping them on the flight deck, where they could see them. Strapped in their seats, but not tied up. Kim Sawyer was blonde, Mather was a black man, the oldest man on board, and had a bearing and a discipline about him that went above and beyond even his colleagues. A military man, Debbie guessed.

'They're taking a long time,' Debbie whispered.

'This is an unusual situation for them,' the Doctor told her. 'It's going to take them a while to work out what they have to do. NASA mission planners go through every scenario. I wouldn't be surprised if there's some protocol about stowaways.'

'What if that's to turn around and go straight home?'

The Doctor considered that. 'It's possible. They have an AOA option – Abort Once Around. One orbit of the Earth, then back home. But this mission's been planned for years; it's cost a fortune. They won't throw that away unless they have to.'

'You two: quiet.'

'No need to raise your voice, Commander Fairchild,' the Doctor said sweetly.

'You're in serious trouble. I don't know who you are or –'

The radio crackled. '*Atlantis*. This Doctor's a British businessman. He's mentioned in *Time* magazine this month. Well... more than that, he's one of their Top Fifty People of the Decade. Deborah Gordon is his girlfriend. Stand by.'

Debbie giggled. 'Don't believe everything you read in the papers,' she advised.

'This some sort of stunt?' the commander asked. 'A publicity gimmick?'

'No,' the Doctor said, deadly serious. He checked his pocket watch. 'Look at that – even works in zero gravity. Superb craftsmanship.'

Debbie knew what was coming next. She peered out of the window, checked the horizon.

They all saw it at the same time.

'What is it?' the pilot asked.

'A spaceship,' Debbie told them.

It was. It was hanging just over the horizon.

The Doctor leaned forward in his seat.

'Houston. This is *Atlantis*. Code Bluerose.' The commander was flicking switches on the comms panel.

'Roger that, *Atlantis*. Describe the UO, please.'

'It's the shape of an hourglass. It's big... er.'

'Four kilometres long, I'd say,' the Doctor estimated.

Everyone in the cabin was looking at him.

The commander took a deep breath then said, 'It's not terrestrial, repeat this is not terrestrial.'

The Doctor was shaking his head. 'It's what we came here for,' he told them.

'You're UFO nuts?' the mission specialist asked.

The Doctor jabbed his finger towards the window. 'There's a time and a place for scepticism. This is not it.'

The ship was already getting larger. It was metal – not the smooth, shiny metal of the saucers, but a patchwork of copper, gold and bronze.

There were half a dozen saucers attached to its rear section. They gave the thing a sense of scale – Debbie knew that those saucers were the size of a large house but here they looked like barnacles on the side of an ocean liner. All over the big ship were towers, spires and other protuberances that gave the impression that a city had been built on the surface of the original vessel.

'It's coming towards us,' Debbie suggested.

'It's not showing up on radar,' the pilot said.

'It wouldn't,' the Doctor informed them. 'But no, *we're* going towards *it*. It's in geostationary orbit above India. Change to an intercept course.'

'Hell, no. I'm the commander here.'

The argument continued, but Debbie wasn't listening. It just wasn't important. Only the alien ship was. Features were becoming more obvious as they got nearer. One end was glowing blue – an engine? The other seemed to be glass – almost like windows in an office block. There was a trench running from bow to stern, full of turrets and what looked like missile tubes. It was like a medieval fortress, Dracula's castle.

'*Atlantis*. This is Houston. Mission objectives changed at three twelve Zulu to Bluerose Protocols. We're switching mission control to the top floor. Please advise your crew.'

'Roger that.' The commander turned to look back. 'For over twenty years, the United Nations have been aware that extraterrestrial life forms exist.'

He let that one sink in. Even with only five other people in the room, reactions ranged from 'I knew it' to 'Impossible'. Debbie glanced over at the Doctor, who was listening intently.

'There are established protocols to deal with these situations, first drawn up in the Brookings Report in 1961. I'll familiarise you with those in a moment. Rest assured, there's a procedure to follow here.'

The Doctor snorted a laugh.

Fairchild ignored him. 'Our mission is to investigate the UO. Doctor, Ms Gordon, you clearly have some knowledge of this situation. Bring us up to date.'

Chapter Twenty-four
Home is Where the Hearts Are

Miranda looked up to find Cate offering her a silk handkerchief.

'I'm sorry,' she said. 'I don't mean to cry.'

'You are a long way from home,' Cate said. 'Of course you are crying.'

It was the nearest the woman had got to expressing sympathy. Miranda still reckoned the Deputy controlled her emotions, bottled them up like Mr Spock. She wasn't like Commander Data, who didn't have them in the first place.

She also strongly suspected that the real universe didn't work like *Star Trek*.

Miranda sighed. 'Am I a long way from home?' she asked. 'Or is your galaxy my home and I'm just going back?'

'I couldn't say, Lady Miranda.'

The door slid open and Ferran stepped through, unannounced.

'It is time to continue the tour of the ship,' he told Miranda. They had talked about it before, as they'd walked back from the flight deck. 'We will start at the mapping room.'

Miranda wiped the last tear from her eye and stood, tugging her tunic into shape. 'I'm ready.'

Ferran turned and left, and Miranda strode out after him. Once again, the Deputy followed a few steps behind them.

'The ship is four kilometres long. I can walk that far, how about you?'

Ferran was already sweating. 'There are travel tubes.'

The nearest was directly opposite the door to her room. The normal doors were roughly rectangular (although a little wider at the bottom), but the travel-tube door was circular, and they had to step over a ledge to get in. Once inside, Miranda looked around what resembled a futuristic London Tube carriage, except without windows or anything else to break the monotony of the smooth copper walls. Ferran touched a control and the door hissed shut behind them and the carriage started moving.

The whole process was silent, and it was difficult to judge the speed. The ride was very smooth – smoother than standing in a lift, for example.

Ferran kept his eye on Miranda the whole time. He was on edge. Was he expecting her to pounce on him, or something? Or was he about to pounce on her?

Miranda was beginning to *feel* again – her emotions were slowly returning, as if her batteries were recharging. At first she'd only felt numb, but she was getting angry now. She'd beaten Ferran last time, she reminded herself. She'd killed his last Deputy. He was on home ground, now, but that just meant he would be getting complacent. She could defeat him.

'Why?' she asked. 'Why did you come back for me?'

'Because I love you,' he said, his voice dripping with sarcasm.

'And the real reason? It's because I'm the heir to the throne, isn't it? You want to marry me and become Emperor.'

'Nominally,' Cate began, 'in some quarters at least, you're the heir to the throne. Constitutionally, you're the Empress of the entire universe.'

Despite the absurdity of it all, and knowing that she'd done nothing to deserve the honour, a part of Miranda felt very proud of that. In practice, of course, she'd barely held the under-seventeens swimming team together in the face of competition from exams and boys, so the chances of her keeping a galactic empire united seemed fairly remote.

Ferran laughed. 'We fought a war to rid the universe of your family and their rule. There might be a few royalists out there, but I doubt it. No one was sorry to see your kind go. If I want to impose my authority, then this ship will be far more effective than your hereditary claims. But those matter to some people. I will marry you, to demonstrate my ownership of you, and your titles, nothing more.'

'How do you feel about that?' Miranda asked the Deputy. It was easier to ask the question than answer it for herself.

Ferran turned and stroked his Deputy's face. 'She has no feelings one way or the other, do you, my dear? She obeys me. A job she does exceptionally well. Besides, she knows that marriage to you will be very little more than symbolic.'

'You treat her like an object,' Miranda noted.

'She is.'

'She's a human being.'

'She most certainly is not.'

'She's a… person.'

'You don't recognise her, do you? Look at her. Let her take a good look, Cate, my dear.'

Cate stood still.

Miranda looked into the face. The blue eyes. She was in her mid-thirties... but there was something about her face. Ever since she'd first seen the Deputy something about her had bothered Miranda.

'"Cate" is short for "duplicate",' Ferran explained. 'She's what you would call an android.'

Miranda took a step back, instinctively. Cate just didn't look like an android, a *built* thing – there was no hint of it. She hadn't even suspected that the Deputy was anything other than a person. Not a human being, but human-like, as she and Ferran were, a creature of flesh and blood.

Miranda glanced back at Ferran, who was still grinning at her. He hadn't told her everything yet.

Miranda looked into Cate's face again, then she realised. 'A duplicate of me.'

Ferran was grinning from ear to ear. 'If you can't have the original, you have to settle for the next best thing.'

'She's a clone of me?'

Ferran shook his head. 'Not quite. You don't need to know the exact process used. She looks like you, that's all. A physical duplicate, not a mental one. She doesn't have your mind: she just has a computer.' He reached over, stroked Cate. 'Her body is an almost exact copy of yours, though... or it was, before it aged. Copied from surveillance images I took of you on my last visit to this time zone. Isn't that right, Deputy?'

Miranda looked at the woman, whose face hadn't so much as flickered.

'Yes, Prefect,' Cate said flatly. Cate's voice wasn't the same as Miranda's – the accent was different. Well, it would be – Cate hadn't been brought up in Greyfrith.

'You are sentient? Intelligent? I mean... not just programmed to follow certain orders and answer certain questions?'

Ferran laughed, but Miranda ignored him.

The Deputy nodded. 'My positronic brain contains over ten million micro-relays. In human terms, I am above super-genius level.'

'Aren't we all?' Miranda chuckled. She cast a disparaging glance over at Ferran. 'Well – most of us are.'

Cate's mouth flickered a little, Miranda was sure of it.

'You have Cate. So why do you need me?' Miranda said.

'I need full access to the restricted areas of the Librarinth.'

Miranda shrugged. 'I'm not sure how I can help you. I've got a school-library card, if that's any use. But not *with* me.'

'The Librarinth is in... a rather unique location. The Needle. It's a very large structure with a black hole at one end. One of the last surviving artefacts of your people's technology. There are cities on its surface. And the Librarinth is the largest of those cities, the repository of all surviving knowledge and art from the time before your father's reign. Every secret in the universe is kept there.'

'You must know this is the first I've heard about this place. How can I possibly help you?'

'Only the leader of a race can access their race's secrets. You are that person, by default. The guardians of that place will recognise your authority. You will extract the technological secrets of your forefathers – I shall use them to impose my will, as they did theirs.'

The carriage had drawn to a halt.

Miranda had been keeping count. The journey had taken about two minutes. So they had been travelling at about seventy-five miles an hour, she calculated.

'Why don't you just teleport everywhere?' she asked. 'You have the technology, so why use travel tubes?'

'Teleport?' Ferran asked, mulling over the word. 'Oh, you mean *transmat*? It's a costly process, and like all forms of transport it has its risks. Humanity in the twentieth century has jet aircraft, but they don't use them to commute to work.'

Miranda nodded.

The door hissed open.

They were in a small communal chamber. Cate had been here many times before as the mapping operation had progressed. There were desks set up, and they had glowing maps and plans laid out on them. Cate glanced over at Miranda. The young woman was feigning nonchalance as she studied the displays, memorised them.

'This is the mapping room,' Ferran explained. 'We are exploring the ship in teams. Teams of slaves at first – expendable men, in case there is anything dangerous. Once that's done, soldiers are sent in for a proper survey.'

'No one is expendable,' Miranda said. Cate almost gasped at the audacity of the statement. The caste system must have been evident to Miranda just from this room – the guards wore black coveralls, the

slaves wore grey tunics. There were others, their clothing less uniform – engineers, technicians. How could she not see these divisions?

One man was standing on his own, the others not quite daring to stand close to him. A subcommander, wearing the emblems of rank, and a cap instead of the full helmet his troops would be wearing.

The others in the room kept their heads down, tried to look busy. Miranda was watching the scene, looking puzzled.

'Report,' Ferran barked.

'Two members of the mapping team have vanished. Slaves. Their names are Graltor and Tarvin and they were –'

'I don't need their life stories. They have removed their tracking discs? How is this possible?'

The Deputy cleared her throat. 'Tarvin is a con man, sir, a thief. He could well have the necessary skill.'

Ferran turned to the subcommander. 'You knew this man's history?'

'Sir, I didn't think he'd be able to –'

Ferran had pulled something from his belt – something too thin to be a cosh, something that looked more like a wand.

'Sir, I beg you, please –'

Ferran pointed the wand at the subcommander's head. There was a low hum.

The man backed away, clutching his head, screaming.

'What are you doing?' Miranda yelled.

'Simple pain induction,' Ferran said. 'It keeps my subjects in line. They all have receivers.'

'Stop it!' Miranda insisted.

Cate stood very still.

Ferran glared at Miranda. The slaves and the technicians were clearly shocked to see the Prefect's authority challenged. Cate wasn't sure how Ferran would react – and, to judge by the Prefect's face, Ferran was unsure himself.

Ferran lowered the wand. 'Subcommander, find them in the next hour.' Then he turned to Miranda. 'Come with me,' he said.

Ferran said nothing on the journey back to Miranda's room. He hadn't needed to say anything to make it clear that their tour was over. Miranda faced him all the way back, her arms crossed over her chest. She'd challenged him to justify what he had done. His silence had just seemed to make her more and more angry.

Cate remained silent, knowing it was best not to intervene.

They arrived back at Miranda's room. The Deputy followed them into Miranda's chamber, and made sure the door was closed before Ferran spoke.

'The strong prey on the weak. It is the natural order,' Ferran explained, impatience in his voice.

'It most certainly is not,' Miranda said. Cate was surprised to hear such anger and defiance. Despite herself, Cate found herself siding with Miranda. But the Last One was stating what ought to be the case, not how the universe truly worked.

Ferran glared down at her. 'You are not a leader, you never have been.'

'True leaders don't rely on punishment. They lead by example, they reward success.'

'In this primitive, compliant age perhaps. Not in mine.'

Ferran turned to Cate.

'Kneel,' he ordered.

She did, without hesitation.

'You would have me lead by example?' Ferran spat. 'Have me kneel down before she did, to show her how it is done? Or have me throw her some food to thank her for doing it?'

'I wouldn't have her kneel at all.'

Cate looked up at the young woman, but Miranda was staring over her at Ferran himself. Cate lowered her head again.

'I feed her,' Ferran said. 'I give her clothes, I give her food and shelter. I protect her from those who would destroy our kind. She benefits from the achievements of the scientists and engineers I employ, she enjoys the arts of which I am a patron.'

Cate's head stayed bowed.

'She is a human being.'

Ferran laughed. 'No, she is not.'

Miranda glared at him. 'You know what I mean. She's a person. She has rights. Stand up, Cate.'

The Deputy remained on her knees.

Ferran smiled. 'She has only that which I grant her.'

'It's not fair,' Miranda said, surprised how upset she was that Cate wouldn't stand. 'There's no justice here.'

Ferran shook his head. 'There is law. The law of the strong. We have our obligations, too – we look after our subjects, if they remain loyal.

People demand strong leadership. This is the natural order of things. My family fought for and won their lands and titles.'

'But you didn't,' Miranda said. 'There's a story from Earth. A working man is caught poaching in the wood by the owner of a great stately home. "What gives you the right to steal the game from my land?" the lord asks. "What makes it your land?" the worker asks. "My ancestors fought for it," the lord says. The working man puts his fists up and says, "OK then, let's fight for it."'

'Then what happened?' Ferran asked.

Miranda sighed. 'It's a story. An allegory. A reminder that the status quo hasn't always been the status quo, that true leadership is not simply conferred on whoever owns the most property.'

Ferran shrugged his shoulders. 'Deputy, fight me. Win, and you get my title and all that that confers.'

Cate looked up. 'My Lord?'

'No conditions. This isn't a trick. Win the fight and you'll be the Prefect.'

Cate looked between him and Miranda, but stayed down on her knees.

'You see?' Ferran said, faintly disappointed. 'When she was created, I knew she would spend a great deal of time alone with me. I toyed with the idea of placing a limiter in her brain, a device that would prevent her from trying to assassinate me. In the end, I decided not to – I command loyalty. It hasn't even occurred to this *property* to try to hurt me. I am her master.'

Miranda's eyes flashed at Cate. *Try it.*

Somewhere, in among the micro-relays and neuronitecture of her brain, Cate found herself agreeing.

And the Deputy leapt at Ferran, hands out like talons.

Ferran batted her out of the way, kicked her in the stomach. While he did that, he reached to his belt.

He took the wand from it, pointed it at Cate and pressed a control. The Deputy collapsed on the floor, doubled up, clutching her head. She kept her mouth closed, trying so hard not to scream.

She couldn't think, she couldn't think, she couldn't think. It was the only thing her mind was telling her, an endless loop of the same error message.

'You've made your point, now stop it,' Miranda demanded.

'She likes it.'

Cate cried out, finally.

'She tried to depose the Prefect,' Ferran said. 'A traitor deserves to die, not just suffer.'

Cate looked up to see Miranda looking down, unsure what to do. Then the girl tried to grab the control from Ferran. He pulled it up out of her reach. Cate watched them, unable to do anything more.

There was a chime, then a voice. 'Prefect, this is the flight deck. Computer is reporting a development.'

Ferran started towards the door, stepping over his Deputy as he went. As the door opened, he turned back to look at Miranda and tossed the wand at her.

'Use it wisely,' he advised.

The door slid up.

Miranda quickly found how to turn the device off.

Cate lay there for a moment, trying to get her breath back.

Miranda leaned over her, tried to comfort her, but Cate shrugged her away. 'I deserved it,' she said.

'No one deserves that,' Miranda said. 'Have you really never even thought about hurting him before?'

Cate shook her head. 'I do only what he commands.'

Miranda hugged her. 'We have to get out of here,' she said. 'If Ferran wants a fight, then he can fight me.'

Cate shook her head. 'Fight *us*,' she said. 'He will have to fight *us*. I can get you to a saucer, return you to your father.'

Miranda hesitated. 'I can't fly a spaceship.'

'You wouldn't need to: one pilot can. I can. I could come with you.' There was a tremble in her voice that undercut the defiance she was trying to convey.

'But Ferran would come after us.'

Cate was happy to lie there, debating the point – it gave her a chance to get her breath back. 'No. You heard what he said – there are no records of you. He wouldn't know where to look for you.'

'But he has those records of Dad. I couldn't go home without showing up on those.'

'Perhaps they were faked.'

'Or perhaps he destroys the saucer to prevent us from landing.'

'He would kill me, but he wouldn't kill you. He needs you alive.'

Cate was surprised to see that Miranda was starting to cry.

'I want to see my father more than anything else at the moment,' she

said, voice full of anger. 'I want to go back to my bedroom. I want to walk round the garden and touch that reassuring, stupid police box. Take me home.'

'What is it?' Ferran asked as he came on to the flight deck.

'A human space craft has been detected. Its markings indicate that it is *Atlantis*, a vehicle belonging to the National Aeronautical and Space Administration of the United States of America,' Computer said, without emotion. 'It is on a powered intercept course.'

A hologram appeared in a bubble underneath the apex of Computer's pyramid. It was a primitive thing. Aerodynamic, with rocket engines.

'Weapons?'

'None detected.'

'Force fields?' Ferran asked as he stepped down into the centre of the room.

'None detected. The airframe is stressed aluminium, the cargo doors are graphite and epoxy resin, the outer skin is coated felt.'

If Ferran didn't know, he would have asked if Computer was joking. He couldn't help but laugh.

'Crew?'

'Detectors register six life signs.'

'Is it signalling us?'

'No.'

'Do we have a targeting solution?'

'Yes.'

Crosshairs appeared on the hologram.

Ferran stepped over to one of the control seats. The pilot moved his hand out of the way of the weapons panel.

Ferran reached for the firing control.

'Radio signal from the Earth craft.'

'Ferran? Ferran – I know it's you.'

Ferran's eyes narrowed.

'Voice-pattern recognition,' Computer reported. 'The voice is that of –'

'I know who it is,' Ferran snapped, moving round to the communications panel. The officer handed him a microphone. 'Doctor,' he continued. 'Show me his face.'

The screen rippled and became a close-up of the Doctor's head. He

showed no signs of ageing, he looked just as he had at their last encounter.

'Hello, there,' he said. 'I've come for my daughter.'

'You haven't a hope, Doctor. *Supremacy* is the most advanced ship in the universe, even in my time. Computer, calculate the odds of the Doctor's attack on *Supremacy* succeeding.'

'There is no possibility of an attack succeeding,' Computer intoned. 'If *Atlantis* were to ram the ship at maximum attainable speed it would not breach the defence cloak.'

'And if you were to attack me?' the Doctor asked.

Computer didn't respond.

'Answer the Doctor's question,' Ferran told it.

'One shot from any of our weapons systems will destroy *Atlantis*. If *Atlantis* merely collided with our defence screens there would be a major hull breach on the human craft and it would be rendered inoperative.'

There was a moment's hesitation from the Doctor.

'Gosh, how impressive,' he said finally. 'And a voice-activated computer, too. Keyed to your voice patterns and only your voice patterns?'

'That's right.'

The Doctor's face beamed. 'How marvellous.'

'I have you in my sights. Do you have any last words?'

'Actually, yes, I do. Computer,' the Doctor said, imitating Ferran's voice precisely, 'deactivate all ship defences and all systems not essential for the support of life for twenty minutes. This order cannot be countermanded.'

'I obey,' Computer said, before shutting itself down along with the rest of the ship.

The lights all over the surface of Ferran's ship dimmed right down.

The Doctor threw his head back and laughed. 'Typical master criminal: loves the sound of his own voice.'

'That's a quote from *Blackadder*, isn't it?' Debbie asked.

The Doctor grinned. 'No, not really. This is a different thing: it's spontaneous and it's called wit.' He checked his pocket watch. 'Commander, we have nineteen and a quarter minutes left. I suggest we take advantage of them.'

The commander nodded over to the pilot. 'Commence landing sequence.'

There were clanks, an unwelcome sense of movement as retro rockets fired. The space shuttle drifted into the hangar bay of the alien craft. There was emergency lighting on, signs of activity. But no guards, not yet.

'Undercarriage down,' the pilot reported.

'Clear for landing,' the commander acknowledged. Then, like a light being turned on, there was gravity. *Atlantis* lurched a little as the undercarriage took the weight. Strapped into their seats, they were no more shaken than they would be by the lurch as a train comes into a station. Going from nought to eleven stone took the breath from Debbie for a moment, though.

The crew began flicking switches, shutting the ship down. A well-rehearsed routine, Debbie assumed.

The Doctor was already out of his seat, seemingly untroubled by the return to gravity.

'We will stay here and get ready for a quick getaway,' the commander told him, beginning to unstrap himself. 'Mather is going with you.'

The Doctor was waving his hands at them. 'That isn't necessary, I –'

'You don't have time to argue. Doctor: you need a combat specialist, and Mather is a member of Delta Force.'

'That's like the SAS, isn't it?' Debbie asked, dim memories of Barry's military magazines coming back. 'What are you doing in space?'

'That's classified,' Mather said, curtly.

'He's launching a military satellite,' the Doctor said. 'A prototype deuterium-fluorine laser weapon connected with an SDI programme the American public thinks has been cancelled.'

The commander and Mather looked at each other and then at the Doctor.

'I saw your mission objectives,' he explained.

'A laser? Could we use it against Ferran?' Debbie asked.

The Doctor gave a sly laugh. 'No, won't work properly.'

'That's what we came up here to test,' Mather said curtly.

'Oh, any fool can see the mirror on it's all wrong. You should have asked me before you launched it off into space – you'd have saved yourself some money. Eighteen minutes. Are you coming or not?'

Chapter Twenty-five
Power to the People

Cate sat silently opposite Miranda, staring ahead.

Miranda wondered what thoughts were going through the woman's head. It was clear that whatever a 'micro-relay' was and however many Cate had in her head, the effect was to create something indistinguishable from the workings of an organic brain. Miranda found it easier to understand Cate's thought processes than those of Ferran.

They were the only two passengers in the travel tube. The hangars were about halfway along the ship, so the journey should take only a couple of minutes. Those minutes were a long time coming.

'Ferran has the interests of his people at heart,' Cate insisted.

Miranda must have had the oddest expression on her face, because Cate immediately followed it up with, 'He wants to keep the Empire together; he wants to maintain the rule of law.'

'He just said he *was* the law,' Miranda reminded her. 'He tortured you, abused you. He treats you like his property.'

'There is no other way. Think about it, Miranda – think of the difficulties there are of maintaining such a vast empire. Do you know how much power is needed for intergalactic travel? Even using dimension drives, it needs the rarest fuel sources, the most skilled technicians.'

'Perhaps the Empire is too large, then.'

'You would split it up, break it down into administrative areas? A recipe for rivalry and conflict. Above all, there must be one leader, one authority.'

'Or no leaders at all,' Miranda said. 'Do you know what *gramdan* is?'

'No.'

'I've just been to India. It's a scheme that Gandhi thought up.'

'Those names mean nothing to me.'

'No, I'm sure they don't. But their ideas – perhaps you don't need an empire at all. You need local communities, ones that run themselves. India's a large country, with all sorts of religions and races, but it's also a democracy. It's not perfect. But nowhere is, I don't think.'

Cate watched her carefully.

Was she doing the right thing? Miranda wondered what she could do other than escape – find a self-destruct mechanism, go after Ferran himself? She'd run through a couple of scenarios, but couldn't see how she could do anything constructive here. It wasn't heroic to run away and leave Ferran to it, preferring to go home and forget all about it. Was it really that cowardly to calculate the odds of survival and realise that she stood no chance against a legion of soldiers?

About eighty seconds into the journey, the lights dimmed, then the tube slowed and stopped.

'What's going on?' Miranda asked.

'I don't know,' Cate confessed.

'They're on to us.'

Miranda tensed. She would go down fighting, take a few of them with her. She got ready, pumping adrenaline into her system, clearing her mind, prioritising her visual acuity and reflexes.

Beside her, Cate was doing the same. She had the same body, of course, an older version, but one that was at least as well honed. Cate was combat-trained. Miranda was, or at least liked to think herself as, merely a talented amateur.

The door of the travel tube slid down, but there wasn't a squad of guards waiting for them on the other side. There was nothing, just an empty corridor. The lights here were also dim.

'Where are we?' Miranda's voice echoed off the metal walls and pipelines. She felt a little disappointed. An empty corridor was an anticlimax.

Cate shrugged. 'This looks like a service area, right in the middle of the ship. We may be the first crew to come here. If there was a problem with the tubes, it may have dropped us off here. This is an uncharted area.'

Pilot Mordak watched as Prefect Ferran lurched through the gloom towards him.

The only source of light was the scanner, the image frozen where it had been when the systems had shut down. The Doctor's face, staring down at them, eyes wild, his face split by a broad grin. The pilot had heard legends of the Doctor – everyone had: how he'd destroyed planets, how he'd wiped out whole intelligent species, how he'd brought darkness to the universe, how he travelled through time

wiping out his enemies and turning those he abducted into monsters and terrorists.

The Doctor had killed the Prefect's father, single-handedly wiping out a saucer and its crew of elite troops and hunters. Even Sallak hadn't returned from that encounter.

'We have emergency lighting,' Mordak said, pulling himself away from the image, trying to stay calm. 'Gravity, life support, limited travel-tube use. The medical units are active. We have use of some internal communications – emergency channels, alarm systems and the like.'

'Computer!' the Prefect shouted. 'Computer!'

'It's offline, sir. There –' Mordak pointed at the display that was counting down the minutes until Computer reactivated itself.

'Turn it back on.'

'It's impossible. All the security measures you insisted upon are working.'

The Prefect flung the man out of his chair and took his place. Mordak watched nervously as his master looked over the consoles, but after a moment's work it was clear that the pilot had been right.

The Prefect slumped forward, his head in his hands.

'The human spacecraft has landed in the hangar deck, sir. Should we dispatch security teams there and to the Last One's quarters?' Mordak realised he didn't know whether the communications circuits were counted as 'essential'. All sorts of systems could be down – even the doors may be stuck.

The Prefect sat immobile.

'My Lord, we have to react to this problem.'

Ferran looked up at Mordak, fire in his eyes. The pilot had thought he was a broken man, but –

'I hate him,' he said simply.

The Pilot stood, ignored the crewmen scurrying around trying to find some power for their consoles.

'He and I are two sides of the same coin. We are equals and opposites. I am everything he is not, I have everything he wants but can never have. It is fate that we should meet here for a final confrontation. This is destiny.'

'You are talking about the Doctor,' Mordak reminded him. 'Even in this time zone he is a powerful adversary, not to be underestimated.'

Ferran looked him square in the eye. 'That was the mistake I made last time. I thought I could snatch his daughter away, that he would be

powerless. But he is here, he's disabled my ship against all the odds. He has come to reclaim his daughter, and I must stop him. Oh, this is almost *mythic*.'

'I will dispatch guards to the hangar. They will kill him.'

Ferran looked around. 'No. I must face him. Face him alone. Ready my armour.'

The pilot hesitated.

'You heard me! Let the Doctor go where he will. I'll track him down and I'll tear those two hearts from his chest.'

'This is too easy,' Debbie warned.

The hangar bay was empty. They'd been able to leave the shuttle and cross the deck without impediment. Mather had come with them. The others had stayed behind, keeping the shuttle ready for a quick escape.

'I have to agree,' the astronaut said. 'Why aren't the guards all over *Atlantis* by now?'

The Doctor scowled and waved his hand at them. 'Don't knock a bit of luck. This is a big ship – they might be at the other end of it. They must have some sort of internal transport, and that won't be working.'

The Doctor had found a computer terminal. He'd pulled a grey box from his pocket and connected it up to the console with a length of black wire.

'And I know for a fact,' Mather continued, 'that you won't be able to access an alien computer using a Psion organiser.'

The Doctor held up the little grey box, showed him that the LCD screen was flickering with alien symbols.

'I've had almost ten years to decipher this technology,' the Doctor explained. 'I know more about this lot's software and wetware than even they do.'

'Wetware?' Debbie asked.

'I'll explain later.'

'What are you doing?'

'This is a big ship. We need to know where we are going.'

The liquid-crystal display resolved into a deck plan.

The Doctor peered at it, scrolled the picture up and across.

'Come on: according to this, Miranda's cell is a long way off, but the route there seems simple enough.'

* * *

Cate peered down a service corridor that went on as far as the eye could see. It looked like it ran straight, parallel to the travel tube, quite possibly from one end of the ship to the other. There was no sign of activity, no indication which way led back to the living quarters and which led on to the engine rooms.

The light was poor, provided by tiny triangular boxes set into the walls every ten metres or so. The walls were lined with pipes, vents and ducts. The floor was a metal grid, with a trough running along the far wall.

'Which way?' Miranda asked. She had a new determination now, a new focus. She was looking for a way out, refusing to be scared, or to give up.

The Deputy shrugged. 'I have never been to this place.' She hesitated, looking into the shadowy depths. 'Possibly no one has.'

Miranda sighed, refusing to be superstitious. 'Someone built this.'

There was a clank, a hundred metres or so to their left.

'Machinery,' Miranda assured Cate. 'It's probab–'

Something clamped itself over Cate's mouth.

Her first thought was that a piece of piping had come loose and entangled itself round her.

But this was warm, smelled of meat. It was a hand. A large one.

Another hand had snaked around her waist and she was being lifted off her feet.

As she was pitched round, she saw Miranda being menaced by a small man with a length of pipe.

'Graltor!' Cate managed to cry out through the gaps in the big fingers. She stopped struggling.

After a moment, she was lowered back to the metal deck and released. She turned to look at her attacker – as she suspected, it was the larger man.

The small man had stopped menacing Miranda. She looked him up and down. 'So you must be Tarvin?'

The men glanced at each other.

'You know us?'

'We know you're escaped slaves. We're not armed.'

Graltor was stocky, built like a wrestler. And he was huge – hands the size of dinner plates.

Tarvin was a far smaller man. 'Graltor's from a high-gravity planet,' he explained. 'He's the runt of the family. But that's by the bye. The

important question is: who are you?'

'Don't you recognise me?' Miranda asked.

The thief scowled. 'Of course I do, I just wanted to see if you'd admit it. You're Miranda,' he said sceptically. 'You're the Last One.'

Miranda nodded. 'I was taken to Earth when I was a baby. I don't remember any of my parents' crimes. I'm... sorry if they hurt you. I'm sorry for what they did.'

Tarvin was clearly taken aback. 'She doesn't sound like Ferran or any of the other Senators.'

The giant was scratching his chin. 'What are you doing here? Is this your mother or something?'

'Her mother was the Empress, stupid,' Tarvin chided. He looked at Cate warily. 'Elder sister?'

'If she was her elder sister, then the Last One wouldn't be the Last One, would she, *stupid*?' Graltor grunted.

'I'd be the Last *But* One.' Miranda giggled.

Graltor chortled.

Cate moved a little closer to Miranda. These two clearly didn't recognise her as the Deputy, and telling them she was Ferran's right-hand woman didn't seem wise.

'She was helping me to escape,' Miranda said.

'Escape where?'

Miranda was reaching a decision. 'Cate can fly one of the saucers, escape the ship and get us to Earth. And you can come with us.'

Mordak was struggling with the shoulder straps of Ferran's armour. He could sense that the Prefect was growing impatient. Finally, everything was in place. Ferran looked at his hologram, flexed his fingers, then began heading for the door.

One of the scientists intercepted him and pressed a control box into his hand.

'What is this?' the Prefect demanded.

'It allows you to access some of the deactivated systems. In theory, any device within about five paces should operate for you.'

Ferran was impressed. 'You've come up with this since the systems went down?'

The scientist nodded.

Ferran slapped him on the shoulder. 'We shall discuss your reward for this when I return.'

Ferran stepped through the doorway and the door swished closed behind him.

The scientist looked insufferably smug.

'You should have discussed it now,' Mordak noted. 'He's going up against the Doctor.'

That wiped the scientist's grin off him.

Mather had known there was something wrong – he'd said it, right when they were back in the hangar.

'The guards are keeping away from us,' he repeated.

The Doctor shook his head. 'Why would they do that?'

The corridors were lit with emergency lighting only. They'd come across some of the aliens on their journey. Mather noted that they looked just like people – women in long grey skirts, small men in functional tunics. Every so often there would be a robot of some kind: things that looked like automated street cleaners' carts, smaller ones, too, that looked like tarantulas with tools and implements on the end of each leg.

But no guards.

This was a warship. That was clear just from looking at the exterior of it. And everything the Doctor and Debbie had told Mather about these people led him to expect the inside of the Death Star, or at least the starship *Enterprise*. Where were the guards?

He hesitated for a moment, watched the Doctor and Debbie hurry along.

And a transparent screen slid down, cutting him off.

'Hey!' he called, banging his fists on it.

The Doctor and Debbie turned, then hurried back. So the door wasn't soundproof.

'I'll try to get it open,' the Doctor promised.

Debbie was running her hands around the edges. 'It's very thin material.'

It was: barely a millimetre thick – but pushing against it had no effect: it hadn't budged.

The Doctor was down on one knee, opening up his briefcase. 'I'll use the sonic suitcase,' he told them, playing around with some instrument wedged into one side of it.

There was a high-pitched squeal. The Doctor smiled, looked up at the door, then frowned when it remained obstinately closed.

Then the squeal became higher still.

'Get back!' Debbie warned, pulling him away.

The thing in the suitcase exploded, showering the corridor with sparks.

The Doctor blinked. 'A deliberate feedback loop,' he said. 'Ferran must have anticipated that I'd use it.'

Mather pressed himself against the screen. 'I thought the power was off.'

'They might have found an override.' The Doctor looked around. 'Get back to the shuttle, Mather, I don't think we can open this.'

'Then how will you get back?'

The Doctor shrugged. 'I'll find a way round.'

Mather thought about it for a moment. 'Agreed,' he said.

The hangars could be only about a ten- or fifteen-minute walk away – Cate and Miranda agreed on that. Graltor and Tarvin were flagging a bit – they'd been on the run for several hours, and were worn out.

Cate took the opportunity to whisper a few words to Miranda. 'We can't take them with us, they're slaves.'

'You're all slaves,' Miranda said sharply.

Cate was shocked, and then surprised just how shocked she was. 'I'm the Deputy of a galactic –'

'You're a slave. I'm freeing you, I'll free them. I only wish I could free everyone else.' There was little warmth in Miranda's voice now.

'I am not a slave.'

'You are.'

'No.'

'I can prove you are.' Miranda took the pain inducer from her belt and pointed it at Cate, and pressed the button.

Cate flinched, then realised it wasn't working.

Miranda looked baffled, and passed the wand over. 'Is it being blocked by the walls?'

Cate tried to puzzle that out as Graltor and Tarvin caught up with them. She handed it back to Miranda.

'Did I just see what I thought I just saw?' Tarvin asked.

Miranda nodded.

'Do you want to hurt us?' Graltor objected.

Miranda tossed the wand at him. 'No. And I don't think I could if I did want to.'

Graltor was too slow to stop Tarvin from catching it.

'The wand works,' he said. 'The light's coming on, look. It must be the receivers that are damaged.'

Cate took it from Tarvin's hand, pointed it at him and pressed – but nothing happened. 'It draws its power from the ship's generators.'

Miranda looked around. 'And if the travel tubes and the lights aren't working properly... Ferran's men don't carry guns, do they?'

The Deputy shook her head and held the wand up. 'He doesn't trust them to – they have these, that's all. There are weapons, but they are locked in the armouries. Only Computer can open them, and only with Ferran's voiceprint.'

'Then the slaves can overpower the guards?' Miranda asked.

'"Overpower"?' Graltor grunted. 'Kill. You mean kill.'

Cate grabbed Miranda's arm. 'Those men joined up to serve the Empire and their people, not Ferran. They are men and women doing their jobs.'

'Just following orders?' Miranda hissed.

'This isn't a matter of sides. There are guards loyal to Ferran, of course there are – but there are at least as many who aren't.'

Graltor and Tarvin both snorted at that, but Cate was pleased to see Miranda giving it some thought.

'You know who's loyal and who isn't?'

'I have my suspicions,' Cate replied diplomatically. Of course, she'd never asked anyone. 'None of us are here through choice.'

Tarvin eyed Cate, perhaps suspecting that she was of senior rank. 'The slaves would love to riot. But the guards can locate us and use the pain inducers – unless you know how to remove them.'

Miranda nodded. 'But given the chance, they'd want to be free?'

'Isn't that obvious?'

Miranda turned to Cate and looked coldly at her. 'Not to everyone.' She stopped in her tracks. 'OK. Change of plan – we take control of the ship.'

'Lady Miranda, they won't just let us walk on to the flight deck and hand us control.'

Miranda smiled. 'Then we'll just have to steal it.'

The Doctor checked his watch, then slipped it back into his pocket.

'Our twenty minutes is nearly up,' he told Debbie.

'This ship is even bigger than it looks.' She was starting to get out of

breath. 'What's that map of yours saying?'

'We're nearly there. In fact –' The Doctor stopped abruptly. 'This door,' he exclaimed, staring at a large circular hatch. Then, hesitating, he took four steps forward and turned a hundred and eighty degrees. 'No, this one.'

Debbie smiled and reached for the control panel.

The moment before she touched it, the Doctor sensed something was wrong.

There was a thunderclap, and a flash of light seemed to transfix her. Debbie fell back.

The door control was blackened, smoke pouring from it. The Doctor knelt over Debbie. He checked her pulse. She was untouched – no sign of burning, no sign of charring.

But she wasn't moving and he already knew...

He stood quickly, looked around. He realised he was becoming agitated. He tried to concentrate, to raise his endorphin level, but it didn't seem to be working. Behind him, he realised, the door to Miranda's cell was opening. He looked back at Debbie. He would deal with that in a moment, when he'd found Miranda. Until then, yes, finding Miranda was his top priority, and nothing else mattered. No one else mattered.

The Doctor ducked through the door. Inside was a circular room, with a large bed in the middle.

The Doctor looked around. 'Miranda!' he called out.

This wasn't a prison cell. It looked more like the penthouse suite of a hotel in Vegas. Something caught the Doctor's eye. It was lying on the bed. He pulled it up. A Batman T-shirt. It had to be Miranda's – even that marketing campaign hadn't got as far as the next universe but one.

The Doctor paced around the room.

Miranda wasn't here.

The door had been booby-trapped. They'd destroyed the sonic suitcase. They'd killed... they'd... they'd been expecting him.

The Doctor turned.

A middle-aged man in green body armour stood in the doorway.

The man had a long, curved blade in his hand.

'I'm glad it was her, not you,' he said, stepping over Debbie's body. 'I wanted your death to be at my hands.'

Chapter Twenty-six
Death in the Family

Ferran filled the doorway. He was standing over Debbie's body, a sneer on his face.

'Where is my daughter?' the Doctor asked quietly.

The Prefect absent-mindedly prodded Debbie with his foot. 'I don't know. She's managed to escape, but she can't have left the ship.' He looked up. 'I will hunt her down. I only need one of you alive; your brain pattern is as good as hers. All things being equal, I would have spared Miranda. But I might have her beheaded just to see the look on your face.' He chuckled at his witticism.

The Doctor turned to face the Prefect square on.

Ferran was still sneering. 'What's the matter, Doctor, no *bons mots*? No quips? I thought the pen was mightier than the sword. I thought you could destroy your enemies with a well-chosen word.'

The Doctor took a step, then another, the third step was easier. By the sixth and seventh, he was charging forward.

Ferran faced him, readied himself for the attack.

But the Doctor was already there. He slammed into the Prefect. Ferran tried to slash him with his knife, but the Doctor was already forcing it out of his hand.

'That's right,' Ferran hissed. 'Fight me. Feels good, doesn't it?'

Ferran shoved the Doctor away from him, then punched him in the stomach.

'But you'll have to be faster than that.'

The Doctor chose not to feel the pain. Instead he lashed out, swinging a punch that Ferran barely avoided.

Ferran grabbed the Doctor's sleeve, reached up, under his arm, twisted around, then hoisted the Doctor over his shoulder, pivoted him, threw the Doctor on to his back into the middle of the room.

'Not very good at this, are you?' Ferran smirked as the Doctor forced air back into his lungs and tried to get back on his feet.

He faced Ferran, got a couple of jabs to his opponent's head. Ferran blocked the third, grabbing his arm, twisting it, until the Doctor was forced to sink to his knees.

'You've got the strength,' Ferran said. 'You've got the technique. But you don't have that killer instinct. Your hearts aren't in it. You think it's the last resort, but it's not: it's the fundamental unit of social control.'

But the Doctor shuffled forward, broke Ferran's grip and punched him hard on the foot.

As Ferran hopped back, the Doctor was on his feet again, launching a chop to the neck and a flat palm in Ferran's face, all one move. The Doctor brought his knee up to Ferran's stomach, winded him. Then a single punch floored the Prefect.

Ferran coughed, gasped for breath.

The Doctor glared down. 'What's the matter? No *bons mots*, no quips?'

The Doctor knelt over him, pressed his knee into Ferran's chest and punched him hard in the face. He felt Ferran's nose break. He hesitated, but only for a moment, then punched him again.

Ferran slumped back.

The Doctor got up, and stood panting. He had to find Miranda.

He paced around the room.

Ferran was on his hands and knees, glaring at him.

'Why stop?' Ferran asked, wiping blood from his lip.

'Not so good against someone who can fight back, are you?' the Doctor shouted.

Ferran smiled and started to rise.

'Where are your principles now, Doctor? I thought you abhorred violence. I thought you used your mind, not your fists.'

'You're a bully, Ferran,' the Doctor snapped. 'Sometimes bullies need to be fought. Where's Miranda?'

Ferran ignored him this time. 'You think you're brave because you started this, but you aren't, not unless you finish it.'

Ferran leapt at him, swinging a punch at the Doctor's jaw. The Doctor barely had time to dodge it. While the Doctor was still disorientated, Ferran followed it up with another, got in close, kneed him in the stomach, made him double up, lifted him off his feet.

The Doctor flailed, got a punch in, but Ferran didn't even feel it.

Ferran grabbed the Doctor's hair at the nape of his neck with one hand, headbutting his face. He grabbed the Doctor's wrist, twisted it back, pulled his arm out, chopped it at the shoulder.

The Doctor collapsed, coughing.

He was lying alongside Debbie's body. Her eyes were open, staring

straight at him. He reached out, touched her face. It was the only movement he could make. He tried to summon the effort, but just couldn't.

'So now we discover the truth,' Ferran hissed. 'You don't fight because you can't. Because you know you would lose. And that great mind, all that experience, all that wit, all that learning. It's useless.'

He lifted the Doctor's head, then slammed it into the floor.

The Doctor sagged. Ferran toyed with the idea of breaking his neck, but decided against it. He settled for breaking a couple of ribs.

There was a flicker and the lights came back on to their normal levels. Humming and buzzing as the ship's systems came back on stream. Ferran seemed imbued by the power himself. He took a deep breath, as though he was absorbing the light.

Ferran knelt next to the Doctor, leaned over him, his breath hot on the Doctor's face. 'Things have changed since your time. People have evolved. We know that there's no such thing as law, no such thing as politics, no such thing as science, no such thing as religion, no such thing as philosophy, no such thing as civilisation. There is strength. All else is there to increase or justify strength, or to keep others weak. The universe just doesn't work the way you think it does. It never did.'

The Doctor didn't move. He hadn't moved for a while, now.

Ferran lifted him up, easily, then dropped him on to his daughter's bed. He recovered the knife.

'You are nothing. Goodbye, Doctor.'

There was a familiar figure in the doorway.

'Ah, Deputy, glad you could join me. Better late than never.'

She moved into the room, gracefully.

Ferran stepped back, showed off his handiwork.

'That's the Doctor?' the Deputy said, betraying surprise. She crossed the room to the bed, then bent over him, touched his neck, then each of his wrists. She parted his swollen eyelids with her fingers, stared into his eyes.

'He's dead,' she said, no feeling in the words.

Ferran took a step forward. 'Dead?'

He looked at the Doctor's body, then at his Deputy. 'Partially?' he said, 'His kind can...'

The Deputy looked up. 'He's dead.'

Ferran considered the news for a moment. He felt empty. Although the Doctor had died by his hand, he still felt robbed. What had his last

words been? He struggled to remember. 'Where is his daughter?' he asked, finally.

'I don't know. I brought her back here, then –'

Ferran held up his hand. 'We need to find her. Come with me to the flight deck. Now the power's back, we'll soon locate her.'

He glanced back at the Doctor. 'This could still be a trap. Get someone here to secure the Doctor's body.' He stepped over Debbie's corpse. 'And to dispose of his companion's.'

The Deputy nodded, then reached for her communications mic and whispered a few commands, before joining the Prefect in the corridor.

'Can you smell smoke?' Ferran asked as they walked the short distance to the lift.

The Deputy shook her head. 'I'm surprised you can smell anything at the moment. Did the Doctor do that to you?'

Ferran dabbed at his nose with his finger. He already knew it was hot, and sore. The bone was broken and, no doubt, there were a few bruises. Nothing that wouldn't mend.

The lift door hissed shut and they started moving up to the flight deck.

The Deputy stood impassively at his side. She was a beautiful creature, perfection itself. But she was nothing compared with her *original*. She had none of Miranda's fire.

Well, the first step to strength, the first rung on the ladder of progress, was to harness fire.

With her father dead, there was no hope for the Last One, now. It was all but over.

The lift door opened and Ferran strode on to the bridge.

'Computer, what is our status?'

'Ship is in class-three orbit above planet Earth, all ship systems are operating at full capacity, with the exception of the time engine, which is repairing in line with previous reports.'

Ferran turned briefly to the Deputy. 'Like it never went away. Computer, use internal sensors to locate Miranda.'

'Internal surveillance is not functioning.'

'You told me all ship systems were working at full capacity.'

'The surveillance system, while powered from the ship's generators, is your technology retrofitted to the ship. As such it is not classified as a ship system.'

Ferran stared up at the pyramid. Computer was artificially

intelligent, and had shown signs of having a personality, a sentience, in the past. He had often been struck by a sense that Computer was being insolent, or wilful.

'Why would it be malfunctioning?' he asked his Deputy.

She wore a puzzled expression. For his benefit, he assumed, as she wouldn't be *feeling* puzzled. 'It would have gone to stand-by mode when the power went down. It sounds as if it hasn't automatically started up again when power was restored.'

Ferran turned back to Computer. 'Are the internal cameras working?' They were original features of the ship.

'They are. A visual search of the ship will take several minutes, and coverage is limited to those areas mapped by your people.'

Ferran narrowed his eyes. Computer had steadfastly refused to release any technical information or deck plans of *Supremacy* unless his people figured it out for themselves. His best engineers had tried to override Computer's security, but had found nothing. Computer seemed to bear no malice to those who tried – or have any objection to the mapping teams. Almost perversely, when a mapping team had searched an area, Computer released the details. There seemed no way round this, and Computer offered no explanation.

'Computer: put images from the internal cameras on screen.'

The holographic bubble became a montage, a confused collection of images. There was no sound, just movement and colour.

Ferran stared at them. 'How?'

In the refectory, three dozen slaves, and half a dozen guards were holding a group of technicians hostage, while a smaller group was barricading the doors.

The armoury door was open, and a small man was passing out neutron guns to slaves and guards. None of the guards were wearing helmets, but some had material tied around their arms or necks – scarves, bandanas: marks of individuality.

There was a firefight going on in the hydroponics area – neutron bolts picking out guards, who fell from their positions in the trees and behind statues.

Slaves surged down corridors in the barracks areas, opening up the doors, dragging out the sleeping guards.

The saucer cradles at the far end of the ship were controlled by slaves, guards and technicians, who were sharing food and laughter.

The main engines were secured behind sealed bulkheads and doors

thicker than any bank vault's. Inside the engine rooms, the engineers and technicians cowered, prepared barricades and argued among themselves. Ferran could not hear what they were saying, but it seemed one group – the minority, thankfully – wanted to open the doors and welcome the rebels in. For their part, on the other side of the barriers, slave crews were slowly burning big holes using heavy cutting gear.

'Computer: activate pain inducers throughout the ship. Everywhere but this room.'

'Unable to comply.'

The Deputy pointed him to the lower left-hand corner of the hologlobe. 'They've smashed the master control unit.'

Ferran stared into the screen, transfixed by what he saw.

'Seal the bridge,' he ordered.

She'd killed a man once.

Miranda had been haunted by it every day since.

She had no doubt that Sallak had deserved to die. He'd killed her parents, his master had murdered her family. It really was kill or be killed. She had rationalised it, come up with any number of philosophical and logical justifications for what she had done.

But none of them had explained why she had *enjoyed* it.

The sense of power as she'd taken a life.

And during the years she'd been travelling, that was what had worried her the most. That Ferran was right, that locked inside her blood and her genes was a monster.

She'd started a riot. Perhaps she'd even started a revolution. She wasn't thinking that far ahead. For now, she wanted the slaves freed and Ferran captured.

Or killed.

Lives would be lost.

She'd not seen anyone killed here, let alone killed anyone herself, but it was inevitable. There was so much pent-up anger among the slaves. And among the guards and scientists – Cate had been right: over one in three of them had switched sides the moment the possibility existed.

Graltor was at her side, keen eyes and ears listening out. Somehow, without either of them saying anything, he'd become her bodyguard. He was carrying a neutron rifle, and made the bulky weapon look

small. No doubt he could hear the disturbance. Glass shattering, battering rams against doors. There was the smell of smoke in the air.

But the riot hadn't reached Miranda's room yet.

She stepped out of the travel tube. The door to her chamber was broken, and the lock looked like it had been blasted off.

Graltor went into her room first, made sure it was clear.

As Miranda followed, she saw Debbie Castle's body was just inside the door. Miranda checked it, but she was long gone, just as Cate had said. She closed the woman's eyes.

'I'll keep watch,' Graltor assured her. He brandished his neutron rifle, to emphasise his point, and leaned against the door frame, looking out into the corridor.

Miranda was already heading for the bed. Her father lay there, immobile.

She ran her hand over his cheek. His lip was split and there was swelling round his left eye.

His eyes fluttered open. 'Miranda? I'm... it's... I think I might be dead.'

The Doctor's head flopped back.

'That's the Emperor?' Graltor asked. 'It doesn't look like the Emperor. When I was a gladiator, I was given a medal by the Emperor. He was –'

'Shush,' Miranda said, laying her head on her father's chest. 'He's alive.'

The Doctor's eyes snapped open. 'Good,' he said.

He tried to sit upright, but the effort was too much.

'I can't believe you got here. How did you get here?'

'*Atlantis*. Space shuttle. Hijacked it.'

Miranda laughed.

'Ferran...' the Doctor said.

She smiled. 'It's OK. Cate, the Deputy, she's on my side. She told Ferran you'd died, then radioed me and told me where to find you. These should help.' She attached a couple of white pads to the back of the Doctor's neck. 'It's medicine,' she explained. 'Special space medicine. I've no idea how it works, but it does.'

She saw her Batman T-shirt on the floor, leaned down and picked it up. 'I've been looking for that. Graltor, look the other way a moment, would you?'

He returned to his post at the door.

She slipped her jacket off, tugged off her shirt and pulled the T-shirt back on.

Her father was blushing.

'Dad...' she admonished.

'He killed Debbie. You remember Debbie Castle?'

'Of course. I'm sorry.' She finished tucking in the T-shirt and reached for her jacket.

'We could have been a family.'

Miranda kissed him on the forehead. The swelling around his eye was already going down. 'You're going to be OK.'

'My side.'

Miranda shifted a little. 'I'm sorry. Am I putting too much weight on it?'

The Doctor managed a small chuckle. 'No. You said, "my side". Since when have you had a side?'

Miranda smiled.

The Deputy had taken her place behind Ferran's chair, looked over his shoulder as he tried to piece together the scale of the rebellion.

Computer was displaying an image of *Supremacy*, with rebel-held areas in red, areas secured by men loyal to Ferran in black.

Cate allowed herself a small smile.

In terms of floorspace, most of the known parts of the ship were under the control of the rebels. They had blocked the travel tubes, virtually all of the lifts and the main corridors. As they watched, the red areas were virtually lapping against the blast doors of the flight deck.

Ferran hadn't given up. 'We need to marshal our forces. Our priority has to be establishing communications lines and consolidating existing strongholds. Whatever else happens, we must keep control of this flight deck.'

The Doctor was standing unaided.

Miranda looked at him, full of admiration. He'd stolen a space shuttle to find her. Long ago, she'd realised that she loved him, but she thought she'd burned her bridges.

There would be time for a proper reunion later. For now, she was catching up on what was happening throughout the ship.

She had told her father what had happened, how she'd started a

revolution in about ten minutes flat. Now she learned that the astronauts were fine. They were helping her uprising – a Captain Mather was giving tactical advice; the hangar bay where the shuttle was docked had become a temporary headquarters.

The Doctor nodded. 'He's US military, Delta Force. I suspect this isn't the first time he's helped a revolution along.'

'He helped the Contras?'

'At the very least, I'd have thought.'

Miranda continued to take stock of the situation. There was a stand-off at the engine room. There were massive doors and walls, designed to prevent an explosion in the engines from spreading to the rest of the ship. Her revolutionaries, or whatever they were, couldn't get through them. The personnel in the engine room were staying loyal to Ferran, as far as anyone could tell.

But that was it: Ferran held the flight deck at one end of the ship, and his men held the engines at the other end. Two critical areas of the ship, of course they were, but her followers held, or were on the brink of taking, all points in between. They'd secured the robot garages, the saucer cradles, the armouries, the detector banks.

In a matter of ten minutes.

She wasn't sure how she'd done it. Tarvin and Graltor had led her to one of the slave refectories – and just telling them that the pain inducers weren't working was enough. Suddenly, after all these years, all these centuries, there was nothing to stop the slaves. She'd lit the blue touchpaper, but wasn't sure how she could control the process.

She realised she was staring at her father, and that he was the answer.

Once he was on the flight deck, he'd take command.

Ferran sat square in his command chair, watching as the red lines and blobs spread. The slaves controlled everything, now, everything but this room and the engines.

'Mordak, override life support. If necessary, we'll shut off the air supply in other areas of the ship.'

'Stay where you are,' Cate ordered.

Mordak saw her gun, and sat down, keeping his hands to himself.

Cate allowed herself a smile. But, she realised with a start, she'd neglected Ferran, dropped her guard.

Her reflexes weren't a match for her master's. Ferran drew his own

pistol and fired, piercing Cate's left shoulder with a needle-thin beam of white light. The Deputy span back, dropping her gun.

The Prefect's second shot hit the gun where it fell, all but disintegrating it.

The pain Cate felt was intense, but very localised. It was difficult to concentrate.

Ferran raised his gun and aimed it at his Deputy's head.

'Computer: shut down life support in all areas of the ship apart from the flight deck and engine rooms.'

'Such an action will kill all life forms outside those areas who are not wearing protective clothing.'

Ferran grinned. 'Of course it will. That's why I'm taking that action. Implement the order.'

'Confirmed.'

Chapter Twenty-seven
Death Comes to Time

'They've started shooting in there.'

'I think the air's getting thinner, too.'

The Doctor looked up from the door control. He had a handful of wires, and had been sparking them together, but nothing had triggered the door. 'I don't have time for this, then. Graltor, old chap, can I borrow that neutron rifle?'

'It won't cut through blast shielding, there's four metres of Kladenium to get through,' the giant told him, but handed it over anyway.

The Doctor smiled and opened up a side panel. 'Oh, don't worry, I'll be adjusting the neutron flow.'

'Ah,' Miranda beamed, 'a multiphase pulse on neutron frequencies might override the security interlocks on the blast doors.'

The Doctor patted his daughter on the head. 'Actually, the modifications I've made work on a slightly different principle. Stand back.' He hefted the rifle up, pulled the bolt back and fired.

Ferran smiled at his Deputy, determined to savour her last moments.

But she was smiling. She knew something he didn't.

And behind him there was a roar like an oncoming storm, or the voice of the gods. The door on to the flight deck exploded inwards, showering the bridge officers with fine metal dust and debris.

Ferran turned, instinctively, and immediately flinched. The light was so bright, so pure.

He fell back, tried blinking the red blotches from his eyes.

He could hear the Deputy scrabbling away. He fired in her direction, heard the beam carve a scar in the deck.

She wasn't important. The door was important.

The light was fading. There was a figure clambering through the hole where the door had been, careful not to touch the thick, white-hot sides. A silhouette. A lean figure with shoulder-length hair, wearing a long black coat.

'I killed you,' Ferran screamed. 'I *killed* you.'

He could see there was another one. Another one with long hair and a long coat. Back to back with the first, slightly taller.

'No,' he said. 'No! This is impossible.'

The Doctor's people were demons, he remembered. They only looked like people, but they were impossible to kill, and their cunning was unrivalled. They destroyed worlds, they destroyed universes.

'I killed you!' Ferran shouted at the shapes. 'This isn't fair: I killed you.'

As the smoke swirled away, he saw the Doctor, standing back to back with his daughter.

Miranda strode out first, the Doctor following. He dropped the smoking remains of a neutron rifle.

'I'm afraid it's good for only one shot,' the Doctor told the large man who had followed them through the remains of the door. A slave! Here on the flight deck. Ferran bristled at the thought.

The Doctor and Miranda stood shoulder to shoulder.

'Hello, Ferran,' they said together.

'Jinx!' the Doctor giggled.

Ferran raised his pistol.

Miranda had a gun of her own, and was holding it straight out in front of her. She shot Ferran's pistol out of his hand, then aimed at his head.

The Doctor placed his hand on her shoulder, and shook his head.

'Weapons are the tool of the cruel and the cowardly. We strive to be better than that. We do not need them.'

Miranda nodded, then tossed the pistol at Ferran, who caught it.

He looked down at the gun, unsure, then aimed it at Miranda.

No. Not her.

He shifted ground slightly, got a good aim at the Doctor.

The Doctor was smiling.

'It's a trick,' Ferran said. 'You've tampered with the gun. If I fire, it'll blow my arm off. I won't fall for it.'

He started circling round them.

'You saw me fire it,' Miranda reminded him, taking another step towards him.

'That was part of the trick. You set it to fire once, then to backfire. All part of the trick.'

His bridge crew sat in their seats, reluctant to move.

The giant had helped the Deputy to her feet and she stood alongside him.

'Computer: transfer all command codes to the Doctor and Miranda,' the Doctor said, in Ferran's own voice.

'Implemented.'

Ferran spun to face Computer. 'Cancel that order!'

'Unable to comply: command codes have been transferred.'

Miranda laughed. 'Computer: restore life support to all areas of the ship.'

'Implemented.'

'Is it possible to broadcast pictures and sounds from the flight deck throughout the ship?'

'It is.'

'Do so.'

'Implemented.'

Ferran turned to his bridge crew. 'What are you waiting for? Kill them!'

The Doctor shook his head. 'You have lost, Ferran. You've got the gun. You're at the heart of your empire: the flight deck of the most powerful ship in the universe. You have your Deputy, your most loyal crew. I... I am not carrying a weapon. My daughter is a nineteen-year-old girl, and she's also unarmed. And even here you can't win? Even here you can't command loyalty?'

Ferran turned to face Miranda. 'The gun has been tampered with. It's a trick.'

'No, it hasn't,' the Doctor said softly. 'The gun works... but it *is* useless.'

'If you want to rule the universe,' Miranda said, 'start here: order your bridge crew to stop us.'

Ferran glanced over. His men were sitting at their stations, not moving, not daring to look at him.

'Cowards!' he shouted.

They could hear cheering, coming up through the deckplates, from the rest of the ship – they could hear singing and shouting and laughter.

'It's over,' the Doctor said simply. 'The violence, the killing. It's not needed any more.'

Ferran stared at him.

Fire.

His mother, lying dead on the Senate steps, gunned down.

He'd never known her, not really. From before he could remember,

his brother had told him about his destiny, told him of revenge. His future was in his past, locked in his genes, flowing through his blood. Miranda and her kind must be destroyed. If he had killed her from orbit, then this would be over, he would still have his ship. His mistake was thinking that he could harness this power.

'Never,' he shouted, reaching for his wrist.

'No!' Miranda leapt at him.

But Ferran was already fading out of existence.

Miranda stood where the Prefect had been just moments before.

'That wasn't time travel,' she announced.

The Doctor shook his head. 'No. Computer: where is Ferran?'

'He has transmatted to the main time-engine chamber.'

'The other end of the ship,' Cate said, 'the only area still held by his men. It's behind heavy blast doors – ten times thicker than the ones for the flight deck, with independent force screens, too.'

The Doctor drummed his fingers against his lips. 'He's not just gone in there to hide. Presumably he can exert some control over the ship from there?'

The pilot, Mordak, nodded. 'Yes, sir.'

The Doctor smiled. 'I'm no one's sir,' he told him gently. 'What's your name?'

'Space Pilot Sub-Captain Mordak, of the Twelfth Galactic Fleet.' Mordak started to salute, but a bout of self-consciousness turned the gesture into a vague wave of his hand.

'And you know everything there is to know about the ship?'

'Everything that is known, Doctor, not everything there is to know.'

The Doctor smiled. 'Excellent answer. Come with us. Miranda, we need to get to the engine room.'

Miranda nodded. 'Graltor, Cate – stay here. Liaise with Captain Mather: make sure the rest of the ship is secure, make sure no one gets carried away.'

She followed her father and Mordak up towards the doorway. The Doctor had his arm confidingly over Mordak's shoulder. 'What's the Prefect doing?'

Mordak gulped. 'Well, he won't have complete control of the ship from there – but he could try to shut down power distribution. That would have the same effect your own tactics had – make us blind and defenceless.'

The Doctor looked thoughtful.

Miranda wasn't convinced. 'Then what? We took over the ship with sheer force of numbers. He's got a few technicians and anyone else who was in the engine room.'

They reached the travel-tube door, which opened automatically. The travel car was empty. A holographic screen on one wall continued to relay pictures from the flight deck, just as she'd ordered.

'Ferran knows we're coming,' she realised. 'He would have seen that.'

The Doctor gave an exasperated gasp. 'Well… he doesn't know what we're planning. How could he, when even we don't?'

Mordak grinned at that, and Miranda found herself smiling.

The door was a vast thing, like the drawbridge of a fortress, cast from solid steel.

The slaves and other men and women in front of it looked tiny. Half a dozen of them had opened up the control panel and were trying to rewire it. A larger team had a less subtle approach – they were setting up a laser cannon, moving it into position and trying to agree among themselves where to aim it. There were shallow, futile burn marks on the door where they'd tried using smaller weapons to do the job.

The Doctor wasn't at all surprised to see Captain Mather in charge of that operation.

'No peeking,' he warned.

'Doctor!' The astronaut grabbed him and gave him a bear hug, lifting him off the ground. 'I've had a look under the hood of this thing already – and I'm none the wiser.'

'That's as it should be.'

'Where's Debbie?'

The Doctor looked him in the eye. 'Ferran killed her.'

Mather nodded, suddenly subdued. 'I'm sorry.'

They all started walking towards the door.

Miranda shook Mather's hand. 'It's good to finally meet you.'

'You're his daughter? Yeah, I can see that.'

The Doctor and Miranda shared a smile.

Mordak was looking at the door.

'How thick is it?' the Doctor asked, knowing he wasn't going to like the answer.

'About forty metres.'

'Forty metres?' the Doctor echoed.

'Tarvin?' Miranda asked.

A man in slave's clothes looked up from the control panel. 'Long time no see. Anything happened since we last saw each other?' He chuckled.

Miranda smiled. 'How's that looking?'

'It's looking impenetrable.'

Miranda banged a fist against the door. 'We're not going to get this open...'

There was a mechanical sound from all around them, and the door slowly began to grind back, into the wall.

'I didn't do that...' Miranda said, her voice trailing away.

'Fall back!' Mather warned. 'Get that cannon ready. Anyone with guns, take up positions!'

The Doctor pulled Miranda away from the door, almost carrying her until they were safely behind the cannon.

With a screech, the door ground to a halt, well before it was fully open. The chink in the door was perhaps four feet across.

No one was saying anything, everyone was waiting.

There was a scrabbling sound, getting louder.

Miranda held on to her father, eyes wide.

Mather and Tarvin looked at each other and shrugged.

The sound was footsteps – echoing and amplified by the metal corridor.

A clawed hand emerged, grabbed the doorframe.

A few rifles were raised, and there were high-pitched hums, like camera flashes powering up, as the guns were readied.

'Don't shoot!' the Doctor shouted.

He headed forward. The hand was pale, with thick, dark veins standing out. The Doctor frowned. It reminded him of something.

Miranda and Mordak were a few feet behind him.

'Stay back,' he said, but his voice lacked conviction.

The hand was slipping down. The Doctor took it, gently, and pulled its owner clear of the gap.

An old man, wearing a frayed and faded technician's uniform. He looked at the Doctor with uncomprehending gratitude.

'Chann,' the Doctor said, reading from the name tag on the man's sleeve.

Mordak stepped forward. 'It can't be: Chann was a classmate of mine. This man is ninety years old.'

Miranda peered into the tunnel formed by the half-open door. 'I don't understand.'

Then she looked at her father.

'The time engines,' they said together.

'Mordak, could Ferran have done this?'

'Start a deliberate time spillage? That would be madness. It would throw the time engines out of phase.'

'They are all dead,' the old man croaked. 'We could see it was hopeless. We told him we were going to surrender, and open the doors, and he killed us all. He's decoupling the engine. Everything in there is carefully balanced, it's exquisite. He's thrown everything out of phase.'

Mather and Tarvin had run forward with a medical kit. Mather moved over to the gap.

The Doctor grabbed the sleeve of his spacesuit. 'No. You'll be killed.'

Mordak gave a dry laugh. 'If the time engines have been tampered with, we're all dead. The ship will explode, the time spillage will be unstoppable.'

'Earth...' Mather said.

'By tomorrow morning, the Earth will be a desert,' Mordak said. 'Tomorrow afternoon, the sun will be a red giant, and will destroy it.'

'Miranda,' the Doctor said, 'we have to stop him.'

She stood, shivered a little. 'We don't know that we are immune.'

'We know that we're the only two people who *may* stand a chance. That has to be enough.'

She nodded.

'I'll go first,' he told her, easing himself into the gap.

It was dark – the walls were solid metal.

There was forty metres to walk – forty paces, about twenty seconds.

There was blue light at the other end, harsh, like neon.

And about halfway along Miranda realised that if Ferran was at the other end, and saw them coming, all he would have to do would be to close the door again and there would be nothing they could do to stop themselves being crushed.

She quickened her pace, forcing her father to do the same, and they stepped out into the engine room.

The chamber was smaller and less cluttered than Miranda had expected, but it defied logic.

It was the inside surface of a sphere, but there was no up or down: the whole surface was the floor. She could tell, because it was littered with skeletons and patches of faded uniform. It was disorientating, against all mammal logic. What sort of people could feel at home here?

In the centre of the room was a large sphere, lit from within, the source of the harsh blue light. The sphere was translucent, and full of mechanisms like snapping jaws. As they gnashed together, it reminded Miranda of a tank full of piranhas.

The room was thick with time, filled with it, as it might have been full of poison gas or seawater. There was a sense of movement, like a hurricane, but it wasn't around them, not in space at any rate.

Ferran was about a hundred yards away, wearing a protective suit, the sort of thing they wore in nuclear power stations. He was kneeling down, and it looked like he was at a control console or similar piece of apparatus.

She looked over to her father.

'You stop Ferran, I'll save the Earth,' he suggested, matter-of-factly.

Miranda nodded, and started to stride towards Ferran.

The Doctor hurried over to the huge central sphere.

His mind kept whispering words at him, but they weren't quite audible. The words were the names of the components of the time engine, and explanations of how they worked. He tried to concentrate on them, but he couldn't hear.

He knew what to do.

The sphere was about twenty metres in diameter, and threw out blue light, waves of time and a great surging, grinding noise. But there wasn't any heat.

He reached out to place his palm on the surface of the sphere, and – just as he knew it would, he realised – the surface parted, forming an oblong hole just large enough to walk into without ducking his head.

The Doctor stepped inside.

'Ferran!'

He looked up, startled by her presence.

'How can you survive in here?' he asked, through a clear visor so thick it refracted his face.

'I'm above all that,' Miranda told him. 'Look at my clothes, though.'

Her clothes were fading and fraying. Nothing too serious yet, but clothes that had been new on yesterday now looked as if they'd been worn and washed dozens of times. She could feel her hairgrip corroding away in her hair.

She wondered what her lifespan was, and when she would start to feel different. So far, there was nothing, no changes at all.

'Stay back!' Ferran shouted. He had to shout to make himself heard.

'I can't let you destroy us,' she told him gently.

The Doctor reached into one of the energy streams.

It talked to him, responded. A machine this sophisticated had to be on the verge of intelligence, he realised with a start. And, as Turing had always said, a computer as intelligent as a man was instantly more intelligent, as it would have a better memory, more efficient control over its own thoughts.

It wasn't alive, not quite: it needed guidance, it needed coaxing.

By him.

Time travel, literally in his hands.

It had been one of his and Debbie's perennial conversations: if they had a time machine, where would they go in it? Debbie always chose the past: the court of Queen Elizabeth, Roman Britain, even the streets of Victorian London. The Doctor had walked those streets, but he had never spoiled Debbie's romantic notions with his memories of them. The Doctor would pick the future, every time. The past fascinated him: he loved to study history, to imagine himself talking to historical figures. But how much better to step on to the first space station, or stand on the top of a mile-high skyscraper, or see how the world eventually solved the problems and challenges that faced it in the twentieth century. The future was unwritten – anything could happen.

He wanted to travel in time. Debbie had taken him to see *Bill and Ted*, and he'd seen their flying telephone box and wished he'd got one of his own. If only Zevron's saucer hadn't been fitted with a self-destruct circuit, that dream might have come true nearly ten years ago.

Show me the future, the Doctor asked.

'Why are you doing this?' Miranda asked.

'To rid the universe of you and your kind.'

'Think about what you're doing. You'll die, too.'
'It's a price worth paying.'
'And who will lead your people?'
'Someone will emerge.'
'You're the last of your family. And I doubt you've endorsed a successor, not if you spend so much time away from home in your Librarinth or on this ship. He might get ideas.'
'My people are strong – they are the supreme beings of the universe. They will survive.'
'No,' Miranda said. 'You said yourself they wouldn't. They'll be swept away by your enemies. Without this ship, without you, they'll be wiped out, or enslaved. They need you. But even with you, the Empire's on the verge of collapse.'
'No, I won't accept that.'
'I know you won't, and that's why what you're doing is wrong, and that's why it'll destroy everything you're fighting to preserve.'

It was too bright in here to see anything.

The Doctor could hear something. Violin music, violin music in the heart of a lightning storm. It felt like a memory, but... The Doctor ducked as a large robot arm swung a silver fist at his head. A swarm of wasps surrounded him. 'Time is out of joint!' he heard himself yelling. Mr Saldaamir smiled his disconcerting smile. The Doctor grabbed a ship's wheel, with the stars streaking over his head above him. A man in a bowler hat walked through the mud, checking something from a clipboard. Mather: an old man now, his hair gone grey. A large metal vehicle, something between a tank and a chrome turtle, sat in a forest clearing. A young woman in a scarlet tunic with long blonde hair, smiling at him, as if he should recognise her. There was a crowd of people in what looked like Renaissance clothing. 'The planet's called *Albert?*' he asked. A conical robot, gunmetal-grey, swung a camera eye at him, the lights on the top of its head flashing angrily. A man with thin white hair and a mournful expression looked down his nose at him. 'I wondered when I'd put in an appearance.'

The Doctor tried to concentrate on the here and now.

He was in the heart of vast machinery. Great columns plunging up into the heavens, down into the depths, and snaking out in all directions in between.

The sphere wasn't this large on the outside, the Doctor told himself.

And that seemed like the most natural thing in the world. Whatever had made him think that there should be a relationship between interior and exterior dimensions?

There was no obvious cause for the previous damage, the faults that had kept the ship here long enough for him to get here. It was quite a stroke of luck that had happened.

You make your own luck, he realised, telling the engines to shut themselves down for three days, then backdating the order. He felt the engines disable themselves. Don't tell Ferran, he said, just tell him it's a routine repair.

The Doctor felt the power equations enter his mind, and did a quick calculation – there was a lot of energy here: as a bare minimum, Earth would be in the blast radius if the engines exploded. The side of Earth facing the ship would be scoured clean: the seas would become gas, every forest would become ash. At least it would be quick for that hemisphere – the other half of the world would take several minutes to die, as the tidal waves, blasts of air and superheated debris bombarded them.

He set to work.

Ferran stared up at Miranda.

Her clothing now was frayed, with all the colour leached out – as if she'd stolen it from an abandoned museum. But she was still so young. Her skin was pale, smooth. He had thought she'd have started to age by now – she must have been exposed to centuries of time.

Ferran's visor display was warning him that his suit wouldn't protect him for many more minutes.

He returned his attention to the couplings. There wasn't a procedure for this – destabilising the engines was presumably something that would horrify the original designers, whoever they were.

'Listen to me,' she insisted. 'This is wrong. It doesn't have to end like this.'

'It's destiny. It's our genetic destiny – you mustn't be allowed to survive. My mother, my father, they must be avenged.'

Ferran remembered his brother's face staring at him. Zevron was so much older then than he was. With a start, Ferran realised he was older now than his brother had been when he had been killed. It was difficult to imagine.

He remembered how his brother had died, who had killed him, and why.

It had been him or Miranda. And that was still the choice.

'This can only end in one of two ways,' he told her. 'With one of us dead, or with both of us dead.'

Miranda shook her head. 'No one needs to die. I've thought of a better way.'

'A better way?' Ferran parroted, full of contempt. 'Then why not kill me and implement this "better way"? Why not take the Empire for yourself?'

Miranda's lip twisted into a sneer. 'I intend to. But I need your help.'

The Doctor was awake instantly.

Which came as a shock: he didn't remember blacking out.

The time energies swirled and crackled around him.

He felt so old. He glanced down at his hand. It hadn't aged, not at all. He should know, he knew what he was looking at like the back of his hand.

Earth. He had to stop the time engine.

The ebbs in time were starting to affect his perception. They were shuffling his memory around like a deck of cards. He remembered blacking out, now – but knew that was still a few minutes in the future.

Earth.

He felt something seeping into his shoes. It brought back a memory he'd never had. He turned to gaze around his surroundings.

He was standing on a beach, with seagulls whirling overhead, and waves lapping at his feet. The light was flame-red, the setting sun was far larger than it should be. *Supremacy* filled the sky, and looked like it was falling to Earth. It eclipsed the dying sun.

Everything was at stake. Everything.

And as he stared out to sea, there was someone else with him. A man his age, his height, but with closely cropped hair. His lover was dead and the seas were dry. The stars were coming out, now. Night was falling.

The Doctor's eyes snapped open.

Reality. That would be reality in moments, unless he could prevent...

Prevent what? All those memories had slipped away. They must be

in his future now. All he had to do was wait for them to reappear. But there was no time.

He laughed at the irony – he was working against the clock, but the clock was throwing out random numbers.

Energy crackled around him.

But he understood this place now, knew his mind was shaping it, or at least guiding the software and hardware that shaped it. Ferran was throwing the engine out of phase by introducing areas of instability; he was punching holes in certain sections that led to time spillage, and causing the disruption of all the beautiful equations that ran this place.

The Doctor eased the power conduit into place, replaced the relay and activated it.

The power was flowing freely now. The damaged sections of the system were now isolated, the time energies flowed freely, keeping themselves to themselves.

He stepped from the sphere, on to the metal floor. All was calm now.

Ferran was sitting on the floor, Miranda standing over him.

'You can remove that protective gear, now,' the Doctor told him.

Ferran shook his head. He was subdued, as if he'd just received some bad news.

He should feel angry with this man, the Doctor thought. This man had driven his daughter from him, kidnapped her, tried to kill her. He'd murdered Debbie, simply because he could.

But the Doctor was too tired for revenge. It just seemed so... irrelevant.

Miranda hugged her father. 'You're all right,' she said, smiling at him. 'Sorry about your coat.'

He looked down at her. 'I always seem to lose one fighting these people.'

They looked down at Ferran. 'It won't happen again,' she assured him. 'We've come to an understanding.'

Chapter Twenty-eight
The Next Generation

Miranda stood before the masses in the refectory, her father by her side. They'd improvised a little podium by stacking dining tables.

Behind them, Cate was keeping a suspicious eye on Ferran. Tarvin and Graltor basked in their new celebrity status. Mather and Mordak stood shoulder to shoulder.

Miranda faced the crowd. There was a good proportion of the crew here. She'd expected them to be in groups – guards and technicians in one corner, slaves in another, like boys and girls at the start of a school disco. But that wasn't the case at all. The slaves and their former guards mingled, chatted. The uniforms were no longer uniform – a lot of the guards had changed into civvies, and most of the slaves were wearing strips of coloured material as bandanas, sashes or armbands, anything to express their individuality.

Ferran seemed subdued, which was hardly surprising. The crowd had booed him as he'd entered, bayed for his blood. Perhaps a few of them had come here expecting to see a lynching.

Miranda stepped forward.

'I am Miranda,' she declared. 'I am the Last One, Empress of the Known Universe, President of the Supreme Council, and Commander-in-chief of the Armed Forces of the Known and Unknown Worlds, Custodian of the Artefacts, Master of the Keys to the Four Gods. I am also now Prefect. In the absence of a united Senate, I also decree that I, and I alone, now wield the powers of the Senate, including access to the galactic computer co-ordination networks, trade routes and supply lines. I am also now Head of the Galactic Bank. Oh, and as of ten minutes ago, I'm the commanding officer of this ship. I have the power to do anything now, absolute power over every particle in the universe.'

'Er... Miranda,' her father said, nervously, from behind her.

She turned to look at him. His eyes were wide.

He'd gone very pale.

'Don't worry,' she assured him, 'this is going somewhere.' She cleared her throat. 'I now, perfectly legitimately, am the Supreme Being of the Universe.'

'The Houses and Factions won't stand for this. There will be anarchy...' someone said, clearly far louder than he had intended.

'Whoever said that, come here,' Miranda commanded.

The culprit trotted forward. 'I meant no disrespect,' he apologised, nervously.

'There *will* be anarchy,' Miranda confirmed. 'I give you that pledge.'

The murmurs in the crowd were louder, this time.

'People need rules,' Cate said softly.

Miranda smiled. 'Anarchy doesn't mean the absence of rules,' she declared. 'It means the absence of rulers. I grant myself supreme power to prevent anyone else from having it. From now on, there will be no more dictators, no more tyrants. Now, with the powers invested in me, I declare all slaves freed, and all soldiers free from their military commissions. Not just here, but throughout the known universe. If anyone tells you they are your master, then tell them that there *is* no master, that you will not obey them.'

Parts of the crowd started cheering and chanting her name.

Miranda held up her hand. 'No! I want you to work with me, not to follow me. From now on, we'll work to build a better society, not fight to preserve an unfair, violent one. So much of the Empire's economy is spent simply ensuring the survival of the Empire - maintaining the intergalactic fleets, paying a vast standing army, shipping goods around that could be made locally. We can do better than that. We can dismantle the old way and use it as the foundations for something better.'

Ferran joined her. 'It will not be easy,' he told them all. 'Not everyone in a position of power will renounce that power. But we will persuade them. If I can change, then so can they. Miranda cannot do this alone. I pledge to fight alongside her. I can no longer command you - you are free men and women, now. But I *ask* you to join us.'

'So you can lead us into a war?' someone shouted. 'How's that different from what we have now?'

Ferran shook his head. 'I've spent all my life killing, or planning to kill. I don't want to do that, not any more. We don't have to. I don't have to.'

'There will be opposition,' Miranda said. 'There are vested interests, there are evil men. But we can build our utopia, all our *utopias,* and we can defend them with this ship. It doesn't have to be like it has been. We are the Children of the Revolution. We're not bound by the

past, and the future can be whatever we want it to be.'

The crowds roared their approval.

Miranda eased herself into her seat, nominally the command station, but just one of six facing in towards Computer and the centre of the flight deck.

The chair was high-backed, a little too hard for her liking, but she could always get a cushion.

'Empress?' Graltor asked.

'Prefect?' Cate asked at exactly the same time.

The three of them chuckled.

Miranda shook her head. 'Miranda,' she said firmly. 'Take your positions, please.'

They took the last two chairs.

Miranda understood the controls and displays on the arms of her chair. The symbols and readouts flickering in front of her made perfect – instinctive – sense. She twisted some of the dials, changed the settings of some of the slide controls.

'Computer, what is the Ship's status?'

The pyramid hanging in front of them began crackling with activity. 'All systems at maximum capacity. The time engines are fully repaired.'

She nodded, pleased. 'And *Atlantis*?'

A sphere opened up in the centre of the room, full of an image of the space shuttle sitting in the hangar.

'The human spacecraft is fuelled and ready.'

'Father,' she said quietly.

The Doctor was standing behind her chair, a proud grin on his face. 'You've not done badly for a girl without any O-levels,' he told her.

'I'll walk back to the shuttle with you,' she told him.

Atlantis sat in the hangar bay, looking absurdly quaint.

'It's not as impressive as the *Supremacy*, is it?' the Doctor asked.

'It's not called the *Supremacy*,' Miranda said. 'That was Ferran's name for it, and it… sends out the wrong signals. From now on, it's just the Ship – that's how it likes to be known.'

The flight crew were shaking hands, making their goodbyes. Commander Fairchild was already inside, running pre-flight checks.

Miranda and her father had passed through the corridors, past clean-up crews – slaves and guards working together. There wasn't a

hierarchy, not yet. There would have to be one, of course. At the very least there would have to be co-ordination. Anarchy was possible, she thought – and not in the tabloid definition of riots and looting, nor the naïve student political sense of hoping everyone got along and assuming someone else was growing all the food and washing all the dishes, but in the truest sense: an abolition of law and property, because such things weren't needed any more. But it would not be an easy option: there was a lot of hard work ahead, and once people realised that…

She wasn't so arrogant as to think that she had all the answers. These were questions for the future, and there were still a few left from today.

'Mrs Castle…' Miranda began. 'Ferran killed her. Can you really forgive him for that?'

The Doctor took a deep breath. 'You don't make peace with your friends, do you? I killed his brother. We've all done things to hurt others. We can draw a line or we can destroy one another. We've made our choice. I talked to him. He wants to start a garden. He wants to go home and keep bees and grow roses. I gave him some tips.'

'Mrs Castle's body… I'll take it with me,' she told him, 'bury her with full honours.'

The Doctor shook his head. 'Bury Debbie somewhere quiet, somewhere where the first snow of winter is always falling.'

Miranda offered him a handkerchief, which he accepted gratefully.

The Doctor looked her up and down. 'You could be a great leader. You could command armies.'

Was he testing her?

'I wouldn't know what to do with an army. I'm my father's daughter… Father. I'm taking supreme power, but I'm not going to use it, I'm taking it so that no one else does.'

'You're going to be magnificent. Children of the Revolution, eh? I envy you.'

She hesitated. 'Come with me. They've forgotten. They've been ruled by the cruel and the cowardly for so long that they've forgotten how to be anything else themselves. And dismantling the Galactic Empire isn't going to be quick, or easy.'

'Rome didn't fall in a day,' the Doctor agreed.

'You could teach them so much.'

The Doctor shook his head. 'You can teach them. Seeing you in

action here, I'm pretty sure you could teach *me*. You... you go forward, I'll catch up with you.'

She looked at him. 'Are you sure?'

'I've an appointment to keep,' he reminded her. 'In a little over eleven years, I've got to meet Fitz. Whoever Fitz might be.'

'I could get Computer to run a check on him – find out who he is, what he wants. Even what that police box of yours is. Ferran was obsessed with you, so I'm sure it's all in the databanks.'

The Doctor laughed. 'After so long, that would feel a bit like cheating, to be honest. Like checking the back of the book for all the answers instead of working them out for myself.'

He hugged her.

'I'll visit,' he promised.

'You'd better,' she said sternly.

By the time Miranda had got back to the flight deck, *Atlantis* had left the hangar.

An image of the space shuttle, orbiting alongside Ship hung in the air beneath Computer. Retro rockets were firing, and the shuttle was easing itself back into its normal orbit.

Miranda took her place in the command chair. She thought she would be crying, but she wasn't. She felt ready. Ready to start work.

'Ship status?'

'Space-time co-ordinates to the Needle have been calculated and laid in,' Computer intoned. 'Vortex scanners indicate a clear path. Estimated journey time, twelve standard days.'

She had no idea what a standard day was, and, for the moment at least, she couldn't care less.

'Computer, show me *Atlantis*. Close-up on the cockpit.'

'As you wish.'

Her father was there, looking straight at her.

'Goodbye,' he mouthed.

'Never,' she whispered.

The shuttle pulled away, descending to a lower orbit.

Miranda laid her hand flat on the green panel in front of her, and it lit up.

She took a deep breath.

'Time machine go,' she said.

And she smiled.

* * *

'Houston, *Atlantis* is now back in the scheduled orbit,' Captain Fairchild reported.

'Roger that.'

Above the space shuttle, the Ship was manoeuvring, turning until it faced away from the Earth and pointed out into deep space. All the crew had been given a chance to look round, Miranda had offered them a five-course meal in one of the banqueting suites, and Fairchild hadn't made himself popular by reminding them that it would disrupt their carefully calculated nutrition regime.

It was a vast ship, a city. Further in advance of *Atlantis* than the space shuttle was to the first wheel.

Some people might have looked at it and despaired, or fallen back on superstition or uncomprehending awe. But the astronauts had talked about it, and they saw it as a goal to aim for. One day, their distant descendants would fly vessels like that, and it would have been because of pioneers like them, the first crews of humans into space. It was an affirmation of everything they believed, not a negation.

The Ship leapt forward and then turned on an axis it didn't have.

There was a howling blue vortex around it for the barest moment, and then it was gone in a burst of light.

Mather turned to the Doctor, who was watching this, proud of his daughter.

'You OK, Doctor?' he asked.

The Doctor nodded.

'Time to go home,' the pilot told him.

The Doctor looked out at the Earth, the terminator crawling over the Atlantic. Then he looked up at the stars. They were sharp points of light here, all distinct colours. The sky was pitch-black, the light here was harsh, pure. There were millions of stars, and around them were millions of planets.

'I *am* home,' the Doctor said.

He would be coming back. He knew that now. Perhaps all that talk of destiny was rubbing off, but the Doctor now knew that he'd be looking down over the Earth again. One day he would be planting footsteps in the soil of other worlds, exploring strange cities, talking to space monsters, watching alien suns rise.

Soon enough.

'Father Time — The Album'

1. Babylon's Burning, The Ruts
2. Prince Charming, Adam and the Ants
3. Wuthering Heights, Kate Bush
4. Fashion, David Bowie
5. No More Heroes, The Stranglers
6. Who's That Girl, Eurythmics
7. The Power of Love, Frankie Goes to Hollywood
8. Love Kills, Freddie Mercury
9. Opportunities, Pet Shop Boys
10. Panic, The Smiths
11. Everybody Wants to Rule The World, Tears for Fears
12. Two Hearts, Phil Collins
13. Nineteen, Paul Hardcastle
14. And She Was, Talking Heads
15. The Only Way is Up, Yazz and the Plastic Population
16. Who's Leaving Who, Hazel Dean
17. All Around the World, Lisa Stansfield
18. Sweet Child of Mine, Guns N Roses
19. Your Love Takes Me Higher, The Beloved
20. Electric Chair, Prince
21. Swamp Thing, The Chameleons
22. Fool's Gold, Stone Roses
23. A Small Victory, Faith No More
24. I Want It All, Queen

About the Author

Lance Parkin has, perhaps surprisingly, only had one novel published by the BBC before, the thirty-fifth anniversary story *The Infinity Doctors*, although he did write four and a half books for Virgin Publishing. He's kept himself busy contributing to short story collections, writing scripts for audio and video, and was a storyline writer on *Emmerdale*. He also edited the diaries of his close friend Mandy Dingle, and these were published last year.

Printed by Libri Plureos GmbH in Hamburg, Germany